# THE IRON BRIDGE

# THE IRON

HARCOURT BRACE & COMPAN

*David Morse*

# BRIDGE

*New York    San Diego    London*

*To Wil Morse and Joan Joffe Hall*

Copyright © 1998 David Morse

Library of Congress Cataloging-in-Publication Data
Morse, David E.
The iron bridge/by David Morse.—1st ed.
p.     cm.
ISBN 0-15-100259-2
1. Iron Bridge (Coalbrookdale, England)—History—Fiction.
I. Title.
PS3563.0879817   1998
813'.54—dc21   97-27849

Text set in Fairfield Medium
Designed by Kaelin Chappell
Map by Georgia Deaver
Printed in the United States of America
First edition
E D C B A

# ACKNOWLEDGMENTS

I am indebted to various people who assisted with the historical research that went into this novel.

David De Haan, Senior Curator at the Ironbridge Gorge Museum Trust, made available the museum archives, generously answered questions, guided me around Ironbridge, and read the manuscript in draft. Barrie Trinder, whose book *The Industrial Revolution in Shropshire* provided a bedrock of fact, helped also, as did John Powell, Sarah Higgins, and members of the staff at the Ironbridge Gorge MuseumTrust. Lady Rachel Labouchere, whose published diary of Abiah Darby I kept always within arm's reach, critiqued certain passages in the manuscript. Pauline Hannigan and Jim Hannigan, of The Severn Trow, were a source of comfort and good cheer as well as information during my visits to the Severn Gorge, and directed me to Tony Mugridge, Ralph Pee, and Michael Berthoud, who helped me track the footsteps of John Wilkinson. I was helped further by staff at the Birmingham Reference Library's Local History Collection, the Bersham Heritage Centre, the British Library, Castle Head Field Centre, and the Royal Society for the Arts.

Michael T. Wright, Curator of Mechanical Engineering at the National Museum of Science and Industry in London, brought to the project an encyclopedic knowledge of early industry and a passionate devotion to accuracy—which proved indispensable in matters ranging from James Watt's steam engine to such arcane details as the kind of wood used to make early slide rules.

To Frank Dawson, whose insights into the character of John Wilkinson are more generous than mine, I owe thanks for spiritual as well as intellectual support—and for the treasure of friendship which he and Fev have extended to Joan and me at the Castle Head Field Centre.

For help at various stages in my research, I wish to thank John R. Harris and the late Janet Butler at the University of Birmingham; Jack E. Harris, member of the Royal Society; Gordon Read at the Merseyside Maritime Museum in Liverpool; and Stephen Jay Gould.

During part of the six years I spent writing this book, I was aided by a grant from the National Endowment for the Arts, and by fellowships at Blue Mountain Center and the Millay Colony for the Arts.

For reading all or part of the book in manuscript or adding to the flow of ideas that shaped it, I thank Harriet Barlow, Sharon Chesler Bernstein, Tanya and Wendell Berry, Carolyn Bloomer, Bruce Cohen, Theodore Deppe, Gary Dorsey, T. C. Karmel, Wally Lamb, Ann Z. Leventhal, Pam Lewis, Heather McWhinney, my sons Bob, Eli, and Scott Morse, Olaf and Sondra Olsen, Bob Parsons, Wanda Rickerby, Barbara Rosen, Alan Shapiro, Joan Seliger Sidney, and Ellen Zahl. Thanks to my agent, Matthew Bialer, and my editor, Michael Kandel, for their valuable suggestions. My father, Wil Morse, has contributed his ideas and nurtured me in countless ways. I am grateful to Storrs Friends Meeting for ideas and for spiritual support, spoken and unspoken.

Finally, words cannot begin to thank my wife, Joan Joffe Hall, whose leaps of imagination and love and irrepressible wit have guided me through the acrobatics of middle age and the sometimes daunting task of creation.

Did the architecture of iron really rival the architecture of the cathedrals? It did. This was a heroic age.

—J. BRONOWSKI,
*The Ascent of Man*

Cheap iron and steel made it feasible to equip larger armies and navies than ever before: bigger cannon, bigger warships, more complicated equipment...Bloodshed kept pace with iron production: in essence, the entire paleotechnic period was ruled, from beginning to end, by the policy of blood and iron.

—LEWIS MUMFORD,
*Technics and Civilization*

And all the while the plow of iron cut the dreadful furrows
In Ulro, beneath Beaulah, where the dead wail Night & Day.

—WILLIAM BLAKE,
*Vala or the Four Zoas*

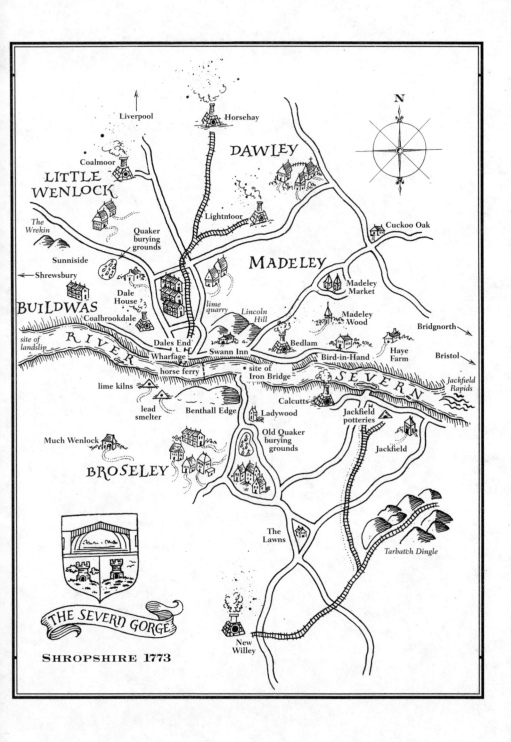

N

Liverpool

Horsehay

DAWLEY

Coalmoor

LITTLE
WENLOCK

Lightmoor

The
Wrekin

Quaker
burying
grounds

Cuckoo Oak

MADELEY

Sunniside

Shrewsbury

Madeley
Market

BUILDWAS

Dale
House

Madeley
Wood

Coalbrookdale

lime
quarry

Lincoln
Hill

Bridgnorth

site of
landslip

RIVER

Dales End

Bedlam

Bristol

Wharfage

Swann Inn

Bird-in-Hand

Haye
Farm

SEVERN

Jackfield
Rapids

horse ferry

site of
Iron Bridge

lime kilns

Calcutts

lead
smelter

Benthall Edge

Ladywood

Jackfield
potteries

Much Wenlock

Old Quaker
burying
grounds

Jackfield

BROSELEY

The
Lawns

Tarbatch Dingle

THE SEVERN GORGE

New
Willey

SHROPSHIRE 1773

# THE IRON BRIDGE

## Maggie Foster

With a bit more sophistication, Maggie might have been able to avoid the earthquake. She might have found some other way to arrive at the Severn Gorge in 1773. Or she might have used the earthquake but managed to arrive an hour before or an hour after—or steered clear of the epicenter.

But as Paul Stanski had explained once in his old-fashioned way, "This is a duct-tape-and-baling-wire operation, Maggie. We just don't know enough about subparticle phasals to fine-tune your arrival." He had peered over his glasses and put a reassuring hand on her knee. "Just remember, it was a minor quake. No recorded fatalities."

Paul was one of the Founders, a physicist in his eighties with a large stooped frame and a shock of white hair—grandfatherly, but a little patronizing, and pragmatic in a way that sometimes infuriated Maggie. Paul saw everything as a set of probabilities; nothing was constant. So neither the words nor the hand was hugely reassuring.

Still, Maggie thought of Paul's *no recorded fatalities* as she lay on the projection table, surrounded by the Circle. "Thank you, ladies," she said, lifting her head to look around at their faces. Erzulie's smile was sad and proud.

1

Maggie was suddenly overwhelmed by a sense of loss, knowing she would never see any of them again. Tears blurred her vision. Then she took a deep breath and got down to business. The Circle spread their hands over her, chanting. She felt their energy join hers. She let herself relax into the alpha state necessary for subparticalization.

Floating as an energy field was like drifting in a fog: you had no reference points, no clues as to direction in time or space. The only means of steering a course was to hold an image in your mind—tiny and indistinct at first, growing as you got closer. Seat-of-the-pants navigation, Paul called it. But such was the state of time travel in the year 2043: an experimental process that combined quantum physics and stochastic resonance, patched together with a little bootleg Jungian psychology.

Her primary beacon was the bridge itself, at the time of its completion at the end of 1779. Because its importance was clear from the very beginning, and because it remained standing well into the twenty-first century, it offered an unbroken link between past and present. Once the image was clear in her mind, it drew her powerfully despite the swirl of psychic disturbances competing for the same band: the natural disasters and genocidal wars that had left deep turbulence in the collective unconscious. In fact, she underestimated the power of the bridge. They all did.

When the famous silhouette came into view—the world's first iron bridge, designed by Thomas Farnolls Pritchard, with its iron ribs and radial braces reflecting in the water to make a full circle—it was scarcely distinguishable from the image she was holding in her mind. Then it began deconstructing. First the railings disappeared, then the roadway. And there was a dizzying jump in perspective, a deepening of colors and crisping of details: the banks of the Severn were crowded with spectators, as she had imagined, but a pair of wooden scaffolding towers stood on either side of the river. It was not the image of the completed bridge, not the famous painting commissioned by Abraham Darby III or any of the later etchings or digifotos, but an earlier gestalt. It appeared to be that moment when the first pair of ribs was being fastened together at the center to create the first arch.

A man suspended in a harness hanging from a boom was intent on tapping an iron wedge in place. Maggie was close enough to see his furrowed brow, a bead of sweat coursing down his neck.

Excitement soared in her. Relief at having made it, gratitude, fear—all in a wave. Too many emotions for her ethereal state. Too many sensations to resist.

She let herself be drawn into the midst of the onlookers, suspended just above their heads. She was on the Madeley side of the river, at what must be the horse-ferry landing, close enough to count the folds in a young woman's full gray skirt, to observe the texture of her gray bonnet—all of it so absorbing that Maggie could hardly attend to the voice of the Circle in her ear, warning her: *Withdraw.* Too soon to reincorporate. She had to go back another six and a half years, to before the bridge was designed. Focus on the earthquake, the secondary beacon.

It was the odors that entrapped her—the first whiff of sulfur dioxide joined by a bouquet of other smells, ale and sweat and scents she could not identify. Most compelling was the delicate fragrance of the woman's hair. *Withdraw,* the voice urged. But she lingered, drifting farther into the sensory realm.

*Withdraw!*

The voice became frantic. Without realizing what was happening, Maggie had crossed the boundary from one energy state to another, vibrating into the fractal-edged frontier of corporeality. Suddenly she felt the gritty cobblestones under her bare feet, heard the clamor of voices. Heard a gasp behind her, and whirled. A man recoiled, bashing his head into the face of another drinking ale from a tankard, bloodying the second man's nose. A dog yapped at her furiously. People were pointing.

"A naked wench!" someone cried out.

In that instant, heart pounding, she might have run. But hearing the voice persist *Withdraw! It is not too late!,* realizing that the energy field was still intact, she resisted the impulse, the hunger to reincorporate. Instead she willed herself back into the alpha state. It was like falling backward slowly, holding her breath, falling back into the calm of the Circle, darkness imploding slowly over the crown of her head, sensation draining away like watercolors under a stream of clear water. Voices dimming around her head. Her parting glimpse like a black-and-white digifoto of astonished faces, the woman's eyebrows puzzled, the man with the nosebleed groping, his fingers looming close. Then only voices in the whiteness:

"I'll be swivel-eyed!" said the man, bloody fingers closing on air. " 'Twas a witch!"

"Nay," said another. " 'Twas an angel."

It all faded like a dream, and again Maggie was floating in mist. *Dummy,* she thought, with as much vehemence as she could muster in her disembodied state. But she managed to turn her self-reproach into an affirmation, *I learn from my mistakes,* and with the help of a few mantras achieved the alpha calm necessary to focus on the earthquake of May 27, 1773. It was trickier than the bridge, being more kinesthetic than visual, and she encountered severe local traumas: a mob carrying torches—was this the Priestley riots of 1791 or the corn riots four decades earlier? Then a flood; but which flood? And a drowned man in a cart, his face a blur, eyes filled with darkness. She jerked back, as in a going-to-sleep twitch. Lost again in the fog.

She gave up trying to summon the sensations of the earthquake. Focused instead on the consequences. The landslip that blocked the Severn. River emptied of water. Boats keeled over. Fish flopping in darkness.

She tried *not* to think of the epicenter, but now it was drawing her; she could feel it, with sudden dread.

This time she was more cautious, waiting until she had oriented herself to materialize. Fewer landmarks here, and it was night. But that pink glow suffusing the misting rain was surely Coalbrookdale in the distance, its blast furnaces pulsing, the glow sufficient to illuminate the hillside around her. Pink glint of river. House and barn located pretty much according to the old map she had memorized.

And now she registered a shiver deep in the earth. She could not think about the forces grinding far below the surface of Shropshire: the Atlantic plate expanding against the Eurasian plate, subducting;

pressures buckling upward through volcanic schists and Silurian shale, shuddering against the Church Stretton fault. Dread deepened in her belly. She said a hurried goodbye to the Circle and let gravity take her. Felt the light rain on her skin, her feet pressing into the cold, damp, trembling soil.

She ran toward the farmhouse. Her feet were tender, she realized, but she had to move quickly. Her plan was to warn the inhabitants of the quake—a superfluous warning, since they would all survive; but they wouldn't know that and might be grateful enough to lend her some clothing. At least that was the hoped-for scenario. Dicey, but better than no plan at all.

The timbers of the barn were already groaning as she ran past it to the farmhouse. Despite all her preparation, she felt cold fear growing in her gut. *No fatalities.* Not yet! She knocked on a window and squatted out of the way, covering her breasts while the vibrations gathering force under her became a rumbling staccato deeper in pitch than anything she had ever dreamed of. The window sash swung open, and a man with a bushy mustache peered out. At that instant the ground jolted powerfully under her. She screamed and took off.

She was knocked off her feet several times, running across the heaving field. All she could think of was avoiding the chasm—drawn in such fine detail on the old map she had downloaded from *Britmuse*—but it was hard to stay oriented. Then she saw pigs and people running up the slope and across the ridge, yelling and squealing, silhouetted in the eerie red light; and suddenly the chasm opened up, separating her from them—and smaller rifts were appearing, each large enough to swallow up one of the armored personnel carriers from her own time.

She crawled along the hedgerow, east, toward the glow of Coalbrookdale, trying to keep her bearings as the ground continued to shake—her bearings and her wits. *No fatalities,* she reassured herself, ignoring the possibility that she might be killed, that her sole change in the historical record might be an additional sentence in the newspaper account. *One itinerant woman lost her life.* Behind her, the hillside was undulating. A thunderous roar filled her ears, incongruously like applause, and she looked back in time to see a grove of trees sliding into the river. Silence. The earth was still. She ran, then walked toward the glow of Coalbrookdale.

Ahead was a pinpoint of light. A house, maybe.

Now that she was over her panic, she noticed her scraped hip and stinging feet. She winced at every step. Forget the feet, concentrate on finding clothing and shelter. She felt exposed. She was about to lose the cover of darkness. She tried breaking off some bushes to cover herself, but they had thorns, so she determined to stay close to the trees and focus on getting to that point of light. Mud caked her right hip and knees. And now that the rush of adrenaline was over, she was shivering from the cold.

Suddenly the ground shuddered again. Her knees flexed; she caught her balance, terrified. Again it was still.

Aftershock.

Erzulie, who had once been through an earthquake in Los Angeles, had warned her that the aftershocks could be more harrowing than the original quake.

Maggie felt a surge of anger. *Minor earthquake.* Well, try getting downloaded into the epicenter of a minor motherboarding earthquake! The anger was more at Paul than Erzulie. But in fact it had been Maggie's decision as much as anybody's. So take responsibility. Just focus on reaching that light.

She came to a small stream and a collapsed bridge. This would be Birches Brook, which had been on the map with the notation *bridge destroyd.* The light appeared now to be coming from a cottage set among the trees on the other side. The throb of Coalbrookdale was louder now. And she could hear something else. Shouts—coming, as nearly as she could tell, from the cottage.

She hesitated before stepping into the dark water, thinking automatically of radiation, then wondering if there was anything that might bite. For all the research she had done, she knew little about the fauna and flora of England. She wished Trevor were here. She tried to hear the calm in Trevor's voice. Gritted her teeth as the cold water closed around her calves and then her thighs. Struggling to keep her balance, she felt her way across the stony bottom. She ducked down long enough to wash off some of the mud. What about leeches? She thought of that old Hollywood *African Queen*. By the time she got to where the other side should be, her feet were numb, her teeth chattering. And where was the damned other side? She could find nothing solid to stand on—slipped on moss-covered rocks, scraped her ankles, sank into cold ooze. She was furious, close to tears.

Another tremor.

She gasped and fell forward, banging her wrist.

Goddamn aftershock!

By the time she floundered onto solid ground, she was crying. She broke off some ferns and tried to dry herself, but they were wet and scratchy. Moaning, she wanted to howl bloody styrofoam. Everything fed her anger and desperation: the weird red sky, the sight of ferns growing in the wild. It was like a motherboarding Hollywood jungle. And her stupid tender feet. Why hadn't she thought of toughening her feet before the journey, walking around Ecosophia barefoot? Why hadn't *somebody* thought of her feet? And what a styro idea it was, arriving in an earthquake! She couldn't seem to suppress this anger any more than she could stop her teeth from chattering.

Get a grip, Maggie. She willed herself to relax. You are in a state of posttraumatic shock. Take a deep breath. Be grateful you made it in one piece.

Under the fear and anger, she could feel an overwhelming eagerness to find safety, warm clothing; not to have to think. And beyond that eagerness, a strange lethargy. She had felt the lethargy once before, during the long trek from California across the desert to Ecosophia, when all she could think about was sleeping in a real bed. Safety. Oblivion.

Horns like conch shells sounded in the distance. The sky was lighter. The pale trunks of trees, aspen or birch, glowed in the blue dawn. Gathering a bunch of ferns to cover herself, she followed a path to the cottage. The shouting had resumed, but as she approached the narrow window, she could make out only one voice, high-pitched and ranting.

The cottage was small. Stone walls, a thatched roof. Inside, a candle flickered in a tin sconce. An old person—a little old woman, from the way she was dressed—was banging on the wooden floor with a stick and yelling incomprehensibly. The one familiar word was "out," pronounced with a long *oo* sound. "Out! *Ooot!*" she yelled at the floor.

Horns getting closer. Holding the ferns over her breasts, Maggie leaned into the narrow opening and called out, "Excuse me! Can I help?"

"Nay, nay." The old woman waved her away matter-of-factly, thumped again vigorously with her staff, addressing the floor. "Out! Out!" Then she turned to Maggie. "Hit's a brock ascrabbling under me house. Digging 'isself a creep-hole. Such a catch-penny creature droiling about'll beggar me swedes!" She cocked her head to listen, then gave the floor another whack, this time maybe for show. "Begone!" She turned to Maggie with arms raised and a toothless, triumphant grin.

"What's a brockascrabbling?" Maggie asked, unable to understand a word the woman had said. Maybe it was Welsh.

"A brock! A brock!"

"What—what's a brock?"

The old woman straightened. "A brock be a brock! A brock be a badger!"

"Oh." An image came to mind. Maggie knew badgers as she knew most animals, from twentieth-century digifotos. The little old woman had straggly white hair and wore a baggy nightgown; fierce ruddy cheeks and pale blue eyes. Maggie supposed she must look a little wild herself, smeared with mud, her hair a filthy tangle of dark curls. Lethargy crept over her again. No fire in the fireplace. Only the sputtering candle, which looked like reeds in what was probably animal fat. Still, it offered some warmth. "Listen," she said. "Can I come in? I'm freezing."

"Eh?"

"Can I come in?"

"May I! May I!" The crone whacked at the floor and cackled. "Mother may I!"

It sounded like gibberish. The old woman drew close enough for

Maggie to see several long white whiskers sprouting from her chin.

It occurred to Maggie that the woman might be hearing-impaired. "I'm cold!" she shouted. "I have no clothes! I need shelter!"

The old woman stepped back and cocked her head suspiciously.

The horns were getting louder. Maggie could see figures advancing along the road. She pressed back from the window so as not to make a silhouette, and wished she had more ferns.

Nothing was going right. Maybe she should mug the old woman. Grab a dress, escape through the woods. But that was no way to start her new career. Maggie took a deep, cleansing breath. She smiled. "How big is a badger?"

"Bigger'n a hedgehog."

"What do they eat?" The window was low. Gradually, as they talked, Maggie managed to climb through the narrow opening, first one leg and then the other, juggling the ferns for modesty. It was awkward, but as long as the old woman was kept busy talking, she seemed not to notice. By the time she was inside, Maggie had learned that hedgehogs could predict weather, although it was not clear how.

She knelt and gathered up pieces of a pottery bowl that had evidently fallen from the mantel. "Where shall I put these?" Make herself useful.

The old woman, who couldn't have been a meter and a half tall, accepted the shards and looked Maggie up and down. "Tha be'est bare-bum naked."

"Yes." Maggie started to explain that she had been attacked by robbers, but the old woman was distracted now by the commotion on the road. Maggie held her hands before the spluttering reed candle. The smell was nauseating. "Listen," she said, when the crone turned back to her. "Do you have a dress I could borrow? Anything. I don't care what it looks like. Something you're ready to throw out?"

The woman frowned and began jabbering agitatedly. Maggie asked about animals again; and while the woman rattled on about bog rats and owls, Maggie found a wool blanket and wrapped herself in it. Finally she stopped shivering. Her eyelids grew pleasantly heavy. For the moment she was safe.

Later she managed to cadge a crust of dark sour bread and a bowl of porridge from the old woman. She was famished. The food warmed her as much as the blanket, and helped settle her stomach. Just as well that the woman was guarded with her food; Maggie's gastrointestinal tract was clinically empty. She should eat cautiously until her gut was acclimated to the local microorganisms. She was also thirsty, but wary of drinking unboiled water.

The old woman was fussing around the door now, which was stuck. Maggie helped push it open enough for her to squeeze through and watched her hobble down the path to the road. Watched her accost passersby, who generally ignored her, which confirmed Maggie's impression that the woman was senile.

Maggie examined the cuts and bruises on her feet. One long scrape along her right side included her hip and breast; it was painful but should heal okay. Her antibodies had been boosted by inoculations. Both knees were abraded. She poured a handful of water from the pitcher and washed them. Combed some of the mud from her hair with her fingers. Helped herself to another little piece of bread, and looked around.

The cottage, about four meters square, had two windows and a fireplace. The furniture consisted of a narrow cot, a table, and a stool. Above the crossed beams she could see smoke-blackened rafters and thatch, with assorted stuff hanging on hooks: bunches of herbs, baskets, a couple of strings of what looked like chili peppers but must have been smoked fish.

Hanging from a row of pegs on the wall were a few articles of clothing. A couple of drab shapeless smocks. Linen, she decided; it had the almost soapy texture of woven hemp. A worn apron. A rust-colored wool cloak. That seemed to be the old woman's entire wardrobe. Everything smelled of smoked fish. Maggie tried on the rust cloak. It wouldn't have looked bad with white slacks. She regarded herself in a piece of mirror she found. Combed again at her mop of curls. Nothing was going to be long enough. And the cloak was probably the priciest piece on the rack, as her grandmother used to say. Better settle for one of the smocks. Her eye went to the dun-colored one—frayed at the hem, barely covering her knees. Could she talk the old lady out of it?

Talk. The success of this whole mission depended on talk. Her ability to persuade. It was all she had. If she couldn't talk a crazy old woman out of a dress, how was she going to change the world?

Voices outside. She was just pulling the smock over her head. She looked out and saw the old woman arguing with a boy whom she was tugging along the path, despite his protests. Maggie wriggled the rest of the way into the dress. It was so tight in the shoulders and bust, she was afraid the seams would split. Just as she got her head clear, she saw the boy wrench free of the old woman's grasp and jump away, poised to run.

"Wait!" Maggie called. "Please, don't run away!" She squeezed through the door. "I need help."

The old woman's eyes widened, recognizing her dress. She scowled. "Thief!"

"Please," said Maggie, appealing to the boy, who was carrying something round, flat, and rusty. Alert eyes framed in a grimy face.

"Thief!" cried the old woman. "Thief!"

"I'm not a thief." Maggie addressed the boy earnestly. "Listen. Can you help me? I'm a stranger here. Can you understand what I'm saying?"

"Aye," he said.

The boy's name, she found out later, was Jeremy Crump. He was twelve. The grime around his eyes was coaldust. It was Jeremy—sweet, clever little Jeremy—who worked out a deal with the old woman: the iron pot lid he had found in the exposed riverbed, plus a copper coin from his pocket, plus a quick repair to the old woman's door, which he freed by pounding a sliver of kindling into a crack under the lintel, using his wooden shoe—all in exchange for this funky, worn-out dress.

Maggie was grateful to have Jeremy's company walking along the crowded road to Coalbrookdale. She was taller than most of the men they passed, many of whom stared at her legs. She tried smiling, but no one smiled back. And the horses, up close, frightened her. But Jeremy chattered excitedly about everything he had seen—the exposed river bottom, the huge chasm. He described how he had ventured into the oak copse and listened to the groaning of the trees and heard the water trickling through the roots. He reckoned he caught a glimpse of old Nicky Nye, which she took to be a sort of water demon. His normalcy was soothing; his enthusiasm lifted her spirits. She had never been around children. After she asked his age and he told her, he asked how old she was, and was surprised to learn she was twenty-nine. What was she doing in the witch's cottage, he asked, and why was her speech so strange? She told him she had been attacked by robbers and that she had come from the Colonies.

"Robbers?" he asked. "Highwaymen?"

"Yes," she said.

The twelve-year-old took her under his wing. He pointed out sights as they entered the smoky brown haze of the gorge: Coalbrookdale descending from their left in a glow of furnaces and forges that teemed with horses and men; to their right, the Ludcroft Wharf and, after that, the horse ferry (whose cobblestones she recognized as from a dream); and across the river in Broseley, the lime kilns and lead smelters throwing more smoke into the air. Maggie's eyes burned. Many of the landmarks were familiar from the old maps, and the geological features were ones she had memorized. But she was on sensory overload. And as often as she had tried to visualize it before, she was unprepared for the intensity of the acrid smoke obscuring the sun.

Jeremy seemed oblivious to it. He was evidently taking her to Madeley Wood, where he lived with his mother and brothers and sisters. They stood for a while surveying the scene, watching men busy prying at hulls with long poles or unloading cargo.

"I anna seen such a sight in me life," Jeremy exclaimed, shaking his head in wonder. "I shall tell me grandchildren!"

This sounded so strange, coming from a child. She would never have children herself. But somehow the words made her smile.

She was here. She had made it!

# Abraham Darby III

He was awakened before dawn by a swaying sensation. The young ironmaster had dreamed he was in a runaway chaise whose wheels were slipping over the edge of a limestone cliff while he fumbled helplessly for the reins. Awakening, heart pounding, he was grateful to find himself in bed. He thanked the Almighty. Then he heard a rumble in the distance and sat up, fearing a dam had burst.

Hearing no shouts or other signs of alarm, Abraham tried to go back to sleep. But by now the demons of everyday worries were besetting him: the dam that must be repaired, the foreman twenty years his senior whom he must reprimand for defects in a cylinder casting, financial details. He banished them from his mind, but they kept creeping back in different guises. Through the window he could see dawn's pale magenta light surmounting the ruddy glow of Coalbrookdale, lighting the crooked columns of smoke. The rain had stopped.

Awake now, he decided to make the most of it. He would ride to the Haye farm. He washed his face at the basin, combed his dark straight hair in the mirror. At twenty-four he was beginning to get the same brown circles under his eyes that he remembered in his father.

He stuffed his nightshirt into his gray breeches, pulled on his stockings, and tiptoed downstairs so as not to awaken his mother or sister. The housekeeper was not yet up. He pulled on his boots, donned his coat and flat Quaker hat, and slipped quietly out the back door.

He was saddling his black gelding when he thought he heard horns from the gorge. He held his breath, trying to hear past the thump of the furnaces. Horns at this hour would signify some calamity. Perhaps he had only imagined them. Blacky, expecting the trot to the Haye farm, tossed his head impatiently. Abraham liked to be present for the farm's awakening—as if the fragrance of new-mown hay rising soft in the mist and the bleating of lambs might swaddle his senses against the stink and noise of ironmaking that he had inherited from his father and grandfather.

But now he heard them. Unmistakable: hollow, mournful blasts rising from the Severn. Cow horns of the sort used to call in workers at the end of a day of haying. But sounded at this hour, they meant trouble. Three days of rain in Wales had left the Severn swollen: a barge might have capsized, someone drowned. But so many horns suggested some wider catastrophe.

They recalled the corn riots, when he was a boy of six made to stay inside with his sisters and baby brother while their father and Richard Reynolds rode off to treat with the ringleaders. The women stayed at home and baked bread for three days, directing the servants to hand out loaves every time the rioters appeared at the gate at Sunniside, lest they ransack the house. So the mournful sound inspired foreboding in Abraham's breast, yet it also brought to mind the aroma of bread baking, and a touch of guilt for feeling cozy and protected amongst the rustle of the women's petticoats.

Abraham set off at a trot down the road that snaked past Coalbrookdale's millponds in an S-curve, past the spewing flames of the Old Furnace, its water wheel turning in the ruddy mist, the great bellows pounding; past the New Furnace, whose pounding eclipsed the first; past the silent blooming mills and the forges not yet fired. Only a few workers had arrived.

Coming out at Dales End, Abraham expected to find the river

flooded. Instead he was greeted by an awful sight. Where Coalbrook flowed out of the dale to join the broad Severn, only its small rivulet continued downstream through the pink mist; the remaining bed of the Severn lay exposed, slick and steaming like a skinned rabbit, from Madeley across to Broseley. Fish splashed among the wet rocks. Sailing barges were tipped on their sides, masts askew, as far as he could see in either direction. People thronged the wharfage—barge men joined by ironworkers; boys running about; a few enterprising fellows gaffing fish into wheelbarrows and baskets—all with such singular excitement that the Dale Company's quarter-till-six warning bell sounded on deaf ears. Church bells had begun ringing. There was talk of an earthquake. Rumors that the castle at Shrewsbury had fallen. A sea serpent in the Bristol Channel. Women fell to their knees praying. A wild-eyed collier ran through the crowd proclaiming the end of the world. Abraham thought of his mother, who often gave testimony that Judgment Day was at hand, calling up the images of the pale horse and pale rider: *And out of his mouth goeth a sharp sword, that with it he should smite the nations, and rule them with a rod of iron.*

Wonder swelled in his breast. Was he prepared to meet the Maker? His mind flashed to his mother, sisters, and brother, to his account books, his uncompleted business: the consignment of pots halfway to Stourport, the new dairy barn at the Haye farm that would never get built. He imagined himself ascending like his father, in Mother's dream, up heavenly steps into the Light. All this flashed through his mind in an instant.

Reason, however, argued for some extraordinary but finite catastrophe. Seeing the crowd setting out on the turnpike toward Buildwas, Abraham decided to observe for himself the extent of the destruction.

He recognized many of his workers. Would the furnace keepers have enough fillers to keep the furnaces in blast? He could not bring himself to do what he imagined Father might have done—rear his horse in their path like a general commanding his troops and order them back to the Works. He did manage to address a few in a properly stern voice, reminding them of the shilling fine for an absence, and when he had seen enough of them straggling back to the Works, he proceeded at a trot. Full of his own excitement, he could hardly cast blame.

People were wading across Birches Brook, where the small wooden bridge was twisted from its stone abutments. The word "earthquake" was on everyone's lips now. The old hag who lived by the fen babbled incoherently to all who would listen, pointing to her hovel in the birch coppice.

A hundred yards ahead lay an even stranger sight: a hillside of rye grass tossed like a blanket, the earth folded and torn so as to obliterate whole segments of turnpike and hedgerow. To the left, where the Severn had flowed from time immemorial, was a copse of oaks. Over the smell of damp earth hung a flinty pungence.

Galloping up the hillside, Abraham could look out and see the new lake that had formed, extending upriver toward the village of Buildwas, and from this vantage it was clear that the copse of oaks had stopped the river like a gate in a millrace. Again he was struck with awe. It occurred to him to wonder if indeed this were some Divine plan. And what if the Severn were to abandon its ancient bed forever? He should have no way to transport his iron, save for the more costly routes overland by wagon. But these practical thoughts were subsumed in a general wonderment.

The hilltop itself was riven by a huge forked chasm, as if the ground, in swelling, had burst open like a potato in the coals. The gelding shied from the sulfury stink that issued from it. The main fissure was of awful size—perhaps three hundred yards long and ten yards deep. Abraham wished now that he had dispatched a boy from the clerk's office to carry the news to his brother-in-law, Richard Reynolds.

Suddenly he felt the ground shudder. Blacky reared. People shouted and rushed away from the precipice. In another moment the earth was quiet. Abraham let the gelding run several paces before reining him to a halt. "Good fellow," he said soothingly, dismounting and stroking the animal's neck. "Good Blacky," he crooned, his own heart pounding like a blooming-hammer. He spoke softly into the erect ears.

*Our Father, who art in Heaven, hallowed be thy name.* By the time he was done, they were both quieted. Shutting his eyes against the powerful neck, smelling its salty fragrance, he thanked the Maker. What an invitation to the soul this was! Abraham determined now to send for Richard Reynolds, who would relish it as keenly as anyone. He recognized a boy from the Works, gave him tuppence and dispatched him to Ketley Bank with a note.

A crowd was gathered around a crofter's cottage. As Abraham approached, he saw that the wattle-and-daub structure had been shaken partly from its foundations. A wall was cracked; leaded diamond-paned windows bulged from their casements. Abraham dismounted so his Quaker hat would not be so conspicuous. A countryman, apparently the master of the house—a rough-shaven fellow with a bushy mustache and a blanket wrapped around his nightshirt—stood outside looking about with bloodshot eyes. He appeared mazed, but responded to questions in a resonant voice.

"Early in the morning, before dawn, I wakes to hear me swine a-carrying on, all adrabble, and a knocking at me window. So's I ope the window, sticks me head out and sees the coppice thrashing about, anna not a breath of wind. But of a sudden comes an awful rumble, and I sees a woman—leaps up and cries out something strange, and runs away as naked as a plucked chicken—and I looks down and sees a crack open in the earth. I collects me wife and children and drives the cows out of the barn, and opens the pigs-sty, and we dunna know whither to run, so's we stands shill-I-shall-I and then follows the pigs up the hill, with the ground a-rollicking under us so's one foot scarce knows where the other'n be. And the sound, oh the sound t'was terrible—I shan't ever forget that rumbling, like a flock of sheep running past yer head. Then we sees the barn commence to move, and everything is heaving like porridge in a pot, the river falling back on itself, and the oaks—" His voice cracked, and he stopped. Abraham felt pity for the man, seeing him tremble.

A child whispered, "He's got snot on his mustache."

Just then a young girl ran up with a kitten, saying it was one of a litter that the mother cat was moving from the ruins of the barn.

"There's mischief!" declared a stumpy woman with a shepherd's crook. "Kits born in May be the worst luck!"

The farmer shook his head numbly. "Barn cat. I dinna know she'd chatted."

"Vigilance, Samuel." The woman spat over her left shoulder. "That crack went for tha barn like a snake after a frog." She held up the kitten and noted that its eyes were still fast shut. "Double bad luck. May kits born in a May flood."

"Drown 'em," an old fellow offered.

"Aye, drown 'em," said others.

Abraham thought to speak against this superstitious cruelty, but he was timid in crowds, unlike Mother, and told himself that his remonstrations would only add to the farmer's discomfort. The farmer waved a rough hand in the direction of the barn. "Do it." The crowd moved to the barn, leaving the man to be comforted by a couple of younger countrymen wearing farmers' smocks.

"What did she say?" Abraham ventured.

The farmer wiped his nose on the back of his hand. "May kits bring ill luck."

"No, no. The woman thou saw'st at thy window."

The man worked his mouth and rolled his eyes distractedly. " 'Twas strange," he said finally, with a look of great perplexity. "She cried, 'Holy shit!' "

The younger of his two companions started to laugh, but seeing the farmer's baleful countenance, grew sober. They all readily attested to the strangeness of the oath.

**B**y the time his brother-in-law arrived at Dales End at noon, the scene had lost some of its terror. A gang of bow haulers was intent on scavenging rusty stove backs from an ancient wreck; a hog had ventured onto a mudflat and was gorging itself on carp. It all looked disappointingly ordinary.

Richard Reynolds was prompt, as always. He was a tall, fair man in his late forties, with piercing blue eyes under shaggy salt-and-pepper brows. The two ironmasters shook hands. The older man smiled grimly in all directions. "This thrills my every nerve," he declared. " 'Tis truly sublime."

"Come," said Abraham, eager to guide him. "Let us view the desolation upstream."

Richard was more father than brother-in-law to Abraham, whose father had died when he was thirteen. Abraham remembered his father as a dark, self-contained man. Perhaps sad. No likeness of him remained, nor of Abraham's grandfather—portraits being counted a vanity—but Mother said they were all cast in the same mold.

Upon Father's death ten years ago, Richard had taken charge of Coalbrookdale. Abraham served his apprenticeship under him, much of it managing the Haye farm. When Abraham took over Coalbrookdale at eighteen, Richard went back to running Horsehay and Ketley, the newer furnaces that were part of the Dale Company's ironmaking enterprise, but Abraham continued to seek his brother-in-law's advice on important matters. It was not just ironmaking that Richard had taught him; it was the Quaker belief in meeting that of God in every man, a hatred of war, love of simplicity and good works.

They found the hillside overrun with people and carriages. A company of Shakers had arrived from Shrewsbury and was singing and whirling about like dervishes, and a congregation of Baptists had waded into the floodwaters. The Vicar of Madeley stood on a hillock before a hundred or so people, preaching in the incantatory Methodist style, his voice rising and falling as he spoke of the "terrible emblems of destruction" placed before them by a Divine hand. Fish were being fried on open fires, loaves hawked, short beer sold from buckets, dogs set against each other on wagers. An enormously fat man known as Little Jake was selling willow baskets from a pole. Buildwas was said to be threatened with flood; yet for all the talk of disaster, the mood was festive.

Upon leading Richard to the great forked chasm, Abraham was disappointed to see men walking casually across the bottom. The two ironmasters tied their horses to a clump of hedge and descended on foot to an expanse of shale that the earth's recent agonies had caused to bulge and split. The smell of sulfur, so rank before, was scarcely noticeable. Abraham described the tremor that had caused Blacky to rear.

Richard listened, enrapt. "Thy nerves must have been quite unstrung."

"So they were." Abraham was pleased to capture his brother-in-law's attention, having no natural gift as a storyteller. He was trying to think of some further detail when the older man reached down and picked up a chunk of shale the size of a teacup, a fossil shell. Richard examined it with the magnifying lens he carried in the upper pocket of his waistcoat, then handed it to Abraham.

"Pray, what dost thou observe about this petrofaction, brother?"

Abraham peered through the glass. "It appears to be an ordinary miller's thumb."

"Exactly! Identical to the miller's thumbs found in the limestone atop Lincoln Hill, two hundred feet up." Richard darted his gaze around the chasm walls and pointed to the strata that had been thrust up. "Consider! 'Tis movements of the earth like this that must account for the topsy-turviness we find today—the seashells on hilltops, and ferns imprinted in the deepest coal seams! Mark thee, if a movement like this took place once every century, why in a few thousand years we should have a mountain the size of the Wrekin!" Slipping the petrofaction into a lower pocket, he gazed around again with a look of fierce determination. "This whole chasm should be accurately surveyed. We must commission a map!"

Abraham was a little piqued to find his own excitement so quickly outdone, although he recognized the vanity of such feelings, for it was all the Maker's handiwork. He agreed to share the cost of the commission. "Come." He tugged on Richard's arm. "I shall show thee an entire barn swallowed by the chasm."

Returning to their horses, they listened to the vicar preach against the sins of the inhabitants of Madeley and Broseley, the *cursing colliers and swearing watermen, the brutish excesses and savage fights which chill the blood of a few righteous Lots among us.* The vicar's themes were not unlike those of Abraham's mother when she felt called to go forth to the market squares and testify against bull baiting and gambling. But while Mother spoke as the Spirit moved her—her humble and sometimes garbled testimony offering proof of the power of Divine love overflowing her heart—the vicar's calculated grandiloquence spoke more of education than faith.

Abraham did not always understand his mother's testimonies; nor did he approve entirely of her ministry, whose leadings had prompted her to journey to distant Quaker meetings even as Father lay dying. But the vicar's elaborate conceits recalled the Pharisees of old.

As they proceeded toward the barn, Richard pointed to a sedan chair carrying a familiar personage—the architect Thomas Farnolls Pritchard, sumptuously tricked out in a blue cocked hat and a yellow waistcoat with large brass buttons that flashed in the sun. Pritchard was said to be of delicate constitution; all the same, Abraham thought the sedan chair an affectation better suited to London.

"Come," said Richard. "He will have enough opinions for two men, and we shall enlist his help in commissioning the map."

At their approach, Pritchard saluted them in his raspy voice, with the customary doffing of hat and elaborate salutations that Quakers avoided—avoided not only for their falsity but also for their putting the creaturely self forward—his blond wig at odds with his wrinkled face. Richard and Abraham responded with simple handshakes and plain speech. After commonplaces were exchanged and Richard announced his intention to commission a map, Pritchard said he was of like mind but that he had just now learned that the owner of the land had already done so for legal purposes. Abraham was secretly glad to be spared the cost.

The three men next speculated as to where the water would most likely find its outlet, the location more evident now that the water was higher and had encroached a little ways into a meadow beyond the copse of oaks. They agreed that once it broke through the meadow, it would curve back like a jug handle to rejoin its old course through the gorge. Abraham did not confess his earlier fear that the Severn might abandon its ancient bed.

Pritchard fancied he could predict the precise hour when the water would break through. Drawing forth a slide rule made of boxwood and ivory, he made a show of estimating the additional height that the floodwaters would have to attain in order to breach the meadow, and what volume of water this would represent, assuming this and assuming that (whisking the little ivory slide back and forth and jotting figures in a little book), until Abraham suspected the architect was quite lost. Pritchard was clearly unpracticed at using the new device, and finally dismissed his own jottings with the admission that there were too many irregularities in the land.

"So, Thomas Pritchard!" said Richard with a grave smile. "Thou submitteth to the infinitude of the Master Builder."

But Pritchard's nose wrinkled with glee, the tip lifting as if hinged. "Mark ye, sirs! The very abundance of unknown quantities argues my case for the bridge!"

Abraham's heart sank. Nothing would stop Pritchard now from making a point more tiresome than Abraham could bear.

Instructing his chairmen to lower the chair onto its legs, Pritchard addressed the Quakers in a raspy whisper. "All this," he said, waving a hand at the lake, "demonstrates the waywardness of the upper Severn, where the flatness of the valley spreads its complications— compared to the gorge, where 'tis funneled through narrow confines. As we speak, sirs, the floodwaters are threatening the Buildwas bridge. I beg you consider: Even if the water should find a new outlet by nightfall, how many days will pass before the barges can trust the new channel, or before you can safely cross by horse ferry from Madeley to Broseley? Hmmm?" Pritchard looked at Abraham with his brow furrowed expectantly, his sallow lips stretched back from his protruding teeth in what was more grimace than smile.

"Several days," Abraham admitted.

"So!" Pritchard now leaned forward, as if he were conferring the greatest of secrets. "Fancy the convenience, sir. Fancy the *reliability*, of a bridge where 'tis most needed, at the gorge!"

Abraham tried to conceal his annoyance. The idea of a bridge at the gorge was hardly unique to Thomas Farnolls Pritchard. It had been talked about for decades. Abraham's own father had essayed to build it, had he not? But Pritchard, wishing to design the thing, had flung himself upon it like a broody hen settling upon a clutch of eggs.

Pritchard offered snuff from a round ivory box, which the two iron-masters declined. "And may I presume—" The architect interrupted himself, sneezing into his ruffled sleeve, and beckoned them closer, addressing them in an insidious whisper. "May I flatter myself to suppose, gentlemen, that you would like it to be—if I may speak frankly—a *Quaker* bridge? That is, a bridge that *Quakers* might find to their liking?"

Abraham wished his brother-in-law would speak. But Richard Reynolds only rocked back on his heels with hands laced behind his back and smiled benignly, while Pritchard waited with his nose poised.

It was a silly question, a ridiculous question. Everyone knew it should be a Quaker bridge! It was his grandfather's discovery early in the century that had turned the whole gorge into a magnet for furnaces! And his father's labors twenty years ago that had made Coalbrookdale what it was today.

Those were mighty accomplishments. Abraham did not imagine that he, the third Abraham Darby, would ever achieve anything so grand. Yet he had known from the time of his father's death that it would fall to him someday to build the bridge.

What did Pritchard intend by his absurd question?

A wariness crept over Abraham. He saw the wrinkles deepen, and guessed what name was coming even before it passed Pritchard's lips.

"John Wilkinson does, of course, have a keen interest in the project."

"Yes." Abraham frowned. "And I am certain that John Wilkinson is especially keen on seeing it made of iron."

Pritchard chuckled. "Surely a gentleman of your lineage might share Mr. Wilkinson's attraction to iron."

"I owe my livelihood to it, but not my soul."

Richard raised an eyebrow at the tone of this pronouncement. Abraham was surprised to hear his own rancor. The truth was, he found it difficult to meet that of God in John Wilkinson. "My interest in iron runs to pots and engine cylinders," he added, keeping his voice evenly deep, "not cannon."

"Spoken as a Quaker, I am sure, sir. But bridges, sir! What of bridges, Mr. Darby?"

"As no man has yet built a bridge of iron, Thomas Pritchard, my interest is tempered by practical considerations."

"Cost?"

Abraham nodded. "Yes. Cost foremost."

"My good sir," said Pritchard, "I should be happy to prepare two sketches. One bridge to be constructed wholly of iron, the other a compromise which shall combine iron with stone. I shan't charge you a penny, sir, but rather offer them as a token of my interest."

Abraham glanced at Richard, who gave a small nod.

"Very well," Abraham agreed. "So long as thou do it at thy own risk."

It was only after they had examined the ruined barn and were headed back to Coalbrookdale that the subject came up again.

"In the matter of the bridge," Richard observed, "John Wilkinson would prove an eager ally."

This was true, Abraham knew. And when the time came to build it, Abraham would need to share the financial burden. But the fact was, he dreaded the whole obligation. He confessed none of this to Richard. An inwardness had taken hold of him. Their stirrups knocked together; Richard's mare was crowding Blacky, as she often did, being Blacky's mother. Abraham withdrew into himself.

He could not think of John Wilkinson without recalling how Father used to frown at the cannon stacked up on the New Willey wharf, on the Broseley side of the river. Father never said anything, only ceased talking and frowned. The sight clearly troubled him. Abraham carried that feeling into adulthood—a great caution in his bowels whenever he found it necessary to be in Wilkinson's presence. Wilkinson's strident tenor grated on his ears. The man's very rotundity offended him, as if the Broseley ironmaster had fattened himself on men's blood.

Now they forded Birches Brook and continued along the turnpike, which was still thronged with sightseers. They passed a tall curly-haired woman walking with a young collier. A Gypsy woman of the poorest sort, she wore a short shift with neither petticoats nor stockings, nor even shoes; yet when she caught him looking at her bare calves, which he was trying to avoid, she flashed a dazzling smile that revealed surprising beauty. With a blush he turned his attention to the steaming riverbed. He thought of the pent-up waters, the bridge, and John Wilkinson.

"It seems that everyone," he said, including Richard in a rueful look, "is in a great hurry for this bridge."

# *Maggie Foster*

Jeremy Crump's mother invited her to eat supper and stay the night. The Crump cottage, overlooking the river, was supported in back by pilings and crowded in front by Bedlam Furnace. Jeremy was the middle child in a brood of five. His mother, Polly, widowed two years ago, took a maternal interest in Maggie; cleaned her wounds, made a poultice of boiled comfrey leaves for her feet, even loaned her a dress.

"Thank you," Maggie said again and again.

They ate with spoons and fingers from wooden bowls—fish fried in butter, boiled asparagus, brown bread. Polly urged her to take more of everything, particularly fish, since the oldest boy, Matthew, had collected more than could be smoked in a sort of tepee he had erected next to the cottage. Putting caution aside, Maggie ate her fill. It was more delicious than anything she had ever tasted.

Over the pounding of the furnaces, which caused the beer to jiggle in the mugs, the children plied her with questions about America:

"Is it true," Jeremy asked, "that everything in the New World be plentiful?"

"Turkeys and deer everywhere," said Matthew, before she could answer, "and cod the size of cows?"

"Hast tha seen an alligator?" asked Helen, the youngest, a five-year-old.

Polly shushed them. "Let her eat." Polly had a lined face with worry knots at the corners of her mouth, small, deep-set eyes in a constant squint, a crimson birthmark on her neck; gaunt frame, stooped shoulders, missing teeth. She seemed too old to be their mother. "They bedaggle thee with their questions, this lot." She chided little Helen: "Thou, Miss Dandiprat! Mind, drink tha short beer."

Shouts came from the river. Horns were blowing, bells clanging. When they rushed out onto the narrow back porch, they saw the torrent rolling toward them in the twilight like a surf, one crest after another lit pink by the smelters and lime kilns that burned on either side, while men struggled with boats or ran to safety.

Jeremy and Matthew scrambled down the embankment, shooed the chickens from the coop, led the pig from its sty under the porch, and began dismantling the makeshift smokehouse. Polly and the oldest daughter, Kate, who was sixteen, began dumping all their possessions into sacks and baskets, which they put by the front door. Within minutes the water was halfway up the pilings, flooding the root cellar. A barrel bumped against the floor boards. Polly sent Matthew next door to see if their neighbor, Mrs. Merryweather, needed help, then hustled everyone out the front door, and they all sat in a row on the narrow strip of land between the cottage and the wagon road, huddled under blankets, their faces lit by the glare of the twin furnaces that constituted Bedlam Furnace.

A wagon rumbled past, the creaking wheels narrowly missing their feet. Maggie yelped. The draft horses were immense. She turned to Polly.

"Is the house in danger?"

"In danger?" Polly gave a short rueful laugh. "Only if it floods."

Helen crawled into her mother's lap. "Ain't it flooding now, Mama?"

"Sorry," said Maggie. "It was a stupid question."

Polly gave her a gap-toothed smile. "Dunna worry. Tha be'est young, and dunna ken the Severn."

Polly could have been the children's grandmother, but she had referred to Helen as her daughter. And Timothy, the next youngest, looked to be seven or eight. All five children like stair steps.

"The biggest fear is trows," Polly said.

"Trows?"

"Aye. Barges. The biggins. If a big trow bumps us, 'twill take the cottage sure."

Helen whimpered and clung to her mother's neck. Timothy looked up with big eyes. Kate sat with her knees drawn up under her skirts. "Is it like three years ago, Mama?" Kate asked.

"I hope not" was Polly's response.

Men were busy stacking sand bags around the hearths of the twin stone towers—each tower thirty feet high and spewing a fountain of flame that lit the bellying smoke. Shadows rippled spokelike across the riverbank from horses plodding in a circle. The horse gin was an emergency measure, Polly explained, to replace the steam pumping-engine that normally raised water from the Severn to turn the water wheels for the bellows. The same thing had happened, she said, during the big flood of '70.

Maggie managed not to cry out as another wagon rumbled past. She checked to see that Timothy's feet were out of the way and asked the boy if he wanted to sit next to her, but Timothy looked at her with his large eyes and shook his head. She was not used to being around children, and could only guess at their needs.

"Where—" Maggie hesitated, not wanting to ask another foolish question. "Where would you live?" Where would *we* live, she was tempted to say—grateful for Polly's shelter, not wanting to leave it.

"The furnace. In the nooks and crannies. This time of year, we moight make shift to live under the bellows arches."

"They'd let us do that?"

"Aye. They'd do us that favor." Polly chuckled wryly. "As long as we dunna get in their way."

"That's nice, I guess."

"Pshaw! They'd love to see it go, this old magpie cottage squatting on the verge. 'Twould give 'em more space to dump their slack."

*Squatting on the verge,* Maggie thought. Sitting here poised between fire and water. It was familiar. It was the way she had lived her whole life—at the margins of corporations. From the time she was Helen's age and her parents lost their fancy zipcode in Texico, and when she entered CALYPOOL, the California Youth Talent Pool. And even after her escape into the desert, to Ecosophia. Ecosophia itself owed its precarious existence to its location in the Radlands, where hardly anybody ventured. *Squatting on the verge.*

Jeremy and Matthew checked periodically on the river. They reported that the water was no longer rising and the brewhouse was safe. Still, Polly declared, they would wait outside until the water had come down a foot.

Their talk drifted to the past. Polly told about coming to Madeley Wood with her husband a dozen years ago, when she was twenty-three, after they lost their rights to the commons where they used to graze a cow and sheep. "Enclosure Act, they called it," Polly said. "They give it a name, but 'twas the rich stealing from the poor, as always. Took it away and fenced it, and called it their own." Polly and her husband moved in with his brother, who had built the cottage and worked in the limestone quarry atop Lincoln Hill. Three years later, the brother was killed in a pit collapse. And then, two years ago, Polly's husband, Matthew, was drowned crossing the river in his coracle. " 'Twas icy," she said, "and he cunna get out of the way of a trow."

Maggie was stunned to realize that Polly was thirty-five, only six years older than she was. Polly obviously took her for younger. Earlier, Maggie had explained, while her feet were soaking, how she happened to be wandering around naked at four in the morning: she had accepted a ride from Bristol with a gentleman headed for Shrewsbury, and they were set upon by bandits, who took her belongings, including her fine velvet dress, and tried to ravish her, but she managed to escape into the woods, and then the earthquake struck. The tale sounded far-fetched as she recited it, and when Polly shook her head knowingly, Maggie thought for a moment that the other woman had seen right through it.

"Tha canna trust such men, lass. Mark me words. This fellow who called himself a gentleman, why he was as thick as two sticks with them highwaymen. 'Tis an old dog-trick in Shropshire, to befriend a young lass such as thaself, fresh off the boat, and lead her into the clutches of punkers and cutpurses."

"Really?" Maggie asked.

Polly nodded knowingly.

Maggie sighed. "And I fell for it."

"Aye. Being from America, and not knowing any better."

Amusing. But now, sitting here frightened by the unfamiliarity of everything, she decided that Polly's assessment was not far off the mark. Maggie was indeed an ingenue. Maybe she should take ten years off her age. She could probably pass for nineteen here, and it might help explain her ignorance. Change her birth date from 1744 to 1754. But she was too bone-weary to alter her story.

"Where was tha born?" asked Polly.

"I don't know. I was orphaned in a shipwreck. I never knew my parents. Only that they were English."

"I expect tha be'st English, then."

Maggie went through her script, how she was taken in by a well-to-do lawyer's family in Baltimore and eventually married a young lawyer. *I've never even been to Baltimore,* she thought. She knew its street patterns only in infrared, from twentieth-century archival aerial photos showing heat loss from buildings.

The part about being orphaned was true: her small body going weightless as her father swung her back and forth once, her stomach flip-flopping as he lofted her over the steel mesh fence. Her mother screaming through the fence. The whump of the concussion grenade. Maggie possessed only a few megabytes of early childhood—memories sometimes indistinguishable from home videos rerecorded on the laser disc that Granny called a family album: her father and mother standing by the swimming pool (whose flecked blue tile she thought she actually remembered). Both holding drinks, both wearing iridescent pink-and-green polaroid glasses, her mother smiling jauntily in a topless suit, nipples cupped in silver pasties, her father's bubbleshirt proclaiming I SUPPORT OUR TROOPS IN TEXICO. According to Granny's voice-over, the video was taken sometime after one of the Petroleum Wars—probably in 2013, the year before Maggie was born. The camera zooming in on their drinks showed the ice cubes fizzing and popping, and you could hear her mother giggling and saying it was twenty-thousand-year-old glacial ice.

Granny herself appeared at intervals, wearing an old-fashioned magenta spandex tank top, sometimes with bubbletights and programmable jewelry, chatting in her airhead way to her "sweet Maggie-Waggie" that the world was going to hell in a handbasket and there wasn't really anything anybody could do about it: *So I'm like, What's my little grandkiddledumps going to do? The best you can hope for is to be one of the lucky ones, Maggie-Waggie, like your mom and dad.* (This was before they got unzipped.) *Be a lawyer; because whatever happens, you will make money. Or be a food designer like me, because people have to eat. Whatever you decide to be, you gotta believe in yourself, Maggie!* That believe-in-yourself styro was something she emphasized so incessantly that Maggie concluded later in life that Granny probably did not believe in herself very much. It was sprinkled in with advice on everything from sunscreen to quality time with your pets, and little riffs like what she was doing when JFK was assassinated (brushing her teeth the morning after a slumber party). All interspersed with old family snapshots, newspaper clippings, and music with Granny as deejay—digitally transferred to the tiny iridescent blue disc that Maggie was clutching when she was thrown over the fence and that she managed to hang on to all those years at CALYPOOL. The disc was her most fiercely guarded possession, not Granny's styro advice, which seemed more and more bizarre as the world fell apart, after the Indian subcontinent and the Middle East were irradiated, and then New York, and with the progression of ecological ruin that left most of the planet hostile to most life except for hypermutating retroviruses. Granny's album was the one constant in Maggie's life, the one thing where the manipulation was at least up-front, where it was just

Granny trying to impress her values on her granddaughter. It was the constancy itself, the very fixedness of it, even the fixedness of Granny's *mishegoss,* while everything else was up for grabs.

Insulated in CALYPOOL from the chaos outside—the breakdown of social services, the privatization, the rampant homelessness after the wars, the collapse of government into corporate fiefdoms—Maggie kept the little disc hidden from the Caretakers, played it surreptitiously, sometimes obsessively, in goggos, under the pillow, relying on those grainy images, those crude audio tracks, to keep her anchored in the past. Even if it seemed like someone else's past, it was a past, and that kept her sane.

Gone now. Lost in a future that she was determined to prevent.

She had dozed off, probably in midsentence. She startled awake. "Where was I?"

"Your husband died of yellow fever."

Maggie nodded. "Right. So I came to England to make a fresh start."

Which was also true, in a way. She was going to be doing so much lying, she was glad to tell some truth.

In the small hours of the morning, she felt a hand shaking her shoulder. Helen was curled in her lap, and Polly was motioning her inside. Maggie struggled to her feet. She carried Helen into the cottage. Polly pointed her to a bed, and Maggie fell into it without a word.

Around dawn, she felt a jab in her ribs—an elbow—and realized she was snoring. It took a while, looking over Polly's shoulder, to remember where she was.

# John Wilkinson

He cracked the wax seal on the letter from Thomas Farnolls Pritchard, tipped back in his chair in the clutter of his office at New Willey, and held the page in a slant of sunlight. He expected to find it amusing, and was not disappointed.

Last month's landslip, according to Pritchard, argued eloquently for a bridge across the Severn Gorge. He wondered was it not perhaps time to give Mr. Darby a wee nudge? If Wilkinson would be so kind as to put in a good word with young Darby on his behalf, then Pritchard would be forever in his debt. *And for my part,* Pritchard said in closing, *I would wholeheartedly recommend the use of iron, since young Darby seems cautious in that regard.*

Wilkinson's belly shook with laughter. Certainly Darby was nothing if not cautious. And the workings of Pritchard's own brain were as clear as carrots in a thin broth. Having designed the stone bridge erected last year at Bringwood Forge, the architect itched to get his hands on a loftier commission—and fancied that Wilkinson would jump at the promise of iron.

In truth, if Wilkinson could but see a way of making money from it, he would undertake the bridge himself. Oh yes. And spring for iron, by God's teeth! Build it of iron, as surely as St. Paul's was built of stone, and call it the Wilkinson Bridge! Ha! But it would be a costly exercise in vanity. Too many uncertainties. And the tolls would never recover the costs. Pritchard was right: better to get young Darby to sink his money into it.

Wilkinson had little use for this new Darby, so wet behind the ears that he fairly glistened—or for Quakers in general, with their drab clothes and sanctimonious pronouncements. They ignored good manners, refusing to doff their hats and addressing everyone with their familiar *thees* and *thous* without regard to social rank. Stiff-necked lot, prideful in their own ways. They forswore oaths and weapons of war and refused to pay tithes like other men. And clubbed together as thick as thieves, they did, so that after eleven years at the Severn Gorge, Wilkinson remained an outsider.

It galled him that Wilkinsons had always followed in the footsteps of Darbys. Seventy years ago, the first Abraham Darby had come up from Bristol and taken over the lease at Coalbrookdale, rebuilding the dam and repairing the ruined furnace, which gave the Darbys the best site anywhere in the gorge, with water flowing all through the dry summer months. And as if that were not enough good fortune for one man, old Darby One discovered how to fire his furnace with coke. Discovered it not by his wits, oh no, not by your least ballock. In the last century, poor old Dud Dudley, the bastard son of the Earl of Dudley, had tried coal and failed. But Darby One had the good luck to happen on to Shropshire sweet clod coal, and the coking coals that it yielded were as good as charcoal. Or nearly so. Oh, it took years of tinkering before he got it right. No denying that. But it started with luck. Luck and Bristol money.

Then fell another piece of damned luck square into the lap of the Darbys. That same year, the blacksmith Thomas Newcomen invented *ye invention for raising Water by Fire:* the atmospheric steam engine. Suddenly the rules of the ironmaking game changed. Now, with a fire engine to pump the water back into his millpond, Darby could keep a second furnace running through the summer drought. And the new pumping-engines permitted sites without plentiful water to be harnessed as well. Darby's son, the second Abraham Darby, was able to build new works at Horsehay and Ketley. Coalbrookdale in the meantime held a near monopoly in supplying cylinders for the Newcomen engines. Thus did the Dale Company grow to become the world's largest ironworks. And thus did Quakers fasten on to the iron trade like piglets to a sow's belly.

Darbys! Short-lived as rabbits, but the goddess Fortune smiled on them. Wherever Wilkinsons went, the Darby footsteps were ahead of them.

Wilkinsons had no such luck. When John was a young chap growing up in the Furness district of Cumbria, his father Isaac had traveled south, purchased Bersham Furnace from the Quakers, and turned it to gun making for the Liverpool trade, and for years struggled to fire it with coke, but the stinking sulfurous coal of North Wales defied Isaac Wilkinson's efforts. It was John who finally succeeded, when he was not yet thirty, John who did the thinking for them both by then, getting the old man's signature on the lease, guiding his drunken hand over various papers. They moved farther south, to the Severn Gorge, to purchase Willey Furnace from two of the Coalbrookdale partners, Thomas Goldney and Richard Ford, who were less pious than some but Quakers nonetheless. So the Wilkinsons came by Willey Furnace as they came by Bersham—purchasing it from the damned Quakers and turning it to gun making.

John Wilkinson had succeeded by his wits. At Bersham, he eased his father into bankruptcy and used his first wife's fortune to take over the Works, where he put his younger brother, William, in charge. At Willey, he replaced Isaac with a syndicate of Bristol businessmen to create New Willey, then juggled the accounts to show scant profit, so that he might use his second wife Mary Lee's fortune to buy out the discouraged investors—all in time to reap the profits to be got from the Seven Years War.

Since then, he had acquired a reputation as a cannon maker of some excellence. Now, at the age of forty-five, he was worth seventy-five thousand pounds, owned three furnaces and a ship as well as interests in tin mines and lead mines in Wales. He kept two houses with half a dozen servants, purchased his wigs in London and Paris, attended meetings of the Lunar Society at the invitation of his famous brother-in-law, Joseph Priestley, and was sending his daughter to study in France. By any reckoning, he was a gentleman. He might have purchased a peerage, as Mary Lee urged. Yet he was restless.

It was not simply that he lacked a male heir. It was some other sense of mortality. A coldness at the very center of his being, a hunger that could not be filled. Always the nagging question, when he thought about resting his boot heels by the fireside: Suppose this is not enough? Well, then, what would be enough? And never an answer. Only the restless thump of the furnace saying, More!

He might have found comfort in the Bible. But he did not believe in the Virgin Birth, or in the Divine Christ either. Baptized a Presbyterian, he counted himself a Unitarian, following Priestley's rational example. His declared belief was in one God, free of papist trimmings. But whenever he tried praying to that solitary, rational God, the picture that crept into his mind was that of His Majesty the King seated on a throne of clouds—benignly indifferent at best, almost certainly helpless, and very possibly mad.

He did not confide this blasphemy to anyone. In old age there would be time enough to ponder eternity and mend his ways. For now, he was determined to beat the devil around the post and seize what he could in this mortal life.

What would be enough? Well, for lack of something grander, it would be a feather in his cap to overtake the Darbys. Ah, yes. It would be a grand satisfaction. For even now it was said:

> Broseley gets the shade,
> Madeley gets the money.

Looking across the river at Madeley, sometimes Wilkinson liked to imagine what he would do with Coalbrookdale if it were his. He imagined rows of cannon stacked up at Ludcroft Wharf, as of old. Imagined the lessons, oh the painful lessons, he should like to teach young Darby!

These were idle, recurrent themes, and yet they informed his scheming like the thump of the furnaces, and Pritchard's letter brought them to the fore.

Now, seeing by the clock on the wall that the time for the afternoon pour was approaching, he grabbed a quill and scratched out a rough draft to Pritchard, concluding, *Indeed, I should be happy to put in a good word with Darby. I remain, Sir, your Obedient Servant, etc.* He blotted the ink with sand and pulled on a bell cord to summon the clerk's secretary.

A boy accompanied Wilkinson to the furnace, hurrying along beside him and helping him exchange his waistcoat for a canvas coat and leather flat-tail hat as he walked. The furnace keeper, seeing Wilkinson arrive, signaled the tapper and his assistant, who used their long poles to pry the bricks and clay from the tap hole. With a final jab, they leaped aside. Through cobalt-blue spectacles, Wilkinson watched the white-glowing liquid gush from the taphole, lighting up the oak-and-tile undersides of the cast-house roof. A pleasurable wave of heat washed over him. He chuckled aloud.

*Iron,* by God! Like liquid sun! Ha! Was there any ejaculation more glorious than this?

The incandescence flowed along the channels pressed into the sand from the feeder channels into the rows of pigs, illumined the perspiring faces of the gutter men working with their pointed hoes to divert the flow this way and that. Once a row of pigs was cast, the gutter men directed the iron to the casting pit, where the cannon molds stood buried and where each of four cannon was poured in turn. The odor of hot metal and scorched loam filled the superheated air. A manly scent, Wilkinson thought. Honest and powerful. It seemed to him he could smell that charged air not just in his nostrils but with his whole body.

When all four cannon were poured, the remaining iron was run into more pigs until sparks flew from the taphole. The tapper and his assistant stopped the taphole with brick and clay. For the gutter men and ladlers, the tension was over. They removed their canvas coats, leather aprons, and flat-tail hats and took turns drinking from a bucket of short beer. The first pigs had cooled to a pale orange heat. Outside, the process was beginning again: the fillers were lined up with wheelbarrows to dump loads of coke, limestone, and ore into the furnace head.

"Beg pardon, sir." A boy from the clerk's office, who had been waiting for Wilkinson's attention, now spoke. "The clerk sends word that Lord Forester's man is waiting outside your office."

"Tell him I shall be there presently." Wilkinson walked among the cannon that were cast some days earlier, now hoisted from the pit, and he savored their continuing warmth. These particular guns were the twelve-pounders ordered by St. Petersburg, with the czarist double-eagle crest on the breech.

He peered into the bores to see if any of the mold cores had slipped off center. Later, when they were fully cooled and sent to the boring mill and polished, the bores would be scrutinized with a candle and a small mirror on the end of a stick to find flaws—voids caused by bubbles or inclusions that might weaken the walls and cause them to explode when fired. Wilkinson undertook such inspections personally in the case of guns for His Majesty's Navy, which had to stand the critical Proof Test at the armory at Woolwich, for the Board of Ordnance took a dim view of failures. With the guns for the Russians it was less important. Ditto the Turks. They paid less per ton, knowing the guns were patched: screw-plugs for the larger holes, iron putty for the small defects. The Russians and Turks were accustomed to their guns flying into a thousand pieces. Life was cheap there. Such were the thoughts that flitted through Wilkinson's mind.

But the presence of the guns giving off their black primal heat fascinated him in another way, a way that had nothing to do with death. Nay, on the contrary, their warmth and newness affirmed life. Was there anything mightier than cast iron? Any surer sign that Man was given dominion over the beasts of the field—and civilized Man given dominion over savages? The Russians and Turks were less removed from savagery, of course, than the English. And then you had your Irish and your Scots, who had only recently stopped painting themselves blue and only recently discovered trousers. And the Welsh, who could not speak straight. It was all a matter of degree.

When Wilkinson returned to the office, walking past the high oak-paneled pulpit from which the clerk oversaw the scriveners and account keepers, Lord Forester's manservant leaped up from the bench and presented him with a letter, saying he had instructions to wait for a reply.

Wilkinson read it on the spot with barely concealed annoyance. Invitation to a fox hunt. Saturday next. Normally he would decline. George Forester owned most of Broseley and was Wilkinson's landlord; fancied himself a patriot and had a few connections among the military, which Wilkinson had used to his advantage; but the man was a blockhead. And although Wilkinson could sit a horse as well as the next man, he secretly hated all that ludicrous galloping about and jumping. He spent quite enough time in the saddle visiting his works in Bersham and Bradley.

One line caught his attention, however. Forester noted that Anthony Bacon, MP, would be riding with the hounds, and that Bacon had referred to "business he hoped to conduct with Mr. Wilkinson."

Wilkinson instructed the servant to tell his lordship that he would be most honored to join the hunt.

What business Anthony Bacon had in mind was anybody's guess. Wilkinson knew him purely by reputation. Bacon had only recently got into ironmaking, but his early years as a provisioner of troops in Senegal and the West Indies had given him a keen nose for sniffing out government money, and he was well connected in London. Six years ago he had built a modern forge in a remote part of South Wales, at Cyfarthfa. He got the leases dog cheap, because the place was so isolated; carried the iron out on packhorses across the mountains and down the valley the twenty-six miles to Cardiff; then, using his influence in Commons, drummed up support for a road and got it built with local money. Now the forge had its own furnace and was prospering quite jollily. Bacon appeared to be a man after Wilkinson's own heart. Wilkinson had use for such a well-connected schemer.

The baying of the hounds suggested that the fox had taken another turn—from Ladywood back onto the Forester estate. George Forester decided that they should wait here, the fox's den being just across the meadow.

Wilkinson, panting, was only too happy to join the seven or eight older riders who waited with Forester, while a party of young squires from Wenlock continued in noisy pursuit. Wilkinson had a cramp in his side, and his arse was sore. He hated jumping. It seemed an unnatural act for horse and rider. Certainly when the man weighed nineteen stone. His big gray mare was of like mind, to judge by her surliness; her hind legs were scratched from the blackthorn hedges, and earlier, when they had crashed through a tenant's clothesline and approached a tall hedge, she had stopped short and nearly pitched him over her neck. Bacon had stayed behind, retrieving Wilkinson's tricorn and accompanying him the long way around, through a gate. Bacon inquired after business in general; Wilkinson replied it was going most jollily. But nothing more was said while they galloped to catch up with the others. Nor did he speak now. Bacon was a distinguished-looking fellow, ten years Wilkinson's senior, wearing his own white hair tied back in two small queues. He was silent while a couple of brandy flasks were passed around amid jocular suggestions in Latin as to how the farmer's wife should be compensated for her goose, which were followed by talk about the rules of cricket now being laid down in Parliament. Supercilious claptrap, most of it. The owners of the flasks, who had attended Oxford together, had rather boozed their jibs.

The hounds were getting near. At that moment the fox appeared through a break in the trees not fifty feet away—looking weary, its tail dragging. Seeing the huntsmen, it turned; but then confronted by the murderously yelping pack, it wheeled, made a desperate run across the meadow, and was overtaken. The master of the hounds waded amongst the pack with his whip—not in time to prevent the fox's being killed, however. He passed the body up to Forester, its lips frozen in a snarl. Forester was angry upon seeing it was a vixen. He cut off the brush and presented it to Bacon. "If it please you, sir, for you have traveled the farthest."

Bacon accepted the tail politely, and the master of the hounds threw the carcass to the hounds. What happened during the frenzy that followed was not immediately clear. Dogs were digging into the burrow. At first it seemed the fox had been torn into several pieces, for fur was everywhere. Then someone cried out, "Kits!" But it was too late. The baby foxes had all been destroyed.

"Damn!" cried Forester, furious now, raising his crop as if to strike the master of the hounds, but thinking better of it. Cursing the ineptitude of the men in his employ, he led the way back.

Wilkinson thought *Good!* It was a bloody piece of work but would leave the fewer to hunt. His arse was numb. As they returned to Broseley Manor at a trot, Bacon rode beside him. They exchanged a few words about the hunt, Bacon confessing some sympathy for the fox. To Wilkinson's relief, they slowed to a walk.

"You have a reputation for accuracy as a cannon maker, Mr. Wilkinson, if you don't mind my saying so. I have heard your name mentioned favorably at the Ordnance Board."

"Why, I am flattered." A few years ago, Wilkinson had been reprimanded by the board for supplying illegally patched guns. The board had gone so far as to cut one apart and counted no less than twenty-three plugs. While he reckoned that he had put that bit of unpleasantness behind him, he liked hearing this affirmation from Bacon—couched as it was with a reminder of Bacon's connections, which meant that Bacon wanted something from him.

Bacon frowned. "And yet—" (For a moment Wilkinson thought he was going to mention the patched guns.) "The present method is by its nature inaccurate, do you not agree?"

"Quite."

They discussed the problems: how mold cores slipped or were crushed; how gas bubbles collected around the cores; how the cutters of the boring machine tended to follow these and other defects in the iron, causing the bore to wander off center. Bacon referred to the difficulties plaguing the Carron works, the big new government-sponsored cannon foundry that had opened in Scotland with great fanfare but whose guns had repeatedly failed the Proof Test. Abruptly, he turned to Wilkinson and asked a very odd question:

"Have you any experience, sir, boring from the solid?"

Odd, because Bacon surely knew the answer, and because the

question was asked a little too casually. Wilkinson responded cautiously.

"No. I bore them in the usual way, sir, from a hollow casting."

Bacon nodded. "A gun would be more accurate bored from the solid, would it not?"

Wilkinson felt a shiver at the back of his neck. "In theory, yes. Muskets are drilled thusly on a lathe. But to put a whole cannon on a lathe, and to bore so large a hole—well." He frowned. "No one has ever tried it, so far as I know."

"The Dutchmen are attempting it, are they not?"

Wilkinson snorted. "In brass, sir. And slowly, in a manner of speaking." His companion was referring to the notoriously methodical Jan and Pieter Verbruggen. The father and son who had been hired to oversee the improvements at the Royal Brass Foundry in Woolwich were trying everyone's patience.

Bacon smiled. "So I am told. But could their method not be adapted to iron?"

Wilkinson shrugged. "From what I understand, the Verbruggens plan to use a single cutting-head. It might do for brass, but cast iron is harder stuff. 'Twould produce too much heat."

"It would seem you have given the matter some thought, Mr. Wilkinson."

Wilkinson affirmed with a glance that this was true. The cored molds caused no end of frustration. And casting in loam was a laborious process. Wilkinson waited for Bacon to come to the point.

As they approached Broseley Hall, Bacon laid out his plan in a straightforward way. He had got word that the Board of Ordnance was about to freeze all orders for Carron guns. "It is not official but will happen soon." Bacon wished to submit a gun bored from a solid casting and to become an approved gunfounder; however, his ironworks at Cyfarthfa was not yet up to the task. Time was of the essence, for once the board's decision became official, other armsmakers would rush into the breach. Would Wilkinson be willing to act as his agent in boring such a gun?

They discussed terms. Bacon would carry the risk; he would pay a good price, a sum in advance and without requiring any guarantee of success. And Bacon was more interested in becoming an approved supplier than in retaining any patents.

"Then we are agreed, sir," said Wilkinson. "I shall act as your agent."

The two men shook hands, Bacon still holding the fox tail in his left. Wilkinson congratulated himself, because there was no risk to him, and if this should turn the whole cannon trade topsy-turvy, then he would end up on top.

## Maggie Foster

During her first couple of weeks with the Crumps, she found herself asking as many questions as little Helen. But she learned how to help with household chores—skills she would need to land a job as a maid in the Darby household.

Polly taught her to spin. Maggie was clumsy at first, but gradually picked up speed. A weaver left bags of flax and paid by the pound for finished skeins. Maggie turned over her coins to Polly, who gave a few back. Maggie's fingers were sore; she dreamed of spinning, dreamed of the movement of flax through fingers and thumbs.

Sometimes other women brought spinning wheels and gathered next door in Mrs. Merryweather's cottage to spin and talk. Mrs. Merryweather, a thickset woman in her fifties, rosily freckled and triple-chinned, wore a mobcap with short durable ruffles. Her travels as a midwife took her all around Madeley parish and beyond, so she was a font of gossip and folk remedies. Superstition filled the talk: peas coming up white signified death; Polly's birthmark was caused by her mother's unsatisfied craving for port wine; and Maggie's clumsiness at spinning came from her mother's having squashed too many spiders.

Maggie's thirtieth birthday went by without her noticing until two days after. The calendar here revolved around Fridays, when the weaver made his rounds, Saturday baths, and holidays. The three older children worked ten hours a day, with Sunday their only day off. Maggie was appalled at Jeremy's description of his work in the coal pit, where he crawled along the seams, dragging great lumps of coal with a girdle and chain.

Maggie's own day revolved around weaving and household tasks and the circadian rhythms of the ironworks: the incessant pounding of the bellows cams, punctuated by the morning pour and the afternoon pour wafting hot dry heat through the Crump cottage. Every few seconds, the heavy oak walking beam on the Newcomen pumping-engine tipped like a seesaw. There was something majestic about those slow silent strokes, in contrast to the chaos of wagon traffic and wheelbarrows crisscrossing one another's paths along the various ramps and terraces crowded into the sloping site. Animals were part of the traffic: not only draft horses and mules pulling burdens but also geese dodging carts, cats hunting mice; even occasional rust-colored flocks of sheep. The official name of the works was the Madeley Wood Furnace, but everyone called it Bedlam.

The cottage consisted of two small rooms below and a loft above where the boys slept on corn husks. At one end of the narrow back porch was the privy, and at the other end, dug into the hillside, was the little brewhouse where they made beer and kept dairy products, and the root cellar. Maggie shared a feather mattress with Polly, Kate, and Helen, which took some getting used to. No privacy. Maggie flossed her teeth nightly using a piece of linen thread, which greatly entertained the Crumps. For the Saturday baths, water was carried to a wooden tub behind a blanket rigged as a curtain. The women bathed themselves, then Helen and Timothy. By the time the older boys had finished, the water was black. The cottage reeked variously of tallow, coaldust, cabbage, and unwashed bodies, to say nothing of the offal and sewage outside; and when it rained, the slag heaps and ash heaps leaked a sour, bitter smell. Everything around the furnaces, including the Crumps' cottage, was coated brown from iron oxide and soot.

"Black by day, red by night," Polly said.

An acrid brown haze filled the gorge when the air remained stagnant for a day or two. Maggie's eyes smarted. When she breathed deeply, she felt a needlelike pain in her chest. Often the visibility was so poor that she could not see across the river, only hear the shouts of the bow haulers on the Broseley towpath or glimpse sails sliding through the pea-soup smog. On the rare clear nights she could look across the river and distinguish the glow of the Calcutts furnace from that of the Jackfield tileworks and make out a few faint stars in the east. But most nights, everything swirled together in a lurid glow that resembled nothing so much as a giant bed of coals.

Whenever she had some time to herself, Maggie jotted down notes from the information she had memorized. She used a pencil stub that Jeremy had found outside the Bird in Hand, the public house just up the road. The stub was too short to use comfortably, so she bound it to a stick with thread. The Crumps were entranced with her writing. The children brought scraps of paper. Helen interrupted often. "What do't *say,* Maggie?"

Despite the lack of time to herself, and despite a general feeling of confinement, Maggie was pleased with her temporary living arrangements. Polly extended an old linen skirt for her with a false petticoat, adapted a top from a shirt that had belonged to Polly's husband, and dyed the whole thing blue so it made a presentable dress, and loaned her an apron, stockings, and a kerchief to tie back her hair. A pair of wooden clogs that had belonged to Polly's husband completed the ensemble. The clogs were too wide, but Maggie padded them with rags, and Jeremy whittled a place smooth where her heel rubbed.

"Tha be'est comely," said Polly with an appraising nod. "With that curly hair and them bewitching green eyes."

Maggie was cold most of the time, being accustomed to Ecosophia's humid warmth and to wearing something soft next to her skin. Here, in this damp, cold climate, her underwear consisted of a linen undervest and underskirt. No panties; the reason was obvious the first time they were walking together and Polly squatted by the roadside. Maggie had difficulty getting used to the bareness combined with the full skirts. In the cottage it offered some privacy for sponge bathing;

but whenever she went outside, the whole getup felt restrictive and a little silly, as if she were concealing something. Which she was, of course: the entire lower half of her body. She felt like a puff pastry.

She liked watching Jeremy paddle his coracle, a small boat constructed like a canoe but round. It was made from a single cowhide stretched across a circular wooden skeleton, sealed with tar, and propelled by means of a paddle held vertically and moved in a figure eight. Being round, the little boat could be made to rotate on its axis. These long summer evenings, when Jeremy got home from the coal pit, he scampered down the embankment with the coracle on his back like a turtle, plopped it in the water, skimmed through the willow shoots, and twirled in circles as gracefully as a water bug. She wanted to ask for a ride, but realized there was no room.

Some of the tasks were particularly repellent: rendering lard, skinning rabbits, wringing the necks of chickens—which recalled the punishment veeries back in CALYPOOL. The first time Polly showed her how to clean a goose, Maggie gagged. And when Polly showed her how to singe the pinfeathers, she recoiled from the smell. Polly chided her. "Where wast tha mother's *knee?*" she demanded.

"I beg your pardon?"

Polly gave Maggie's kerchief a sharp tug. "Tha shoulda learnt these things as a child!"

"I—" But Maggie stopped herself. It was easier, she had found, not to make excuses. Just concentrate on learning.

Once she was working at Sunniside, she would be in a position to observe Abraham Darby III and devise a strategy for influencing the design of the bridge. But first she had to get hired.

She missed Ecosophia. The people. The great fig tree sprawling from the atrium, its boughs following the steel catwalks. She missed the Beethoven string quartets and access to databases. She felt a kind of numbness in her heart, knowing all those things were lost to her forever.

Yet she sensed a vitality here that was missing back home—most obvious in the children. She had never had the opportunity to watch children play. She watched those who were too young to sort ore and coal, the four- and five-year-olds still engrossed in play. It called up a dim memory of making dolls with scraps of red-and-white-checked cloth, investing them with pretend life that was somehow more vivid than the life around her. It must have been after her parents got unzipped, when they lived in the metal quonset hut, but all she remembered was the feel of that red-and-white-checked cloth, and how absolutely real those dolls had seemed.

One day a woman whose baby Mrs. Merryweather had helped deliver brought the infant for them to see. She let Maggie hold it—a girl, three weeks old. The tiny, perfect features, the miniature pink fingers grasping her own finger, the fragrant, downy hair against her lips, all sent a thrill through Maggie's body.

"Aw, Maggie wants one," the woman teased.

Maggie caught her breath. She handed the baby back, not out of fear that she would drop it, but from the intensity of her own response. It came from too deep a place.

The old people had the same vitality. It showed in their hard edges, mobile faces, twisting postures; their tenacity bargaining at the Madeley market. Certain workers at Bedlam stood out sharply: the clerk with his clean white stockings and curled wig; the one-armed man who operated the Newcomen engine; the big woman with the raucous voice and rust-streaked face who worked with the men breaking ore. There was a heartiness in all that idiosyncrasy, even among the maimed and the impoverished. Maybe because they at least had a future.

One evening, taking a moment to stand at the porch rail looking out into the pink mist, Maggie heard birdsong from nearby, probably from the crab-apple tree—a liquid trill so unexpected, so miraculously clear over the thump of the furnaces, that her heart soared. It was a nightingale. She recognized the sound from an old disc of birdsongs they used to play in the atrium at Ecosophia. Hearing the living bird filled her with joy. She wished Trevor could hear it.

From inside the cottage, she heard Helen's soprano piping "Where is Maggie?" a question she dreaded. And yet at that moment it was part of the same melody. The sound of a world still intact. Simply to stand outside in the mist like this—even one that stank of rotten

eggs—and to breathe without fear of radiation or retrovirus, was painfully exhilarating.

She got her period on a Friday. She was helping Polly bake pies
for the Bird in Hand—they baked twice a week, fruit pies on
Tuesdays, meat pies on Fridays—when she felt something run down
her leg. Polly shooed her out of the kitchen, gave her some rags, and
warned her to stay away from the beer, or she would spoil its fermen-
tation. Maggie tied the rags as best she could, making one serve as
a belt. Later Polly showed her where to wash them and hang them
to dry, next to the privy—all in the whispered voice befitting "the
curse." Cautioning Maggie not to "walk abroad," Polly delivered the
pies by herself. And Maggie, aware of her own ineluctable odor, did
feel unclean, and sad. Sadness always accompanied her menstruation.
She would never conceive: her chromosomes were too messed up, her
tubes laser-fused.

But menstruation gave her license to seclude herself. She put the
pencil stub and scraps of paper in her apron pocket and walked down
the terraced slope to the river's edge, to the willow stump that Jeremy
had showed her—what he called the withey. The stump was half in
the water but reachable from a stepping stone and surrounded by
sprouts—the stump itself broad enough and flat enough on top that
she could mount it comfortably in her full skirt and sit partly hidden
from the river by the scrim of green leaves, and hidden from Bedlam
by a slag heap. She took off her shoes. At intervals she watched the
pink-stained sails of the barges as they tacked back and forth across
the Severn. She listened to the chanting of the bow haulers as they
scrambled along the opposite bank with their tow ropes. But mostly
she wrote, ignoring the occasional cramps, scribbling the facts she had
memorized: names, with birth dates and death dates and marriages,
and all the dates relating to the construction of the bridge. Every twist
in the careers of Abraham Darby III and John Wilkinson. Geological
information. She wrote furiously, unpacking the one piece of baggage
she was able to bring with her: the contents of her mind.

It had been strange memorizing so much, accustomed as she was to storing data electronically. But maybe what Trevor said was true. She was pacing around their apartment one morning in June, repeating facts from note cards, stopping to complain about the limited storage capacity of her brain, and Trevor observed that the mind was efficient in unexpected ways.

"Lookit Chief Joseph," Trevor said. "Lookit Charlie Parker."

Trevor was half Hopi, half Dineh—ecumenical enough to have great admiration for Chief Joseph's brilliant retreat from the U.S. Army in 1877 and for Charlie Parker's improvisations on tenor sax in the 1950s. He looked up from the bronze valve he was polishing with little swirling motions of his fingers, sitting cross-legged and barefoot on his workbench like a Buddha, wearing faded hemp jeans and one of his rare smiles—a smile more often in his voice than on his lips. "Lookit how you and me figure out what to tell each other."

She had registered the irony in his last comment. Trevor's reticence, compared to her need to talk, was an issue between them; he kept so much hidden, or at least unspoken, while she had to process things. "You will never know me," he told her once, "because you are too busy talking."

"I will never know you, Trevor, because you don't reveal yourself."

She was willing to concede that the truth was somewhere in between. It was the solid curve of Trevor's jaw that she loved, his understated humor, the unexpected turns of his mind. Not his silence. There was too much of it. She felt swallowed up in it sometimes.

She deposited a little stack of note cards on Trevor's knee and recited the names and dates of the Darby children. Mally, Abraham, Sarah, Samuel. The note cards were the old-fashioned distillation of all the information she had gleaned from various databases—mostly the classic 2011 edition of *Britmuse* available on disk in Ecosophia's library, but also some docuveeries that had turned up at the Albuquerque Commune bazaar and found their way into the Navajo trade routes. The docuveeries were flashy, but so heavily biased toward the corpo myth of progress as to be untrustworthy; they did, however, help her visualize the gorge and the bridge three-dimensionally, with actual and simulated flybys. She spent hours poring over maps and satellite false-color digifotos to assess the geology of Shropshire.

Less glitzy but more intriguing were the few primary sources that had been digitized: Abraham Darby III's careful account-book entries, John Wilkinson's letters to James Watt, Abiah Darby's diary. Maggie was particularly drawn to the handwritten documents. She practiced her own handwriting, using an old buzzard feather that she turned into a quill. She copied John Wilkinson's flowery signature. She even began to like the note cards, the tactile ordering of information. Liked shuffling through them, arranging them in different piles, thumbing their velvety worn edges.

"You know, Trevor, you don't have to hang around for this." She meant he didn't have to help her study. But it came out sounding preemptive.

This was an awkward time for them. They had lived together three years in this apartment, which was separated from its neighbors by yucca mats and a lattice of flowering vines and potted herbs. They had not got around to marrying; it seemed to Maggie too much of a commitment. Trevor said nothing, but was probably waiting for her—another part of himself that he kept hidden. She at least expressed her doubts. They were monogamous, but not by declaration. Their connection remained unofficial, tentative.

"I guess it's love," she told Erzulie with a shrug. "I don't know." When she described her feelings, Erzulie grinned.

"Child, what are you waiting for?"

Maybe they did love each other. But somehow she always thought there would be more time, that something would happen; she would *know*. And now she was about to disappear from this world forever. The finality of it was hard.

Trevor shuffled through the note cards. "John Wilkinson."

Maggie made a face. She didn't know whether she had the patience for Wilkinson.

"Do you think Wilkinson was really 'iron mad'?" Trevor was going to tease it out of her.

"No. I think he was just very aggressive at applying innovative technologies. He helped shape the First Industrial Revolution."

"So you believe in the First Industrial Revolution."

She shrugged. "I'm using the term loosely. The gradualists always argue that some of the innovations in the fourteenth and sixteenth centuries were just as important as what happened in the eighteenth, and that's true. But *something* came together in the 1770s, in the Severn Gorge. An explosion. Something like what happened two hundred years later in electronics, and at the turn of the century in biotech. Everything suddenly reached critical mass."

"Sounds like Paul."

Maggie colored. *Critical mass* was in fact Paul Stanski's metaphor. Paul, who looked so saintly with that halo of white hair floating around his head, had spent most of his career in a corpo weapons lab before he made an about-face thirty years ago. He was—as he was fond of saying, with the self-deprecating humor that made him bearable—part of the brotherhood of Old White Men who had totaled the planet.

Maggie liked Paul. It was his leadership as much as Erzulie's that had built Ecosophia. Trevor found him arrogant and Eurocentric. *They destroyed everything, all those Old White Men. And now they want to redeem themselves.*

Maggie shrugged. "Whatever you choose to call it, it was powerful. Watt's steam engine. The bridge. That whole shift in the scale of technology. And Wilkinson was at the center of it."

Trevor applied a thin coat of oil to the mating surfaces of the valve and carefully slid one piece inside the other. "Synergy." He worked the pieces back and forth gently. "Wouldn't it have come together without Wilkinson?"

Maggie stuck her hands in the hip pockets of her jeans. "Maybe. But it might not have had the same explosive force. The old atmospheric steam engine would have gone on for another generation or two, limited to pumping water. And without the bridge, you might not have had that jump to large-scale iron structures. It wouldn't have had the same impact."

"But..." A hint of a smile entered Trevor's voice. "Don't those things evolve? Wasn't it just a matter of time?"

Maggie chewed her lip, annoyed. This was the issue they had all argued back and forth, and continued to argue in the weekly meetings as the mission grew closer: whether she could divert the process of industrialization from its destructive path—not merely delay it by a generation or two but actually accomplish a paradigm shift. It was a tall order. But they had finally reached consensus—no small achievement for the one hundred and forty-one inhabitants of Ecosophia. She was proud of them. And impatient now with Trevor's questioning.

"Suppose you stop the bridge?" Trevor persisted. "What's to prevent the next guy from building it?"

"Nothing, Trevor!" she snapped. "And I'm not trying to *stop* it!" She grabbed her note cards from his knee. "And this whole effort could be pure styro! All for nothing!" She paced away. "Is that what you want to hear?"

She stood at the balcony, looking through the atrium at the dazzle of sun on glass. The silence grew. She could feel it draining her energy. She needed to get outside.

She was overreacting, she told herself. But she wasn't ready to be civil. Maybe a walk would help. Maybe a hike up Fajada Butte. The weather was clear. She slipped an elastic around the note cards. "I'm sorry." She said it flatly, unconvincingly. I'm sorry *but*. "Trevor. What's going on? Suddenly you're opposed to any kind of intervention."

Trevor laid the valve aside and swung his legs off the table. "Hell, I'm the one who said we should go back to when the Europeans first arrived here, and tell them thanks but no thanks."

"You were being facetious," she reminded him. "Weren't you?" A little sardonic edge to her voice. Had Trevor actually harbored that fantasy? "You yourself admitted it was impossible—carrying that message to all the Indian nations on the coasts of two continents and the islands of the Caribbean, and getting them to agree. It was too broad a front. Too many languages. The bridge may not be a big thing, but it's workable. It gives us a choke point."

Trevor was silent, frowning at the valve.

She grabbed one of his big toes. "And I'm not trying to stop the bridge. Give me that much credit. The idea is to get it to fail. If we can change the design, tweak it for failure, then we've changed the package! Paul says—" Annoyance flickered across Trevor's face. She pulled his toe. "Paul says it's like designing a bomb. You shape an explosion. If we can change the package, we can change the direction of the explosion."

Trevor grunted. "Not an image of healing."

"Not in a traditional sense." She might have gone on talking, arguing. But she stopped herself. Finally, without a word he opened his legs and embraced her, and they remained like that for a long time, his thick arms and legs around her, their faces burrowed into each other's necks. She felt him nod.

"You got your work cut out for you," he whispered.

She sighed. "You're right, it's a little crazy. We've always known that. But we've got to try, Trevor."

He nodded.

What made the bridge workable was its uniqueness. It was not as technologically profound as Watt's steam engine, but unlike the steam engine, which went through a succession of inventors, the bridge was a one-time occurrence. The first demonstration of structural iron, it excited the public imagination and influenced the direction of engineers. Americans were especially taken by it: Thomas Paine proposed a similar bridge over the Schuylkill River as a symbol of the new republic, whose capital was then in Philadelphia; Thomas Jefferson had a print of it hanging on the wall at Monticello; Robert Fulton visited it in the 1790s, and later promoted an ironclad warship.

Prior to the bridge, cast iron was used for objects such as cannon and frying pans. The idea of using iron castings to build a large structure was so avant-garde, and surrounded by so much trepidation, it was ten years before anyone was willing to build another one. Not until the flood of 1795 wiped out every other bridge on the Severn was the new bridge deemed a monumental success. After that came the cast-iron building frames, suspension bridges, and ironclad ships of the nineteenth century—which led to the huge steel skyscrapers and nuclear submarines of the twentieth.

But what if she could turn the bridge into a monumental failure?

That was the plan. It might be a little crazy, but nothing could be crazier than the present path: forests and topsoil gone, portions of the globe radioactive, the ozone layer destroyed, the massive extinction of plant and animal species continuing unabated into the twenty-first century. Until as early as 2030, estropoisoning and genetic damage was so widespread that human reproduction was tenuous outside the laboratory; and now most of humanity was dying from the rapidly mutating retroviruses that had made the jump from disappearing species.

Maggie snuggled into Trevor's warmth. Someday, she would miss him more than she could now imagine. Someday, she would long to relive even this sad embrace—to sniff the faint, undefinably familiar smell of his neck, to feel the pulse that made that little jump of flesh against her eyelid. Someday. Someday in the past, when all this would seem like a distant dream.

# Maggie Foster

What she remembered most vividly from that day was the hike she took afterward to Fajada Butte.

Her need to get outside was suddenly urgent. She trotted down the open steel steps three stories to the bottom of the atrium, avoiding the few people conversing by the waterfall or doing t'ai chi with Mr. Ho, but she managed to brush the fig tree's trunk with her fingertips as she walked past. She stepped into the hydroponic greenhouse that enclosed the atrium on two sides, its air bright and thick with the pungency of the tomato vines. She walked by the air filters, by people tending plants. She didn't want to get into a conversation.

A woman with dark, almond-shaped eyes glanced up from tying eggplants, then looked away. Maggie hurried past. This was the woman who had argued against the mission, who in a tearful outburst had told everybody that she was trying to become pregnant. She accused them of giving up hope. *I am a survivor!* she cried. *You are committing suicide!* For a time she stood in the way of consensus, but in the end stepped aside. Maggie knew she should talk to her, but the woman's pain was like a flower opening endless petals. Maggie had kept clear of it.

Arriving at the inner air lock, she stepped from her sandals into green recycled-plastic slippers. Pushing open the door, she felt the air suck past the rubber gasket. From a shelf she took a pair of disposable coveralls made from nonwoven fabric, a wide-brimmed hat fitted with a fabric cowl and dust mask, and a pair of goggles. She applied sunscreen paste to her face and the backs of her hands. Punched the keypad on the wall for weather info. Wind from the west at three to five kilometers per hour; no sandstorms predicted; visibility good. She recorded a message on the audio log, giving her destination, Fajada Butte. She started to call Erzulie but thought better of it. Instead, she logged her destination on the clipboard, giving the date, 06/21/43, and the time, 09:40. The redundancy was part of the protocol. She hesitated, pencil in hand. Again, that funny feeling.

She punched up Erzulie.

"Erzulie, do I have an appointment with you today?"

"Don't you wish!" Erzulie's deep chuckle filled the air lock. Maggie pictured her tipping back in her rocker, starting to work her fingernails through her short, nappy, gray hair, the way she did when she welcomed an interruption. Erzulie was a psychophysicist whose pioneering work had formed part of the conceptual basis for projecting energy fields. She was older than Paul and on occasion liked to zing him with the street jive she used to "discipline the white boys of old," her colleagues at Princeton's Center for Paranormal Studies. That was back in the teens, before the whole university system collapsed into privatized research parks and corpo networking.

Maggie grinned. "Well, were you thinking about me a minute ago?"

"Girl, I think about you 'most every minute. But not that particular minute. That minute I was thinking about loops."

"Loops?"

"In space-time. What happens when you get an oscillating pattern, like a repeating decimal, within an otherwise linear energy flow? In fluid dynamics, that'd be an eddy. You'd get a larger repeating pattern until something came along to destabilize it. The question is, what happens to the energy? And what happens to time?" She sighed. "Just another wrinkle in the theory."

"Does it—involve me?"

A moment's pause. Humor gathering in Erzulie's voice. "Is this something you need to worry about?"

"No. And I didn't call to chat. I just had a funny feeling."

"Listen to your feelings, girl."

Maggie nodded. Hesitated. "You're tipped back in your chair, scratching at your hair with your left hand."

Erzulie's laugh cascaded through the speaker. "You got it, girl. You got it." Maggie imagined her face lit up.

"Good. On that note, I'm out of here." Maggie punched out. She knew she was forgetting something, but she had to get outside. She pushed through the door to the outer air lock, trading the green slippers for brown—color-coded against contamination. From her locker she removed a pair of boots that were half expired and put them on, securing the cuffs of the coveralls with peeltabs.

Loops.

Erzulie had assured her it wasn't necessary for her to understand the whole theory behind time travel. Good thing, because Maggie was lost once she got past the principles of subparticalization, by which every atom of her body would be converted into pure energy. "Forget about quantum mechanics," Erzulie told her. "Practice your gift."

Maggie's gift—an anomaly occurring in about two percent of the population, most commonly among those who reported out-of-body experiences as children—was the ability to bend energy fractiles. Prior to Erzulie's experimental work with brain waves, it was not even a measurable skill. But with the right software it showed up on a CRT, and subsequent computer simulations proved that Maggie could effectively move her own energy field through the space-time continuum.

They had tested it spatially. Maggie succeeded in projecting herself to the other side of the atrium. It was unnerving, that journey of forty-three meters. A floating sensation, like lucid dreaming ending in a powerful urge to reincorporate.

The experiments were kept brief, owing partly to the drain on Ecosophia's limited power supply and also to the risk of paradox involved in short trips. Maggie learned to relax, learned to direct her passage and resist the urge to reincorporate. That was where the Circle came in—a group of women (there was no rule concerning gender, but it worked out that way) helped her focus and keep her field stable. Her trips provided practice and answered certain questions. She was physically unchanged: the childhood scar on her knee was still there, her teeth remained straightened, her fallopian tubes remained fused. Her DNA was not altered; her antibodies were intact.

The actual journey would be one-way, since the electronics necessary for her return would not yet exist. They were putting all their eggs into this one basket.

Maggie alone had the gift—although Erzulie assured her that the gift was by no means the only qualification. "Ain't nothing about this that's by the numbers, Maggie. It needs a gal who trusts her gut."

Maggie's gut said to ride with the gift, which belonged, in a real sense, to them all. Whatever the risks, she felt that she embodied their collective will. As an orphan, she had never had such a feeling before, of carrying a communal presence, of representing something larger than herself.

She wheeled a sun trike out of the storage bay into the dazzling light. The broad floor of Chaco Canyon threw back the glare of a pale blue sky, cloudless except for the brown striations of dust near the horizon. A couple of kilometers to the south was the purple palisade of the opposite canyon wall. Beyond were the Radlands. Six kilometers to the east stood the distinctive silhouette of Fajada Butte. Everything was crisp. No sign of dust squalls. She wouldn't need the goggles, but she peeltabbed them to her shoulder anyway.

Pedaling hard, she arrived at the butte drenched in sweat, her mask popping in and out with her breathing. The trike batteries were half fried. Eleven years ago, when she arrived at Ecosophia, the trikes were almost effortless to pedal. Stored solar energy had supplied two-thirds of the cranking power, making it possible to carry heavy loads even in the sandy desert soil. Now the batteries were getting old, and so were the bearings. She parked the trike among the boulders scattered at the bottom of the talus slope, then climbed up to the vertical cleft where the trail began.

She liked following that prehistoric trail, liked its familiarity, the logic of the switchbacks, the sense of the accumulated ingenuity of generations operating like water in reverse, searching out the path upward of least resistance as it spiraled clockwise around the butte. On a clear day like this it felt good to be outdoors, despite the restriction of the mask.

She got most of her exercise indoors, where the air was cleaner. Ecosophia eschewed automation wherever possible: human muscle took the place of servomotors and automatic sensors in performing such tasks as opening and closing vents and watering plants; exercise equipment was designed to generate rather than consume electricity. Menial tasks were rotated, to foster mindfulness and community.

But Ecosophia could make you antsy. Maggie liked the vastness out here. The enormity of the sky. The sense of connection with the Anasazi, who had struggled to eke out an existence in this canyon nine hundred years ago.

She stopped to rest in the shade of a sandstone overhang, took a swig from her canteen, and looked out at the expanse of saltbush and greasewood stretching purple and olive to the northwest, to where the ancient pueblos were nestled at the foot of the far canyon wall. Chaco had probably not changed all that much in a thousand years. The arroyo that zigzagged down the middle—a miniature of the canyon itself—had deepened in the last century, lowering the available surface water, and the climate was a little hotter and less predictable in this century. Even so, a sward of green cottonwood from the arroyo signaled the presence of water.

The Anasazi had screwed up too, of course, as Trevor always observed. They had cut too many trees, exhausted the thin desert topsoil—like traditional cultures in Asia Minor and elsewhere. But those were local screwups compared to the global destruction in the past seventy years.

Maggie had never understood the paralysis that seemed to grip everyone during the Second Industrial Revolution, though Paul, Erzulie, and the others who had lived through it had explained it often. By 1990, the United States had consumed more resources than the rest of the world in all previous history. And then China had to have its turn, pumping billions of tons of carbon dioxide into the atmosphere. The corpo democracies were unwilling to scale down, or even to help newly industrializing nations find appropriate technologies. Was it simply the logical outcome of capitalism, or was the paralysis intrinsic to the human condition?

*It all happened more quickly than we predicted,* Paul always said. But who was the "we"? Erzulie observed it was mostly corpo scientists, supporting do-nothing politicians. Entertainment as usual.

Global warming brought more violent weather patterns, which devastated farmlands already treated as disposable and exacerbated the ravages of war. In her own life, during the three years she spent at CALYPOOL as a teenager analyzing satellite digifotos, Maggie had watched the Sahara creep south through most of Tanzania, the American desert creep east to include Iowa and Illinois. Much of the world now looked like Chaco Canyon.

Laying the canteen aside and replacing the filter of her dust mask, she picked out the white of Pueblo Bonito at the foot of the palisade. Next to it was the triangular shadow cast by the awnings jutting from the cliff that protected Ecosophia from the sun at its zenith and from aerial surveillance. At the edge of that shadow was a telltale slant of glass. She told herself it would not be easy to spot at this distance if she did not know exactly where to look. Ecosophia was protected by the surrounding desolation—the Radlands to the south, the single access road from the north with the fence across it and the signs warning of mines. Still, looking at Ecosophia from afar, she was always struck by its vulnerability.

Judging from the shadow, it was nearly noon. She glanced at her watch, and continued up the trail.

Usually she felt it before she saw it. A game she played when she was here alone. Walking past and sensing it, as though with her back. This time she could hardly wait. Turning, she looked up and saw the three tall boulders leaned up against one another at a slant: the solstice marker.

She approached the spiral incised in the stone at breast height and started to trace it with her fingers, as she often did. This time her heart was pounding. Before she knew what she was doing, she unfastened the peeltab under her chin, tore off her mask and hat, and pressed her forehead to the stone. Crouched there against the rock, she listened to the pounding as though it were coming from the spiral and tried to discern what was inside her head and what was outside. Then she felt something else. Twisting around, she looked up to see a flash of sun through the interstices of the three silhouetted boulders. She backed away from the spiral and saw it: a tiny wedge of light entering the top of the spiral, lengthening slowly downward.

The solstice!

Slowly the dagger of light descended, bisecting the spiral. Then, in the space of a few minutes, it thinned, broke in two, and disappeared.

She felt blessed, but also puzzled. Today was June 21. Normally at least a small group came up here to observe the solstice. What did it mean that they had all forgotten it? What did it mean that she alone, in her peculiar fashion, had remembered?

On the way down, she stopped again in the shade and gazed at the sparkle of glass, which had moved a little. She imagined the sun pouring in on the soybeans, lighting up the red peppers and the green-marbled algae pools. She felt a wave of affection for it.

Ecosophia required constant tinkering: dealing with the white flies and fungus, keeping everything in balance—not just the physical entity but also the spiritual life. The constant reinterpretation of its four guiding principles: Openness, Sustainability, Mindfulness, and Community. The frustration of having to decide everything by consensus. Yet somehow they muddled along. And they might muddle along for many more years. But there were no children. The average age of Ecosophia's inhabitants was sixty-six. Maggie was one of the youngest.

And Ecosophia maintained its isolation at a cost. One whole bank of photovoltaics had been cannibalized in order to maintain the other three; spare parts for machinery had to be obtained on the free market at exorbitant prices and usually at some risk of revealing Ecosophia's location.

The commune's existence was known to relatively few people.

Among the Dineh, eleven—Trevor among them—had joined; the others continued to honor the treaty that allowed the Ecosophians to live on tribal land in exchange for medical services. From the Navajo traders Ecosophia obtained computer chips, clothing, bricks of guano and other fertilizer, and bales of plastic trash for recyling—in exchange for the few commodities that Ecosophia was able to offer, such as genetically engineered fruit trees. But as the world outside continued to deteriorate, the secret of Ecosophia's location grew more precarious. Only last week, the commune outside Santa Fe had been wiped out by a gang of bikers using rocket launchers supplied by a corpo warlord.

A movement in the corner of Maggie's vision became a small lizard. She sat perfectly still. The lizard's long toes were splayed haphazardly. Its soft, scaly sides moved in and out barely perceptibly, its body stonelike in profile except for the tiny, black, glittering eye. The creature was probably low enough on the food chain to outlast its warm-blooded predators, coyote and hawk.

When she looked again, it was gone.

She was startled by the shouts of the bow haulers from across the river. Gazing through the blur of leaves at the Severn's brown current, looking down at her own hands pressing the scraps of paper against her apron, she was surprised—as though those chapped hands belonged to someone else. She missed her turquoise ring. She missed Trevor. She missed the desert.

A breeze made her aware of the rags in her crotch. So strange. Like going through puberty all over again. She gathered the scraps of paper together, folded them in half and stuffed them in her apron pocket. She tried to put herself again in Trevor's encircling arms and legs, recover the smell of his neck. But it only sharpened her isolation.

Somewhere in that other time, *her* time, a marauding motogang might be attacking Ecosophia. She would never know.

And anyway, she was here to be the agent of Ecosophia's undoing. Their sending her here was an act of self-sacrifice. Not suicide. There was a difference. If she succeeded in reshaping the industrial explosion, then Ecosophia would cease to exist.

# Abraham Darby III

**I**n truth, Abraham was less interested in the actual making of iron than in keeping the account books. Oh, he liked watching those gaudy rivulets of molten iron, and he liked seeing the pots broken out of their box molds and glowing dull red. But he was content to leave the operation of the furnaces to the furnace keepers. The parched air of the casting house awakened a dread in him, and tickled his asthma.

He preferred the solitude of his office, where he could sit at his father's old oak desk, going over the accounts, corresponding with customers, and contemplating improvements at the Haye farm. He spent more time daydreaming than he should, standing at the window gazing out at the Old Furnace, which lay three rods away—a stone's throw—and whose fiery head rippled in the wavy glass with interesting optical effects. Or he would peruse the worn leather-bound ledgers that went back to his grandfather's day, deciphering the different handwriting.

As a young boy he had spent his happiest hours at the small farm attached to Sunniside, the three-story brick house built just after he was born. His older sister, Mally, used to take him to play hide-and-seek in the barn and to watch the milking and help feed the chickens. By the time he was six, old enough to venture over by himself, he was a favorite of the tenants, who called him Master Abey and gave him an orphaned lamb to raise. He fed the lamb with a glass teat-bottle and kept it warm in flannel on the kitchen hearth. Afterwards it followed him about, nuzzling in his pockets with startling force. When he went away to boarding school at Worcester and returned at Easter, the lamb did not recognize him. It had joined its brothers and sisters in the flock—or so he was told by Mrs. Hannigan the housekeeper and Nehemiah the stable keeper, who had a blue knotted vein on the tip of his nose that frightened Abey, because Mally told him it would burst if he looked at it with any sin of pride in his heart.

On Easter First Day—what Mrs. Hannigan called Easter Sunday, for she was not Quaker—when they all climbed the Wrekin to watch the sunrise and came back to Sunniside to eat the big meal in awful silence, and Abey saw the roasted lamb garnished with cloves and Robin-run-o'-the-hedges, he was certain it was his. He fled to his chamber, where Uncle Third—who was not really his uncle but Thomas Goldney III, his name grown from the jest that they were both "thirds"; a big man with white hair in his ears and great pink hands—coaxed him to return and gave him a piece of eight, a wedge of pure gold which he said was Spanish pirate money chopped with a broadax. Uncle Third showed him how smooth the edges had worn; but the gift only made Abey feel more wretched for sulking. Then Baby William cried in the nursery, and Abey heard Nurse's feet answering up the stairs. When Abey followed Uncle Third back to the table, he felt everyone's eyes on him, and could not bring himself to eat the lamb, and kicked his younger sister, Sarah, under the table for making faces.

After dinner, he sat by the fireplace in the parlor listening to the adults talk, with his hand in his pocket feeling the gold soft as satin. The adults were talking about the coming marriage. Hannah, his half sister, who was a grown woman, was soon to marry Richard Reynolds. When their father proposed a toast, Hannah's and Richard's faces turned the brightest red. Father was jolly; the brown circles under his eyes crinkled into tender webs when he laughed. It was Abey's happiest memory. Yet all he could think of at the time was how the gold piece could not buy back his lamb. Then came the lonely ride back to boarding school in the Goldneys' big black shiny coach, he wedged among the five big Goldneys, falling asleep to their voices droning about the prophets. (It was years before he realized they were discussing *profits*.)

That summer, Baby William fell ill with a swelling and died. Mother gathered all the children and thanked the Great Name for providing a "safe little bed" for Sweet William, who was without Sin and would sleep with Jesus. That night, Sarah whimpered for the longest time, because Mother had taken their next youngest brother, Sammy, to sleep with her, and Sarah was afraid it would be her turn next to sleep with Jesus. Mally told her to bite her tongue. Abey did not want to sleep with Jesus either, but he kept silent, biting his tongue to keep from whimpering. Afterwards, the house seemed empty, with Baby William gone to Jesus and Hannah gone to live with Richard Reynolds at Ketley Bank.

When Abey was older, he was given responsibilities at the Haye farm, where horses and fodder were raised for the ironworks. The Haye lay on the eastern side of Madeley parish, three miles away on a broad knoll fringed with orchards overlooking the lower Severn Gorge. There, with the furnaces only a distant throb, he could lose himself in the cut hay and turned earth, in each spring's new crop of foals and lambs, whose orphans he fed again and warmed in flannel. He began to understand, even if he could not quite put it into words, that it was all the same lamb, the same foal. Every spring, a new Creation.

From Thomas Sparrow, the tenant at the Haye, the boy learned the crafts of husbandry—how to tell the weather from the way the midges darted, how to cure split hooves and graft fruit trees, what time of year to dig up thistles, the signs of readiness in brood mares, and what to do when bees swarmed.

When Abraham was twelve, Hannah died suddenly. A year later his father died. After his father's death, Abraham was allowed to stay home from boarding school and work at the Haye. Its dark, welling rhythms of birth and death became a refuge. When Abraham was fifteen, Richard, who had remarried, turned the farm over to him to manage as part of his apprenticeship. "Thou art half a farmer," Reynolds observed, "and 'twill teach thee economy." Abraham's shoulders broadened, and his voice deepened. His shyness was thought seemly in a Quaker youth, but he felt awkward, ashamed of his fleshly yearnings, and, confined in the Darby mold, had little knowledge of himself even when he peered guardedly in the mirror.

When he entered the Works officially at eighteen, he had already showed as much aptitude for ironmaking as he had for husbandry. With Richard's help, he learned the qualities of the different kinds of coal—doubles and deeps, fungus and flints; how to cast in sand using the box-mold method developed by Grandfather's foreman, John Thomas; how to cast in loam (although he hated the smell); how to take a furnace out of blast, as was required after several years of continuous operation; and how to blow it in, using holly root mixed with the charcoal and brays until it was hot enough for the coke. Yet for all this, he never entirely lost his old dread.

What he remembered were the voices.

Father: "Hand him down to me, Abiah."

Mother: "Dost thou have him?"

"Aye, aye." Big hands closing around him; his father's voice resonating, "I've got him." And the parched smell rising like dust all around him in the gloom. "Dost thou know where thou art, little man?"

Above, a round hole of daylight framed the silhouette of his mother's bonnet. Still higher, another, smaller hole dazzled his eyes. He blinked. His gaze wandered over the scaly yellow-ocher walls enclosing them.

Father's voice whispered close to his ear: " 'Tis all round in here, like the inside of a Rhenish bottle."

Fear. His father's voice echoing strangely.

"Dost thou know where thou art? 'Twill all be thine someday."

He could not talk. Something about the confines, the smell coming from the peeling, mustard-colored bricks, terrified him.

"Thou art in the fiery furnace, Abey," said Father gently. "Like

Shadrach, Meshach, and Abednego. Feelest thou, how the walls be warm?"

The big hand took Abey's, pressed his palm to the rough surface. Suddenly a sob struggled up through that crushing, tormented smell, and his own wails were echoing around him, his mother was calling, he was being passed upward into her hands into the light, where he gulped air.

Much later, Abraham realized that this must have happened in the summer of 1753, when the New Furnace was taken out of blast and relined. So he was three years old. Whether the asthma began then or later was unclear. But afterwards, with every attack, he remembered that feeling of confinement and of unspeakable dryness; the evil of dust tortured beyond dust. Whether that was the cause of his dread, he could not say, but the seed of that feeling stirred in him every time he watched his father come home from the Works and wash his hands and face in the basin, turning the water ocher or rust—the smell of sulfur carrying with it the knowledge as certain as death that his turn was next.

# Maggie Foster

She was beginning to feel like a prisoner. Some of it was the cramped cottage, the hours of spinning. Some of it was Polly's warning: "Dunna walk too far abroad, where thy face be strange, lest a churchman or constable stop thee and inquire thy business." Maggie complied, restricting her walks to the neighborhood.

On a clear day, she could see the smoke from Coalbrookdale rising over the next hill. Coalbrookdale was only a mile and a half away, but it seemed quite inaccessible. John Wilkinson's New Willey furnace seemed even more remote, since it was across the river in Broseley, its smoke visible beyond the plumes from the Calcutts ironworks and the potteries of Jackfield.

Sometimes, as she sat spinning with the other women—listening to medical complaints, recipes, the history of feuds, floods, and pit collapses from decades ago related as though they had happened yesterday—she felt both the narrowness of this world and her strangeness within it. Also the confines of her gender and class.

"What do I have to do," she asked Polly, "to be able to go where I want to in Madeley?"

"Tha must have permission." But Polly was vague.

Mrs. Merryweather was more knowledgeable in such matters. She said Maggie would have to appear before the church warden to obtain settlement papers. The other women agreed, and prepped her for the questions the church warden would ask: her place of birth, parentage, marital status, religion. It gave them an opportunity to pry. They were curious about Trevor, her deceased husband. Had he beaten her? How many chairs in their household? How many bedsheets? How many chairs had Trevor's *father* owned? Odd questions. She was tempted to reveal that, by Trevor's account, his father, Charlie Two Clouds, had owned a Salvation Army La-Z-Boy recliner inhabited by mice. When she told them four chairs, they seemed impressed.

Polly accompanied her to the parish church. They wore clean kerchiefs and their best aprons, and carried baskets on their arms—emblems of purpose and respectability. Polly took her inside the church and showed her the dark old altar panels carved from chestnut that depicted Eve being tempted by the serpent, Adam and Eve being expelled from the Garden.

The church warden was an avuncular, white-haired man with a drooping eyelid. His questions were aimed mostly at determining that Maggie would not end up on the Poor List, a burden to the parish. When she explained how she made her living spinning, he asked to see her articles of indenture. Polly explained that they had no articles but were paid by the pound. The church warden asked to see their thumbs. Evidently satisfied with Maggie's calluses and warning her to keep to Christian ways, he granted her permission to remain in the parish of Madeley. When she entered her own name *Margaret Foster* in the church register—using the double-loop flourish she had practiced, inspired by one of John Wilkinson's earlier signatures—the church warden tipped the page in the light, screwed up his brow, and gave her a respectful nod.

Jeremy offered to walk the bounds with her, so that she should know the parish. It was a welcome suggestion, offered with a real sense of what was needed, much as he had offered the willow basket he made her to hold her few possessions. They started out along the wagon road on a Sunday morning in August. Jeremy had scrubbed the coaldust from his face, except where it remained stubbornly embedded around his eyes and ears. He told her what she already knew, that the river, to their left, formed Madeley's southern boundary. During these summer months, the water was so low that only the smaller barges could make it past the Jackfield Rapids.

The gorge was greener than she remembered from her arrival last May. No big trees but numerous small ones. And now she was able to attend to the geology. Up ahead, she saw limestone workings on both sides of the river. "That must be Lincoln Hill," she said, pointing to the bluff on the Madeley side.

"Aye."

"And that must be the Benthall Edge, over there in Broseley."

Jeremy nodded.

What she knew—and Jeremy would have no way of knowing, even if he were educated—was that the two bluffs were part of a single escarpment of Silurian limestone laid down four hundred million years ago, when most of Shropshire lay under a shallow tropical sea.

The gorge was formed in comparatively recent times—a mere ten thousand years ago—when water from the melting glaciers cut through a fault. It was still relatively unstable. That instability was the key to her plan for sabotaging the bridge.

From where they stood, the sounds of the different ironworks converged. The sky was gray. She tried to imagine the gorge when it was first formed. It must have been spectacular, beginning with a nearly three-hundred-foot-high waterfall. She tried to see it through the eyes of Paleolithic hunters. It must have been a sacred place. A place for driving game; a place for erecting fish traps woven from willow. And now it was ideally suited for ironmaking, with its exposed limestone and coal and with swift tributaries like Coalbrook descending into the navigable Severn. An accident of geology had given the gorge a special place in human history. And that same accident of geology would, she hoped, undo the damage.

The road climbed as the river narrowed. They stood looking across at Benthall Edge. Jeremy seemed to read her thoughts. "This be the place," he said, "where they'll build the bridge."

Maggie looked at him, startled. "How do you know?"

Jeremy shrugged. " 'Tis what they say."

"Who? Who says it?"

"Why, everybody."

"So it's common knowledge."

"Aye. 'Tis common as weeds." He looked at her with those clear eyes. "The Darbys shall build it."

They followed the wagon road downhill. She was feeling the momentum of Jeremy's words in the pit of her stomach. When they passed the horse-ferry landing and she saw the cobblestones, she felt a frisson of recognition—recalled the feel of them on her bare feet, the dizzying glimpses of the bridge, all like snatches of a dream lost from memory.

Jeremy pointed out landmarks. Ahead was Ludcroft Wharf. Dales End. Across the river was the glow of the lead smelter, the limestone kilns, and smoldering piles of coking coals. Once they got past Lincoln Hill, Coalbrookdale opened up before them, the clanking din of the forges joining the deeper pulse of the furnaces.

Suddenly Jeremy grabbed her arm and pointed to the wharf, where a man was being lifted from a rowboat. "A drowning!" he exclaimed.

They took hands and ran to the wharf. Two men were holding the drowned man upside down while another squeezed his stomach. Water flowed from his mouth and nose. Maggie heard Jeremy catch his breath, almost a sob, and she remembered how his father had died.

"Put him down," she said, surprised by the firmness in her voice. "Lay him flat."

They obliged. "He's a goner," one of the men said. Another man tore at his own beard and keened helplessly.

The drowned man had a dark beard, pale skin. Maggie stuck her fingers in his mouth to make sure it was clear, and turned him onto his stomach. Keeping her arms straight, elbows locked, she leaned forward, then rocked back, pulling on his shoulders; then forward again, with all her weight. Water gushed from his mouth. "When did this happen?" she asked, rocking back and forward again.

"Only now. Tangled 'is foot in a line, poor bugger."

She rolled the man onto his back and, holding his nose, overcoming some revulsion for the cold lips, she took a deep breath and blew. She had never actually done this, only seen a training video. She felt the chest inflate. Then, centering her hands on his breastbone, she rocked forward again. Heard the air escape through those purple lips. Again she inflated the lungs. She remembered a warning about vomiting, but at least this world was not so filled with disease.

Someone laughed. "What the devil?" She ignored the blur of people around her. She kept up a steady rhythm, counting silently. Half-conscious of newcomers asking what had happened. The man's dark beard and eyebrows stood out against his coarse waxy skin. She could see every pore, every follicle. A crease formed between the brows.

Suddenly his eyes blinked open. He convulsed, coughing.

She helped him sit up. From stunned silence, a clamor arose. Then a cheer. Looking around, Maggie saw a couple of dozen people standing around. The men who had brought him ashore waved their arms and whooped at others watching from a small barge, and there was an answering cheer.

"Get a blanket," Maggie said. "Something to keep him warm."

But the man's friends started pulling him to his feet over her protests, wrapping their arms around him, knuckling his head. Someone produced a bottle of rum, which they forced on him; he took a swallow and choked. Abruptly he collapsed.

"You'll kill him!" Maggie cried.

"The doxie saved tha life, Mikey boy," someone told the drowned man, dragging him to his feet. "Tha was a goner, sure as shit." The drowned man was clearly disoriented. His friends tried to explain what had happened. The man who had been tearing his beard threw himself to his knees before Maggie.

"Thank ye, miss. This be me brother ye brung back from the dead."

Maggie froze at the phrase. She had made a mistake. A terrible, stupid mistake.

"Was he really dead?" someone asked.

"Dead as a doornail!" someone exclaimed. "Old Nicky-Nicky Nye had him by the toes!"

"Who is she? Who's the doxie?" Questions floated through the crowd. "Kissing him, was she?" "Aye, or stealing his soul!"

"Let's go," Maggie said to Jeremy.

"Thank ye, miss!"

"A water witch!"

Jeremy took Maggie's elbow and whispered, "Tha must needs thank the Lord."

"Thank the Lord," she said.

"Aye," Jeremy sang out. "Praise the Lord." Others took up the refrain.

They managed to get free of the crowd and continue on their way. The whole wharf was abuzz, people pointing after them. Maggie quickened her steps. "Which way?" she asked nervously.

The parish actually went a little farther, Jeremy said, its corner bounded on the west by Birches Brook. But realizing that she wanted to escape the crowd, he proposed walking straight up the dale. Maggie agreed, glad to avoid the old woman at Birches Brook.

"How did tha do it, Maggie? How did tha bring him back from the dead?"

"I only helped him breathe, Jeremy. He wasn't dead. He just needed help breathing." They passed forges, hammers ringing on anvils, and followed the road that snaked between the ponds and millraces of Coalbrookdale.

"Help breathing," Jeremy echoed.

"Don't think about it, Jeremy." But she could hear him repeating the words under his breath.

Great. Just fucking great. Back in Ecosophia, they had agreed on two restrictions: *Introduce no new technology* and *Limit the intervention strictly to the bridge.* Two simple rules they had all agreed on, and she had violated both of them!

The danger of either introducing new technology or widening her agenda was that even the tiniest deviation could have great repercussions. A whole sequence of events could unravel and generate new chains of causality, spreading in unpredictable directions through the fabric of history. The classic example was the butterfly flapping its wings in China, giving rise to a hurricane across the globe.

"Remember," Paul used to say, "you are wielding a scalpel, not a cleaver."

So what damage had she done?

At the very least, she had saved one man's life, and his future progeny. That was bad enough. But suppose, in addition, someone witnessing it were to master the technique and it were to become widespread? The field of probabilities would change vastly.

*Surely it would be for the good,* she imagined herself protesting, back in Ecosophia, *introducing a technique for saving lives.*

But she knew the answer:

*What other technology might be introduced as a result? And what of the thousands of individuals who might be saved over the next two hundred years, who might enter the flow of history with unknown consequences?*

Jeremy said something she didn't catch. She asked him to repeat it.

"Said I wish tha wast here when me father drowned."

She smiled and squeezed his hand. How could she confess her own desperate hope that no one had observed her closely enough to duplicate the technique?

"Was tha blowing or sucking, Maggie?"

"This place is huge," she said, avoiding his gaze, standing aside while a wagon passed, looking around at the millraces and water wheels of the various mills, and the blast furnaces ahead. "You could fit five or six Bedlams into this place."

"Aye, aye. Was tha blowing or sucking, Maggie?"

She shrugged. "I don't know, Jeremy."

Life sucks. That was what she was thinking.

That was what Granny used to say. *Life sucks!*

Granny, who really had it all. Boomers, she called her generation. Maybe because they came right after the Bomb. She was a food designer, whose big achievement in life was developing a fake whipped cream that did something in the microwave. Maggie forgot exactly what—but Granny thought it was the greatest thing. *And I'm like, You kids will never have what we had!*

Right, Granny. You didn't leave us much.

Near the top of the dale, they took the road past a row of houses and the Quaker meeting house, until they were over the crest of the hill and out of the main smoke. To their left was a grove of trees followed by a carriage lane lined with tall cedars, at the end of which stood a large three-story brick house.

"Yonder lives the third Abraham Darby. And his mother, the Widow Darby."

So this was Sunniside.

"Tha wilt see her, mehaps at Michaelmas," Jeremy added.

"Who?"

"The Widow Darby."

"What do you mean?"

"At the Wakes."

"Wakes?"

"Aye, the Madeley Wakes." Jeremy laughed, seeing her puzzlement. "Oh Maggie! Tha hanna seen gaiety like the Madeley Wakes at Michaelmas! Three days of frolic! A bull baiting each day. Pine torches at night. Stilt walkers and jugglers and rope dancers. Punch and Judy. Dancing bears! Fights everywhere. But ye must have wakes in the Colonies!" Those bright eyes waited.

Maggie shook her head. "I mean, I don't know. I suppose we do." She thought of the Instagrat orgies at the simulation arcades, and airbladers rampaging through the old urban zipcodes high on synzymes with names like Mayhem and Mindfuck. "But not in Baltimore."

Jeremy waited for something more. "Withal," he said, "tha moight like it." He seemed disappointed.

"Maybe. But what does this have to do with the Widow Darby?"

"Tha'lt see. Just come to the Madeley Wakes."

"Oh don't be a tease, Jeremy."

"Tha'lt see. Tha'lt see."

They were following the horse-rails north, in the direction of Dawley. They could make out Lightmoor Furnace, and beyond it the more distant plumes of Horsehay and Ketley—all part of the Dale Company empire. Jeremy chose a footpath east, which kept them within the bounds of Madeley, and then onto a road that led to the Cuckoo Oak, at a crossroads where the stagecoach regularly stopped. There they shared a kidney pie for tuppence. Maggie was glad to rest her feet. They proceeded to the more rural northeastern corner of the parish, then south through farmlands, following a public footpath past the Haye farm, which commanded a panoramic view of the lower gorge.

"The Darbys own all this," said Jeremy, pointing to the cornfields and meadows descending into orchards. They watched a hawk cruise an updraft from the valley. It was beautiful. They removed their clogs to descend a steep path, laughed running part of the way down, and came out at the river across from the Jackfield Rapids, where they picked blackberries and watched a small barge being poled past the rocks. Maggie's legs hurt, but Jeremy seemed unfazed. They came out on the wagon road, just east of the Bird in Hand, and stopped to rest on an outcropping of shale. Maggie rubbed her feet. She asked him how far they had walked, and he supposed eight miles. He looked happy. She was happy too, to have expanded her little world.

"Jeremy, if you tell your mother about the drowning—" She sighed. "Well, maybe it would be a good idea if you didn't make it sound too—weird."

"Weird?"

"Yes. You know what I mean? I mean—"

"Aye. Aye. He dinna be drowned."

"Right. Exactly."

He nodded, glanced up with those disarmingly clear eyes and then down at his blackberry-stained fingers. They were both silent. She tried to guess what was going through his mind. She put an arm around him, and to her surprise he threw both his arms around her and hugged her tight.

# Maggie Foster

By the time they got home, word had got to Polly that a drowned man had been saved by a water witch.

" 'Twasn't a witch!" Jeremy told his mother. " 'Twas Maggie!"

Maggie reddened. "Jeremy's right." She explained as vaguely as she could what she had done. Polly seemed satisfied. Jeremy listened intently, frowning but keeping a discreet silence.

Mrs. Merryweather was eager for particulars. Her sharp little blue eyes danced. "Oh, I never thought for a trice that a man could be fetched back from the dead. Not me. And I've seen many a strange thing in my day. But I am ever so watchful for remedies that might save a Christian life." She leaned over her spinning wheel. "Is it true tha put something in his mouth?"

"No."

She narrowed her eyes. "How, then, didst tha tempt his soul back into his body?"

Maggie demurred with a faint smile of the sort she had seen Mrs. Merryweather affect upon being asked to divulge the secret ingredient in her bladder-infection tea. "It's just something I learned in the Colonies."

Jeremy was more difficult. That evening she was down at the willow stump, watching birds skim across the water in the twilight and missing Trevor, when she felt a presence. Or maybe she caught a glimpse of Jeremy's coracle without registering it. Anyway, she felt his presence, and then he appeared in the withey, holding the coracle steady in the current, his features murky in the rose-colored, reflected light. Mouth somber, she guessed. His silence was intimidating.

"It's too dark for you to be on the river, Jeremy."

He took hold of a willow branch and stopped paddling. "It ain't fair."

The accusation hurt. She could think of nothing to say. "I'm sorry, Jeremy."

He waited for more. Revolved a few times and then shot away. Later she saw him scamper up the embankment with the coracle.

The truth was, she didn't know what to do with her feelings toward Jeremy. She hated lying to him more than anyone. Jeremy had a kind of purity. Things mattered to him. She spent the next day trying to sort this out.

There was something else, if she was honest. Mixed into it were impulses she could hardly bring herself to acknowledge, impulses she had comfortably ignored until yesterday, when he hugged her and she felt her body respond in a way that surprised and embarrassed her. He was only twelve. These twinges were inappropriate. And yet she indulged them now in fantasy, sitting on the stump with her knees drawn up under her skirts, the willow stump prickling her buttocks. Eyes shut, she imagined the boy in her embrace: she was his coracle, cradling him, turning around and around and around.

By September, Maggie's restlessness had grown. She had not worked up the nerve to apply for work at Sunniside. The cottage was more cramped than ever, every available space taken up with preparations for winter: the making of applesauce, pickles, and jams; the drying of beans and pumpkin chips; bundles of parsley and onions and chamomile bristling under the eaves; turnips and marrow packed in straw in the root cellar. The boys trapped rabbits, and Maggie helped Polly bake tarts to sell at the Madeley Wakes.

Jeremy seemed to have forgiven her. She had put her fantasies aside, but they raised disturbing questions. Why was she fixated on a twelve-year-old boy? True, he would be thirteen next month, but the feelings were still inappropriate. She wished she had someone to talk to—Erzulie or Trevor. Some of it surely had to do with missing Trevor. Some of it, with the fact that Jeremy seemed wise beyond his years. But it also had to do with the purity that she so idealized in him, a purity missing from her own childhood. She found herself longing to possess it.

Her childhood had been corrupted in ways she probably still could not fully comprehend. She supposed it started even before CALYPOOL. CALYPOOL, like most of the privatized, fast-track orphanages for the intellectually gifted, was designed to mold its young charges into programmable technicians and scientists. Virtual Family, they called the dorms, with a V-Mom and a V-Dad on every floor. What she remembered was not flesh-and-blood people but the software that colonized every corner of her imagination and left little else.

At an early age—seven or eight, maybe even younger—she sensed something was wrong. She distrusted V-Mom and V-Dad, whose antiseptic praise echoed the learning programs. They were like advertisements for happy families. V-Mom pretended to bake, and V-Dad took them on simulated fishing trips. But it was all styro. Underneath was the gnawing fear that she was unlovable. Why else would her real parents have abandoned her? And if she was *not* the good, competent, obedient little girl that V-Mom and V-Dad said she was, then who was she?

In her dreams, she often took to the air. Flew around the halls looking for something, she didn't know what. Awake, observing V-Mom and V-Dad and her teachers and custodians, she watched for those flashes of spontaneous feeling—anger or laughter—that might reveal the truth. Not surprisingly, she got into trouble provoking such responses.

The punishment veeries gave her nightmares; she woke up screaming. The reward veeries were powerfully seductive but left her feeling degraded. By the time she was eleven, she feared there was nothing at her core, no feeling that she owned. Years later, there was a name for what she had suffered: electronic abuse. But naming it did not free her from it.

During adolescence she discovered other ways to rebel: to dwell in her own changing body; to play Granny's little blue disc again and again, searching for clues to who her parents were and who she might be; to seek out among her peers and teachers those individuals who deviated from the script; to discover heresies, forbidden drugs, forbidden pleasures—antidotes to the electronic manipulation. But it was too late. Something had been taken from her. Later, with Trevor, when their barriers were down—moments when they revealed themselves to each other—she felt tantalizingly close to recovering it. Yet it always eluded her. What remained was a feeling of incompletion.

None of this was new to Maggie. But in Jeremy she saw for the first time what was missing from her childhood: not just love, but *innocence*.

She could not get it from Jeremy. She knew that. But acknowledging her need helped put the fantasy in perspective.

An uneasiness remained between woman and boy. How much was his and how much hers, she couldn't tell. She wanted to say something about the drowning but could think of nothing.

Polly began hinting that it was time for Maggie to end her mourning and look for a new husband. "Wear tha apron lower," she advised. " 'Twill trim tha height." The women in the spinning circle began recommending their nephews and other promising young men. Had her secret stirrings somehow announced themselves?

One night, lying in bed between mother and daughter, the three of them sleeping like nested spoons, Maggie awoke to find herself in an embrace—Kate's young, pointed breasts pressed against her back, her own arm thrown over Polly's hip. Maggie smelled their mingled odors and felt desire.

Polly was a puzzle. She seemed to have extinguished her own sexuality, to have given up any hope of ever marrying again, considering herself too old. She claimed her womanhood was a "cross to bear," yet she bought the whole idea of a woman's life revolving around a man and was always talking to Kate of marriage as a *destiny*. Lying there sandwiched between them, trying not to move, savoring that young breast against her shoulder blade, Maggie felt, in her own amorphous yearning, an unutterable loneliness.

Erzulie had told her once, "Girl, it's going to hit you more than once. Nobody's going to know you. Nobody, nobody, no*body!* Survivor of a world that ain't never been!"

The light of a blurred three-quarter moon shone dimly through the open window. Maggie missed the night sky over Chaco. The days were getting shorter. She could smell the dried parsley hanging from beams. Winter coming. She had to get busy. Get a job at Sunniside. She was stalling. Out of fear? She thought of those scraps of paper filled with notes, which she had sewn together in a sort of book that she kept at the bottom of her willow basket. If nothing came through at Sunniside, she would try for a job at John Wilkinson's. Too bad that neither household had children young enough to require a governess. As a governess, she would start out with higher status. But anything would be a start.

*I'm trying to change the world!* The audacity of it caused her heart to pound, although she tried not to stir. She thought of the church warden examining her thumbs . . . Adam and Eve being expelled from the Garden, the flaming sword of the archangel raised against them . . . the gilded chestnut carvings blackened by worm holes and candle smoke . . . the women spinning their endless advice.

Shortly before Michaelmas, a dozen people appeared at the cottage door with a cart. In the cart was a drowned man. It was the moment Maggie had been dreading, when she would have to choose not to save a life. Mrs. Merryweather hobbled over from her cottage.

To Maggie's relief, the man was stone cold. "Too late!" she announced. Their eyes remained fixed on her. "Aye," she called out more loudly. "The Lord has taken this man!"

There were muttered amens. Reluctantly, they wheeled the man away.

That night she dreamed of an endless procession of drowned men in carts. She could never make out their faces.

The whole family set out together for the Madeley Wakes: Maggie, Kate, and Polly carrying baskets filled with pies and tarts; Matthew and Jeremy with a couple dozen rabbits—some alive, some gutted—tied by their ears to a pole; Timothy and Helen carrying small baskets. By the time the bull baiting was announced, they had sold all their wares and were visiting the gaming stalls set up on the green. Maggie wanted to avoid the bull baiting, but she finally gave in.

"There she be," said Jeremy while they waited in the crowd gathered outside the bullring. He pointed to a pair of women in gray dresses and gray bonnets holding up placards outside the gate. "The Widow Darby!"

"What do it say, Maggie?" Helen asked.

"I can't see yet." When they got closer, Maggie read the large type aloud.

A
SERIOUS WARNING
TO THE
INHABITANTS OF MADELEY

"Repent!" cried Abiah Darby, a thin woman approaching sixty, her face made narrower by the brim of her Quaker bonnet. She had sharp features: a thin aquiline nose, prominent eyelids, thin pursed lips. A scrubbed look. The other woman was considerably younger.

Maggie stooped to read the smaller printing: *I am concerned in great Love to your never dying Souls, to warn you to consider your Ways and be Wise, and to remember your latter End, that you must in a little Time be called upon to give an Account of your stewardship, of the Grace of God bestowed upon you.*

"This is lovely," Maggie said, looking up. "I like the part about stewardship."

The younger woman must have been the widow's daughter, Sarah, who was twenty-one—and who looked perplexed, or perhaps it was the dark eyebrows that met under her bonnet.

Maggie read the remaining text aloud—a diatribe against Drunkenness, Rioting, Chambering, and Bull Baiting. Snickers from others pushing past.

"Thou art a fluent reader," said Abiah.

"Thanks." She corrected herself. "Thank you." She was about to inquire about work, but the Crumps were all pulling at her sleeve.

"What's chambering?" Maggie asked as they proceeded.

"Fornication," Polly whispered. "In Broseley they call it fooking around." She chortled.

Polly gave the gatekeeper a few copper coins, and they entered the bullring, a temporary enclosure about thirty meters across made from posts strung with ropes; planks were woven into the ropes. Within this compound was a smaller ring, marked by posts and ropes, in the center of which was a large bull chained by one foot to a stake driven into the ground.

Maggie was still thinking about Abiah Darby. She would follow up this encounter tomorrow—look for her in the same place, or walk to Sunniside and ask for work. She followed the Crumps up onto some tiered wooden benches, which were occupied mostly by women and children. Matthew wanted to stand with the men at the edge of the ring, but Polly insisted he stay with them.

The bull, a shaggy red animal with horns nearly a meter across at the tips, was being restrained from either side by teams of men with ropes, while others took turns jabbing it with sharp sticks until it bellowed and tossed its head with such ferocity that the men holding the ropes were nearly jerked off their feet. The dogs, mostly short-legged mastiffs with spiked collars, lunged against their ropes, while men walked around taking bets.

The men at the edges were clustered by vocation. The laborers wore pantaloons, the colliers were recognizable by the coaldust ringing their eyes, the bargemen by their long hair and striped jerseys, the bow haulers by their more ragged clothing. Occasional fights broke out among them. The farmers, in their smocks, conducted themselves with more dignity, as did the skilled tradesmen and shopkeepers, who wore breeches and wigs. Occasionally one of the laborers would dart close to the bull and leap away, provoking laughter from his fellows.

"I'm leaving," Maggie told Polly.

"Please, Maggie!" Jeremy begged her. "Wait till tha seest it!"

Against her better judgment, Maggie stayed.

"I dunna like it," Polly confided.

"Why do you go, then?"

Polly shrugged, gave her gap-toothed grin. "For the sake of the children."

Family values.

The first dog released was a stubby, spotted animal that must have weighed fifty pounds. It hurtled low, stopped short as the bull tossed its horns, lunged at the bull's left foreleg, and managed to seize it. Maggie felt sick as the bull bellowed, eyes rolling. The crowd roared. Lifted off its feet by the bull's horn, the dog hung fast. Suddenly the bull twisted its head sharply; the dog's belly opened, a glossy gray-pink, and the animal went flying. It landed with a thump, entrails trailing wetly in the dust as it attempted to raise itself on its front legs—only to fall back, writhing and snapping. Maggie hid her eyes. The men in front of them were laughing.

"Will it die?" she heard Helen ask.

"Hush," Polly said.

Maggie looked up to see a couple of men wedge a stick between the dog's jaws and drag it away.

The bull was limping. Maggie felt disconnected from her body. A part of her seemed to inhabit the bull, centered on the pain in its left foreleg, while another part of her registered the confusion around her, unfocused images mingled with the smell of rum and a sudden, rank, sour odor that she associated with fear.

A second dog—smaller, with an uglier, blunter snout—was released, and it made several feints at the bull's rear legs. The bull kept turning, its mouth frothing. The spectators rose to their feet, the benches creaking and flexing, the stamping of boots and clogs rising to a crescendo. Maggie tried not to look as the dog made repeated charges. But when she shut her eyes, she got dizzy and saw flames. She was going to be sick to her stomach. It was the crowd's glee that she found most repellent.

Hearing the bellowing of the bull rise to a suddenly higher pitch, she looked up to see the animal dancing backward on three legs, eyes bulging, a dog fastened to its neck slick with blood, both animals shaking their heads in a terrible frothing frenzy. Darkness rose around her, containing her, enfolding her. The yells were deafening. Blackness. Dizzying. Somewhere in her mind, flames leaping.

Suddenly she was gulping for air. Jounced off her seat by the mad stamping, she pitched forward, was pushed back roughly. The crowd was chanting something. She was going to be sick. A small hand gripped her arm in time to restore her balance. She pressed her forehead to her knees, but everything kept lurching.

*Why?* From the chant surrounding her the only word she could make out was "throat." *God. Why?* She was ashamed of her species.

The hand belonged to Timothy, who regarded her with somber eyes. She glimpsed a fountain of orange arterial blood, felt her gorge rise. She vomited, struggled down the planks. Something hard—a fist or elbow—struck her on the back. She scrambled over people, jumped to the ground, twisting her ankle, and ran past the gatekeeper.

She saw the gray bonnets. Breathless, she stared into Abiah Darby's scrubbed pink face. "Please," she said, not knowing what she was going to say—realizing from the other woman's expression that she must look a fright. "Please." She wiped her nose, brushed the hair from her eyes. "I want to work for you."

# John Wilkinson

John Wilkinson had long ago decided there was more money to be got from scheming than from ironmaking. Accordingly, he devoted as much time to improving the products of his brain as to the products of his furnace.

Every evening, while other men were wasting time in their cups or prayers or conjugal pleasures, Wilkinson took tea with his wife, Mary Lee, and then sequestered himself in his study, in a heavy oak chair equipped with a desk arm. There—with paper and pencil or quill at the ready, along with abacus and maps and a copper bowl on the floor beside him—he endeavored to see what ideas he might fashion in the forge of his mind. Whenever he began to feel drowsy, he picked up an iron ball, a two-pound shot, and held it over the copper bowl, so that if drowsiness loosened his fingers, he would be startled awake by the clatter. Thus was he able to scheme late into the night.

Occasionally the excitement of these calculations gave rise to lusts, which were received more readily by the upstairs maid than by Mary Lee, albeit with some grumbling. At other times the direction of inspiration was reversed, lust supplying the motive power to his brain.

It was by this latter sequence that Wilkinson arrived at a partial answer to the commission put forward by Anthony Bacon—a method for boring cannon from the solid.

Wilkinson's dealings with his wife were cordial. It was a second marriage for both, entered in midlife some years after the deaths of their respective spouses, and with few illusions. Their courtship was brief. Mary Lee possessed a substantial fortune; Wilkinson had wealth but was looking for cash to buy out the Bristol businessmen who owned New Willey. They married in 1762, and he purchased New Willey the same year.

Mary Lee was barren. Wilkinson had reckoned as much, her first marriage being childless. He had a daughter named Mary from his first marriage but would have liked a son to carry forward the Wilkinson name. He made occasional forays into Mary Lee's bed— not with any real hope of producing a male heir but out of itching desire, husbandly duty, and the challenge of her tightly crossed legs. He mounted these expeditions using military tactics, often employing a diversionary assault or a temporary retreat, which culminated in a final breathless effort to storm the citadel.

One evening, failing to breach her defenses, and dissuaded by the maid's insistence that it was her time of month, Wilkinson withdrew into his study and in a state of nervous agitation began scribbling ideas for the new boring machine, grappling with the problem of heat and friction—until it came to him that the challenges were similar. In the case of a woman, one was best off not storming the citadel at once but, rather, proceeding more subtly—inserting first one finger and wiggling it about craftily, then two fingers, and so forth. Thus would he overcome the resistance of cast iron: not all at once, as the Verbruggens were attempting in their blunt, Dutchmen's way, but by drilling first a small pilot hole and then expanding it with successively larger bits.

The next day Wilkinson refined the sketch. Like the Verbruggen machine, his would work on the principle of a lathe, the solid casting being made to spin on a horizontal axis while the cutting-head remained fixed. The cutting-head would contain multiple cutters of the best Huntsman steel.

He gave orders for the machine to be built. While work proceeded, he removed two of his existing boring machines from the boring shed and caused walls to be erected so that the experiments could take place in secret. He might have spared himself this trouble, for the new machine answered poorly. The cutters chattered and the boring bar wandered off center.

In the meantime, the Ordnance Board made its official announcement: all Carron guns in storage were to be frozen and those in the fleet were to be called in. Anthony Bacon wrote, demanding to know of Wilkinson's progress.

The race was on. What was he to do?

It occurred to him to pay a visit to a fellow he knew who ran a small forge and lathe shop a few miles away at Leighton—one Sniggy Oakes, who turned carriage bushings and musket barrels and who enjoyed a high reputation among local squires for the accuracy of his fowling pieces.

This Oakes was a spindly fellow with stooped shoulders and bedraggled mustache, who lived pretty much in his leather apron and was lost to all else but his work and his small family. Wilkinson had cultivated the man in the past, supplying him with good bar iron from his air furnaces, asking his opinion on matters pertaining to lathes, and finding him quite canny. Now the Broseley ironmaster persuaded Oakes to accompany him to New Willey to observe the difficulties he was having with the new machine.

"What think you, Mr. Oakes?" said Wilkinson, after the fellow had stood for some time observing how the cutting-head was deflected from its path.

Sniggy Oakes straightened and pulled thoughtfully at his mustache. "Well, sir, I have no experience boring large guns. Only muskets. But if it was left to me, I would shrink the cannon."

"Ha! You would, sir? Shrink it, you would? Ha!"

"Aye, sir, shrink the cannon to the size of a musket."

Wilkinson fumed, determined not to waste another minute in the company of so whimsical a character. "Very good, sir. I thank you for your opinion, and shan't take any more of your time."

But Oakes was strolling all around the machine, examining it from different angles. "There is only one way to shrink the cannon, and that is to make the machine bigger."

"The machine bigger?"

"Aye. Two or three times bigger. Heavier carriage, to conquer the vibration. And a much thicker boring bar. Then ye can bore your cannon like muskets."

Wilkinson was planet-struck. The idea made perfect sense. And perhaps this Sniggy Oakes was just the fellow to carry it forward. He persuaded the mechanic to come work for him for the summer, observing that the pool at Leighton was low (and Oakes of course lacked a fire engine to pump him through the drought) and offering to pay him fifteen shillings a week. He quickly raised it to sixteen.

Thus did Sniggy Oakes labor at New Willey the rest of the summer and into the autumn, with a few trusted workmen assisting him and Wilkinson supplying the heavy castings he requested—an enormous flywheel, and gears and bearings of like size—and Huntsman steel for the cutting blades. Wilkinson made light of the secrecy surrounding all their work—the keyhole stuffed with oakum, for example. "Distractions!" he said with a cheerful wave of his cane. "Outside that door, my dear Mr. Oakes, is a mob of workers! Country fellows, with manure on their shoes. Just yesterday one of them went raving mad, and would speak nothing but Welsh. You, sir, shall not be subject perforce to their interruptions!"

The mechanic seemed flattered by these attentions. Wilkinson permitted nothing to stand in Oakes's way, and often sent him home with a quarter round of cheese or a jug of cider to take to his wife and children. The ironmaster prevailed on him to stay into October, after the rains resumed, increasing his pay by half a shilling, because Oakes was still perfecting a method for supporting the tip of the boring bar to keep it from wandering. Wilkinson wrote Bacon, assuring him that the difficulties were nearly overcome.

Every afternoon at two, Sniggy Oakes was invited to Wilkinson's office, to a little side room where a table was laden with food: cold venison, squabs, short beer, black pudding, currant cakes, and other delicacies. Wilkinson often joined him for these repasts, conversing with an erudition and gentility to which the mechanic, mindful of his fork, might only aspire. Wilkinson spoke modestly of his other operations —his furnaces at Bersham and Bradley, his mining operations in Wales, his ship, the *Bersham,* sailing out of Liverpool. He bestowed bits of worldly knowledge—of London, where Oliver Goldsmith's *She Stoops to Conquer* had captivated Drury Lane, and of the new dance, the waltz, that was sweeping Vienna. These meals were conducted with an almost conspiratorial air. Wilkinson assured the mechanic that their project, while not actually a secret, was best *regarded* as a secret, for reasons left obscure.

"Jealousy," Wilkinson said, cracking the small bones of a squab with his teeth, "is rampant among the ironmasters. The less said about this"—his hand took in the workroom and made a barely perceptible dip over the currant cakes with clotted cream—"the better."

Oakes nodded. "Ere I obtain me patent."

"Ah, my dear Mr. Oakes!" Wilkinson chuckled. "The Royal Patent Office is filled to the rafters with patents, most of them worthless, for an idea must be quite unusual for the patent to stick—or at least one must have the money to defend it. No, no, no, 'tis simply—how shall I put it? 'Tis simply that I have to get along with my neighbors. Lord Forester, and all of those Quakers. Jealousy, and all that. You do understand, don't you, my good fellow?"

Oakes wiped his mustache uncertainly. "But what of the boring bar?" he asked. "Mightn't it be unusual enough for a patent?"

"We shall see, my good sir," said Wilkinson with a wink. "We shall see!"

Finally, in November, the new boring machine was ready for its trial. The ironmaster and the mechanic were alone in that section of the mill. Wilkinson had latched the door and left strict orders for them not to be disturbed. A solid cannon, a thirty-two-pounder, had been locked into collars made of hornbeam and was spinning at about twelve revolutions to the minute. The day before, Oakes had drilled a small pilot hole, then enlarged it by means of successively bigger bits, until it was three inches in diameter, to accommodate the boring bar.

Oakes's boring bar was round, a masterpiece of ingenuity: just small enough to be inserted in the pilot hole yet rigid enough to overcome the problem of vibration. Now, with a crank, Oakes advanced the cutting-head along the bar until the cutters began to engage, and the first brittle, intricately fractured curls of metal spilled from the bore. A weighted handle kept the head advancing slowly.

Wilkinson watched with the keenest interest. He was seated on a stool, his hands resting on the iron knob of his cane and with cotton wool in his ears to muffle the sound of the cutters, which was like the hissing of angry geese. With growing excitement he watched the cutting-head advance into the muzzle. Ha! He relished the gleam of that new bore, the acrid fragrance of cut iron prickling his palate like gunpowder. He picked up a handful of tailings and crushed them to powder, experiencing the same galvanic thrill he felt when he clenched the black ball of his cane in his moist palm—an exuberance that caused his blood to sing. The evenness of the tailings and regularity of the sound testified that the new boring bar was performing flawlessly.

When the cutting-head reached the end of its track, Oakes cranked it back out and readjusted the blades to enlarge the bore further. He lubricated the tip of the bar, which continued to rest in the socket of the original hole, and proceeded. Wilkinson excused himself to go about other business, but returned at intervals, each time gratified to see no sign of vibration, even when the blades were extended nearly full length.

Watching the mechanic, Wilkinson felt compassion stir in his breast. Something about the droop of the fellow's mustache, the head cocked like a terrier's as he attended to various adjustments, awakened Wilkinson's sympathy. This Oakes was the sort whose restless brain conceived of any mechanical process as perfectible. Such a mind was both a blessing and a curse to its owner, for the most agreeable method of production was soon found wanting when measured against its cousin, Perfection, and every manufactory became an endless series of problems to be solved. Wilkinson liked to think that he himself possessed such a mind, but that it moved in a grander orbit, around a higher abstraction, where the perfection lay in making Money. Thus it was Wilkinson who saw the vastness of the opportunity that lay before him, while Sniggy Oakes, moving in his smaller orbit, would remain encircled in his leathern apron.

When the cutting-head had completed its final advance, the sound of the cutters ceased. Oakes cranked the head backward along its toothed track, threw the clutch handle, and the flywheel began to slow. He looked at the Broseley ironmaster expectantly.

Wilkinson consulted his timepiece, a thick pocket watch of the sort known as a turnip, made for the Turkish trade, with a hinged tortoiseshell case. Today's boring had taken just under seven hours. Add yesterday's drilling and setting-up time, and the whole process had taken thirteen hours. Not bad, considering they had saved all the labor and uncertainty of a cored mold!

Oakes beckoned him back from the noise of the machine. "What think ye?"

"It answers well. 'Tis as good as any iron I've cast."

"But the machine. Does it answer?"

"Well, sir. Let us see." Once the cannon had stopped turning, Wilkinson laid a brass straightedge along the bore and confirmed that it was indeed bored to truth. Not the least glimmer of light showed under the brass, by heaven! It was all he could do to conceal his excitement. " 'Twill do, Mr. Oakes. 'Twill do. You've stopped the cutters from chattering. You've conquered that great enemy, vibration, quite jollily. Now, if you will forgive me, I must leave for an appointment." He held up the key, meaning that the mechanic would also have to leave.

Oakes took his coat from a peg and followed him to the door. "What think ye, sir, Mr. Wilkinson? Might I could obtain a patent for the boring bar?"

Wilkinson chuckled. "Ah, well, Mr. Oakes. You and I appreciate the value of your improvements. We are men of industry." He threw an arm over the mechanic's narrow shoulders. "And I assure you no one in all Christendom appreciates your cleverness more than John Wilkinson. But—" He dropped his voice. "To those witless clodpates on the Privy Council, 'twill appear nothing more than a lathe, plain and simple. Not so different from the Dutchmen's, which was patterned—dear me—after the Swiss. And though by Heaven I can't abide the ignorance of such drazels, I am forced to admit that they do have a point. For laudable as your improvements may appear to you and me, sir, they do not depart *in substantia* from the lathe—which has been around, oh, dear me, since the ancient Romans, I expect. You might as well suggest to my friend Wedgwood that he patent the potter's wheel."

"But . . ." The mechanic's shoulders lifted helplessly.

"Take heart, Mr. Oakes. You are a worthy engineer. I have a need for someone with your abilities right here at New Willey, and will make it worth your while. Will you do me the honor of quitting your forge and remaining in my employ? I will give you another shilling." The man must not fall into other hands.

A flush crept up from the mechanic's collar and around his mustache while he watched Wilkinson lock the door.

"Sleep on it, my friend. The cannon trade has never been worse than it is now. Peace, you know. We all want peace, of course. But since the Treaty of Paris, the world is awash in cannon. The Carron partners face bankruptcy. Still, I can offer you a snug port." While the man fumbled for words, Wilkinson put on his greatcoat and steered him outside to the stables, where he ordered the mechanic's horse brought with his own. "A snug port! Do think about it," he called as he rode off.

Wilkinson was so inflamed by success that he scarcely felt the November chill. He had, unbeknownst to Sniggy Oakes, already applied for a patent. It might not stick. What he had told Oakes was to a great extent true: the process might be judged insufficiently unique. But he had the money to defend it, and if by such bluster he could keep his hooks in it for three or four years, why then he could make another damned fortune!

He slowed the mare to a walk, looked up at the crescent moon, and shivered with a moment's sadness. The moon drifting through the coke haze recalled the glint of that new bore. But it also brought to mind the ruined cannon at Backbarrow when he was but thirteen— the shattered iron, one shard curled like a twisted fingernail paring;

the despair written on his father's face. Tension filled the house in those dark days, while they waited for the word on the guns that had been sent to Woolwich for proving. Isaac Wilkinson, pot founder, struggling to enter the cannon trade, had constructed a deep casting-pit in the Backbarrow Company's casting house and paid for hot metal on credit against his wages. More than that, he had put his reputation on the line, the old cock. And when word arrived from the Ordnance Board confirming that half his guns had burst on proving, Isaac collapsed into a kitchen chair and in a frenzy smashed a butter crock against the fireplace. Young John was hurried out of the house by his mother, along with his younger brothers and sisters. They stayed under the linden tree, the baby crying, and then his sister, who was three, got bitten by ants, which left red welts on her legs, and it grew cold —until finally Isaac came to the door and called out hoarsely, and they all trudged back inside.

He would never forget the defeat in his father's face, the sense of something shattered. Some tenderness in the boy wished to defend his father, smooth the pathetic frazzle of hair that stuck out over his waistcoat collar, seize the big, work-toughened hands and forgive him—if not for the beatings then for the shortcomings he could not fathom then (for it was only later that he was able to catalogue his father's vices); but stronger than the sympathy was a contempt he felt knowing even at thirteen that he would see his father brought to ruin more than once. He resolved never to let that happen to him.

Now these feelings hardened as always in his breast as he flicked the reins, urging the big gray mare back into a trot. Sniggy Oakes would not know what to do with the patent. Such a fellow was best off not rising too high. He, John Wilkinson, was a generous provider. The mechanic's family should never want, as long as John Wilkinson should live.

As for the cannon trade, well, it might be slack at the moment, but Denmark was arming against Russia, Constantinople against Damascus. The Boston colonists were rebelling, the rajahs of India making cause against the East India Company—and there was always the Balkans. Always a bloody war somewhere. If ever there was a truth in the affairs of Man, it was that war begat more war. Even now, France, smarting over the loss of colonies in the last conflict, was looking to regain them. War was the natural condition of man. Easier to maintain than peace. Peace required patience and craft; war required only jealousy and vengeance. If he were a gambling man, which he was not, he would wager on war.

Blood and iron, iron and blood! If he could not get an heir, he would get himself another damned fortune!

As his house came into view, Wilkinson thought again of the cutting-head advancing into that whirling orifice, spilling its bright seed, the scent of it in his nostrils. He thought of Mary Lee in her big four-poster bed, the maid in her garret, and was once more filled with lust.

# Abraham Darby III

From his study, he could hear the murmur of voices ascending the central staircase. The new housemaid had arrived earlier this evening, her indenture to start tomorrow with the New Year, and Mrs. Hannigan was taking her around the house and explaining her duties.

He stood looking out the window, holding a damp chamois, discouraged by his efforts to repair his electrical machine. Snowflakes danced in the pink night beyond his reflection, fading into the blur of snowy pastures. Early tomorrow morning, he would ride to the Haye farm to bring in the New Year, then sail down the Severn with Richard Reynolds to the quarterly meeting of ironmasters in Stourport. He looked forward to seeing the new, unsullied snow.

For the moment, however, his frustration with the electrical machine dampened his excitement. He had done everything he could think of—polished the glass globe, changed the brush, cleaned and lubricated the brass gears, tightened all the fittings—and the spark was weaker than ever.

He hung the chamois over the fireplace fender to dry. He felt wretched. He would have to direct an inquiry to Ramsden's shop in London, where he had purchased the device. Or have a word with Joseph Priestley next time John Wilkinson brought the renowned electrician around to Coalbrookdale. But what if the problem turned out to be something embarrassingly obvious? Abraham paced about his study. Oh, vain pretensions—to have purchased such a worldly plaything! Did he fancy himself a philosophe? Everywhere his eyes fell, he saw superfluity. The Adams weatherglass; the Persian-lined café full of books he scarcely understood, including Priestley's history of electricity; his silken partridge net draped across two brass hooks: all emblems of worldliness and vanity. The words of Isaiah came to mind: *Their land is full of idols; they worship the work of their own hands, that which their own fingers have made.* Laden with such worldly goods, he might no sooner get to heaven than a camel squeeze through the eye of a needle. He had an impulse to pitch it all into the snow.

To calm his nerves, he took a long-stemmed pipe from the mantel and filled it with tobacco, opened the sash a crack to help the smoke escape up the chimney—his mother did not like the smell in the house—and lit it with a splint from the fire. The medicinal effects of the tobacco were soothing to his lungs, although it made him think as always of naked savages with feathered hats.

Mrs. Hannigan's familiar knock sounded at his door, a flutter of light taps. He opened the door to the housekeeper's broad smiling face lit by a candle.

"Not wishing to disturb ye, Abraham, but might ye have a moment to greet the new girl?"

"Yes, of course."

Mrs. Hannigan presented Maggie Foster, the tall young woman who had lately been attending Meeting and whose soul his mother was interested in bringing to Truth. He had seen the woman only from a distance. Now her large eyes met his in a gaze quite as penetrating as Sarah had described. For a moment he thought he had seen those eyes before. But perhaps it was only the boldness of the gaze that flustered him.

"My mother speaks well of thee," Abraham said. "I understand thou art from America."

"Yes."

He thought to inquire which colony but did not know what he would then say. "Well," he said awkwardly. "Thou art welcome here." It seemed insufficient. What was needed, he supposed, was some firm but kindly word of advice. "Thank thee, Mrs. Hannigan," he said with a nod. Maggie Foster smiled, flashing a spectacularly even set of teeth.

The two women had turned to leave when Abraham stepped into the hall, suddenly inspired. "Follow my mother in all matters spiritual, Maggie Foster," he said, "and follow Mrs. Hannigan in all things kitchenly, and thou canst not go wrong!" The words were scarcely out of his mouth than he withdrew back into his study. He closed the door, mortified. *Thou art a blockhead! Why didst thou say that?* He lay for a moment against the door, in extreme agitation. Waited for their footsteps to fade. *Abey, Abey, Abey, thy middle name is maybe! Thou art a jack pudding! Merciful heaven.* He seized his pipe, but was too agitated to smoke and put it back. He felt like leaping in the air and capering. He lifted the partridge net from its hooks, tossed it into the air, and felt the silken strands slip down his face.

Getting free of the net proved troublesome. He gathered up what he could of the weighted perimeter; then, dipping low and raising his arms—feeling extremely foolish—he set about teasing the strands past each cloth-covered button, until finally after much effort he was able to gather up the net in his moist palms and return it to the hooks.

Maggie Foster. Was it her smile that so addled his brain? And was it that of God or that of the Enemy that shone from those eyes?

Arriving at the farmhouse, Abraham took the jug of cider from his saddlebag and stuck the mistletoe in his hat band. He made sure his boots were muddy before he knocked. He heard scurrying inside. Then the door swung open; he stepped carefully upon the threshold, which had been sanded. He was nearly deafened by the shouts.

"Our dark man comes!" the Sparrows chorused, taking his jug. "Master Abey! Master Abey!" the young ones cried. "What news have ye?"

"Good news! Good news!"

Then the two oldest sons, whom he'd known as lads, strapping fellows now, picked him up bodily and carried him through every room in the house to shake the muddy sand from his boots—January butter, as it was called in Shropshire—amidst great laughter and drubbing on saucepans, while he held up his sprig of mistletoe like a scepter. By the time they had finished, his stomach hurt from laughing. None of it was very Quakerly, but it was surely the most predictably pleasurable of his visits to collect the quarterly rent—all from the accident of his dark complexion.

Thomas Sparrow offered him a dram of apple brandy made from the first pressing of apples last autumn. Then they all went down to the dairy barn to burn the old mistletoe and feed what was left to the cow that had last calved. Abraham's head felt light from the brandy as they trooped outside to the orchard and wassailed the trees, chanting:

> *Stand fast, bear well top,*
> *Pray God send us a howling crop;*
> *Every twig, apples big,*
> *Every bough, apples enow,*
> *Hats full, caps full,*
> *Full quarter sacks full!*

Next they presented gifts to the bees, pouring a small libation of the cider into an eggshell wedged in the top of each straw hive before returning to the house. Ann Sparrow insisted, as she always did, that he take a basket of hot pop-lady buns with him, along with the goose, which was his due, and he rode off with his saddlebags full.

At Sunniside, the celebration was more discreet—so that his mother might not hear. He rattled the latch, allowing the servants time to scurry into place. In silence they watched him cross the threshold—Mrs. Hannigan, Jane, and the new girl, Maggie Foster, as well as Andrew and Joseph come in from the stable.

"What news?" they whispered.

"Good news!" He held up the goose and passed a sprig of mistletoe to Mrs. Hannigan, who conveyed it to her apron pocket. He gave another sprig to Andrew, for the stable. Sarah watched from the staircase and joined them parading silently through the downstairs rooms. They all ended up in the kitchen to eat the pop-ladies and wish each other a pink and prosperous New Year. Then Mother's footsteps sounded upstairs, and they all dispersed, the maids sweeping up the January butter and everyone going about their business.

After breakfast, taken in the customary silence, they exchanged gifts. Abraham gave Sarah a paper of pins and his mother a tatting frame, and received a pair of hose and an ivory comb. Mrs. Hannigan presented them with colored eggs and received marzipans that Abiah had wrapped up in tissue paper with a silver piece. Richard Reynolds arrived then, bearing a tin of Fothergills' tea, whose fragrance they all admired before Abraham and Richard were driven by Andrew to Ludcroft Wharf.

Locating their barge, the two ironmasters settled themselves in the aft cabin, warmed by a salamander stove. With only the mizzen sail unfurled, the barge glided downstream past the furnaces—Bedlam on the left, Calcutts on the right—and the potteries at Jackfield, where the river widened and the topsail was raised. Once they got outside the smoke and soot of the gorge and the river curved south, the sun refracting from the snowy valley was quite dazzling.

"Didst thou play the dark man for the Sparrow brood?" Richard asked.

"Yes," said Abraham, a little cautiously. They did not talk much about those old pagan customs.

But Richard smiled. "As thy father did, being dark too."

Abraham recalled sitting on the steps with Sarah and Sammy, whispering, hands clasped on their knees, watching Father bring in the New Year. He had a dim memory of being awakened while it was still dark and riding behind his father to the Haye farm. "Did he— did he once take me to the Haye farm and send me across the threshold with a bag of . . . ?"

"Macaroons. 'Twas I who carried thee to the Haye." Richard grinned. "Thou wert but eight. 'Twas the winter thy father fell from his horse and injured his knee."

Abraham remembered little more than the macaroons—only being awakened in the dark and sitting behind his father in the saddle. Yet it held magic for him, a sense of adventure. To learn now that it was not his father but Richard Reynolds was a little disconcerting. Sometimes his childhood felt like a house through which others roamed freely—Mother, Richard, Mrs. Hannigan, even his sister Mally—but whose rooms remained for him a mystery.

# Maggie Foster

**H**er first impression of Sunniside was of darkness and gloom. She arrived on the last day of December, carrying her few possessions in the willow basket that Jeremy had made for her. It was midafternoon, the sun below the trees, the tall cedars casting the carriage lane in deeper twilight. A smell of snow in the air, Jeremy said.

He had insisted on accompanying her, but the reticence between them only deepened the chill in the air. Some of it was the awkwardness of parting. Things had not felt quite right between them since the bull baiting last September, and since she had started attending Quaker meetings. The cruelty of the bull baiting brought to mind Trevor's observation that it was the English, not the Spanish, who first gave smallpox-infected blankets to the Indians, the English who had promoted slavery most aggressively. Abiah Darby's offer of employment, when it came Sunday before last, was so welcome that Maggie felt guilty for leaving the Crumps. All these feelings were mixed with gratitude when she said goodbye to Polly outside the cottage—hugging her, letting her cheek fall on the port-wine birthmark, *You were like a mother*—and now, walking along that dark carriage lane, preparing to say goodbye to Jeremy, she realized she was a little frightened.

At Jeremy's suggestion, they followed the formal clipped hedge around to the back door, where they were received by Mrs. Hannigan, the housekeeper, a short, squarely built woman with graying blond hair and squinty blue eyes. A few flakes of snow danced in the air.

"Come, come," said Mrs. Hannigan, holding the door open impatiently, after Maggie had hugged Jeremy goodbye. *Thank you, Jeremy.* The housekeeper instructed Maggie to leave her clogs in the brick-floored entryway. "We wear shoes in the house."

"I have only the clogs," Maggie said.

The housekeeper raised her eyebrows at this.

Barefoot, Maggie followed her into the kitchen, which was as big as the Crumps' whole cottage and smelled of apples and spices. She was introduced to a lean, redheaded woman with a freckled face and amused eyes whose name was Jane. "Yer a tall one," Jane observed, tossed her braids, and went back to chopping parsnips.

Maggie followed Mrs. Hannigan through the house, taking in its spaciousness. The Darbys were not at home but expected back shortly. Mrs. Hannigan showed her the pantry off the kitchen entry. Next to the pantry was the housekeeper's own tidy room, and down a few steps was the buttery. Off the kitchen in the other direction were the dining room and downstairs parlor. The furnishings were surprisingly ornate, given the Quaker belief in simplicity. The windows were handsomely curtained, the dining-room chairs mahogany Chippendale, the dinner service decorated with blue-and-white Chinese landscapes. Simplicity in an era of ornamentation.

In the parlor, a door opened onto a greenhouse. "A great extravagance," Mrs. Hannigan remarked. "All that glass."

Maggie could not tell whether "extravagance" reflected the judgment of the housekeeper or her employers, but the criticism carried a hint of pride.

Next was a library, with a couple of shelves of books that had to be dusted every week. Mrs. Hannigan pointed to a door she said was an ash closet, whatever that might be, then led the way up a wide central staircase with walnut railings and carpeted steps that branched in either direction from a landing. She showed Maggie the upstairs parlor, which had blue striped wallpaper, Abraham's study, which included a few pieces of scientific apparatus and some fossils, Abiah's sitting room, a separate bedchamber for each of the Darbys, two guest rooms, and the door to another ash closet.

"What is an ash closet?" Maggie asked.

The eyebrows went up again. "What is an ash closet?" Mrs. Hannigan opened the door to reveal a privy seat. "Tha be'est a country lass, methinks." She explained how Maggie was to change the ashes and empty the chamber pots daily, and went on to describe the weekly schedule, beginning with laundry on Monday.

Before taking Maggie back downstairs, she pointed up a steep winding staircase to the top floor, where Samuel, the youngest of the Darby children, had a study and where Jane had her bedchamber. The housekeeper had offered no hint of where Maggie was to sleep.

They descended the main staircase. The house conveyed an impression of wealth and solidity. And now that she was over her initial surprise at the degree of ornamentation, Maggie sensed an element of restraint. Except for the blue wallpaper in the upstairs parlor, the colors were subdued. No sign of musical instruments. The walls were bare except for two framed prints: one, hanging by the first landing, portrayed William Penn "treating with the Indians"; the other, fastened to Sarah Darby's door, showed the floor plan of a slave ship, the silhouettes of bodies filling every available space.

Returning to the kitchen, they encountered a fat, toothless woman scrubbing the hearth—Martha, the scullery maid, her bare feet a reminder to Maggie to lose no time getting shoes.

Maggie ate supper in the kitchen with the other servants, who included an old man and a boy who took care of the horses. Later, after the Darbys had dined, Maggie was summoned to Abiah Darby's sitting room to discuss her articles of indenture. Sarah, sitting beside her mother, scarcely looked up from her mending. Maggie and Sarah had exchanged words one Sunday after the rise of Meeting. The young woman had taken the initiative to ask about antislavery sentiments in the Colonies, but she seemed shy.

Reading the document, Maggie saw that in addition to her tasks as a maid she was to "assist in reading and writing." She decided not to ask what that meant; she hoped it would offer a chance to improve her status. She was to be paid five pounds eight shillings a year and to have First Days off. Altogether it looked as though she would be working eighty hours a week.

Abiah asked if all this was satisfactory.

"Sounds good," Maggie said, immediately realizing that was too colloquial. "I'm very grateful," she added.

Abiah nodded and then shut her eyes, evidently praying. After a long time, she looked up. "Thou art replacing another maid, who professed herself a Quaker but who strayed from the path. I pray thou wilt find the Light, and keep thy precious soul in Jesus' grace." After another, shorter silence, she rang a little brass bell.

Sarah looked up from her mending. "Dost thou need anything for thy comfort?"

Maggie thought quickly. "A Bible, if you have one I could borrow. And, ah, a pair of shoes."

An inspired response, she thought later. Abiah handed her a Bible from a nearby shelf. Sarah promised to inquire among Friends about shoes.

Mrs. Hannigan appeared, evidently in response to the bell, and witnessed their signatures on the articles. The housekeeper waited while Sarah traced Maggie's foot on a newspaper, and then took Maggie upstairs to be introduced to Abraham.

Abraham Darby III impressed Maggie as painfully earnest—a slender, athletic man, with his mother's eyelids and sharp nose but without her scrubbed look. He was dark, almost swarthy, with close eyebrows, like Sarah's, and brown eyes. And he was shy, which struck Maggie as being at odds with the prominent role he would play in building the bridge and with the fact that at the age of twenty-three he was in charge of the world's biggest ironworks. When he popped out of his study to suggest that Maggie follow his mother in all things spiritual and Mrs. Hannigan in all things *kitchenly,* and then popped back like a cuckoo in a clock, she could have sworn he blushed.

Mrs. Hannigan had taken her downstairs and showed her the little room under the main staircase where she was to sleep. It was no more than a walk-in closet, windowless, with only a ventilation grate. A brick chimney formed most of the tallest wall, against which the ceiling sloped. A narrow cot had been squeezed into that triangle. The housekeeper left her with a candle stub and a chamber pot.

The room was so tiny, Maggie had to gather her skirts just to turn around. But it was warm and dry. For the first time since she had arrived in Shropshire, she had a space of her own.

Sarah Darby was gone the next day, but returned that afternoon with a pair of old black leather shoes that fitted Maggie quite nicely.

"Tha be'est lucky," Mrs. Hannigan told Maggie when she saw the shoes, "to find service in a Quaker house. They be frugal, preferring to do some of the work themselves and expecting two servants to do the work of three. But they be honest and fair."

During her first week at Sunniside, Maggie got a sense of the dynamics at Sunniside. Mrs. Hannigan, who had worked there seventeen years, was unswervingly loyal to the Darbys. Jane, who had been there three years, cultivated two distinct styles—one for serving the Darbys, the other more rambunctious. Maggie wondered about the young Quaker maid who had left under a cloud, but nothing was volunteered.

The Darbys took their meals in "awful silence." They had frequent guests, Coalbrookdale being a favorite stopping place for traveling Friends who made the circuit from London through Wales and the North Country or oversaw the businesses in which Quakers excelled—ironmaking, banking, chocolate, tea—commercial and spiritual concerns interwoven with friendships between families. It was a tight little world, the Quaker subculture, with its distinctive dress and speech, a minority even here in Coalbrookdale.

The servants ate in the kitchen, exchanging gossip at low volume. That was how Maggie learned of the comings and goings of the Darbys and the Reynoldses, and first caught the whiff of scandal surrounding

John Wilkinson. The Broseley ironmaster, it seemed, "enjoyed one of his maids in the bed, as well as in the kitchen." This whispered intelligence came from Andrew, the old man who managed the stable and drove the carriage.

Jane was the prime source of news from within the parish, and from Dawley, the next town north, where she had grown up and where her mother lived. Jane was in her thirties. Her wit ran to the sardonic, mirth enlivening her sometimes startling blue eyes and downward-sloping smile. A lively storyteller, she did imitations of village characters that made even Mrs. Hannigan laugh out loud.

Abiah, preoccupied with her ministry, had a reputation among the servants as an "airling." "She dunna tithe, nor pay taxes," said Jane. "On conscience. What they call sufferings. But ere they clap her in jail, the Dale Company ups and pays the money. 'Tis all a sham, really." She tossed her braids with a smirk. Mrs. Hannigan gave her a disapproving look.

This sort of talk was generally the province of the inside staff—the two maids and the housekeeper—and occasionally included Andrew. It excluded Martha the drudge, who was said to be simple, and the outside employees—Andrew, under most circumstances, his nine-year-old nephew, Joseph, who assisted him as a stableboy, and the gardener and groom.

Mrs. Hannigan drew a clear line between herself and the servants, censuring them whenever family business was discussed too openly in the hearing of outsiders—servants from other households, or fishmongers and grocers who tarried at the kitchen fire.

Once, after observing Maggie and Jane laughing together, the housekeeper took Maggie aside and warned her to mind her step with Jane, who was thought to have exerted "a corrupting influence" on the Quaker maid. " 'Tis a spirit of impudence," Mrs. Hannigan said, her ruddy cheeks so close that Maggie could see the little broken capillaries. "Mind she don't lead thee astray."

Maggie promised to be careful.

In fact, she found Jane's iconoclastic wit a refreshing break from the seriousness of the Quaker household. Jane had names for each of the Darbys, which she used outside Mrs. Hannigan's hearing. Abiah was "Queen of the Air." Abraham was "Master Shill-I-Shall-I" because of the way he paced back and forth in his study, the squeaking of floorboards audible in the downstairs parlor. Sarah was "Miss Mousie" for her retiring ways, although Jane claimed to have seen her dancing in the deer park in the moonlight.

One day, when Mrs. Hannigan went to market and Jane and Maggie had the house to themselves, Jane led the way into Sarah's bedchamber. Opening the armoire, she pushed aside the gray Quaker dresses to reveal a fancy green gown. It had full skirts, the outer layer of silk gathered up in scallops to reveal an inner skirt of painted cotton with a green-and-white floral design. Puff sleeves done the same way.

"Wow," said Maggie.

Jane removed the dress from its hooks.

"Are you sure you should do that?" Maggie asked.

"Tut, she'll never know." Jane held the dress up to herself and flashed her eyes coquettishly—transformed, her eyes set off by the freckles and red hair.

"You look gorgeous," Maggie said.

The freckles crinkled. "Gorgeous?"

"It's a good color on you. Better than on her, I imagine." Sarah was a plain young woman; her complexion, like Abraham's, ran to the sallow.

Jane clearly liked having an audience, and Maggie liked Jane's verve. Still, this felt like an invasion of Sarah's privacy. She was relieved when the dress was back on its hooks and they were safely out of the room.

On another occasion, when Jane took her up to Samuel's study and leafed through his pencil drawings—mermaids with laboriously drawn breasts, dragons with vaguely phallic snouts—Maggie expressed some uneasiness.

Jane shrugged. "Them with servants gives up some privacy."

"I suppose."

"But mind thee, if tha'rt of a mind to snoop in Abraham's study, he keeps it tidy and notices anything out of place."

Useful advice. Jane should be the spy. Probably she was cut out for it better than Maggie was. Her energy might have found an outlet on the stage had she lived in another time and place. It seemed barely contained in this Quaker household. But for Maggie, Jane's irreverence made the long winter bearable.

Samuel Darby, who was in Liverpool serving his apprenticeship, already had a reputation for erratic behavior. Jane did an imitation of him outside Mrs. Hannigan's hearing. "When he's brash, everything tickles him. But when he's in a sulk, he walks like this." She demonstrated, squinting nervously and scuttling crabwise with her back to the wall.

Mrs. Hannigan herself voiced concerns about the youngest Darby. Samuel had been a difficult child, she said. Always in trouble. Suffering seizures. Setting fire to the barn. Shamming. "But he'll grow out of it," she insisted.

Maggie knew otherwise. She knew that at the age of twenty-one Samuel would be put in charge of the Dale Company's London office; in his mid twenties, he would suffer a breakdown, described in his mother's journal as a "nervous condition," and have to be cared for for the rest of his life.

Her knowledge of the future was a burden now that she was among people who were part of the historical record. The kitchen gossip might be titillating, but it was nowhere near as creepy as being introduced to the Reynolds family and knowing that young William would grow up to disowned by the Quakers for marrying his first cousin. Or knowing that Abraham would die at the age of thirty-nine, the same age as his grandfather. Or knowing that Sarah Darby would never marry but have a long-time female companion named Sukey Appleby.

Maggie tried to forget the death dates, which were all safely recorded. Her notebook stayed hidden at the back of her sleeping closet, in a space between the brick chimney and the paneling. She tried with mixed success to blur the dates in her mind. Over time, she supposed, she would acquire a professional detachment. But for now, the cold precision of those dates added to the chill of her first winter.


**M**aggie herself was the object of some curiosity. She was glad that her stay at the Crumps' had given her a bit of personal history that was safely in the past. Her years in the Colonies were harder to account for here at Sunniside, where American Quakers occasionally visited and where her accent was perceived as strange.

Once, while she was clearing the table, some Philadelphia Quakers on their way to Shrewsbury asked her views on the recent Boston Tea Party. She responded tactfully, knowing it was a matter of some controversy—knowing, too, that American Quakers were being criticized for refusing to take up arms in the revolutionary cause. The challenge, she said, was to explore "nonviolent alternatives" (they liked this phrase), and she observed that at least the demonstration in Boston Harbor involved violence against property, not against people. She thought she acquitted herself fairly well. There was some talk then about John Woolman, the famous American Quaker who had died last year, who had refused to wear clothing dyed with indigo or to otherwise support slavery. His white hat and coat made him stand out amidst the Quaker gray. No, she had not met him. And then someone caught her totally off guard by asking where exactly in Baltimore she had lived.

"You mean, what street?" A cold lump of fear high in her belly.

"Yes," the man said, "for I have spent some time in Baltimore."

"Well," she said. "It wasn't a street with a name. I mean we lived outside Baltimore, in the direction of—" Blood rushed to her face. For an instant it was as though she had taken flight from her body; all she could think of was satellite digifotos: the lacy fingers of the Chesapeake Bay zigzagging into the eastern shore of Maryland. Then the Mediterranean, then the Red Sea emptying into the Gulf of Aden; she was orbiting out of control. "Toward Annapolis," she managed.

"Aye, we lived in the direction of Annapolis."

"Ah, Annapolis. I have been there."

"But you see—we moved west. My husband and I traveled to the Western Territories. Have you been west?"

"No."

She talked effusively about the hardships of the trip west, until Abiah thanked her and gave her leave to return to the kitchen. Her armpits were wet. She leaned against the wall.

"What happened?" asked Jane. "Tha lookst pale. Did tha drop something?"

Maggie shook her head. "Almost."


**H**er ability to read and write set her apart from the other servants, as did her interest in Quakerism. Abiah gave her tracts to read and loaned her a copy of George Fox's *Journal*. Fox had founded Quakerism in the last century, during Cromwell's time; his journal served as a basic text, along with the Bible. Abiah also gave her letters to copy, which Maggie executed in her most careful hand.

She attended Meeting with the family. The meeting house was a plain square building that had separate entrances for women and men. Inside was dark wood paneling, and straight-backed benches facing each other in a square. Worshipers entered in silence and often remained silent the whole two hours, the women wearing bonnets with brims often so constricting that the visible portion of their faces was hardly bigger than an egg. The men's faces were shadowed by dark, flat-brimmed hats, which they removed only when they stood to testify.

It was all very staid. Later, Quakers would refer to this as the "quietist" era. The ecstatic trembling and prayerful outpourings associated with the earlier Quakers were now rare. Quaker evangelism had ebbed. And, commensurate with their success in business, few Friends actually went to jail for their beliefs.

And yet Maggie found herself drawn to the Society of Friends. They retained a radical social agenda: working to reform prisons and schools, protesting slavery and war. Local meetings were linked to a network strengthened by visits of traveling Friends and by exchanges of letters. The meetings gathered regionally four times a year. In the interim, individual meetings passed resolutions, or "minutes," on various issues, which were carried to the Quarterly regional meetings and which the Quarterly meetings often forwarded to the Yearly meeting held in London. So the network had a potential for rallying great support around a cause, at least within the Society of Friends.

Quaker principles overlapped with those that guided Ecosophia. It was no accident, she realized. Quakers were among Ecosophia's original founders. Still, she was surprised to see how many of those principles were in place. Friends decided things by consensus; they were committed to nonviolence; they emphasized mindfulness and community.

And Maggie grew to like the shared silence of worship. Often an hour passed without anyone speaking, so that a simple utterance had special force. But apart from any spoken testimony, the silence itself seemed full. Trevor would have been right at home here. She supposed someday she would join the Society of Friends. But she was content for now to be simply an attender—waiting, as Abiah had made it clear she must wait, for Convincement.

"Every seed," said Abiah, "hath its time of ripening."

She was invited to attend family meetings for worship. These were held once or twice during the week, usually in the casting house of the Old Furnace. They stood in a circle: the Darbys joined by members of other Quaker families—the Thomases, Roses, Fords—who kept the furnaces and occupied other skilled positions at Coalbrookdale. The silence included the roar of the blast and the whump of the bellows. Abiah occasionally spoke, although Maggie could rarely get her drift. Sometimes visitors testified, inspired by the fiery spectacle of the Dale. Abraham and the furnace keepers testified only rarely, prompted usually by the death or injury of a worker, asking for Divine mercy.

Prayer. She used to get into arguments with Erzulie over prayer. Maggie could never bring herself to pray in the Christian sense of asking for this or that. If she prayed *to* anything, it was to something larger, more amorphous, and certainly less gender-bound than either the old-guy-in-the-sky of the Judeo-Christian tradition or the

Goddess that Erzulie prayed to. If Maggie prayed to anything, it was to Life. The Great Mystery. But never comfortably. Always with the feeling that by the time you worked your way across the spectrum from the loquacious chauvinism of homo sapiens to the mute intelligence of earthworm and legume, the life force became so remote as to defy imagination, let alone answer human prayers. You could see why Christians and Muslims and Hindus got hooked on their avatars and saints—little ombudsmen who bridged the gap to the Unknown.

Mostly she meditated. Used the time to gather herself: to see past the details, to locate herself in the circle of life. What Trevor called the hoop.

H er ability to read caused some friction in the kitchen. One morning Abiah came in with a book of recipes entitled *The Country Housewife* and asked Maggie to read aloud the instructions for pitchcotting eels, for the benefit of Mrs. Hannigan and Jane—to improve their minds. Maggie began reading dutifully. When Abiah left, Maggie saw them looking at her crossly.

"Shall I continue?" Maggie asked. "You probably know how to pitchcot eels in your sleep."

Mrs. Hannigan insisted she carry on—obviously furious, interrupting to disagree with this point or that, which she imputed to Maggie. Later that morning, the housekeeper ordered Maggie to prepare a calf's stomach for rennet—a singularly loathsome task, worse than cleaning geese. Maggie had confessed her revulsion earlier to Jane.

Hunkered over the copper washtub with the fleshy bag of the stomach and forcing herself to reach inside to scoop out the curds, which smelled like vomit, Maggie caught Jane's eye. Jane smirked.

The rat! Maggie wiped the curds into a bowl. To get on Mrs. Hannigan's bad side bummed her a bit, but Jane's betrayal cut like a knife. Maggie had been counting on that friendship. By the time she had picked the hairs from the curds and scoured the bag inside and out with salt, the hurt turned to anger. Anger made the task easier, guiding her fingers across the limp, rubbery flesh. And by the time she had finished cleaning the curds and stuffing them back into the bag, she was furious. She spread the stomach to dry in a roasting pan. She carried the scraps to the pigpen and threw them as hard as she could at the pigs. When she returned to the kitchen, Jane looked up, her expression a little softer. *Screw you!* Maggie thought. The fury was part of her loneliness. Might as well get used to it. She was never going to fit in.

The next day, things were back to normal. After breakfast, when the Darbys left, Jane gave a hilarious account of the time the Fothergills paid one of their cherished visits to Sunniside for three days, and afternoon tea became such an occasion for reminiscing and carrying on that no one could bring himself to stop for a silent supper.

"Tea!" Jane hooted. She slapped her thigh and stamped her foot. "The first night, they kept putting off supper, they cunna stop talking, with a suckling pig on the spit, till they'd et up every sweetmeat and biscuit in the house, and all the time one story just a-leading 'em to the next! Finally Abiah lets 'em have the suckling pig! 'For tea,' she tells 'em, just as sober as a judge. Says it twice, lest there be any doubt! *'We be having tea!'*" Jane shrieked, her braids dancing, tears rolling down her cheeks. Mrs. Hannigan chortled. Maggie laughed till her sides hurt, laughed partly out of relief.

# Maggie Foster

In building their sacred bridges, the Japanese used no iron. "Not because they lacked nails," Paul Stanski told her. "It was only the blast furnace, the ability to liquefy iron, that they lacked. They could work small quantities of iron in their open forges to produce nails and even fine steel for swords. But to keep the bridges pure, they built them without nails."

From what she could hear, eavesdropping on the Darbys' conversations that winter, the bridge was hardly mentioned.

Then one day in March, she answered the door to find a large portly man. She knew immediately it was John Wilkinson: not so much by his appearance as by an animal energy, a humorous ferocity around the eyes. Polished cheek ridges descended from either side of a Roman nose, which had a wart just above the right nostril. The ridges swelled into florid, pendulous jowls. He announced himself in an imperious manner. His voice surprised her. She had expected a baritone or bass, but what came out was a ringing tenor:

"Please inform your master that John Wilkinson wishes the pleasure of an audience." He smiled lasciviously.

Maggie invited him into the foyer and trotted upstairs, aware of Wilkinson's eyes following her. Later, she tried to overhear their conversation in the parlor, but Mrs. Hannigan assigned Jane to serve them coffee. When Maggie quizzed her afterwards, Jane only shrugged. "Something about the bridge."

Three weeks later, one dark, rainy afternoon in April, old Andrew showed up at the kitchen door in his oilskin coat, his bushy gray eyebrows and mustache dripping. As he warmed his hands at the fire, he announced that he had overheard something while driving the carriage from the Cuckoo Oak, where the ironmasters had met.

Rubbing his hands, he turned to the room. "They are going to build a bridge of iron."

Mrs. Hannigan had been instructing Maggie how to scrub the copper pans with lemon hulls and fine sand, Martha being out sick with the flu. She looked up sharply. "Which bridge is that, Andrew?"

"At the gorge." Andrew squeezed the water out of his mustache with scissored fingers. "The place everybody talks about, I warrant."

The housekeeper shook a spoon at him. "Mind tha dunna drip in that pot of custard, Andrew. Iron, didst tha say?"

"Aye, iron!"

Maggie had got goose bumps upon hearing *iron*. "Who was talking about it, Andrew?" she asked.

"Why, Richard Reynolds and John Wilkinson. And Abraham. But 'twas Mr. Reynolds and Wilkinson did most of the gabbling. They had plans."

"Plans?"

"Aye, aye. Drawings of the bridge. They kept passing 'em back and forth."

*Pritchard's drawings?* Maggie could hardly contain herself. *Actual plans, or rough sketches?* "Did you see them, Andrew?"

"Enough to see 'twas a bridge."

She was asking too many questions. Mrs. Hannigan grabbed her hand and stuffed a lemon hull in it. "Easter is Sunday next. Guests be coming up from Bristol, the pots must shine!"

Maggie scoured furiously. Her hands, already chapped, stung from the lemon juice. She had to get busy. Winter, the sense of everything frozen, was giving way to flux.

She had to see those drawings.

P aul's words kept coming back to her. *Remember, this is a surgical operation. You are wielding a scalpel, not a cleaver.*

Maggie wished she could forget half of Paul's advice. Erzulie's comments were cryptic but expansive; they planted seeds. Paul's were prescriptive and often made Maggie feel boxed in. It was Paul's words that came to her this morning, as she stood at the top of the stairs with an armload of bed linens, listening. Finally, hearing the housekeeper's muffled voice instructing Martha, she dropped the sheets in a pile and tiptoed into Abraham's study, mindful of the squeaky floorboards. Today was Monday, wash day. Blue Monday, Jane called it. Maggie could not wait for Wednesday to dust Abraham's study, and anyway he might be occupying it then. Today the house was empty except for Mrs. Hannigan and Martha. Jane was visiting her mother, and the Darbys were out. It was as good a time as any to search for the drawings. Still, her heart pounded as she approached Abraham's writing table.

Everything was meticulously laid out: on the left, a neat stack of letters weighted by a fossil trilobite; on the right, a pair of silhouettes in oval walnut frames and a magnifying glass; in the middle, a ruler placed symmetrically.

She listened again, stock still. It would not do for Mrs. Hannigan to hear her creaking around in Abraham's study, where there were no linens. Finally she heard the murmur of voices in the kitchen. That would be Mr. Hannigan instructing Martha. She turned her attention to the wide drawer flanked by two narrow ones. Slowly, silently, she slid it out.

No drawings. Maybe they were too large for the drawer. Or maybe he kept them at the Works. Her eyes went past the electrical machine—a sort of stunted spinning wheel, with a glass globe instead of a spindle—to the glass-fronted cabinet where he kept his books and fossils. She tiptoed across and, finding it unlocked, carefully opened the doors. Inside, lying across a row of books, was a long packet wrapped in burlap. She removed it, untied the ribbon, and opened a pair of boards. Inside were two drawings. Her heart leapt.

Neither drawing resembled Pritchard's final design. They appeared to be preliminary sketches. Signed *F. Pritchard.*

She laid them side by side for comparison.

Both designs were based on a single arch, the only way the river could be spanned without impeding barge traffic. One drawing portrayed a stone bridge; its arch formed around a semicircular iron hub. The other bridge was made completely of iron. Pritchard was giving them a choice—the choice that Abraham and the committee would wrestle with for a year and a half.

As she studied the drawings, she saw that Pritchard was trying, with that second design, to show how the traditional Roman arch could be abandoned, or at least flattened, using all iron. It anticipated Thomas Telford's proposed bridge across the Thames a generation later. She wondered if Telford would see this sketch.

"Maggie!" Mrs. Hannigan called from the foot of the stairs.

*Damn!* Maggie closed the boards and rewrapped them, hurriedly tied the ribbon, returned the packet to the bookcase, tiptoed out of the study, and sprinted softly around the corner just as Mrs. Hannigan emerged, puffing, at the top of the steps.

"We must needs turn the mattresses," Mrs. Hannigan said, eyeing the pile of sheets as she wheeled past.

"Yes ma'am."

That evening, in her little room under the stairs, Maggie stuck a candle stub on a protruding brick, fished her notebook from its hiding place between the chimney and paneling, and sat at the end of her cot, facing the chimney. The journal on her knees, she turned to a blank page. With a pencil she sketched Pritchard's two designs as accurately as she could from memory.

Next she turned to her notes on the local geology. The sketches of substrata showed the instability of the gorge: soft brown clay overlying hard blue mudstone and shale, all of it under thousands of tons of pressure from the strata above and slipping toward the middle of the riverbed, which had been carved at the end of the last Ice Age. That was the key.

The gorge would suffer numerous landslips during the nineteenth and twentieth centuries. The instability was well enough understood by the end of the twentieth that when a new steel bridge was built at Jackfield in 1994, it was constructed with one end fixed, the other end permitted to move in a slot.

But in the eighteenth century, people didn't know about such movements—any more than they knew about the expansion and contraction, with temperature changes, of large iron structures. That ignorance was nearly the bridge's downfall. They built the abutments on the soft brown clay atop the mudstone that was creeping inward at the rate of two or three centimeters a year—fast enough that within five years of the bridge's completion, cracks appeared in the cast-iron arch.

Fortunately—or unfortunately, depending on one's point of view —the bridge was overengineered. Five pairs of ribs were used where three might have sufficed. So when three of the ribs cracked, the redundancy saved it and gave the builders time to make repairs.

Even with that redundancy, the bridge would have failed had they used one of the newer methods available for joining the members: bolts or rivets would have given the frame more rigidity. Cast iron was brittle stuff. Movement would generate hairline fractures. And then, under the lateral delta force of wind or of high water during a flood, all five pairs of ribs would have cracked in quick succession as the load got transferred from one failed member to the next, and the whole thing would have toppled over.

But once again, the bridge was saved by the conservatism of its builders. They reverted to the ancient techniques of carpentry:

mortise-and-tenon dovetail joins, wedges—all of which permitted a little movement.

She had to get them to use that shallow, more vulnerable arch. Or to reduce the redundancy. Or to create more rigidity in the frame. Any one of those things would probably do the trick. Two would virtually guarantee it.

The candle stub was guttering, perfuming the interior of the closet with the sweet cloying fragrance of beeswax. Maggie watched the light dance on the bricks. She felt confined, keyed up. She wanted to stretch her legs, go for a run. It was the kind of nervous energy that used to send her to the treadmill at Ecosophia, or out into the desert on a clear night. She felt both exuberant and scared.

It was time to raise her status here at Sunniside. Time to impress the natives.

At the family meeting for worship at the Old Furnace, she focused on positive images. Tried thinking of herself as the foremost molecule at the crest of a great curling wave. She thought of the forces gathered behind her, the human tide that had brought her to this point, that had made this detour backward in time. She tried to think of those forces as irresistible, imagined herself gathering strength from the consensus that had sent her back, saw herself as the expression of great purpose and power.

She once asked Erzulie if she believed in destiny.

"Destiny," Erzulie snorted. "Destiny is one of the most abused words in the English language. My ancestors were slaves because somebody insisted it was their destiny. Your great-grandfather died in Auschwitz because somebody said it was his destiny. Our planet was brought to ruin in the belief that it was Man's destiny to conquer Nature."

Maggie was startled by Erzulie's vehemence. They were walking through the rain forest, carrying umbrellas, looking up at the forest canopy; beyond was the dazzle of sun on glass. Maggie had been admiring Erzulie's face, the yellow of the umbrella reflected on her dark skin. Maggie hadn't meant to strike a nerve. "So." She proceeded cautiously. "Destiny is just a human construct. You don't believe in some larger inevitability?"

"Dunno. Can't say. As a scientist I see an order to the universe that lies outside our comprehension. What Mr. Ho calls *li*. But I'm not comfortable giving it a name. And what human beings call destiny or God's will or Natural Law is a spit in the ocean compared to that orderly flow. Invariably those terms become political."

"Okay," said Maggie. "Politics aside, what's going to happen if we succeed in getting industrialism onto a less destructive track? Will humankind show any more wisdom the second time around?"

"You mean, is humanity *destined* to screw up?" Erzulie made the loose palm-up gesture they all used to indicate the ruined world outside.

Maggie shrugged. "Or gain wisdom."

The little downpour was ending, thanks to whoever was doing rain that day. Now there was only tree drip. Erzulie tipped her umbrella aside. "Well, we sure are out of control now, girl. The human species. Been out of control for a long time. It may be a law of evolution that intelligence will extinguish itself. Intelligence in the wrong species." She sighed. "I suppose if I truly believed it was our destiny to mess up, I'd say forget trying to go back and change it. Go with *this*." She made the other gesture, palm curved in to embrace Ecosophia. "This little miracle." She knocked on a thick bamboo trunk; after a couple of seconds, a miniature shower came from above. She grinned.

"But not a day goes by I don't thank my mama and daddy for refusing the destiny that was offered them. If you ask me do I believe in free will, in our ability to change things, I don't have an answer— but I live *as if* we did. My daddy was barely literate—I mean it was a struggle for the man to read a newspaper—but he used to quote Gandhi. *What you're doing may seem insignificant, but it is terribly important that you do it.*"

Those words were a comfort to Maggie now, standing in the circle, trying to focus her own power. Not only to have Gandhi's words, but to have them from Erzulie's father.

Next to her, someone's stomach growled audibly over the thump of the furnace. Abiah, head tipped up. Abraham, head bowed.

*Look at us, standing here on our hind legs, looking for comfort against the abyss of meaninglessness. Looking for external salvation. That's the pitfall of Christianity—the idea of Christ coming and saving us from the mess we've made. Judaism with a credit card.*

*Do I really believe in Gaea? In the planet as a living whole, a composite of dynamics rhythmically adjusting its chemistry and temperatures within the range necessary to sustain life? And if I accept as an article of faith the sacredness of the life not only on the planet but of the planet, then isn't it the height of presumption to suppose the planet wants to be habitable for humankind?*

A furnace keeper sneezed.

*Mr. Ho used to say that compassion is for all creatures, not just for our fellow humans; that the universe is not human-hearted. A person who wishes to be in harmony with the universe will not be human-hearted.*

Her own stomach growled.

She thought of all their bodies respiring; semifluids and gases moving through their gastrointestinal tracts; atoms of minerals and heavy metals tumbling slowly through the plasm of hair follicles; the oxidation of sugars to power muscles; hearts pumping blood, the iron in its hemoglobin carrying oxygen to cells.

Iron moving within them and without them. Iron shaping the planet for life; iron in the earth's core generating electromagnetic fields; the moon swinging tides of iron; magma forced up through seabed rifts that caused continental plates to shift; diatoms billions of years ago digesting iron; the oxidation of iron freeing oxygen to accumulate in the atmosphere, permitting complex life to evolve; the planet a rusty spaceship hurtling through the void.

# Maggie Foster

Her plan was to demonstrate her knowledge of geology. She would start with Abraham's interest in fossils, then make herself useful at a practical level by showing him exactly where to dig for iron ore and coal.

Once she had established her competence in geology and gained his respect, she would parlay that respect into a position of influence. In an era not yet given over to specialization, she had enough knowledge of engineering, rudimentary as it was, to pass for an engineer, enough scientific understanding to buttress her arguments, and this should enable her to affect the design of the bridge.

It seemed a fairly modest goal.

The challenge was not to give away any important information. There was some risk, admittedly, in telling Abraham Darby III where to locate new coal pits, but the risk would be increased exponentially if she were to alter his understanding of geology or suggest improvements in mining technology. Chaos theory, again. The law of unintended consequences. She would have to watch her step.

She began by inquiring about the fossil that he used as a doorstop.

She had already identified it as a gastropod, and after studying it under a magnifying glass, determined on the basis of the coral inclusions that it was from the Silurian era—which would make it perhaps 400,000,000 years old.

"Begging your pardon, Abraham," she said, as she dusted. "Do you mind if I ask a question?"

"Not at all."

"This limestone fossil," she said, stooping to examine it. "Where did it come from?"

He responded oddly, explaining that it was limestone and had once been a living creature—somehow failing to notice that she had used the words *limestone* and *fossil* when she asked the question.

After listening carefully to his little lecture—which was reasonably accurate, considering that his time frame was vastly compressed—she tried a more direct approach. "It's a *Gastrioceras,* isn't it? I once had one like it, in shale."

He looked blank.

"A type of gastropod?" she asked. *Gastrioceras* might belong to a later taxonomy. But surely *gastropod* was current.

"This creature," he said uncertainly, "is thought to be a sort of marine snail."

Right. "Where was it discovered?" she asked, rephrasing her original question.

"Discovered? Ah. On Lincoln Hill."

"I thought so," she said brightly. "I would have guessed either Lincoln Hill or the Wenlock Edge." *That* might get his attention. Like, "Why did you pick those two places?" And she had an explanation all prepared, one that would not give away too much yet should impress him.

But again he looked puzzled, and went on to explain the significance of a marine snail's being discovered so far above sea level. Another little lecture. He was of the opinion that Lincoln Hill may have lain underwater thousands of years ago. "Some philosophes have put forth this theory. Perhaps it was even *tens* of thousands of years." His eyes twinkled, as if this might surprise her.

"Philosophes?" she asked. Then she remembered the term was fashionable among English scientists who were emulating the French.

"Dr. Darwin, among others. I have sent him specimens. Petrofactions like this one."

"Ah." This would be Dr. Erasmus Darwin, the grandfather of Charles Darwin. And now she remembered that *petrofaction* was the operative word these days; *fossil* was simply something dug up. "Well," she said, "I agree with Dr. Darwin. It's the most likely explanation." What Abraham could not know, of course—or Erasmus Darwin either—was that it was millions of years ago; that England had drifted over the equator; and that the band of Silurian limestone known as the Wenlock Edge was thrust up as a result of the collision still going on between the Eurasian plate and the Oceanic plate, several kilometers under their feet.

"It's all really fascinating, isn't it!" she said, allowing some intensity into her voice. "The whole geological record."

"Yes."

"The questions it raises!"

"Yes."

But his voice had tightened. She could feel him withdrawing. It happened every time she tried to project a little warmth. The tips of Abraham's ears reddened, and he was suddenly in a great hurry to be somewhere else.

Her efforts were interrupted by the arrival of house guests over Easter—not just any house guests but the legendary Goldneys. (Samuel had sent word that he would not be coming from Liverpool, after all. Abiah and Sarah seemed disappointed, Abraham irritated, and Maggie was more curious than ever about the youngest Darby.) The Goldneys drove up from Bristol, braving the muddy turnpikes in their coach-and-four, with its wrought-iron leaf springs, plush interior, and family coat of arms emblazoned on each lacquered door.

Gabriel Goldney was seventy, tall, and stooped, and he dabbed continually at his rheumy eyes. Ann Goldney, his sister, was three years younger; she presented Abiah with a crock of herring from the Bristol fair. They were accompanied by Gabriel's wife, Martha, and their two cousins, who wore wigs more flamboyant than any Maggie had seen, one more or less blue, the other orange.

Gabriel and Ann were, she knew, the last survivors of the twelve children born to William Goldney II and his wife, Martha, around the turn of the century. At first they impressed Maggie as phlegmatic and a little goofy, like two old turkeys strutting slowly about a barnyard. Both were powdered and rouged. Ann spoke in a warbly alto, and Gabriel's ornate wig called attention to his close-set, hooded eyes. But everyone deferred to them. The Darby and Goldney families had been entwined for three generations, and the stories told over coffee were fascinating—Gabriel spinning a loose narrative, Ann filling in details and keeping him on track.

"When thy grandfather came up from Bristol in 1708," Gabriel told Abraham, "the whole gorge was filled with trees. Big elms and oaks grew all the way down the banks of the Severn. And Shadrach Fox, whose furnace exploded when the dam broke—his wife, I should say, for Shadrach had run off to Russia to make cannon for the Czar and left his affairs in a terrible mess, oh a terrible mess. But I forget..."

"The floors," said Ann.

"Oh yes. This Shadrach Fox lived in a house with oak floorboards as wide as your arm is long, and straight-grained for twenty feet." Gabriel chuckled, dabbing at his eyes. "My father used to say that the iron-making business followed the badger. Fleeing to the wilderness of Shropshire! For all the great woodlands were gone. Sherwood Forest, the Weald, the Forest of Dean all cut for charcoal and timber. And the price of charcoal was rising like a Cornish tide."

Maggie overheard all this while serving coffee and "standing post" just inside the parlor door, holding a silver tray at her side and acting invisible, as she had learned from Jane.

The Goldneys' stories rambled from the chicanery of barge owners to fortunes made and lost in the West Indies sugar trade. Gabriel was a prodigious user of sugar himself, ladling three and four spoonfuls into his coffee. Whatever the digressions, his stories never strayed far from the true subject, which Maggie finally realized was money.

It was not clear why the cousins were there. They showed little interest in ironmaking. They were in the clothing trade, and not Quakers, to judge from their speech and their outfits—satin with cut-steel buttons and extended coattails. The older cousin, who was perhaps fifty, wore a pale blue wig curled tightly like a cauliflower. His younger brother wore a massive orange wig with three tiers of curls around the sides; he kept trying to catch Maggie's eye.

Abiah, to judge from the corners of her mouth, disapproved of some of Gabriel's stories about the West Indies trade. Maggie saw her once in the hallway engaged in urgent whispered conversation with Richard Reynolds. Something was afoot. This was more than a social call.

That night, Maggie went over her notes—which confirmed her memory that the first Abraham Darby had been a better inventor than businessman. He had turned to the Goldneys for money; and the Goldneys, who had started out as the Dale Company's salesmen, ended up as its bankers.

When the first Abraham Darby died suddenly in 1717 at the age of thirty-nine, he left no will, a son only six, and a widow strapped for cash, who died a year later. The secret of coke firing nearly died with him.

Thomas Goldney II, who owned a controlling interest of eight shares, hired an ironmaster named Richard Ford to run the Works. Conveniently, Ford married the eldest Darby daughter, who was eighteen, and took over her shares, this only a year after her father's death, and about when her mother died. It was all very quick. Savagely quick, Maggie thought. Poor young woman.

The Darby family might have lost its hold on the Dale Company at that point. But three shares had been left in trust for the children. When Abraham Darby II was old enough to enter the Works, he was only a salaried employee. But through hard work and determination he managed to improve on his father's technique of coke firing to produce a more malleable iron that could be worked at the forge as well as cast. Finally, in the early 1740s, with Ford's health declining, Abraham Darby II took over the Works.

Maggie had always identified with the second Abraham Darby because he was orphaned and had to prove himself. As she read over her notes, she was flooded with her own images: the tall steel-mesh fence, the deafening voices of the crowd all around her, the sensation of weightless falling, everything momentarily suspended upside down, the hands of a uniformed man catching her. Breathless terror. Her mother was screaming through the fence, face white, hands gripping the galvanized mesh to keep from being swept away by the press of bodies. "Say it! *Say it!*" Her father's voice yelling over her mother's, "Tell them your test scores!" Her mother crying, "Say it!" The fence bulging before the press of people. Until there was the whump of what must have been a concussion grenade, and the whole crowd fell flat, as though under a crushing weight. Where were her mommy and daddy? Then, before terror could overwhelm her, she recited the words she had memorized: *I am Maggie Foster. I am American. I am five years old and I scored nine hundred thirty-one on the CAC Inventory. Take me to the American ambassador.*

She understood abandonment: the empty space that could never be filled, the feeling that love had to be earned and was never quite solid.

Abraham Darby II married Abiah Maud in 1745—a second marriage for both—and it was a race against the biological clock to produce heirs. Abiah, beginning in her mid-thirties, gave birth to eight children in the span of a decade. Half died in infancy, but the Darbys ended up with two male heirs: Abraham and Samuel. And the Goldneys, despite their larger brood, produced no heirs. Upon Gabriel's and Ann's demise, the Goldney shares would go to their cousins.

The cousins. Of course! That was why they were here.

So this was the buy-out agreement. Sometime this year, Abraham, with the help of Richard Reynolds, was going to arrange to purchase the Goldney interests.

M aggie had little chance to eavesdrop the following morning. She was stuck helping Jane and Mrs. Hannigan prepare an elaborate dinner: carp and rabbits that would surround a swan, flanked in turn by an array of pickled pheasant eggs, stewed fruits, breads, and sweetmeats. Mrs. Hannigan bustled around, orchestrating. Her face flushed, she talked to herself and smoothed her apron continually, saying, "Dear, dear, dear."

When the fishmonger arrived with half a dozen live carp in a wheelbarrow, Maggie was assigned the task of preparing them. It was a messy job, so she and Joseph, the stableboy, worked outside near the pigsty.

Maggie laid a carp on the plank, apologized as she stuck the knife blade into the brain behind the staring eyes, ending its life with a crunch. She remembered to save the liver, as Mrs. Hannigan had instructed. As always, Maggie was struck by the abundance of life here. This would be a particularly barbaric feast: the cooked rabbits were to be displayed in attitudes of jumping; the swan would be cloaked in its own feathery skin (an invitation to salmonella). It all seemed profligate and at odds with Quaker simplicity. Done, she supposed, to impress the Goldneys. *Putting on the dog,* Granny used to say. What the hell did that mean?

Distracted by these thoughts, Maggie forgot Mrs. Hannigan's other instruction, to bleed the carp first and save the blood. Later, when Mrs. Hannigan discovered there was no blood for gravy, she threw up her hands, then rapped Maggie on the head smartly with a wooden spoon.

Jesus! Maggie resisted the impulse to grab her wrist. "Sorry!" she said.

Mrs. Hannigan looked up at her fiercely. "Sorry! Sorry!" she mimicked. "Foolish be the wastrel who knows how to read and not how to talk! Or bleed a carp! A sorrier wench I anna seen."

Maggie hung her head. "Pray thee," she said, "forgive me."
*Asshole.*

The housekeeper seemed mollified. She put Maggie to work on the stuffing. Face hot, Maggie set about chopping the fish livers, an eel, a dozen oysters. Her scalp still smarted. Nobody had ever hit her like that. She reminded herself that Mrs. Hannigan was under pressure. And when it came to violence, nothing here could compare to Maggie's time. Not even the public hangings. Nothing here was as grotesque as the genocide and tortures of the twentieth century or the warfare and retroviruses inflicted on the poor in the twenty-first. Here, the violence was just more personal.

When everything was chopped up, Jane showed her how to mix it together with eggs, bread crumbs, melted butter, and sweet marjoram and stuff it all in the fish. In the dining room, Mrs. Hannigan was helping Abiah lay out the best china: the blue-and-white Nankeen oval plates, the tureen on its stand, the cut-glass decanters and silver candlesticks.

"Can she do that?" Maggie whispered to Jane. "Bonk me with a spoon like that?"

"Only if tha deserve it."

"Did I?"

Jane grinned. "Aye." She laughed and thrust a hand into the back of Maggie's skirt.

Maggie jumped. "Jesus fucking Christ!" she yelped, nearly dropping the carp.

Jane shushed her. "What's the matter?" she giggled. "Ne'er been goosed?"

"Sure." Maggie laughed nervously. What was *normal* around here?

But Jane frowned. "Mind tha speech, Maggie lass. Be glad Abiah dinna hear tha blaspheme."

They sewed up the fish and laid them on damp willow splints, bound with a spiral of salted eel fillets, and fastened the whole business to a spit with wet twine. Maggie watched Jane's hands at every step and tried to duplicate her motions. "Jane," she said, "Mrs. Hannigan is going to give me some really shitty job after dinner, isn't she?"

"Tha wish to stand post again, eh?"

"Yes."

Jane smirked. "I seen that Goldney cousin with the red wig rolling the old sheep eye."

"It's not that. I just like hearing their stories."

Jane jerked a thumb at the spit. "Take the other end," she said. They lifted it into the iron notches. "I'll do what I can," she said.

Jane was as good as her word. When dinner was over, it was Maggie who ended up standing post. When she entered the dining room, a hush had fallen; Gabriel Goldney was speaking slowly, dramatically. This was the story—evidently a familiar pièce de résistance—of how their father, Thomas Goldney II, acquired his wealth. Abiah, a little grim about the mouth, left the table.

"The year 1708 was an extremely fortuitous year," Gabriel began, "for not only did my father provide the financial backing for the first Abraham Darby's venture in Coalbrookdale, but"—Gabriel waggled two fingers—"in that very same year he also invested in a pair of ships cruising out of Bristol. They were named—" He looked to Ann.

"The *Duke* and the *Duchess*," Ann warbled.

"They ended up sailing around the globe."

Ann nodded. "Under Captain Rogers."

"Indeed so. And Captain Rogers brought back the most remarkable prize. An absolutely remarkable prize."

Abraham and Sarah exchanged glances, and Richard Reynolds and his wife Rebecca caught their teenage sons' eyes.

Gabriel went on. So civilized were his intonations, so circumspect his account, and so respectful of the vast wealth aboard that prize, that it was not immediately clear to Maggie that he was talking about the capture of a Spanish galleon.

"*The Manila-Acapulco,*" said Ann.

Gabriel's father nearly doubled his money, eventually receiving 6,826 pounds from his original investment of 3,726 pounds. The figures rolled off Gabriel's tongue as he smiled around the table. "Which proved fortunate," he added, with a nod toward Abraham, "for thy grandfather's experiments with mineral coal were to prove costly. Costly indeed."

Now it was the cousins who exchanged glances.

Ann took her brother's arm with her skinny fingers. "Selkirk," she whispered hoarsely, loud enough for everyone to hear.

"Ah yes. Selkirk." Gabriel chuckled. "Among the less remunerative but more celebrated exploits of the *Duke* and the *Duchess* was the rescue of the marooned sailor Alexander Selkirk from the island of Juan Fernandez. 'Twas Selkirk's account that inspired Daniel what's-his-name to write his book. *Robinson Crusoe.*"

"Defoe!" Ann chortled. "Daniel Defoe. The book has become quite famous."

Now it dawned on Maggie that this family connection was why *Robinson Crusoe* was permitted in the Sunniside library.

Gabriel's little blue eyes watered. "When, as a wee chap, I was invited to shake this Selkirk's hand, I stubbornly refused. My mother asked me what was the matter. 'Art thou frighted of the gentleman?' she asked, thinking I did not understand he was a Christian. But alas, nothing could persuade me to shake the fellow's hand. I said finally that he could not possibly be Alexander Selkirk, for the true Alexander Selkirk was maroon! Ha, ha! Maroon in color!" Gabriel wheezed.

Abiah, returning to the room, directed Maggie to fetch a pot of hot chocolate and a tray of tea biscuits. When Maggie returned, Gabriel was reminiscing over the first Abraham Darby's funeral, when the only Quaker burying ground was on the Broseley side of the river. The river was swollen with rain, the path steep and muddy, and the pallbearers—including Gabriel himself, who was thirteen—suddenly lost their footing. The coffin slid down the hill, coming within inches of plunging into the Severn before it was stopped by Richard Ford, who had slid with it and managed to seize hold of a sapling.

Congratulated for his heroism, Ford thanked the Maker and responded with true Quaker modesty. " 'I had no choice,' he said." Gabriel cackled. "I had no choice!"

Everyone laughed, anticipating some humorous outcome. Gabriel took another bite of tea biscuit. "Only later did he—" Gabriel coughed, tried to finish, and fell into a fit of choking. Yet he persisted in trying to deliver the punch line.

"What *is* it?" his wife Margaret cried. "Selkirk?"

Gabriel shook his head vigorously. Margaret wrung her hands.

"Not Selkirk!" Ann spat, waving her talons. "Ford! Richard Ford!"

Gabriel nodded vigorously. Stood up, face crimson.

Ann finished in her warbly alto. "Only later did Richard Ford confess that his arm was caught in the coffin handle!" A droll conclusion. Her brother nodded wildly. His face was nearly purple, eyes bulging.

"Water!" cried one of the cousins. "Fetch water!"

"No, no!" the other countered.

Maggie watched with dread. The old man's windpipe was clearly blocked. Another minute or two, and it would all be all over. Her impulse was to administer the Heimlich maneuver, but she restrained herself. Who could say what would happen if the Heimlich maneuver were to be introduced a couple hundred years ahead of schedule? She tried to consider the options, heart pounding. If Gabriel were to die now, before the buyout agreement, then the cousins might be part of the bridge decision.

Gabriel was clawing at the air, his eyelids fluttering.

If, on the other hand, she were to save his life, then events would proceed along the historical path that led to the bridge.

Then it occurred to her that she didn't *have* to save his life, because somehow Gabriel Goldney was going to survive this! He would live another eleven years!

Okay. So do nothing. She clutched the silver tray against her breast. Then another realization came to her. She had traded places with Jane, standing post. That was an intervention, however slight. What if something she had done—some unknown variation in the way she served the tea biscuits—precipitated the choking?

Margaret was shrieking hysterically for water. Maggie ran into the kitchen. By the time she returned with a glass of water, Gabriel's eyes had turned up. Maggie could stand it no longer; she elbowed past

Richard Reynolds. But at that moment Abraham delivered a substantial whack to Gabriel's back. That was *not* what you were supposed to do; but something flew from the old man's mouth.

Gabriel collapsed into his chair, gasping. When he had recovered his breath, he wiped his eyes and accepted water from Abraham. Swallowed several times. Squeezed Abraham's hand, Margaret's arm. Looked around the table to reassure everyone.

Abiah held up a hand. "Let us pray to the Maker."

During the silence, Maggie let loose a long shuddering breath. She felt weak.

Later, when they were all sitting in the parlor, the Goldney cousins suddenly took a more active role in the conversation. They inquired about last May's landslip, then brought the subject around to bridges, prodding Gabriel to recall the various stone and timber bridges on the Severn that had been washed away by floods. The cousin in the blue wig solicited Abiah's opinion, suggesting that the absence of a bridge at the Severn Gorge must hinder her travels. He seemed to be driving at something.

Abiah replied that she was not unduly hindered, that the bridge would be built more from duty than convenience.

"Are we to understand, then," said the cousin, "that this duty will fall to the Darby family, much as 'tis said the towpath will be undertaken by the Reynoldses?"

Abiah deferred to the men. Richard Reynolds deferred to Abraham. Abraham looked up from his coffee cup, his shoulders tensed. "Yes." His voice cracked.

"Rumor has it," said the orange-wigged cousin, "that the bridge will be made of iron."

Abraham smiled. "I fear the bridge is more rumor than iron."

After some further probing, the cousins determined that the plan was to build the bridge by subscription.

"Ooh," exclaimed the blue-wigged cousin. "Then you will sell shares?"

"Indeed so," Reynolds assured him. "For 'twill be too costly for one man to bear."

"Costly," echoed the orange-wigged cousin, eyes shrewd.

"But one man must guarantee the final cost, is that not so?" asked the other. "Else you will have no subscribers."

Reynolds nodded. "Thou art correct."

"And that one man will be—" The blue wig nodded toward Abraham.

Abraham nodded, ears red.

The two cousins exchanged a look. They clearly wanted no part of the bridge. You couldn't really blame them, Maggie thought. The bridge would very nearly bankrupt Abraham, and they all seemed to have some inkling of the danger.

The next day, after all the legal proceedings had been completed, the parlor reeked of pipe smoke. The Goldney coach drove away, and a general sigh of relief was breathed among the Darbys. Abiah seemed elated. " 'Tis better," she wrote in a letter, which she gave Maggie to copy, "to have bread in our own houses and water in our own cisterns."

Elation did not altogether describe Abraham's body language. He knew perhaps better than his mother the sacrifices that lay ahead.

# John Wilkinson

Assurance. That was the word.

Matthew Boulton wore an assurance that Wilkinson had never acquired—the invisible, affable cloak of old wealth. Wilkinson had met him socially a few times, twice at gatherings of the Lunar Society, which Wilkinson attended as Priestley's guest. Mostly they met on business, for Wilkinson supplied castings to Boulton's factory at Soho, on the outskirts of Birmingham.

Boulton was a big, hearty fellow like himself, but better liked—for reasons that escaped Wilkinson, apart from that assurance of older wealth, and Boulton's living in Birmingham, where everyone's paths crossed. Wilkinson had little opportunity for such sociability, living here in darkest Broseley and surrounded by Quakers.

And Boulton was a better-looking specimen than he, or at least possessed of even features, which some would call handsome. He had a deep voice, a broad forehead tanned with freckles at the edges, a ready smile, and a gentle humor that cushioned the quickness of his mind. Boulton was an able engineer, interested in philosophic matters—electricity, Priestley's discovery of dephlogisticated air, and such. But Boulton's real gift, in Wilkinson's view, was in organizing men.

Wilkinson could not help feeling some jealousy toward an individual with nearly a thousand workers under one roof—whose factory at Soho was a showcase of modern methods for making buttons and baubles, the "toy shop of Europe," as Edmund Burke called it—and who also served as a magnet to the great scientific minds of the day. The Broseley ironmaster had neither time nor inclination to exchange letters with the likes of Dr. Franklin or open his doors to the parade of learned visitors that traipsed through Soho, and it annoyed him that Boulton did. Wilkinson was sick of hearing that Boulton had dined at Windsor Castle or advised Her Majesty the Queen how to furnish her chimneypiece—for what was this fellow Boulton, finally, but a toy maker? Yet Wilkinson found himself drawn to the man, and valued his good opinion.

For all these reasons he was both flattered and irritated when Boulton showed up unannounced one afternoon in late May.

"What ho, Mr. Boulton!" he called out, recognizing the larger of the two men, once the clerk's boy had got his attention. He bustled out to greet them, removing the cotton wool from his ears. "To what do I owe the honor of your presence?" Under his genuine pleasure was the suspicion that Boulton's main business was at Coalbrookdale.

Boulton smiled. "The honor is mine." He presented a calling card, of the sort now fashionable in London, and introduced his smaller, darker companion—James Watt, of Glasgow, whose name was known to Wilkinson.

"What ho!" said Wilkinson. "Mr. Watt! My brother-in-law Priestley has been singing your praises."

Watt flashed a sardonic slash of a smile. The Scotsman had a prominent brow, a mobile mouth with a long and poorly shaven upper lip, and he wore a goat-hair periwig of the sort one could purchase on the street at Covent Garden. He looked a bit like a monkey, although said to be absolutely the most brilliant of the young Scottish engineers now invading England.

They bowed and, following the practice common among those who did business with Quakers, also shook hands, Watt being a bit clumsy at both. Ha! It was enough perhaps for the fellow to be wearing breeches.

Wilkinson turned to Boulton. "You take me by surprise, sir," he said with a note of reproach.

"Forgive me for not writing in advance, my friend. But Mr. Watt here will be joining me at Soho, and I wished to waste no time bringing such idea'd gentlemen as you together." Boulton smiled broadly and clapped a hand on both men's shoulders.

Flattered in spite of himself, and assured by the warmth of Boulton's hand on his shoulder, Wilkinson agreed to show them around. He began with the lathe shop and grinding shed, where a dozen or so workers were putting the finishing touches on engine castings. He kept his voice unobtrusive until they were well past Sniggy Oakes, who was busy installing bearings on a new lathe made wholly of iron and whose skills Wilkinson had no wish to display.

"You have taken Mr. Watt to Coalbrookdale?" he inquired of Boulton, as he held the door for them to step outside.

"Quite so." Boulton nodded.

"Aye, sir." Watt's simian lips twisted in a sneer.

"My friend Mr. Watt," Boulton explained, "requires more precision than Coalbrookdale can offer."

"They are living in the past, man!" declared Watt contemptuously.

Wilkinson felt a sudden fondness for this impudent fellow. The day was warm and clear; the sun shining through the smoke marbled the ground with shifting shadows. "I understand, sir," he said to Watt, "that you have in mind some considerable improvement to the common fire engine."

Watt laughed abrasively. "Not only in mind, sir, but in metal! Every jot and tit of it! We built a small engine, with an eighteen-inch cylinder made of block tin!"

Boulton beamed. "It works far more economically than the common atmospheric fire engine."

"Even with Smeaton's improvements?" Wilkinson was dubious.

"Smeaton!" Watt hissed. "Smeaton has merely tinkered with Newcomen's engine! My engine works on a different principle entirely! 'Tis the steam that pushes the piston down, not atmospheric pressure. And I waste not one bit of it!"

Boulton nodded. "We calculate 'twill use one quarter the coal."

Wilkinson perked his ears at this. At New Willey his profits were constrained by the cost of coal. "And could it blow a furnace directly, Mr. Watt? Work the bellows directly, instead of pumping water back to the pond?"

"Aye. I do not see why not. Your iron bellows requires the same reciprocal motion as a pump, does it not?"

"Quite so." The prospect of blowing air directly was dear to Wilkinson's heart. He had tried such an experiment, using an atmospheric engine, but found it insufficient.

"You are on the right track, Mr. Wilkinson," Boulton agreed. "It is my firm opinion that we shall see the fire engine transformed from simply pumping water to performing all sorts of work—grinding corn or running a lathe."

"Rotative motion?" asked Wilkinson.

"Precisely, sir. Steam mills in the middle of London! Someday, perhaps steam carriages on the turnpikes. In our lifetime!"

"Pssh!" Watt scowled, picking his nose. " 'Tis enough to pump water!"

Wilkinson said nothing, but it seemed to him that Boulton saw the possibilities as he did. The reciprocal action of a steam engine, with its walking-beam, could be made to turn a wheel; it was simply a matter of finding the best way. If not a crank, then some other way. And once rotative motion was achieved, there was no limit to what could be done with steam! But clearly something was preventing Watt from proceeding. They had come to him with a purpose. He turned to Boulton. "What, sir, is the catch?"

"The catch, my friend, is the cylinder. We must have an accurate cylinder in order to build a full-size engine."

"*Pressure!*" cried Watt, knotting both hands into fists, the sibilants escaping from his mouth like water dashed on hot coals. "The cylinder must be accurate enough to hold the *pressure!*"

The Scotsman began scratching a diagram in the dirt, explaining the principle of the new engine, showing how the valves opened and closed in turn; how, unlike the existing atmospheric, whose cylinder had to be cooled down with jets of cold water for each stroke, his new engine used pipes and valves to transport the steam to a separate cooling chamber, which he called a *separate condenser.* Thus the cylinder could remain hot and immediately receive a new batch of steam, vastly increasing its efficiency.

And its speed, thought Wilkinson. Could such a machine not go faster? He listened in wonder. Steam had always mystified him. As a child, watching the kettle boil, he had felt the steam condense to water on his fingers. Now, hearing Watt talk about steam's expansive properties—the *elasticity* of steam—he realized he was in the presence of a man who understood steam as perhaps no one had understood it before.

"Twenty pounds of pressure to the square inch!" said Watt. "Think of it, man!" He reached into the drab tweed vest that he wore under his waistcoat, produced a slide rule, and used it to calculate the force that would be exerted against a piston the size of Wilkinson's present engine. It came to thousands of pounds. "The power of eight horses," Watt observed. "And using a quarter the coal!" He clapped the slide rule shut and looked up at Wilkinson, eyes gleaming.

"Ye can understand now, Mr. Wilkinson, why the new engine needs a cylinder bored to truth. In the old atmospheric engine, the cylinder wall can wander, with half an inch gap betwixt piston and cylinder—why, a mouse can get through it!—and nobody cares a fiddly fartkin, because the cylinder is open at the top, with water to seal the leather gasket. But the new cylinder is closed, and stays so hot that water would boil off. It requires a cylinder true enough to hold the pressure."

"What degree of truth do you need, sir?" Wilkinson asked.

"I mean"—Watt held up his thumb and forefinger so they very nearly touched—"accurate to the thickness of a worn shilling."

"Good heavens, man. On a forty-inch cylinder?"

"Aye, sir!" Watt thrust out this chin.

Watt's arrogance was irksome, but his demand for precision might work to Wilkinson's advantage. The ironmaster could carve out a pretty future for himself if he could capture the market for the new cylinders—much as Coalbrookdale had managed fifty years ago to capture the market for the old.

His mind worked on the problem as he showed his guests around

New Willey. He invited them to examine the new air furnaces that he used for remelting pigs, and impressed on them how much more up to date it was than Coalbrookdale. But he delayed showing them the cannon-boring mill, for a plan was taking shape in his mind. Indeed, he professed modesty when it came to the business of boring cylinders, for he had seen enough of Watt's scorn to want to avoid it. "I fear, sir, that you will find my cylinders not much better than Mr. Darby's." Chuckling to himself, enjoying Watt's impatience, he hinted that theirs might be an impossible errand, that Mr. Watt's engine, designed in some Platonic heaven, might be doomed for lack of a cylinder to be found on earth. He continued in this vein, all the while noting the glances exchanged between Boulton and Watt and delighting in Watt's rueful countenance.

Boulton took Wilkinson aside. "Be gentle, sir," he whispered. "Watt's wife died last year, and it has brought him quite low. I must tell you that for all his excitability, the man is grieving in his heart. And his former partner, Dr. Roebuck, went bankrupt the year before. For eight years, the poor fellow has been struggling in vain to bring this engine into the world. Now that we have an extension on the patent, there is hope. But 'tis not easy." Boulton shook his broad, freckled head. " 'Tis not easy."

"Roebuck?" Wilkinson's belly shook with laughter. "The same Dr. Roebuck who was a partner in the Carron works? Ha! I had forgot he had an interest in steam as well as cannon!" Wilkinson was elated at the idea of besting this Roebuck twice.

Boulton took Wilkinson's arm gently but firmly. "I beg you, sir, remember my friend's nerves are highly strung. I repeat, it has not been easy."

"Well, sir," said Wilkinson, reining in his mirth. "I have something for your amusement." He hailed Watt, who had ambled ahead with a most morose countenance, and suggested they visit the casting house. There he showed them some cannon recently lifted from the sandpit. "Do you observe anything curious about these guns, gentlemen?"

Watt furrowed his brow. "Why, they are cast solid." He glanced at Boulton.

Wilkinson chuckled. "Quite correct, sir." He smiled mysteriously and bade them follow him to the end of the boring mill where the finished cannon were being polished. He stopped before the largest—a fifty-six pounder, so the bore was sizable—waved a couple of workers aside, dragged a boy out by the rope tied to his ankle, and tapped the cannon with his cane. "Gentlemen." He smiled. "Be my guests." He provided them with calipers, straightedge, and candle lantern and stood back, smiling, while they examined the bore. Boulton dropped to his hands and knees, reached in as far as he could, and took a long swipe with his fingertips. Watt did likewise. They exchanged wondering looks. As they examined the cannon more methodically, using the straightedge and calipers by candlelight, the two engineers muttered to each other with growing excitement.

" 'Tis bored to truth," Watt exclaimed.

Wilkinson shrugged carelessly. "I offer it only for your amusement, gentlemen. Obviously it is not of a diameter sufficient for your purposes. Still, I daresay my method is unique."

Boulton lumbered to his feet. "What of Anthony Bacon, at Cyfarthfa? We heard that he was boring from the solid, and are headed there next."

Wilkinson chuckled. "Ah. Well. Dear me. I can save you the trip into South Wales, for 'tis I who bore Mr. Bacon's guns for him. And as every one sent to Woolwich has passed proof, the Ordnance Board has taken quite a liking to my new method. 'Tis only a matter of time before they shall accept nothing else." He beamed. "Bacon, you see, has no such capability at Cyfarthfa." Wilkinson leaned back triumphantly. "Nor will he. For 'tis I who invented the new boring machine, and I who hold the patent!"

Watt's fists danced with excitement. "Will ye show us the boring machine, man?"

"Well, gentlemen. If this interests you—" He leaned on his cane and swiveled, observing how they held their breaths. "And I see that it does." He had them quite by the ballocks and wanted them to appreciate it most fully. "Then I should be happy to show you the machine. Once we have an understanding. Indeed, I will do better than that. I will undertake to bore a cylinder to your specifications—provided that if I succeed, I shall be your sole supplier."

They readily agreed.

When the contract was drawn and signed, he invited them to his home to sup and stay the night. The next morning, they breakfasted in a leisurely fashion. Boulton displayed the ease of his breeding, inquiring about last year's landslip, which had stopped the Severn, and described the activities of his famous Lunatic friends—Withering, Wedgwood, Darwin, and the others—while Watt was awkward buttering his toast.

After seeing his guests off, Wilkinson sat down again for a second breakfast of venison sausage and eggs, fried fish, apple dumplings, and a leg of lamb with gravy, washed down with coffee. He found the upstairs maid making the beds in the spare chamber, where, after talking prettily to her and finding her compliant, he dropped his breeches and blew off a few loose corns. Then, as it was a fine morning, he took himself for a walk up the cobbles that led through Broseley, past the bullring and the parish church, smiling beatifically and tipping his tricorn to those he met, continuing uphill until he reached the old Quaker burying ground. He stood savoring the breeze and looking across the gorge at Coalbrookdale, with its myriad plumes of smoke drifting across the brow of Lincoln Hill, and he felt not the usual envy but, rather, elation. Almost a contentment. This new engine would transform the world. He could feel it in his very bowels. Steam mills in the middle of London! And he would be part of it, by God. He ambled into the Quaker burying ground, stood before old Darby's grave and gave it a friendly thump with his cane. More than friendly. Ho! Listen to that hollow sound. Rest thy moldering bones, old fellow. Leave me to teach your grandson the ways of the world.

Now is the time, he thought. Before young Darby understands what is what. Now is the time to get him ensnared in that bridge. Get him wedged tight as a bung in a barrel.

# Abraham Darby III

**H**e had taken work home from the office on this splendid morning in order to escape the noise and smell of the Works. Yesterday was spoiled by a visit from Matthew Boulton and James Watt. One remark by Boulton, delivered genially, had nevertheless stung. Discussing the challenge posed by Watt's new engine, Boulton praised Father's resourcefulness: "Coalbrookdale was a great works," he said, with just the slightest stress on the *was*. The two engineers were headed next to New Willey, so Abraham supposed Wilkinson would be dropping by Coalbrookdale today—to complain or to crow, or both, in his fashion. Another reason to avoid the Works.

Sitting here at his study table with the window open, Abraham smelled the fragrance of the first mowing of hay, a welcome distraction from Boulton's remark and from the columns of numbers before him. *A wet May brings a good load of hay.* He heard a sedge warbler and saw it darting about in the boxwood hedge. He watched the deer browsing on tender new shoots.

Maggie tapped on the doorway, asking permission to dust. Nodding assent, he returned to his calculations, distracted only slightly by the curve of her hip—until she startled him with a question.

"Excuse me, Abraham. Have I been dusting this correctly? It looks delicate." She was standing before his electrical machine.

"Too delicate, alas. I fear the problem lies not with your dusting."

"Something the matter with it?"

"Yes. It produces no spark."

"None at all?"

"None." For months he had put off writing to London for instructions. He was annoyed at himself, a little annoyed at Maggie for her incessant curiosity. He went back to entering his various loan payments onto a five-year calendar.

"I'm familiar with these things," Maggie said, examining the machine more closely. "My husband had one. I'd be happy to check it out."

"Check it out?"

"Examine it. See if I can figure out what's wrong."

Abraham nearly snickered at this audacity. She was a most peculiar member of the female tribe, to pretend to an understanding of scientific instruments. "Thou needst not trouble. I simply have not taken the time to attend to it." He turned back to his loan schedule.

"Not to worry. Really. It may be something very simple. Trevor used to say I had a knack—"

Abraham frowned. "Please! I am quite occupied."

She opened her mouth again to speak but, seeing the sternness in his countenance, resumed her dusting without a word.

When she was gone, Abraham was too vexed at himself to concentrate. He should not have lost patience with her. She was a strange woman, this Maggie Foster, strange in speech and manner. She moved and walked like a man, taking long, purposeful strides; yet there was no mistaking her womanliness. And that bold gaze, ever since she arrived at Sunniside, had haunted him. Lately she had begun plaguing him with questions—about petrofactions, coal deposits, astronomy—questions to which he did not always know the answers and that seemed at times intended to demonstrate her knowledge. And yet she betrayed her ignorance more than once with humorous effect (referring to the *rings* of Saturn, for example, as if there were several), and in general she resorted to the most whimsical words to express her thoughts. Her questions would have been unsettling in any case, coming from a woman. Occasionally his heart beat faster.

He had asked himself, when she first arrived last winter and he felt that fluttering in his breast, *Would I feel differently if she were not a housemaid but an equal?*

What if she were a Friend traveling under the care of some distant meeting? Or related to a weighty Quaker family—as was Becky Smith, the Reynoldses' niece? The truth, which he recognized in his heart, was so troubling that he tried to hide it from himself: if Maggie Foster were a Quaker suitably recommended, then he would seek her company. And if she were marriageable—ah! but he must put aside these idle thoughts, for they were only that. Flights of fancy, at best. At worst, seeds sown by the Enemy. Maggie Foster was, after all, a maid in his mother's employ. An odd creature. Comely, but an inch or two taller than he, and older by six years. And although she attended Meeting and dressed in Quakerly fashion, she was not yet a Convinced Quaker. He would think about her no more. For a while he watched the warbler rustling about in the boxwood, then returned to the column of numbers.

He was to pay the Goldneys a total of ten thousand pounds in equal installments over five years. These and other payments amounted to a substantial sum. And on top of that would come the expense of the bridge. He wished to delay the bridge; but everyone around him seemed intent on moving it forward. It would add perhaps another two thousand pounds to his burden, spread across two or three years.

The figures were of such magnitude as to seem unreal. Yet the purchase of the Goldney interests was a good thing. As Mother put it, *Best to have water in one's own cistern.* Best to be freed at last from the West Indies trade. And if he could not meet his loan payments, then Richard had promised to stand surety for him, in effect replacing the Goldneys as the Dale Company's banker.

Abraham liked to suppose that he was purchasing something for Father, reclaiming something lost, although he did not know altogether what. It was an unspoken sentiment, shared by Mother and

Richard, and however vague, it carried more weight than any column of figures. *I am doing it for Father.* The good of it was clearer now, as he gazed at the hayfield, than if he were in his office at the Works. Someday he should like to do nothing but farm.

His thoughts were interrupted by a knock.

Maggie, her face flushed (still from his vexation?), told him that John Wilkinson was waiting downstairs.

Wilkinson! Abraham shuddered. He considered saying he was indisposed but instead conveyed word that he would come momentarily. He plodded down the steps. One could never tell what was on Wilkinson's mind. The first impression was often deceiving. The last time Wilkinson had called on him, supposedly to discuss a wrecked trow that was impeding navigation, they had ended up discussing so many other matters, that after Wilkinson left, Abraham was mystified as to the purpose of the visit.

This time was no different. The Broseley ironmaster began by asking if he might inspect Abraham's greenhouse—which he did, after requiring Abraham's repeated insistence that it was no trouble. Wilkinson was a man of excesses. His effusive solicitations, rendered in that high, ringing voice; the surfeit of words; the very abundance of flesh that seemed to amplify a boundless energy—all took up so much space that little room was left for anyone but Wilkinson. Abraham tried nevertheless to meet that of God in him.

Saying that he planned to build a greenhouse himself, Wilkinson asked about its construction and method of heating. This reminded him, he said, of Matthew Boulton, who was a great champion of greenhouses. He inquired about Boulton and Watt's recent visit to Coalbrookdale.

"Did you give them any satisfaction?" Wilkinson asked, and before Abraham could answer, he added, "I must confess I was out of sorts. A cylinder bored to truth!" He went on, thumping about annoyingly with his cane and suggesting that Boulton's quest for an accurate cylinder was akin to Ponce de Leon's quest for the fountain of youth. He stopped thumping at intervals to ask Abraham's thoughts on the matter. "What measure did you take of Watt?" he exclaimed. "I warrant, the Scotsman has enough opinions for ten men!"

Abraham found himself assenting to much of this, although reluctant to speak ill. He might have asked Watt's help with the electrical machine, had the engineer not proved so arrogant. Wilkinson's views, however uncharitable, were reassuring. Yes, Abraham agreed with Wilkinson that neither Boulton nor Watt fully grasped the problem of obtaining accuracy in large cylinders. And no, he had no hope of achieving any greater accuracy himself. It was doubtless a vain quest on their part.

Over tea, the Broseley ironmaster announced that he wished to discuss a subject of the highest importance. It was, as Abraham feared, the bridge. Wilkinson wished to see Pritchard's drawings once again, *if it would not be too much trouble,* etc., and went on at such length that Abraham was forced to produce them and to listen while Wilkinson argued the case for the bridge made wholly of iron. "But for one change," Wilkinson added. "The arch should be a proper Roman arch, do you not agree? That is, it should conform to the ancient laws of proportion."

Abraham felt a headache coming on.

"But," said Wilkinson, seeing reluctance writ on his host's face, "it matters not. The important thing is the bridge itself." He went on nevertheless to press the case for iron, which he supposed would best advertise their wares. " 'Twill show how men can build anything with cast-iron that they now build with timber or stone."

"Perhaps," Abraham said.

Wilkinson argued that the timing was right, the price of iron being depressed, as they all knew.

"Perhaps," murmured Abraham. The headache stabbed his right brow like a needle.

Wilkinson, seeing him wince, assured him once more that it was the bridge that was the important thing. They must attract ample support for it, so that no one man—meaning of course Abraham—*should bear too great a burden.* They must draw up a list of the gentry whose names would encourage local investors as well as gain support in Parliament. The next thing Abraham knew, Wilkinson was proceeding to scribble names on a sheet of paper he took from his waistcoat pocket. And although Abraham at first resisted the offer, he finally agreed to let Wilkinson begin approaching those "worthies," as Wilkinson called them, residing on the Broseley side of the river.

Abraham's headache was so excruciating that it was all he could do to see Wilkinson to the door.

# John Wilkinson

Timing, John Wilkinson believed, was everything.

He had lost no time pressing his case for the bridge with Darby. (He would have liked to press his case with their new maid, a tall young woman with the most captivating green eyes.) To his surprise, he had got Darby to agree to his approaching the titled gentlemen on his list—a key step, for it served to announce the banns, as it were. Wilkinson had spent the past week talking it up in Broseley. So the project was all but launched.

Boulton and Watt's visit to New Willey had come at precisely the right moment—while Wilkinson's new method of boring from the solid was carrying his reputation to new heights, and before Sniggy Oakes had got wind of the patent.

It was in fact Boulton and Watt's visit that lit the fuse to Sniggy Oakes's murderous rage. A worker had evidently overheard Wilkinson boasting about the patent, and word reached Oakes. From later accounts it seemed the mechanic had seethed for much of the day. He had begun muttering aloud and showing signs of great agitation. Wilkinson, upon returning from Sunniside, was walking through the

lathe shop when Oakes lunged at him, waving a spanner and screaming, "Ye stole my boring bar!"

Terrified, Wilkinson dodged behind his foreman until the deranged
mechanic could be subdued by a couple of apprentices. The constable
was called, complaints were sworn against Oakes, and the fellow was
brought to some semblance of reason. Two days later, Wilkinson sent
him a magnanimous offer: Oakes could return to his employ, and
would receive an extra shilling a week to redress any imagined wrongs.
But the mechanic would have none of it.

So it is that opportunities come and go in a flash. Sniggy Oakes,
who might have obtained the patent himself, had he been a little
sharper—and who, failing that, might have been paid as handsomely
as any foreman at New Willey—retired instead to the bitter solitude
of his own small forge at Leighton. And he, John Wilkinson, who but
for a few seconds' delay might have had his skull cracked by a mad-
man, was free to comport himself in his full power and dignity. Ha!

Timing!

In the weeks that followed, Wilkinson entertained the fear that
Oakes would carry his complaint to the Privy Council, for although it
would be the mechanic's word against Wilkinson's, the complaint
might be seized upon by those who would like nothing better than
to see the patent overturned. But by Midsummer, Wilkinson had
pretty well concluded that legal redress lay beyond the poor fellow's
scope.

In the meantime, Anthony Bacon was busy winning adherents to
the new method. Bacon's guns all passed the proof test, so he was
added to the list of official gunfounders. Bacon persuaded the
Ordnance Board to approve the new method, having negotiated a
price of eighteen pounds per ton for the new guns, the going rate for
those bored in the old way. Wilkinson thought this too cheap, but
Bacon reckoned it would speed acceptance of the new method, and he
was quite right. The Ordnance Board placed an order with Bacon for
three hundred tons of ordnance, including fifty-six thirty-two-
pounders, which Wilkinson began making immediately. A clever gentleman, was Anthony Bacon, MP.

Wilkinson built three more of the new cannon-boring machines and began soliciting his own orders. Using the new method exclusively would mean fewer workers. More tons of cannon produced per man. Let others supply inferior guns to the Russians and the Turks!

Now he set about applying the new method to the boring of cylinders. He tried using the cannon-boring machine itself, to see how large it might bore, but encountered too much vibration beyond a diameter of twelve inches. Watt insisted on eighteen inches for his trial cylinder, and the machine would have to bore cylinders much larger than that if it were to be practical.

Wilkinson designed a completely new machine, based on the Oakes principle, viz., he would effectively shrink the cylinder by making everything bigger: bigger flywheel, bigger boring bar, bigger cutting-head. The machine would be built at Bersham, under the direction of his younger brother, Will. At Bersham it could be better kept secret. Oakes's assault had left Wilkinson feeling vulnerable. For all he knew, there might already be a spy amongst his workers at New Willey, and the last thing he wanted was for Darby to get wind of his machine. Bersham, being two days away, just north of Wrexham, was more secluded.

In August, Wilkinson rode to Bersham to go over the plans with his brother and assure himself that the strictest measures would be taken to keep the new machine safe from prying eyes. The work would be done by a team of four men—foundrymen and machinists—with articles enjoining them to secrecy, and all keyholes would be stopped.

"Remember what happened to Huntsman," he cautioned Will. Everyone knew the story of how Benjamin Huntsman's secret for making crucible steel was stolen by the lowest of tricks—a rival disguised in rags begging permission to warm himself by the furnace on a wintry night. Wilkinson himself had resorted to such a ruse to get information about the Verbruggen machine; he had sent a man professing an artistic interest in the younger Verbruggen's intricately detailed pencil sketches. Such were the rules of commerce. One kept a hand always on one's purse.

Upon returning to Broseley, Wilkinson found new orders for guns awaiting him, and a letter from Bacon complaining of his slowness. The truth was, Wilkinson had more orders than he could handle. He had inquiries from a Prussian prince, a polite note from the French embassy. The four new cannon lathes were running all day, making a formidable shriek, deafening the workers despite the cotton wool. He would have run them all night too, but for the inability of the pumping-engine to return water to the ponds fast enough.

If only he had Coalbrookdale! By God's wig, would he produce cannon then!

Throughout all this, he took care not to neglect the bridge. Whenever he had an hour to spare, he jumped on his horse and rode off to win new converts. Darby had finally approached the blue bloods on his side of the river, and now it was a matter only of attracting subscribers. Wilkinson tried to appeal to each man's greed in various ways. For some it was a share in the tolls; for others, the chance to make money on land holdings; for others, the opportunity to fatten their sense of self-importance. To those whose opinions might carry special weight with Darby, Wilkinson suggested that the young ironmaster's ardor might be encouraged for his own good. Ha! He had kept the heat on Darby for half a year now, and was jolly pleased with himself.

Shortly after Michaelmas, the Ordnance Board decided in favor of the solid-bored method. Now the grumbling from other armsmakers rose to a noisy chorus. All that autumn, Wilkinson kept them at bay with threats of legal action. When Anthony Bacon wrote, saying that he was preparing to bore his own guns at Cyfarthfa, Wilkinson wrote back tactfully but firmly, regretting that he could not allow this.

Bacon was stunned. He fired back an angry letter accusing Wilkinson of ingratitude. In November, Bacon and the others (encouraged in all likelihood by Isaac Wilkinson, who would lose no chance to do mischief to his own son) lodged a complaint with the Ordnance Board that Wilkinson was restricting competition. The board began an inquiry. Wilkinson directed his solicitor in London to throw up whatever roadblocks he could, but the case was clearly going against him.

He should not have cozened Bacon. Greed had got the better of him. But it was too late. His enemies were clamoring for his downfall. Time was more precious than ever now. If he was to obtain the monopoly with Boulton and Watt, then he must lose no time boring a cylinder to truth.

# Maggie Foster

She was getting nowhere with Abraham. She knew she was doing something wrong but didn't know what.

The May 27 anniversary of the landslip had come and gone. It seemed more than a year since she'd arrived, so much had happened, and yet she had accomplished so little. Not true, she corrected herself. She had become acclimated to the eighteenth century, got into the Darby household. And the actual construction of the bridge was more than two years away!

Two years away, but it was hard not to panic.

On June 5, her birthday, Mrs. Hannigan fixed Maggie's favorite dessert—sillibub, a mixture of chopped fruit, nuts, and cream—and Jane gave her an alphabet printed on pasteboard, suitable for a child learning its ABCs, with little homilies. *A is for Adam.* Maggie laughed. Tears welled in her eyes.

"If it ain't what tha want—" Jane said, rubbing her nose with the heel of her hand.

"No, no. It's perfect. I love it!" She hid her face in her apron. Under all her anxiety about accomplishing enough lay the simple fact that she was thirty-one years old and alone in a way that she was only now beginning to comprehend. The finality had sunk in that her life was here, in this time and place. She felt weepy and giddy. Neither Jane nor Mrs. Hannigan could figure out whether she was laughing or crying, and she couldn't either.

F ailing to make progress with Abraham, she shifted her focus to Abiah—spent the summer cooped up in Abiah's sitting room whenever she wasn't doing her regular chores, helping Abiah write a horrible little pamphlet entitled *An Exhortation in Christian Love, to all who frequent horse-racing, cock-fighting, throwing at cocks, gaming, plays, dancing, musical entertainments, or any other Vain Diversions.*

This was the part of Quakerism that Maggie couldn't stand: the Puritanical assumption that not only was bull baiting bad but anything *fun* was bad. It was that, probably, that kept her from joining the Quakers. But she gritted her teeth and volunteered extra hours, with an eye to improving her status. She spent most of July and August confined with Abiah—the windows usually shut, the air stuffy from the coal grate (Abiah kept a coal fire going on all but the hottest days) and the smell of Abiah's liniment—copying drafts or discussing tedious variations in wording.

At first she simply corrected Abiah's spelling. But when she encountered muddled grammar, she raised questions—always diffidently, in the guise of not quite understanding Abiah's meaning. Gradually, without either of them acknowledging it, she took on the role of editor.

Abiah, unlike her husband and sons, had little formal education. Quakers and other dissenters were excluded from the universities as well as from political life, but the men could at least attend dissenting academies; the women could not. Abiah, like most women of her class, had received tutoring, but she had difficulty writing coherently. And for all her avowed humility, she resisted criticism. "If the Light shineth within me," she liked to say, "then the Great Author fills me to overflowing with words." When she did follow Maggie's suggestions, she credited the improvement to the Divine Author. So Maggie's was a thankless job. And it never seemed to occur to Abiah to give Maggie time off from her regular tasks, so Maggie often ended up working a sixteen-hour day.

But Maggie persisted. These hours weren't so bad, she told herself. During the short winter day, Jeremy never saw the sun. And in the 1970s, Erzulie's father worked double shifts at a textile mill, plus had a janitorial job, in order to put Erzulie through Catholic school and then college. Still, Maggie envied Sarah, who sat outside in the deer park whenever she could, going through the motions of mending while engrossed in the novel she kept in her sewing basket.

Occasionally on the long summer evenings, Maggie managed to get out for a walk, alone or with Jane. Sometimes, screened by the hedges, she lifted her skirts and ran in place. Not a very fun way to get cardiovascular exercise, but Jane thought it hilarious.

"I just don't want to have a heart attack when I'm sixty!" Maggie panted.

Jane guffawed. "So tha canna wait?"

Jane was a reliable counter to Abiah's sobriety. She took Maggie places where they could be alone: the stable, where they were out of sight, or the well, where they were at least out of earshot. Maggie looked forward to Mondays, when she and Jane did the laundry together. They piled everything into a cart and took it to the laundry house, where the water was heating in a big copper cauldron with a brass petcock, from which the hot water drained into a wooden tub. They stirred and pummeled the wash with forked paddles. The interior of the laundry house was whitewashed and sunny, with drying racks suspended from pulleys. When the steaming sheets were wrung out and hoisted aloft, the two women were surrounded by whiteness, cut off from the outside world.

Inside that damp bower, their talk turned intimate. Sometimes it was the exchange of fantasies; their ideas of heaven and hell, the perfect life. But often it had less to do with words than with the freedom from decorum and with the force of Jane's presence—her freckled forearms working the paddle, her lilting voice, the way she threw her whole body into the telling of a story. The two of them giggled over the steamy water, Jane's hair falling into limp coppery strands, Maggie's dark hair drawing into tight curls.

Once Maggie looked over to see that Jane had stripped to the waist, her bodice thrown back on her hips. Small pear-shaped breasts bobbed pale against her freckled chest, their areolas bright pink. Maggie looked at her in wonder.

Jane grinned. "Tha can'st do it too." She threw an inviting glance at Maggie's buttoned front. "If tha darest."

"But—" Maggie's mouth went dry. "What if somebody comes in?"

" 'Tisn't so strange. They say that in the Black Country women nail makers work bare-titty all the time."

Could this be true? It wasn't the England Maggie had expected. She unfastened her top button but went no further. Too much at risk. She felt vaguely excited, though, watching Jane's breasts and thinking about herself and Sandi Kalowicz as thirteen-year-olds fondling each other under the laser deck. Her thoughts went to the Quaker maid.

In July, Samuel Darby sent word that he would be arriving on the Saturday afternoon coach. Abraham drove to the Cuckoo Oak to meet him, but Samuel was not on the coach, which caused some consternation. Maggie overheard Abraham in Abiah's sitting room bemoaning Samuel's irresponsibility, and Sarah defending him.

Samuel showed up the following day, walking from the Cuckoo Oak, carrying a valise. Maggie was shelling peas when Mrs. Hannigan greeted him at the kitchen door.

Samuel looked a lot like Abraham, but with coarser features. The same swarthy coloring, but Samuel was a little taller and looser, had fuller lips, a longer jaw, and heavier eyelids. His thick, dark hair was tied back like Abraham's in a couple of queues, but there was more of it. A few pimples at nineteen. Under his gray Quaker waistcoat he wore a blue-and-yellow vest of brocaded silk.

Mrs. Hannigan introduced Maggie. Maggie would have preferred being introduced in her other role, as Abiah's secretary. When she took his hand and met his eyes, she thought she saw a flicker of uncertainty, thought she felt an undefinable tremor go through him. Maybe it was only her prescience, but she had the eerie sense that *he* knew the tragic direction his life would take in a few years' time. His gaze darted away.

The atmosphere at Sunniside changed with Samuel's arrival. Sarah seemed to come out of hiding; Abraham was edgy and drew closer to his mother; Abiah seemed protective of both sons, although Samuel was clearly the baby. Samuel's side of the exchanges sounded dutiful, occasionally sullen. His fancy brocaded vest prompted scorn from Abraham, who called it "contrary to Truth" and accused him of looking like a macaroni.

Samuel and Sarah took long walks together. They played cards when Abiah wasn't around. Sarah, at twenty-two, between her two brothers in age, seemed not to make judgments. From what Maggie could pick up, Samuel voiced a smoldering impatience with the family—including their older sister, Mally, and her husband, Joseph, to whom he was apprenticed. He had a year remaining of his apprenticeship. He complained of Joseph's and Mally's restrictions and of being short of cash.

Samuel brought out a whole different side of Sarah. In her mother's presence Sarah was lackluster, inclined to hunch her shoulders. Around Samuel she was more animated and at the same time more languid, inhabiting her body more freely. He teased her, whispering things that alternately scandalized her and made her laugh.

Maggie found Samuel obnoxious. The first time she was alone with him, in the dining room—serving him breakfast when he had slept late—he sprawled in a loutish way he never would have assumed in the family's presence. He glanced at her furtively from under heavy lids, a gaze both insouciant and guarded.

"So. Maggie," he said, buttering a muffin. "Art thou liking the ironmonsters?"

"I beg your pardon?"

"Ironmonsters. Ironmonsters. It must be my Liverpool accent. Or thy American ears." He leered over the marmalade. "What thinkest thou of the shenanigans in Boston?"

Before she could respond to either question, he plunged a finger into the marmalade crock and sucked it lasciviously. "But thou art from the western lands, as yet unsettled. Not settled by Quakers at any rate, unless I'm mistaken. A wild and comely land whose virtues are"—he gave a final lick—"untested."

Maggie might have been amused if she were an equal, not a servant. Her heart was pounding. "Samuel," she said sternly, hands on her hips, "how old are you?"

"Nineteen."

She nodded. "Then you are old enough to know not to put your finger in the marmalade."

She left for the kitchen as coolly as she could, but she was shaking. This was the first time she had challenged Darby authority. When she returned to clear the dishes, Samuel was subdued. He stayed out of her way the rest of the morning.

Later, cleaning his room, she found a copy of *Gentlemen's Magazine* folded open to illustrations of the Roman statuary unearthed at the Herculaneum. It occurred to her that the engravings of naked women might have some erotic appeal.

She found something else on the floor under his dresser: a scrap of newspaper folded in quarters.

*Faggergill, late Mr. Shafto's; he was got by Old Snap, his dam was called Miss Cleveland, got by Regulus; his grand dam was the famous Midge, got by a well bred son of Bay Boulton, his great grand dam by Barlet's Childers, his great great grand dam by General Honeywood's Arabian, out of the dam of the two True Blues. Midge was own sister to Sir William Middleton's Camilla, Squirrel, & Thwackum, all horses in high form.*

*Signed Jack Weatherby, match-maker.*

At the bottom was a list of horses running in a race at Bridgnorth. Some names were circled, others scribbled in the margin. Checking the date of the race, she saw it was Saturday, the day Samuel had failed to show up at Sunniside. She refolded it, deliberating whether to leave it where she'd found it. She tucked it in her apron pocket.

Later, when Samuel was sitting alone in the upstairs parlor, Maggie handed him the folded clipping. "I found this under your dresser."

Samuel half unfolded it, reddened, and slipped it hurriedly into his pocket. He looked up. "Thank thee, for returning it." He searched her face. "My mother—"

Maggie nodded. " 'Twill be our secret."

He looked relieved. "Thank thee." Again, that flicker of fear.

Samuel treated her with more respect after that.

It was a break, a little one, the problem of course being that Samuel Darby was only a bit player. But if she could establish herself as a person to Samuel, maybe she could get through to the others.

W hen Abiah finished her manuscript in September, she thanked Maggie for her scrivening and inquired in a kindly way, "Didst thou receive some educationment from it, my dear?"

She was a tough nut, Abiah. Maggie asked what she thought was a penetrating question about Barclay's *Apology*—an abstruse Quaker treatise that she had read at great labor—but Abiah seemed unimpressed. Whatever her interest in bringing Maggie into Convincement, Abiah was possessive of Quakerism, and content to have a clever maid with editorial skills.

In October, when the pamphlets came back from the printer, Abiah felt a "great weight" to attend Monthly Meeting in Shrewsbury. And, since Sarah was helping tend sick children at the Reynoldses, Abiah invited Maggie to accompany her. She made it clear that she was asking for something beyond Maggie's role as a servant. Maggie readily accepted. Maybe this was the payoff to those long hours.

They set out early on a Saturday morning in the chaise, the two women in their bonnets, Abiah driving, the pamphlets stowed at their feet. As they set out west on the turnpike, they crossed Birches Brook on the bridge that had been rebuilt since the earthquake. The scars were evident in the canted trees and rumpled hillside—vivid enough reminders for Maggie to feel a twinge of the earlier terror. They rode through Buildwas and past the Wrekin, where the Darbys and Reynoldses went for family outings. Now, well beyond the pall of the gorge, the air smelled fresh, the upper Severn Valley stretched out under a blue sky.

The trip took two and a half hours, most of it through pleasant, fertile countryside—silt-rich flood plain founded on glacial till, through which the river flowed in wide, meandering loops that took it in and out of view. Farmers were preparing for winter: animals were being slaughtered, walls repaired, cottages rethatched, fields spread with manure. Mole catchers were at work, hanging the dead moles on fences for counting. Maggie was struck by how medieval it seemed, and by the vibrant colors: the yellows of linden and sycamore, and hawthorn hedges bright with red berries. Occasional panoramic views of the valley were breathtaking.

"It's so beautiful," Maggie said, "it almost hurts."

Abiah smiled. "Praise the Maker."

Abiah spoke of the melancholy she felt sometimes with the fall of the leaf. Her last baby, a girl born three years after Samuel, had died in October, and Abiah's autumn pregnancies had gone badly: the "two Rachels" and William all died in infancy. Maggie talked of the sadness she felt about her own inability to conceive but said that she liked the fall, the sense of everything shutting down for the winter. She tried to describe to Abiah the desert seasons.

At Shrewsbury they handed out pamphlets in the market square, then moved on to Hangsters Gate, a seedy neighborhood where a man called them "shit sacks" and threatened to turn his dog on them, after which a trio of boys pelted them with rotten apples. Maggie chased after the boys, and they scampered out of sight.

The women's dresses were plastered with apple pulp. "Abiah," Maggie said, "maybe we should go back to the market square."

"Go, if thou art afeared, my dear. I will hold my ground, in the power of the Light." She looked surprisingly calm.

Oh well, Maggie thought. At least it was apples, not assault rifles.

Abiah seemed energized by the confrontations. Her face was flushed. Wearing the faint, stoic smile Maggie recalled from the first time they met, at the bull baiting a year ago, Abiah marched through the ancient streets of Shrewsbury, "carrying forth the Light," as she put it, asking everyone to repent, decrying false doctrines to anyone who would listen—while Maggie (after they had a near miss from a chamber pot) kept an eye on the windows overhead. A few listeners seemed persuaded, or at least were entertained enough to follow them. "They are shaken a little," Abiah told Maggie. Outside the parish church, a crowd of thirty or forty people gathered to hear Abiah and the rector engage in a disputation over the bearing of arms, which Abiah said was contrary to the will of a loving God.

"You Quakers," snarled the rector contemptuously, "depend on others to do your fighting!"

"Unwillingly!" was Abiah's response. "War only begets more war." She talked of beating swords into plowshares, of Christian love. "To slay another," she cried, "is to slay that of God, for God is present in us all!" Abiah was radiant.

The rector retreated into the parish church and slammed the heavy door. People took the pamphlets eagerly, until they were all gone. Abiah, her cheeks flushed, grasped Maggie's hand and swung it like a schoolgirl. "Praise the Maker!"

They spent the night with a Quaker family, sharing a bed, Abiah keeping Maggie awake with her snoring. The next day, Abiah testified at the Shrewsbury Meeting. At the women's meeting that followed, she told how she was filled with the Holy Spirit and prayed that she might have turned even one soul toward the Light of Christ. Then she spoke in a more rambling way against the millenarians, against dancing and singing and the refusal to bring forth children. It wasn't until others spoke that Maggie realized that Abiah was referring to the Shakers, who were about to depart for America, under the leadership of an illiterate mill worker called Mother Ann Lee.

On their way back to Coalbrookdale, Abiah seemed relaxed. She talked about her husband, Abraham, what a good man he was, and how after his death she dreamt he was on a staircase, ascending like Jesus into heavenly light.

She handed the reins to Maggie and showed her how to put the horse through its paces, what to watch for in its ears and gait. As they passed a cart loaded with apples, Abiah chuckled. "Thou poor dear! I fear that I led thee into harm's way, and thou art not even a Friend."

Maggie smiled. "I was glad to come." The trip had given her a new glimpse of Abiah. She cleared her throat. "I just wish I had more time for this kind of work."

"Thou wilt find the time, if thou art Convinced." Abiah spoke metaphorically of the harvest: how the spiritual ground first had to plowed, the seed of Truth sown, and the tender plants weeded before the harvest of souls could take place. She herself was a birthright Quaker rather than one brought into Truth by Convincement, and yet she had had to discover her own Light within. As a girl, she wanted desperately to speak in Meeting, but her tongue was stopped—and remained so for years. Not until she was thirty-two was she finally "seized upon with the power to declare the Truth."

Listening, Maggie was moved. "I can understand that." She was thinking of when she was seventeen and finally decided to run away from CALYPOOL. The sense of release she felt.

"What was thy girlhood like?"

Maggie felt herself blush. "Different from yours. Probably not as strict." *Repressed,* she meant. "Or strict in different ways. My teachers didn't understand me." *How could they? They were computers.* "I can't explain. I just felt freed once I realized the truth and that I could act on it. That I had a choice."

Abiah nodded. "And so dost thou have a choice now." She put a hand on Maggie's hand.

It was true, Maggie realized. Looking down at Abiah's hand, with its liver spots, she knew that she was being hustled but thought *Why not?* This might be the moment to let Abiah save her soul. Why not just proclaim herself Convinced?

*Because it felt sleazy.*

Which was weird. She was, after all, a spy in the Darby household; she had lied about everything from her birth to her marital status. Why couldn't she lie and say she'd had a religious experience?

"How—how will I know?" Maggie's heart was beating double time.

*Because this was important to her, at a level that had to do less with her mission than with who she was.*

"Open thy heart, and listen for that still, small voice."

They were silent the whole way back to Coalbrookdale.

Maggie drove. She liked feeling the horse move in response to her commands, liked the elegance of this mode of transport. She was grateful for Abiah's silence. She tried to open her heart. And by the time she turned into the carriage lane she knew the answer.

# Abraham Darby III

Winter arrived early. Bitterly cold winds on the heels of a freezing rain left the Dale encased in ice. The ore and limestone, even where it was protected under shed roofs, had to be broken apart with pickaxes and piled against the furnace to thaw before it could be used. Men had to be assigned the task of breaking up the ice in the millraces. Horses slipped. Men's hands froze. The furnaces required an extra hour for each heat. The forges and rolling mills were shut down, and work crews doubled so they could take turns warming themselves at bonfires. The young children who sorted brays were sent home or allowed to huddle under the bellows arch.

Abraham was in the Dale Company office with three of his foremen, standing around the salamander stove drinking chamomile tea. His toes were still numb, and he felt an ominous ache creeping into his body, for he had stayed out in the wind too long inspecting the millraces and conferring with each of the furnace keepers. He hoped he was not coming down with something. The warmth revived his spirits. Scriveners and assistant clerks talked softly, sitting on their tall stools at the double row of tables, under the watchful eyes of the clerk. Occasional gusts of sleet rattled against the windows.

Through a window Abraham saw a man approaching, wearing a black greatcoat and riding a gray mare. His heart fell. As if the day were not wretched enough! It was John Wilkinson, his bulk distorted through the wavy, acid-etched panes but unmistakable as he dismounted—approaching like death itself.

"What ho!" Wilkinson called as he stepped through the door.

Abraham felt a tightening of the guts. He made space for Wilkinson at the stove and signaled a boy to bring tea.

"Your boring mill is shut down, I see," said Wilkinson merrily, cane tucked under his arm while he rubbed his hands.

Abraham nodded. " 'Tis all we can do to keep the furnaces in blast." Was Wilkinson *immune* to this weather? Could he think of nothing better to do on a day like this than pay social calls?

"This place is too big," cried Wilkinson, opening his greatcoat and flapping it out like a raven landing on carrion. "Too big! Ha, ha! All these launders and leets to freeze! In times like these I am thankful that New Willey is small. Manageable. Tight as a bung in a barrel." He pitched his cane upright into the corner, startling the clerks. "On the other hand," he said more confidentially, "I am spread about hither and yon. I was on my way to Bersham, but have decided to wait out this wretched cold. Whilst in your neighborhood, I thought to drop in."

"Of course." Abraham managed a wan smile. He felt the ache intensify in the small of his back.

The foremen excused themselves to go about their work. Wilkinson talked about the bridge, about how the bridge committee must meet in a formal way as soon as the weather permitted. Abraham watched the minute hand creep across the face of the clock and the achiness spread through his body. He must get off his feet, but he was afraid to sit down, lest Wilkinson sit down too. The man would talk him to death. In vain he focused on Wilkinson's slate-colored eyes and ruddy jowls and tried to see that of God. What was the man blathering? How they should build a hotel at one end of the bridge, for there was no doubt that the *Vigilance*'s route would be changed so that passengers could see the spectacle of an iron bridge. A hotel would make pots of money. Pots of money.

Abraham had started shivering. "If it please thee, John Wilkinson," he said at last. "I must excuse myself. I fear I am taken by a fever."

All but throwing himself into his office, he collapsed into his chair, shivering. Finally he rang for a boy, sent for a blanket and his horse. By the time he reached Sunniside, he was shaking like a leaf.


The doctor prodded him. Sarah at his bedside. Voices faded in and out.

"What sayeth the doctor?" Abraham asked, waking in a sweat.

"He said 'tis either influenza or what the French doctors are calling the grippe. Dost thou not remember?"

"Was it this morning?"

Sarah smiled and shook her head. "Yesterday."

Another interval passed. Someone tended the coal fire. Sarah's cool hand touched his cheek. "Abey. Maggie is going to stay here with thee."

He nodded. Felt a cold, wet cloth on his forehead and heard a kind of lullaby sung softly in his ear.

Something about a Sun King.

The sound of water being squeezed from the cloth into a bowl.

The Sun King again.

And words like Latin, which he could not make out. Or Spanish. *Mi amore. Corazón.*

Latin dripping into the bowl. Or blood. Father was dying. The glow from the coal grate was a sickly, lurid yellow. Like the ocher seeping into Father's washbasin.

Sound of pages turning.

Maggie sat in a chair near the foot of his bed, reading a book in the lamplight. He wanted to ask what book she was reading but could not get the question past his lips. She took off her mobcap, spilled a mass of dark curls.

Maggie Foster. Had he called her name aloud? She looked up, flashed a smile. The sight of her face smiling, surrounded by dark curls, reminded him of a face he had seen once. A Gypsy woman walking along the turnpike during the landslip.

"Good," Maggie said. "You're awake. Your mother asked me to read something to you." She put aside the book she was reading, which he could see now was *Robinson Crusoe*, and read from Mother's small leather edition of George Fox's journal:

*I saw also that there was an ocean of darkness and death, but an infinite ocean of light and love which flowed over the ocean of darkness. In that, also, I saw the infinite love of God....*

The words lulled him. As a child he used to imagine himself in a rowboat, a silvery ocean flowing all around him.

He awoke, or dreamt he awoke, in a ship's hold. It was dark and stifling hot. He could feel the ocean beyond the hull, could hear the waves crash. But he did not know whether this was the ocean of darkness or the ocean of light. The crew cast lots to see who should be thrown overboard.

He heard his own voice asking, "Which one of us is Jonah?" Loudly and self-righteously: "Jonah must needs step forth!"

"Why, thou art Jonah," they told him, all staring.

"No!" he protested. "My name—" But he could not remember his true name. They seized him. He struggled as they carried him to the rail. "My name—" They were waiting. "Abraham!" he cried finally. But the sound was filled with vanity. It tore his throat.

"Shh. It's okay."

He pushed off blankets, threw himself on his stomach. "Where am I?" he asked when he was able.

"In your chamber," came her voice. Cool hand stroking his back.

He listened again. Were those his furnaces, or a beating surf? A cold cloth wiped his neck, wrists, and hands. His mind fixed on the coolness until it became an idea. "Fetch me," he said. There was a long silence, while he fixed on the idea.

"Fetch you?"

He pulled up the blanket. He was cool now. "My electrical machine."

When he awoke again, the electrical machine was standing near his bedside. Maggie was asleep in her chair, mouth open. When he opened his eyes again, she was gone. Daylight, and Mrs. Hannigan offering a cup of hot barley broth. He took several sips of the broth. After she left, he used the chamber pot; then, feeling chilled, he burrowed under the blankets again, shivering, peering out at the electrical machine. Peering from the belly of the whale, or from the needle's eye.

"Destroy it," he told Maggie, when next she came. He pointed to the electrical machine.

"Why?" she asked gently.

He frowned and shut his eyes. *Vanity. Superfluity*. But he could not shape the words, he could only shake his head. "Destroy it."

When he awoke again, she was bent over his washstand, which she had brought next to the bed. He lifted his head enough to recognize the pieces of his electrical machine. She had taken it apart and spread the pieces out before her.

"I thought," she said, "I'd check it out."

*Check it out*. She would never get it back together, he thought. And though he recalled ordering the thing's destruction, he regretted it. Regretted having purchased it in the first place, regretted the vanity. Now he regretted its loss. He burrowed under the covers.

Maggie was asking Sarah for a penknife, a scrap of leather.

"What art thou doing?"

"I'm making a new insulator."

"Insulator?"

She nodded. "Put out your hand." She laid a small leather lunette in his palm. "One of these," she said. "This little washer, you see, got soaked with oil, so it was conducting instead of insulating. That's why you weren't getting a spark."

Abraham gazed at the damp little ring and tried to fathom her words, but his brain was not equal to the task. He watched her hands at work, aligning one brass gear with another. How would she ever get the pieces back together? And yet they were skilled hands. He somehow trusted them.

Sarah came in for a while to watch. She said it was warmer outside; the wind had died. Abraham asked how the furnaces were doing, and she said they were fine. They continued watching in silence while

Maggie tightened all the connections. The glass globe was in place, the wheel and the crank. Finally, she turned the crank. A bright spark crackled across the globe.

"Voilà!" said Maggie.

Sarah clapped her hands with delight.

Abraham grinned. He looked at Maggie in wonder. "I have never heard of a female electrician."

Maggie wiped her hands on a rag. "There's a first time for everything."

In the days that followed, as Abraham's health returned, he requested various materials in order to appraise their electrical properties. He and Maggie played a sort of game: she would predict the conductivity of such things as green wood, feathers, lead, and ice. She was almost invariably correct. He invited her to stay longer than was necessary and to read Joseph Priestley's *The History and Present State of Electricity with Original Experiments* at his bedside, which she did, and they discussed it. She agreed with Dr. Franklin's theory that lightning and electricity were one and the same. As to the great hullabaloo over lightning rods that had erupted in Parliament—King George favoring rounded ends over Dr. Franklin's pointed ends—she supposed it more a matter of politics than science. Finally, he asked the question that interested him the most and whose answer always eluded him. He asked it in a scholarly manner that would not, he hoped, reveal his befuddlement.

"What, in thine own opinion, *is* electricity?"

Her large green eyes regarded him carefully. "Before I answer that question, Abraham, may I ask you one?"

"Certainly."

"Well. Don't you think it's a little strange that I'm working here as a housemaid?"

"Why, yes," he said slowly. The question was unexpected, and yet he had indeed begun to wonder. "Yes, I do think it strange."

She shrugged. "I needed work. But . . . I wish we could rewrite my articles of indenture. I could be much more useful to you in other ways. I could help with lightning rods, with geology. That's where my training is, you see. I could be a consultant."

"A consultant?"

"An advisor. I could check things out for you, give you professional advice. Show you exactly where to dig for coal, for instance. You're going all the way to Dawley for coal. I can show you places closer to Coalbrookdale, which would save you all kinds of money."

Those eyes—the irises dark at the rims, sea-green in their depths, with a hint of amber—pulled him in. Embarrassed, he looked away. Saw his own reflection in the electrical machine's glass globe.

"A consultant," he mused. Why not? "Very well. Thy old articles of indenture expire in a few days. We shall draft a new contract." He leaned back against his pillows. "Now, please give me thy opinion on the true nature of electricity. Is it, as Priestley says, a liquid?"

# John Wilkinson

**B**ad news—damnable news!—from his solicitor in London. The Ordnance Board had recommended to the Master General of Ordnance that steps be taken to overturn Wilkinson's gun-boring patent. And from Bersham came word that the new machine was plagued with difficulties.

Wilkinson had set out for Bersham on a bitterly cold day in December, everything covered with ice, but got no farther than Coalbrookdale, where he stopped to pester Darby and talk up the idea of a hotel, figuring the young Quaker's heart would be warmed by profits. *Money will make the pot boil, though the devil piss in the fire,* the old man used to say. But Darby claimed to have a fever. A cunny-thumbed lot, those Darbys, suffering from asthma and whatnot, their blood growing weaker with every generation. Wilkinsons were made of sterner stuff. Lived into their eighties. Suffered only from teeth and gout. But no rest for the Wilkinsons, by God, no rest. It was too cold to travel, so he headed back to Broseley, taking the Buildwas bridge, the ferry being shut down for ice.

When he finally made it to Bersham, in early January, he saw that the problem was that old goblin Vibration. On account of the large diameter. Even this small cylinder—cast hollow with a wall two inches thick that they intended to bore down to one—weighed half a ton. He tried adding little friction wheels to support it. To no avail: when they tested again, the results were disastrous. The cutters chattered, lost their edge, and drove the cylinder off center, the friction wheels shrieking and the collars thumping louder with every revolution, until the whole thing threatened to break loose. A machinist jumped back in fear. Wilkinson signaled the operator to bring it to a halt. When the casting stopped rotating, they saw a ragged bore indeed.

"Looks like old Roby Douglas breaking wind," laughed Will.

"God rot it!" Wilkinson cried shrilly, smiting the floor with his cane.

What to do? The Sniggy Oakes principle had failed him, and he lacked Sniggy Oakes the man. He strode around in the greatest agitation, imagining Watt's sneer.

The men were looking at him, awaiting instructions.

"Take it down," he snarled, with a wave of his cane. "Break it up for scrap."

Watching Will—thirteen years his junior, broader in the shoulders, slimmer in the waist, working alongside the men with levers to relieve the strain while they freed the hornbeam collars—Wilkinson felt a great black weight on his own shoulders. Will had grown up easier than he. Suffered fewer beatings. Had an older brother to break the way. John felt the weight of his own age, and something else: the dark and malevolent hunger that lurked in his breast. In his twenties he had feared it, feared he might be consigned to the fires of hell. But after years of familiarity with blast furnaces, hell seemed less terrible. In his thirties he came to recognize the wolf within, whose dark appetite prompted him to snatch opportunity from other men's jaws, and saw that it was precisely this instinctive longing for *what he did not have* that animated the higher motions of his brain. Now, in his forties, he perceived that this longing was the font of civilization. Were not Romulus and Remus suckled by a she-wolf? Had that same black cunning not raised the Greeks and Romans out of barbarism? And, inspiring Progress thus, was it not a force for the Good?

But none of these musings lifted Wilkinson from his quandary. He kept seeing Watt like Diogenes carrying his lantern in search of a cylinder bored to truth—its light perhaps falling on Anthony Bacon, or worse, on young Darby. A loathsome thought!

Wilkinson spent all of February at Bersham, trying to conquer the vibration. He dispatched encouraging letters to Boulton, hinting at victory around every turn—but in truth he was stymied.

One night, he was sitting alone by a peat fire in his library at Bersham, listening to the wind howl in the chimney, gazing into the glowing ash, and dwelling, as he often did these days, on the subject of Sniggy Oakes. He wished the mechanic had not been so stubborn. He recalled the suppers they took together—the mechanic's rapt attention, his own erudition—and thought for the hundredth time that it was he who had been stubborn. He should have offered Sniggy Oakes two shillings instead of one. Even four. What had seemed generous then seemed short-sighted now. If he had it to do again, he would offer him half the royalties on what remained of the patent. But it was too late. Oakes abominated him. The world abominated him, and he deserved it. He was a loathsome fellow. The most desperate sort of knave. And worse, a fool.

Suddenly a loud pop shattered the air like a pistol shot. Wilkinson sprang from his chair and clutched his chest, convinced in that instant that Oakes had stalked him to his lair. Oh, ignominious death! Then he realized it was merely a pebble exploding in the peat. But the image still in his brain was of Sniggy Oakes lunging with the spanner, screaming, "I'll kill ye!" Veins bulging in his neck. "Ye stole my boring bar!"

And it dawned on Wilkinson, even before his pulse returned to normal, that it was in fact the boring bar that was at the heart of the invention.

Perhaps his mistake lay in trying to imitate the success of the cannon-boring machine too closely. A cylinder was too large to be turned. But what if he were to do the opposite, hold the cylinder fixed, in the conventional way, and cause the boring bar to turn?

He stayed up most of the night scribbling designs, his brain on fire.

He remained at Bersham long enough to redesign the boring bar and supervise the completion of the new machine. Upon its trial, it answered perfectly: the straightedge lay so flat against the bore that he could see no light under it. They all threw their hats in the air. He ordered rum to celebrate, instructed Will to raise the machinists' pay by a shilling, and made them swear again by the strictest oaths—for this time he was determined to put his trust not in a patent but in secrecy. He sent the finished cylinder to Soho by fast wagon and set out for Broseley.

Two days after he got home, he received an ecstatic letter from James Watt, declaring the bore to be accurate to the thickness of a worn shilling. Just in time, because in April Wilkinson received word that his cannon-boring patent had indeed been overturned, on grounds that the idea was not sufficiently different from the Verbruggens' and that his monopoly was not in the national interest.

The national interest, ha! It was the interests of the other arms-makers! But no matter. The patent had served him well. And now, even defunct, it might serve in the fashion of herring laid to distract hounds—for his competitors, knowing the principle on which his cannon-boring lathe worked, might assume that the new machine worked similarly. A merry thought indeed.

# Maggie Foster

**H**er station, as they put it, was elevated by means of a few strokes of the pen. Abraham seemed to enjoy the task, his face pale in the cold sunlight that sliced across the dining table and illuminated the white top of his quill as it scratched and dipped, spelling out her new terms of employment:

Consultant to Abraham Darby III concerning Electrical and other Matters, her responsibilities to include the propagation of new Whims, and also Secretary charged with scrivening and Other Assistances to be rendered to Abiah Maud Darby. Maggie was to cease being a housemaid and be raised to such a Station as befits her new Duties.

Richard and Rebecca Reynolds were on hand to witness the document. Reynolds chuckled at the phrase "propagation of new Whims," which Abraham had borrowed from the charter of the Royal Society. He peered at Maggie over the tops of his reading spectacles. "What, art thou now a philosophe?"

Maggie reddened. "I know a little about geology and electricity."

"So I have heard."

While the others adjourned to the parlor, Maggie copied the document over twice in her most careful hand. From the parlor came laughter. Reynolds. Should she have responded differently to his inquiry? More humbly? More assertively? She couldn't tell.

The servants were brought in for the signing. Reynolds scrutinized her signature with a frown. "That is no Quaker signature, Maggie Foster. 'Tis bold as a man's."

"I'm from the Colonies," she reminded him, a knot in her stomach. Was Reynolds simply amused or trying to keep her in her place? She felt both annoyance and fear. When the servants were dismissed, however, and she was invited to join the Darbys and Reynoldses for tea, and Jane served them, avoiding her eyes, Maggie knew that she had finally crossed over a line of class—tentatively, perhaps, but crossed it nevertheless.

J ane was a problem.

Everyone else took it in stride. The Darbys, whose chamber pots Maggie had been emptying for a year, had no trouble treating her like a lady. And Mrs. Hannigan, who had rapped her with a spoon, was inquiring if she would like coffee. Jane was the holdout.

When they encountered each other alone upstairs, Jane's eyes flashed. "Tha moight be a gentlelady, but I'll not empty tha twiss!"

"You don't have to," Maggie said quietly. "I'll empty my own twiss." She smiled. "Listen, Jane—"

But Jane flounced away.

O n Christmas morning, Maggie set out for the Crumps. In her basket was a plum pudding that she and Sarah had baked, a little tin of Turkish tea that she'd purchased for eight and a half pence, and a marzipan wrapped in tissue for each of the children. She wore her old clogs, the dress that Polly had sewn, and a secondhand wool coat given to her by the Madeley Women's Meeting—none of which announced her new status.

She had not seen the Crumps in the past year, despite their living only a mile and a half away—except for a chance meeting with Polly at the Madeley market last spring. Something had always stopped her from paying a visit. But as she turned onto the wagon road that led to Bedlam, she felt a gathering excitement.

A sprig of mistletoe hung on the door. Polly's face broke into a grin upon seeing her; she had lost another tooth. Helen was shy at first, but quickly made up for it. Jeremy was taller, more reserved at fourteen; different in some way Maggie couldn't define. Kate had plans to marry. Matthew was off visiting his girlfriend. Maggie handed out the marzipans. "Where's Timothy?" She felt a twinge of foreboding.

"The Lord took him," Polly said. "Pneumonia, last spring."

"Oh, Polly." Hugging her, Maggie felt the stooped shoulders stiffen and remembered the hardness she used to take for callousness. "I'm so sorry."

Maggie helped with dinner preparations, peeling, mixing, trussing the goose for the spit: all things Polly had taught her. Polly filled her in on the local gossip: births, deaths, a cottage lost in the spring flood, Mrs. Merryweather going blind with cataracts, a baby born in Bridgnorth with cleft feet.

Jeremy took her down by the withey and showed her a coracle he had made to sell. He had already sold two. He showed her a pile of timbers he had captured from the river, also to sell. Resourceful as always. He had a new habit of flipping the hair from his eyes. Admiring the curve of his neck, she realized what was different: he was clean.

"You've left the pit," she said.

He nodded. " 'Twas thy doing."

"Mine?"

"Aye." His eyes sparkled. "Tha told me if I wished to die later than sooner, I best get out."

She felt her mouth stretch with pleasure.

"I ain't sorry," he assured her. "I catch rabbits and botch coracles, and betwixt this and that I make as much as I did at the pit."

"Super."

"Aye. Super." He grinned and flipped his hair.

As they talked, she recalled how the bull baiting had come between them. In the past year she had grown to realize it was partly a matter of class. The landed gentry had their blood sports. It was only the more visible blood sports of the poor, cockfighting and bull baiting, that Abiah and the Reverend John Fletcher railed against.

When they returned to the cottage, the air was redolent with cooking. Maggie played with Helen, chalking words on slate for her to sound out while they turned the goose on the spit. Maggie relaxed into the familiar blanket of smells and sounds. Over dinner, she announced that she had become a Quaker. As she said it, she realized that this was partly what had brought her here. She had no one else to tell. She told them about her new life at Sunniside. Most of the stories came from Jane or involved Jane. She felt the loss.

Darkness fell. Polly lit a rush candle and heated up some elderberry wine and spiked it with applejack, and the two women sat talking by the fire. Maggie thought how different the gossip was at Sunniside, how tied to employers. She felt relaxed here, not having to watch what she said. Polly refilled their cups. The elderberry wine was going to Maggie's head. When Matthew came home, she gave him his marzipan. She looked down at the marzipan remaining in her apron pocket and remembered how Timothy used to sit by the fireplace watching with his big eyes. She divided the marzipan with Polly, but as she chewed it, she felt the sadness well up in her throat.

To her surprise, she was weeping. She had had too much elderberry wine.

Polly and Jeremy walked her back to Sunniside through the damp pink night. By the time they got to the carriage drive, the alcohol had worn off. Under the darkness of the cedars, Polly gave her a clove to sweeten her breath. Maggie hugged them both for a long time.

H er new bedchamber seemed palatial. It was the room next to Sarah's: roughly twelve feet square, with a south-facing window, and furnished with a real bed, an armoire, and a dry sink. A fresh spray of orange blossoms from the greenhouse was left in a pitcher to welcome her. Sarah helped her move her few possessions. Later, Maggie went back to retrieve her notebook, which she hid behind the armoire.

On New Year's morning she answered a soft tap. It was Sarah, inviting her to watch Abraham play the dark man for the servants. While they were sitting on the steps, Maggie asked if it was she who had left the blossoms. Sarah hunched her shoulders and nodded shyly.

Watching the new maid, a young woman named Rachel, Maggie saw herself a year ago and remembered how strange it had all seemed.

From her window, Maggie could look across the top of the greenhouse at the pasture with its fringe of berry bushes and orchard descending into the dale. On the rare clear days when the wind swept the smoke from the dale, she discovered she could see all the way across to Broseley.

And the moon! The first clear night, she awoke to a patch of cold light painting the oak floor. She had missed the moon, living under the stairs—occasionally seeing a tease of light through the ventilation grate, longing to get up and ramble around the sleeping house but restraining herself. In Ecosophia she used to sneak out of bed without waking Trevor, climb to the highest catwalk, sit in a lotus position with eyes closed, and feel the moon through her eyelids, feel invisible tides rising through her body. Now she could stand naked at her own window and feel it in her breasts. From Sarah's room, she heard the floorboards creak; from across the hall, Abiah muttering in her sleep.

Odd to consider that she was the only person on the planet who knew what the backside of the moon looked like.

She squatted on the chamber pot, elbows and knees bathed in the cold light, the porcelain cool on her bottom, heat rising from the powerful stream of her pee.

In the silence that followed, listening to the rhythmic squeak of the floorboards, she realized that Sarah was dancing. She imagined the swish of green silk. Abiah talking to her dead husband. Jane looking out at the moon over her white, pear-shaped breasts.

Her period had started.

In March, Becky Smith came down from Yorkshire to pay a visit to the Reynoldses, and the two families saw a lot of each other in what seemed to be a matchmaking campaign by Abiah and the Reynoldses.

Becky was twenty-three, only two years younger than Abraham, but seemed childlike. It was partly her small stature and fair complexion —earlobes and fingertips almost translucent, blond eyebrows giving her a blankness across her high forehead like a China doll—but it was partly by design too: she took mincing steps and deferred to Abraham with a tinkly laugh. When she and Maggie were introduced and Becky offered a tiny gloved hand, Maggie realized her own hand was gloveless and chapped. She felt hulking, dark, opaque.

Abraham invited them both on a tour of Coalbrookdale. Maggie had seen most of the Works by now, in the course of planning with Abraham where the lightning rods were to be installed. She was a little annoyed now to share a formal tour with Becky but supposed it was part of her new role—which she was still figuring out. Abraham clearly enjoyed introducing Maggie to people as his consultant, but her scope seemed to be pretty much limited to electricity, and she was also supposed to act like a lady.

She helped Becky get gussied up in double-width canvas aprons, borrowed from the malt mill, to protect their petticoats, and together they strapped on the wooden overshoes called *pattens* to keep their shoes out of the mud. Becky giggled. Maggie felt somehow tainted by Becky's helplessness. Observing how Becky leaned on Abraham's arm, how she exclaimed over everything and squealed with delight or fear, Maggie tried taking smaller steps herself, and took Abraham's arm whenever he offered it, but she felt awkward. She was not helpless; nor did she want to pretend to be. Yet she was intimidated and—quite unexpectedly—jealous, knowing this was the woman Abraham would marry.

Why? Did she fantasize replacing Becky?

Major weirdness.

Marriage, of course, would make her task easier. Like, *Oh, Abey, sweetheart. This is the bridge design I adore!*

But as she watched Becky needing to be rescued and asking silly questions in that chirpy voice, it seemed the whole idea was not to be taken seriously. No, better to be herself. Depend on her intellect to influence Abraham. She wasn't a matrimonial contender, anyway, since she was sterile. Better get clear on that point.

"Abey says thou art a proper philosophe," Becky exclaimed while they were waiting for Abraham to confer with the furnace keeper.

Maggie shrugged diffidently. "I guess so. That is, mostly with electrical things." She realized she was hunching her shoulders like Sarah. She straightened. "What I mean is, I know it's unusual for a woman to be interested in electricity." She wrinkled her nose. "I hope *you* don't mind."

"No!" Becky protested.

"I'm relieved. I was afraid you wouldn't like me."

Becky assured her this was not the case and confessed to the same worry. They declared a wish to become friends. They even ended up talking about clothes. Maggie, complaining about the awkwardness of full dresses in the Works, was interested to learn that riding habits for women were becoming fashionable in London.

Abraham reappeared, crooking an arm for each lady. They worked their way down the Dale, from the blast furnaces, where crude pig iron was made, to the various finishing operations. They saw air furnaces, where the pigs were reheated and combined into a red-hot mass called a *bloom;* blooming-hammers, which pounded that mass to squeeze out the slag; rolling mills, which rolled the bloom into finished bars malleable enough to be worked at forges; slitting mills, which slit the bar iron into strips of varying thickness suitable for making horseshoes or nails.

A small quantity of bar iron was refined further to make steel. But steelmaking was a laborious, expensive process. All this would change in eighty years, with the Bessemer converter. But for now, steel was a rare metal, used mostly for cutlery, musket barrels, springs, ornamental buttons, and other small objects. Most of Coalbrookdale's output was in crude iron cast directly into flat shapes such as firebacks, or hollowware.

What impressed Maggie as she watched the workers—some four

hundred, according to Abraham; and that didn't include those employed elsewhere mining and transporting the raw materials—was the social organization required to produce iron. No wonder the European blast furnace, developed in the fourteenth century, had conquered most of the world. No wonder the Japanese—isolated for now—would be so traumatized by Commodore Perry's cannon in the middle of the next century that they would devote the century after that to catching up, beginning with adoption of the Western blast furnace.

Abraham showed them the mold shop, the steps required to make a bellied pot, how wooden mold patterns were fashioned and then used to produce sand molds in three sections clamped together in an iron box. These box molds, he explained, were his grandfather's great innovation, along with coke firing. "The box molds allow us to cast bellied pots in sand instead of loam."

When they entered the loam shed, they encountered a sour, humid stench. Becky gasped and covered her nose.

"What *is* that?" Maggie asked.

Abraham chuckled. "That's the loam."

"It smells like fresh manure," said Maggie.

Abraham nodded. "Mixed with coaldust and fine sand." They watched men plastering the greenish mixture over patterns and baking them in open ovens. "We still use loam for certain difficult shapes," Abraham said. "But 'tis painstaking work. Thou canst see why my grandfather's invention was such an improvement."

Maggie smiled. "He must be revered as a saint."

"Abraham." Becky was still holding her nose. "May we leave?"


When they got back to Sunniside, Abiah looked grim. She asked to speak to Abraham in the library. While the three Darbys conferred in hushed tones, Maggie and Becky sat in the parlor drinking tea.

Maggie tried not to appear to be listening to the snatches of conversation that drifted from the library—*Samuel, Liverpool*—while

Becky showed her the embroidery she was doing for her aunt Rebecca. Maggie admired the smallness of the stitches, complaining that her own were clumsy. Becky commiserated, but not excessively. On the whole, she was more bearable when Abraham was not around. Still, Maggie was relieved when Richard Reynolds showed up to take Becky home.

When the Darbys gathered for the evening meal, Maggie sensed tension. Realizing her presence at the table was awkward, she left, took a walk, and retired afterwards to her bedchamber. She would have learned more as a servant. She wished she were on better terms with Jane. An awkward tension remained between them.

By now Maggie had an evening regimen. In the privacy of her room she stripped naked and did squats, lifts, and sit-ups. Then she sponge-bathed. Tonight, she did an extra round. She had just finished and was still out of breath when she heard a light tap on the door. She toweled off hurriedly, slipped into her nightgown, and opened the door. It was Sarah.

The younger woman stood silent for a moment, as if deliberating. "I fear we have been rude."

"Not at all. I just figured it was family business."

Sarah nodded. " 'Tis Samuel. We got word from Mally that he left his apprenticeship without permission."

Maggie waited for more. "Any idea why?"

Sarah shook her head. She seemed at the edge of tears. "A quarrel."

Maggie motioned her inside. The room smelled a little of sweat. "With whom?"

"With Joseph. Mally's husband."

"Over what?"

Sarah threw up her hands. "I know not. Mally insists 'tis Sammy's fault. But Sammy claims—" She shook her head. She seemed conflicted about how much to tell.

"Sammy claims . . . ?"

" 'Tis not my place to judge. I will tell thee only that my brother Sammy is a great admirer of your John Woolman."

"John Woolman?" Maggie could hardly keep the incredulity out of her voice. The American was admired among Quakers for his principled stances: his opposition to the slave trade; his refusal to ride stagecoaches because of the brutal treatment of the horses and boys who rode postilion.

"Thou must needs think it contradictory. But under his bold talk and gay apparel, my brother Sammy is full of ideals. Some I share. Others I take for failings, or perhaps in my ignorance do not understand. I—I wish—" She stopped, frowned. Maggie had always considered Sarah an innocuous young woman lost in Abiah's shadow. Only now was she coming to appreciate Sarah's depth. Sarah sighed sharply. "I fear for him. I fear the conflicts warring in his breast."

Maggie put her arms around her, on impulse. Sarah received the hug, then straightened. There was a moment's awkwardness. She murmured a hurried good-night and left.

Listening to Sarah's preparations for bed, Maggie wondered if she had overstepped her bounds with that hug. She hoped not. It occurred to her that Sarah had told her nothing about the quarrel.

# John Wilkinson

Wilkinson was girded for war. One would not have supposed it, to watch him dining with his wife and the distinguished French officer who was their guest. Oh no. Outwardly all was politeness. Wilkinson appeared in the most civilized attire: black velvet breeches, steel-buttoned waistcoat with white ruffled shirt, and freshly powdered wig. Mary Lee sat at the opposite end of the table wearing a low-cut canary-yellow silk gown with a floral silk stomacher. Seated between them, to Wilkinson's right, was Brigadier General Marchant de la Houlière, a tall thin man of aristocratic bearing, elegant in blue satin. They were eating trout poached in white wine in the French fashion, served with white bread and onion soup. Three maids waited on them. The afternoon sunlight sparkled on crystal goblets and German silver.

But in Boston last month, British troops, supported by thirty-two-pound Navy carriage guns likely made at Wilkinson's own New Willey works, had dislodged the American militia from Breed's Hill. In London, Parliament was busy hiring twenty-nine thousand Hessian troops to work its idiotic will—a vastly foolish undertaking, in

Wilkinson's estimation: a squandering of blood among Englishmen that would lead inevitably to war with France. It was all avoidable with enlightened policies. But good for the iron trade. Yes indeed. And Wilkinson hoped to capitalize on the senseless slaughter while it lasted— for he knew what Marchant de la Houlière was after. And, for all the politeness, Wilkinson knew himself to be as filled with bloody designs as any painted savage.

Houlière had been sent by the French government to find out why British guns were outperforming the French.

"Our guns," the Frenchman said with a flare of those delicate hands, "go *poof!*" He shook his head. "And on the deck of a ship, amongst all these sailors crowded together, nothing is so, so—how do you say?—dispiriting."'

Houlière had been introduced by the French ambassador to Matthew Boulton, who hinted in a letter to Wilkinson that their guest's tour might prove beneficial to all concerned. Houlière had already alluded twice to the new armament works that the French were constructing on an island in the river Loire, at Indret, just above Nantes. Pointed references, whose meaning was unclear.

Now, at dinner, the general referred almost playfully to the activities of French privateers sailing from New Orleans. He asked Madame Wilkinson whether she shared Monsieur Boulton's sympathies for the colonists. It was a way, of course, of ascertaining Wilkinson's position. Wilkinson broke in to assure him that Madame Wilkinson had not the slightest understanding of politics but that he himself shared Boulton's sympathies, being a liberal and believing in Liberty, as long as it did not come too close to home.

Houlière applauded this sentiment, which reassured Wilkinson that his guest possessed, under that ridiculous wig with its intricate cascade of glossy sable curls pranked out in magenta ribbons, a brain as freethinking as his own. Never had he met such a cynical fellow. Yesterday, while touring the Works, the Frenchman had referred haughtily to his own monarch, Louis XVI, as "that little cunt." Wilkinson concealed his surprise. Wilkinson's brother, who had come from Bersham, hooted aloud (revealing his lack of sophistication), and

Houlière had rewarded him with a rich chuckle. Now, in the presence of a lady, Houlière was solicitous and courtly—half woman himself, like that species of New World lizard that changes color according to whatever leaf it sits upon.

Although neither man spoke directly of the likelihood that their two nations would be drawn once again into the fatal embrace of war, their exchange was spiced with the contest of cultures.

"Madame Wilkinson," said Marchant de la Houlière, "you must prevail on your husband to carry you to Paris. Your daughter is studying in France, no? So you will have two reasons, for it is worth the journey to see Beaumarchais's *Le Barbier de Seville.*"

Mary Lee glanced at her husband, as though for permission; but it seemed to him that her eyes slid past his too quickly.

Houlière leaned toward her. "There is so much in Paris to do and see. The new *restaurants.* You have not such in London, I think. Only these chophouses, is that not so? And the theatre!" He went on in tones unctuous and conniving.

Mary Lee chuckled, tipping her head in a manner that Wilkinson found unfamiliar. Or, rather, too familiar. Her laced bodice exposed the tops of her breasts, of which the left sported a beauty spot he had not noticed before.

"I beg to disagree, sir," Wilkinson interjected before his wife could respond inanely. "We have Goldsmith. Have you seen *She Stoops to Conquer?*"

"Ah yes," said Houlière. "But such a pity, Monsieur Wilkinson." He clucked mournfully.

"A pity?"

"So sad. The death of Goldsmith."

"Dead?" said Wilkinson. "Goldsmith?"

"Yes, yes, yes. A great loss. He was so, how do you say, so genial!"

This information jarred Wilkinson—not because he cared a fig for Goldsmith but because he did not wish to appear uninformed. "Sheridan," he said stubbornly, stabbing at his plate. "Sheridan is among the greatest."

"Ah yes, Sheridan." Houlière's lips curled indulgently. "Sheridan is so, so, so French."

Mary Lee laughed with him at this, snapping open her ivory fan and leaning forward. Beauty spot, indeed. She was not acting her age. Wilkinson rang for the next course. The maids took away their plates and brought out new ones laden with quail encircled by their own eggs in alternation with brandied cherries.

"But Madame Wilkinson," purred the Frenchman, "you will see for yourself, no? Your husband makes my point exactly. London is not Paris!"

These attentions to the hostess were intended of course to flatter the host; but they smacked of that infuriating French assumption that Englishmen do not understand women. The ironmaster attacked his quail so noisily that Houlière abruptly abandoned the arts for the sciences—expressing his admiration for what he called "that happy wedding" between philosophy and practicality that he observed in England, and whose absence he lamented in his own country.

"But what of Cugnot's steam traction engine?" Wilkinson demanded with a crooked smile. " 'Twas French genius that first put a steam engine on wheels. Two of them in fact! One for each wheel!"

Coloring, Houlière hastily set down his wine. "A disaster! For the military and for steam! An attempt made too soon! Cugnot's truck was a—a—monstrous waste of government money! It consumed a ton of coal to travel a few feet, and a child was killed."

"Ah, but 'twas a brilliant failure, was it not?"

Houlière grimaced. "I fear that it—how do you say?—put steam enginery in retard by twenty years."

Wilkinson chuckled, pleased now to be found defending the French from the French. "But of course," he could not resist adding, "the problem with the Cugnot engine is that, lacking a separate condenser, it had to build terrific pressure and then proceed all in one great fart." He leapt from his chair, lifted his coattails, and pretended to break wind.

Houlière was aghast. Mary Lee glared at her husband from behind her fan. Sitting down, Wilkinson rang for more wine and, as it was being poured, spoke with the greatest solemnity. " 'Tis true," he told the Frenchman, "to be first with a novelty can cost one dear. I myself prefer to go second."

"But you, sir, were first with the machine to bore cannon from the solid."

Wilkinson responded as modestly as he could under the circumstances. He remembered with what eagerness Houlière had tried to examine the cannon-boring machine more closely, so that Wilkinson was obliged to bar his way with his cane—politely—and a reference to the possibility of some agreement between them. Ha! Let the *monsieur* court his wife, for all his foppish curls and padded stockings. It was he, John Wilkinson, a bluff-spoken, beef-eating, English ironmaster, who possessed what the French desired.

The next day, Wilkinson took Marchant de la Houlière across the river to Coalbrookdale, impressing on him that while Darby's was the biggest ironworks in the world, it was not so far advanced as New Willey. From the horse ferry, he described the bridge that was to span the gorge—thanks to his planning, although Darby would provide most of the money.

" 'Twill be a hundred feet long or more," he boasted, "and made entirely of cast iron."

Houlière marveled at this. The grizzled ferryman, whose name was Danny Day, glared as he leaned against the tiller.

Proceeding in the gig, they found Darby standing outside his house with some workmen and a woman whom he introduced as Mrs. Foster, his electrical consultant. To Wilkinson's surprise, it was the same young woman who had greeted him a couple of times at the door. He had taken her for a mere housemaid, but she was now supervising a workman attaching a braided copper wire to an iron stake. What would Priestley make of this, Wilkinson wondered to himself. A female electrician!

The copper wire, Darby explained, led to one of four lightning conductors that this Maggie Foster had installed at each corner of the double-gabled roof. At Darby's invitation, Mrs. Foster herself explained the principle on which they worked.

Houlière was quite taken both by the lightning conductors, which were similar to those being erected in France (the French of course preferring the pointed ends recommended by Dr. Franklin), and by the lady.

"Do you mean to say that *you* climbed up there?" he asked incredulously.

She smiled a dazzling smile. "With a ladder."

"But how—?" He looked at her full dress.

Darby chuckled. "She wore a riding habit."

"Ah," said Houlière, but he was still perplexed.

Wilkinson prevailed on Darby to show them Pritchard's sketches of the bridge. And while the Frenchman and the lady discussed them in some detail, Wilkinson took Darby aside and assured himself that Darby did plan to travel to London next month, as they had discussed, in order to petition for the act of Parliament required for the bridge.

After obtaining Darby's permission to show his guest briefly through the Works, they bade farewell to Darby and Mrs. Foster and proceeded down the dale, Houlière all the while ejaculating over the singular impression that Mrs. Foster had made on him.

"*Mademoiselle l'électricienne est très belle! Mon Dieu!*" He kissed his bunched fingertips. "Those eyes! Those teeth! And she says she is a widow!" He went on in this fashion, and ended by inquiring, "What is this *riding habit?*"

Wilkinson explained it was the latest craze to sweep England. "They are breeches of a sort for ladies to sit a horse in the manner of a man."

"Ah, like the peasant women. But breeches?" Houlière said. "Surely they are not your *ordinaire*—how do you say—farting crackers?"

"Oh no," said Wilkinson. "They are not tight like a gentleman's. They swell out at the top." He traced a shape with his hands.

"Ah." Houlière shook his head in wonder. "French ladies would never consent to such a strange costume." He giggled. "Only in England!"

No accounting for tastes, Wilkinson thought. Houlière himself wore pads under his hose to make his calves appear larger, and high heels and buckles of a sort to catch in a stirrup with possibly fatal consequences. A man might easily give up his life to fashion.

He showed him Darby's cylinder-boring mill, as an example of the inferior kind, and took the opportunity to mention in passing that James Watt had declared Wilkinson's new cylinder-boring machine a work of genius.

The Frenchman, however, kept returning to their encounter with Mrs. Foster. "This bridge," he said after some further reflection. "She believes it will triumph the Romans."

"Surpass them. Yes. Quite so. The Romans for all their skill had the poorest iron and never learned to cast it. They lacked the blast furnace, you see."

"Ah, but she had another point. She said with iron you can—how do you say?—eliminate the Roman arch."

Wilkinson frowned. He himself believed in the classical forms: Greek columns, Roman arches. But as his companion babbled on, the ironmaster privately relished the thought of Mrs. Foster in her riding habit scampering about like a monkey.

# Abraham Darby III

He invited Maggie to see the old account books, which went back to his grandfather's time. Immediately upon entering his office, she sat on the floor to peruse first one ledger and then another, her skirts spread around her, and he joined her—the two of them sitting in that childlike fashion.

She showed herself surprisingly knowledgeable, exclaiming over certain entries and asking questions. She insisted she wanted to know every detail of the operation, so that she could be more useful as a consultant. He was delighted at her interest. Her hands, spread on the pages, were as long as his but more finely tapered. He had come to trust the skill of those hands. He liked watching them.

Tomorrow he would leave for London, to engage a solicitor and begin other arrangements for the bridge. He would miss her, he realized. The realization came as a surprise.

He showed her some of his favorite entries, and how the writing could be distinguished. Here in the first ledger was Grandfather's careful script, faded to brown. Here, the clerk's. And in the next volume was Richard Ford's, taking over when Grandfather died in 1717.

And here, beginning in the 1730s, were his father's entries. By the end of that decade, Ford's hand appeared only rarely and with obvious labor.

She smiled. "You've obviously spent some time with these."

He nodded. "I like it better than making iron." He blurted it out without thinking, and realized it was true. "What I mean is, 'tis all part of ironmaking. The keeping of records."

She smiled again. "And it gives you pleasure."

"Yes," he admitted. "But 'tis all necessary."

She laughed. "What could be better? To take pleasure in what is necessary!"

He did not know whether to smile. In truth he felt guilty about the hours he spent perusing these old records and gazing dreamily at the furnace through the wavy panes of glass. Idle moments. And Maggie's laughter excited a sensation in his stomach not unlike what he felt when Becky Smith clutched his arm to cross a mud puddle. A dangerous, rippling sensation, but also very pleasurable. He was aware of their being alone together, sitting in this childlike way on the floor, her head inches from his.

Maggie loosened her bonnet and fluffed out her curls. Coming from a man, some of her questions might have seemed insolent. One query especially startled him:

"Did the Dale Company ever make cannon?"

"Why dost thou ask?" He felt alarm.

"When you were sick, I read *Robinson Crusoe* and noticed that his wrecked ship had carried six guns. And the ship that rescued him was also armed. Anyway, knowing Defoe was inspired by the Goldney ships, I wondered."

Abraham confirmed that indeed the Goldney ships had been armed. "The early ships," he somehow felt it necessary to add.

"Not the later ones? The ones trading in the West Indies?"

Reluctantly, he admitted that those too were armed. "Only for defense. They did not sail under letters of marque." He reached for one of the daybooks, hoping to interest her in the early inventories. " 'Tis not something we like to talk about."

"So." She smiled impishly. "Did the Dale Company make cannon, or not?"

Abraham's heart gave a thud. It was long ago, he reminded himself. "Yes. Briefly. Richard Ford made cannon at Coalbrookdale, but only for three or four years. How long exactly I cannot say, because that ledger is missing."

"Missing?"

"Yes. The volume for the 1740s. It has been missing ever since I can remember. All for the best, I suppose. None of us likes to think of cannon being made here at Coalbrookdale. Still, I would examine it if I could." He searched her eyes for some hint of malice but could not fathom those agate depths.

And now another question came to her lips. "How—if you don't mind my asking—how did it happen? The cannon making?"

He took a deep breath. "The Goldneys began selling cannon to merchant ships during the war with Spain. And then, owning a majority of shares in Coalbrookdale, they pressed Richard Ford to make cannon at Coalbrookdale." He felt an old flare of anger. Anger at Ford as much as at the Goldneys. "They brought some wooden cannon patterns up from Bristol by barge in January of 1740. Soon after that, Richard Ford began making cannon for profit."

What he could not convey in words was how, despite all this having happened before he was born, the knowledge of it cut to the center of his being. Why hadn't Ford stood up to the Goldneys? Abraham frowned at the floor. His face was hot.

"Your father—"

"My father put a stop to it the moment he took over from Ford!"

Her cool fingertips touched his hand. "Abraham, I'm sorry. I can see this is . . . I only meant to say that your father must have found it very painful."

*Why dost thou ask so many questions?* He almost shouted it aloud. But after a moment's reflection in silence he realized she was making no accusations. Her green eyes were full of sympathy.

"Yes," he agreed. "Please understand, Father was in his middle age, but Ford still had charge of the Works."

Perhaps she would stop now, seeing his discomfort. But his own questions continued to resonate in his mind, now that she had stirred them up. Father had gone along with the cannon making for that brief time. Was it to spare Ford? Mother did not like talking about it. When the subject came up, she would talk only of the goodness of Christ in Father's breast and the swiftness with which he put a stop to the cannon making once he was in charge.

Alone, he might have prayed. Now that Maggie had declared herself Convinced and been admitted into Madeley Meeting, he might have suggested that they give themselves over to silent prayer. Instead, he got up from the floor, walked over to the window, and looked out at the flames leaping from the furnace head as the fillers dumped their loads.

He wished he knew his heart better, and wished that he were not so alone. Whatever trials Father had undergone, however incomplete Abraham's own understanding of the Darby legacy, the burden was his to bear. His brother was little help. Samuel was in fact part of the burden, lacking the steadiness to make an ironmaster. Samuel was best off in the Dale Company's London office, as Richard suggested. Most of the arrangements were made. To Abraham, as usual, would fall the duties of governing the whole. To him, the burden of debt. And now the bridge. Sometimes the burden was the only thing that felt real.

Finally he spoke, without turning to face Maggie, and was surprised at the calm in his voice. He was speaking as much to himself as to her. "I fancy that I am doing it for him. For my father. Buying out the Goldney shares in Coalbrookdale." As he said this, he could feel Father's presence in the room. *For thee,* he thought. *I am doing it for thee.* He imagined the dark greatcoat. Father's voice: *That is good, Abraham. That is good.* Behind him, the rustle of skirts and Maggie's soothing voice.

"That's good, Abraham."

The words brought a soaring in his brow, yet he did not turn to face her. The furnace was a blur. He longed for the cool, unbidden touch of her hand once more, yet he could not will himself to turn and face her. He stood stiffly, arms folded tightly across his chest. What was he afraid of? Finally, he felt it. The touch on his shoulder, like an answered prayer, sent a shudder through him.

"That's good, Abraham," she whispered. "That's really good."

Why was his stomach a ball of ice? He was relieved to hear her go back to the ledgers. Relieved and disappointed.

Later, when they were walking home from the Works, Maggie turned to him. "Where do you suppose the missing ledger could be?"

As though *she* might find it! Vain creature! And yet she stirred hope. "I have searched everywhere," said Abraham. "And Richard has searched at Horsehay and Ketley. Mother supposes it was burned in a fire." No, he had given up on it. But as they continued walking up the orchard path, past the ripening apples, he tried to think where else indeed he might look, upon his return from London.

# John Wilkinson

After entertaining Brigadier General Marchant de la Houlière
for a fortnight and observing his guest's interests, Wilkinson
realized that he, Wilkinson, possessed not merely the boring machine
but something more elusive and more magical—the very gleam of
Progress.

The French, for all their science, had always lagged behind the
English in practical ways. Isaac Wilkinson used to say that if the silly
*monsieurs* ever left off their fiddling and dancing and turned to industry, Englishmen would shake in their boots. As it was, for a nation
about to go to war with England, the French were at a terrible dis-
advantage: short of charcoal and ignorant of how to fire with coke.

Wilkinson played on all this. After taking the Frenchman to
Horsehay and showing him Reynolds's great pumping-engine, whose
cylinder weighed five and a half tons, he observed that the castings for
the bridge would likely be heavier. The bridge had captured the
Frenchman's imagination. Wilkinson wished he had a model to show
him. He resolved to badger Darby on the matter.

At Brymbo, the farm he owned near Bersham, Wilkinson showed

off the latest principles of modern agriculture: fields limed and drained, pastures planted with Dutch clover, improved breeds of cattle, a horse-powered threshing machine. The officer scribbled notes in the little notebook he carried in his waistcoat pocket and seemed planet-struck by everything he saw.

From Bersham they traveled east to the river Trent, to visit Josiah Wedgwood's modern pottery works. It was during this leg of the journey, driving past fields of ripe grain, that the Frenchman finally came forth with his proposal.

The French government wished to obtain Wilkinson's help in building the new arsenal at Indret. Wilkinson would be paid a handsome salary and provided with a home on the river Loire for the two years for which his presence would be required.

It was a handsome offer. While Wilkinson pretended to consider it, Houlière sweetened it with the suggestion that a mistress might be provided in the bargain. They spent a pleasant mile discussing the qualities desirable in a mistress: shapely limbs, sound teeth, sweet breath, firm breasts. She must be clever but not too clever, coquettish and yet discreet, and she must not interfere with one's life. But when this game was played out, Wilkinson assured his guest that he had wealth and women aplenty, that what he needed was contracts. Volume contracts.

He explained his reasoning, while the other man listened intently. As the day was warm and dusty, they agreed to remove their wigs. The Frenchman's head was shaved; he looked smaller, older, almost wizened. Wilkinson's own naked scalp dried in the breeze. He spoke candidly of the information he possessed which he might sell dear, much as a grocer offers prize truffles. But the iron business, he said, depended on volume. And for a works such as New Willey, whose supply of water was limited, the volume must be in more profitable finished goods—hollow castings as opposed to flat—which might fetch eight pounds per ton or better.

Wilkinson glanced at his companion to make sure he was following. The Frenchman looked up from grooming his wig, which lay in his lap—his fingers nimbly combing the road dust from its locks with a little ivory comb and retying the ribbons—the mass of floppy curls looking disconcertingly like a lap dog. The ironmaster went on to his next point.

"Hollow castings in the retail trade means mostly pots. However, the Quakers have locked onto the hollowware trade so tight, 'tis hard to prize them loose."

"But surely, Monsieur Wilkinson," interrupted Houlière, "you do not aspire to cast pots!" He snickered.

"My father was a pot founder."

"An honorable calling, monsieur. But, but—"

"My point is simply that the Dale Company, after three generations, has got its hooks in every Midland market town from Liverpool to Bristol—all by hard work, thrift, and honesty, to be sure. But they leave no room for others!"

"Such as yourself."

"Such as anyone!"

"Ah, so you intend to—"

Wilkinson snorted. "I intend nothing of the kind. I mean only to suggest that, through no fault of my own, cannon are my hollowware!" He scowled at the road ahead, presenting a profile he fancied as noble as an emperor's on an old Roman coin. "Make no mistake, my friend. John Wilkinson is an armsmaker, first and foremost. And proud of it. But 'tis the only course open to him, thanks to the Quakers. 'Tis a path pursued from a sense of duty."

"Well put, monsieur! Bravo! Someone must pursue it. If not you, then—" Marchant de la Houlière shrugged.

"Exactly. The Russians or the Spanish. The Quakers themselves, if their beliefs did not restrain them!"

"But of course!" Houlière clapped his hands with delight. "It is so profitable!"

"So," said Wilkinson. "As a military man, you understand the problems facing me."

"Yes, yes. Of course."

Wilkinson smiled patronizingly. The truth was quite the opposite. Military men, actually, were fools in the marketplace. Having a bottomless purse at their disposal, they wanted the best new toy regardless of cost. And they were as stubborn as they were impractical: the Ordnance Board had taken decades to acknowledge the advantages of iron cannon over bronze, decades more to accept coke in place of charcoal.

Wilkinson went on to make his point. The great impediment he faced as an armsmaker was fluctuating demand. At the moment, he could scarcely keep up with cannon orders. "The admirals are all insisting on the new solid-bored guns!" He chuckled, knowing that Houlière was salivating. "However, what if I were to invest in more cannon-boring machines? Give up engine castings and make cannon exclusively? Why, then I should be more captive than ever to the caprices of war!"

"I see. Of course." The Frenchman jotted in his notebook, bald head nodding. "It is a trap."

Waiting for him to finish scribbling, Wilkinson went on to observe that once demand for the new solid-bored cannon was satisfied, then it too would fall prey to the vicissitudes of the market that plagued the armsmaker.

"What is needed," chuckled Houlière, "is permanent war."

Wilkinson smiled grimly. The general had intended it facetiously; but this was the very concept that had begun to take shape in Wilkinson's mind after the Seven Years War ended and iron prices began to decline. "I am convinced, my friend," said Wilkinson, "that in a future run by businessmen, this is exactly where 'tis all headed. Permanent War."

"Businessmen would want this?" Houlière raised an eyebrow, uncertain whether Wilkinson was continuing the jest.

"It would be sold, of course, in the usual way."

"Sold?"

"As always sold. In the guise of patriotism and religion. Keeping the world safe for honest trade. Christianizing the heathen. All that rot."

"But—but the bloodshed!" Houlière stared at him in dismay, his forehead wrinkled back to the crown of his head.

At that moment they crested a hill and were suddenly looking down on Stoke-on-Trent, the smoke of its potteries rising in magnificent columns. Wilkinson stopped long enough for his guest to admire it.

This done, Houlière returned to their original theme. "We shall find something for you, Monsieur Wilkinson. Volume contracts. Something to your liking."

"Splendid. I should like to do business with you. In all candor, however, I must tell you I have been approached by others." As he said this, it did not seem to him a lie—for eventually it would be true.

"Others?" The Frenchman donned his wig.

"Oh yes."

"The Russians? Prince Potemkin?"

Wilkinson gave a noncommittal shrug. "I fear I have already spoken too candidly, my friend."

Peering into a pocket mirror, Houlière powdered his face. "What if we order cannon, an order so large it would take you years to complete?"

"Ah, I fear we do not have years. Our nations are close to war. We are but a heartbeat away from an embargo on military goods."

"So. So! We must find something else!"

At last the Frenchman had grasped the point. As they drove into Etruria, Wedgwood's new industrial village completed two years ago, Wilkinson pointed to the workers' row cottages and the pottery kilns all laid out in a neat plan. The most modern village in the world.

Houlière admired the ceramics displayed outside Wedgwood's office, the embossed Grecian figures with flawlessly even borders and blue backgrounds that he said were all the rage in Paris. "Not because they are original," he explained, "but because—how do you say?—this *copie exacte*? Every one so precisely the same! So like a machine!"

Josiah Wedgwood beamed upon hearing this flattery. A cherubic man precisely dressed in a blue-and-white waistcoat, he resembled one of his own porcelain cups, his wooden leg painted in the same blue-and-white scene. He was being assisted that day by his old friend and family physician, Dr. Erasmus Darwin, who was helping design a horizontal windmill for grinding flints. Darwin shambled forward to greet them; he was a great bear of a fellow, with rumpled clothing, an old scratch wig tied up in a little bobtail, and a pocked face nearly buried in his sloping shoulders. Wilkinson had met him only once, at a meeting of the Lunar Society in which Darwin had demonstrated a clever talking machine that he had constructed in response to a challenge from Matthew Boulton. The thing had a wooden jaw, leather lips, and the larynx of a goose, so that when a bellows was squeezed, it could utter the words "Mama" and "Papa." This demonstration prompted some hilarity among the Lunatics. Darwin himself seemed much beloved by his fellows. Despite a stammer, the man was said by Priestley to possess a graceful, flowing wit.

"Mr. Wilkinson! Boulton tells me you have bored a p-p-perfect cylinder for our estimable colleague Watt."

Wilkinson was gratified by the warmth of this greeting, although annoyed that Watt should have found favor so quickly in the Lunar Society himself.

After they had taken the Frenchman through the potteries—where Houlière admired the mechanization of slip making and glaze grinding, and the scores of craftsmen sitting on identical stools—Darwin, at Wedgwood's insistence, showed off his specially built chaise, which was outfitted with a skylight and little compartments for books, eyeglasses, and sweets. "My next one," said Darwin, with a wink for Wilkinson, "shall be p-p-powered by steam!"

They ended up at a public house called the Wayward Crow, where they took a table by a window in an alcove framed by dark timbers and white plaster. Houlière was prevailed upon to talk about Rousseau and other French philosophers whose liberal ideas appealed to "some of us," as Wedgwood put it, with a wink that included Wilkinson. While the Frenchman extemporized as engagingly as he could on the state of philosophy in France, the three portly Englishmen attacked the cheeses and tongue and rolls set before them.

Houlière's account consisted chiefly of gossip, ranging from the Paris salons to Diderot's exile in The Hague to the ménage à trois in which the decrepit Rousseau, his wealthy benefactress, and her husband were said to disport themselves in scanty peasant garb.

Erasmus Darwin cocked his shaggy head. "Is it fair to conclude then, sir, that Rousseau's democratic ideas are g-g-gaining acceptance?"

The Frenchman chuckled. "Among the intellectuals, yes."

"But what of the Bourbon court?" asked Wedgwood, in his earnestness missing the irony. "Do you see any sign of the new principles of Democracy being accepted at Versailles?"

Houlière, who had finally managed to get a morsel of cheese into his mouth, shook his head no.

"But they are living in a world of dreams, sir!" declared Wedgwood. "Can they not see the peasants will one day rebel, as they did in Bohemia?"

"As indeed our own c-c-colonists have thrown off the yoke of tyranny!" Darwin raised his glass in salute.

They all raised their glasses: "To Liberty!" Wilkinson glanced around the room, apprehensively catching the landlord's eye.

Houlière, draining his glass, tore a piece of bread from the loaf. "In France, always there is talk and nothing else. Everyone discusses the need for change, but nothing changes. Everyone sees the *tragédie* unfolding, but always they talk, talk, talk. In the end, I fear it will be very bloody."

Wedgwood nodded. "Thank God, in England, for the constitutional monarchy."

They all fell silent. Wilkinson reflected on the mob of sailors that had rioted a few days ago in Liverpool, against cuts in wages. The sailors had broken every window in the Merchants Exchange and threatened it with a cannon before the Royal Horseguard arrived. He shuddered. For a moment he fancied a mob outside his own door, blowing horns, beating on pots and pans. He saw himself perspiring at the head of the stairs behind a three-inch swivel gun doublecharged with scattershot, a brace of pistols at the ready. He was startled from this fantasy by Wedgwood's inquiring after his daughter's studies in France.

"Mary returns this autumn," said the ironmaster. "My friend the

General de la Houlière is trying to persuade me to cross the Channel to meet her, so that we can visit a certain barber in Paris."

"Barber?" asked Wedgwood, puzzled.

"I believe," said Houlière, "that Mr. Wilkinson is referring to a certain barber of Seville."

"Oh ho!" chuckled Wedgwood.

"Gentlemen," said Erasmus Darwin, "I see we are in a p-p-playful mood." Opening his waistcoat widely, the physician exposed several rows of small pockets sewn into its lining. He produced a glass vial and from it poured a pale yellow powder into a spoon. The others watched while he used a miniature pestle to grind this powder, whose Latin name he gave and which he said came from Bengal, from the Nawab of Oudh's royal pharmacy. From another vial he added a small amount of "dried essence of neckweed, or *Cannabis sativa.*" Finally he added a pinch of ordinary snuff and mixed it all thoroughly. After inhaling a pinch and pronouncing it satisfactory, he offered it around. He called it a "temporary humour elevator" and cautioned them to refrain, if they could, from sneezing.

Wilkinson regarded the mixture curiously. It smelled strange. But seeing Darwin smile expectantly from the other end of the table, the ironmaster put aside his doubts, took a generous pinch onto his thumbnail, and snuffed it powerfully.

When they were done sneezing, Darwin recited a poem of his, a humorous composition about amorous plants. They applauded mightily.

"And what of the iron bridge, Mr. Wilkinson?" asked Darwin. "Have you any news?"

"Good news! Good news!" cried the ironmaster. "Young Darby is about to take the bill to Parliament." Was he talking more shrilly than usual? The room seemed strangely quiet, adrift in time. How many minutes had elapsed since he had spoken? Then he observed something he had never seen before. A subtle light emanating from his nose. And as he looked into the faces of his three companions, he saw the same glow issuing from their noses. By Jupiter! Was it possible he was detecting a phenomenon hitherto unknown?

"Gentlemen," he whispered, struck by a giddy sensation of what it must be like to stand in the shoes of a Newton or a Galileo. "Gentlemen, I am engaged in the most profound observation." The Frenchman was listing in his chair; Wedgwood's mouth hung open; Darwin leered like a crocodile. "Pray, mark my nose, and take note of anything exceptional." Wilkinson looked at each man keenly.

Darwin leaned forward. "It appears to be the expected nose."

Wedgwood cleared his throat hesitantly. "It has a wart, sir. But you surely know."

*They are as blind as bats!* Wilkinson thought. *Or I alone have the faculty of perception.* He turned to Houlière.

The Frenchman shrugged. "It is an English nose."

"Hark," said Wilkinson, impatiently. "Observe, if you can, an extraordinary manifestation issuing from it."

They leaned across the table to peer more closely.

"A luminescence," Wilkinson declared, when they continued to look mystified, the oafs. "An effulgence of malleable light."

"Yes! Yes!" Wedgwood exploded into raptures. " 'Tis lit up like a jack-o'-lantern!"

"You do see it then!"

Wedgwood nodded wildly, bereft of speech, tears running down his cheeks.

Wilkinson declared he should write an account for the Royal Society. Darwin, however, began to propound a more sober view, based on Hume's principles of Cause and Effect, which they were all finally led to accept: (1) the phenomenon had to do with the afternoon sunlight entering the window opposite, and (2) they were all inebriated, if not to the extremity produced by nitrous oxide, then to the distortion of their reason.

"I feel like dancing," said Houlière, abruptly standing. "But not the minuet. Perhaps what they dance in darkest Barbados." He gyrated languidly.

Wilkinson sat perfectly still, clutching the iron ball of his cane and feeling the juices of his palm tingle against the warm, pitted surface, a galvanic dialogue between flesh and iron. Wedgwood was babbling about glazes. Darwin sat with his eyes closed. Houlière meanwhile danced a slow bagatelle beside his chair, rocking his pelvis suggestively and mouthing soft, rhythmic sounds:

*bum-bum-bee-dum deedee-BUMdee-bum*
*bum-bum-bee-dum deedee-BUMdee-bum*

Finally Wilkinson, remembering the original subject of his discourse, lifted his cane and banged it smartly on the floor. Everyone's eyes flew open. "Gentlemen, we were speaking of the iron bridge."

"Quite right." Houlière lowered himself into his seat.

Wilkinson leaned over the table and waggled his eyebrows. "Iron!" he whispered, and sat back. "Pray, let us weigh the implications of building a large object with cast iron."

"In general," asked Darwin, "or in p-p-particular?"

"Let us say in general."

"The *idea* then, of a l-l-large object."

"Quite."

"Good, good," said Darwin, tipping his scratch wig askew and hunching forward eagerly, as though he were sitting down to a game of chess. "And by large, what d-do you intend?"

Wilkinson was enjoying this. "Large, let us say, even by the standards normally applied to stone or timber."

"*Any* large object?" asked Wedgwood. He proposed several large structures, to which the others added examples. Lighthouses. Canal locks. Barges. Even churches. All could be fashioned from iron.

"But let us return to the *idea* of very large objects, or structures, c-cast in iron," said Darwin, "for I suspect that our friend Mr. Wilkinson has a rather more interesting p-p-p-point in mind."

"Indeed so." Wilkinson returned his cryptic smile. Two great minds at work here. In actual fact, he had hoped Darwin would come up with something. He gazed around at the other two men, as if he and Erasmus Darwin shared an amusing secret.

Houlière was first to speak. "It will be a test, this large object."

"Quite so," agreed Wedgwood. "If it succeeds, 'twill increase the demand for like structures."

"If it fails," countered Houlière, "it will be a disaster, no?" Doubtless he was thinking of the Cugnot affair.

Wedgwood was undaunted. "Assuming it succeeds, it will be a powerful advertisement for the new age."

Darwin cocked his head. "The Age of Reason?"

"I had in mind the Age of the Machine," said Wedgwood.

Houlière chuckled. "They are one and the same."

"How can you say that?" demanded Wedgwood. "Do you mean to suggest that Aristotle and Plato were engineers?"

"*Oui, oui!* Precisely. Plato and the steam engine, they are going—how do you say?—down the same turnpike!"

Wilkinson voiced wild approval. Heads turned at other tables. He was screaming, he realized.

"If what we have said is true," said Darwin, ignoring Wilkinson's outburst and Wedgwood's disgruntlement, "then it follows that this very *largeness* will put a singular stamp on the new age, whatever we choose to c-c-call it."

"Are you forgetting the pyramids of Egypt?" cried Wedgwood. "Or St. Paul's cathedral?"

"Excellent point, Josiah." Darwin patted his friend's arm.

"Nonsense!" Wilkinson sneered. "The pyramids were constructed of stone! A natural material! A God-made material, if ye will. The bridge shall be the first built of a material made by Man!"

Wedgwood whirled on him. "But we are discussing largeness!"

For the most fleeting instant Wilkinson pictured the iron knob of his cane smashing deep into Wedgwood's skull. "Come now, Mr. Wedgwood," he said cheerfully, "can we not entertain both attributes at once, that the object in question should be both large and made of cast iron?"

"A noble thought," declared Darwin. "For as the cathedrals advertised Stone and God, so shall the new bridge advertise Iron and Man."

Houlière proposed a toast to the bridge, that it might exceed the achievements of ancient Rome. He proposed a second toast to the female electrician whom they had met at Darby's.

"Female electrician?" Darwin cocked his shaggy head, whereupon Wilkinson and Houlière exclaimed at length over Mrs. Foster's learning in matters electrical.

Wedgwood chuckled. "Ye jest, surely! To understand electricity requires higher powers of reasoning than those found in the female brain."

Darwin disagreed with his friend, citing the botanical drawings of Maria Sibylla Merian, who rendered the lives of certain plants and insects in the most exquisite detail, her work surpassing that of any man.

They proceeded then to argue over what constituted Reason. But a torpor fell over them, and Wilkinson, looking at his watch, announced that he and Houlière must begin their journey back to Broseley.

After what seemed like hours of driving, each man lost in his own thoughts, Wilkinson, dozing at the reins, was startled awake by the Frenchman seizing his arm and repeating a single word excitedly.

"*Tuyaux! Tuyaux!*"

"Hold!" Wilkinson croaked. "Good heavens, man!" The mare had settled into a walk, with the setting sun spread bloody red across the sky. Flicking the reins, Wilkinson urged her into a trot. "Where are we?"

"Alas, I do not know."

The fool was little help. They must find a place to spend the night.

Houlière sighed explosively. "Ah! How do you say it in English, these *tuyaux*? These—ah!" He waved his hands helplessly.

Wilkinson's mouth was parched, his nostrils dry. A flock of sheep standing under an oak looked sinister, their black noses reminding him of the masks worn by highwaymen. What was the Frenchman babbling about?

"*Tuyaux!* Ah! Do you know *conduites d'eau?*"

"Water pipes?"

"Yes, yes! Water pipes!"

Yawning, the ironmaster listened to his companion babble about how the Périer brothers were redesigning the old gravity-fed Paris waterworks with a system requiring more pressure in the pipes. "These

Périer brothers, they shall employ the newest methods, using pumps and reservoirs. They must replace the old wooden pipes. So there you have it! You, Monsieur Wilkinson—you can make large cast-iron water pipes, can you not?"

"Of course!"

"Voilà! These are the hollow castings you wish, no?"

"How many pipes do they require?"

"How many?" The Frenchman laughed, flinging his arms into the soft summer twilight. "They need *forty miles!*"

Wilkinson whipped the mare to a gallop. "General de la Houlière," he yelled, "you are a genius!"

# Abraham Darby III

From the moment he stepped off the stagecoach onto the cobblestones of St. Paul's Church Yard—Paul's Yard, as Quakers preferred to call it—Abraham was distracted as always by the bold tempo of London, the vainglorious fashions. Wooden French heels, painted bright red, went clicking past, with ladies' wigs as tall as grenadiers' hats; enormous wheels of phaetons rolled by, mounted on springs so absurdly high as to require a ladder to climb into them; and shopwindows were filled with earthly temptations, which he had to keep reminding himself he did not need. Eyes alert, he held his purse snug to his breast. Gawking, he was nearly run over by a coach-and-eight arriving on the heels of the *Diligence.* He was accosted by peddlers and by punks in soiled laces, jostled by chairmen, and pros-elytized by a ragged, wild-eyed man reeking of lavender and rum, who took a swipe at his hat and declared himself the last of the Ranters. "We know God by our sin!" the man cried, whirling in circles.

Abraham reminded himself he was here on business: to obtain a solicitor to shepherd through Parliament the act that would authorize the bridge. All the same, he lingered outside a famous trunk maker's shop to admire a portmanteau with little drawers trimmed in calfskin and silver. He walked inside, smelled the new leather, and toyed with the idea of replacing the valise he was carrying. It had belonged to his father.

In a bay window he saw a pair of silver sleeve buttons that made him think of Maggie Foster and Becky Smith. He considered purchasing them—sixteen shillings—but could not decide for which lady. Plain oval buttons. Still, a dangerous touch of luxury! Flushed at the thought, he moved on, caught up again in the crackling rhythm of the city.

The Lloyds were expecting him. Resolving not to tarry further, he followed Ludgate Street past the Bull's Head Coffee House. Laughter inside. A gathering place for Freemasons and Druids, it was said. He crossed the stone bridge that spanned Fleet Ditch. To the right loomed Fleet Prison; to the left, the waterfront, with the new Black Friars Bridge and the masts of ships filigreed like lace against the broad Thames. The smell of sewage mingled with coal smoke in the damp September air. Abraham thought of the Ranter whirling about on the cobblestones, denouncing "stinking chastity." He pictured Rebecca Smith's pale smooth brow and the almost giddy way she had clutched his arm on her last visit—unnecessarily, he was tempted to say. Yes, it was the very unnecessariness of it that excited him—the insistent pressure of her fingers affecting him like some mysterious perfume.

And Maggie Foster. Her endless questions. Eyes like green agate pouring forth the inquiring energy of her mind. The purposefulness of her long strides. Her voice freighted with meaning, firm and delicate. *That's good, Abraham.*

None of them reasoned, the thoughts tumbled through him: the fragrances, the poised limbs, the magic. Until he saw those sleeve buttons, he would not have supposed himself in any turmoil—although it was true that during the coach ride both women's faces kept coming to mind. The heaps of golden corn made him think of Becky's hair, her tinkling laughter. Maggie's hand on his shoulder. These secret thoughts occupied him dreamily the whole journey. The pleasurable feeling in his stomach worked its way downward, where, to his dismay—the coach being crowded—the mischievous flesh began to gambol and strain. He kept his coat on his lap, listened to the fat merchant snoring next to him, watched the woman with two young children sitting beside a pock-faced draper with a bolt of calico standing between his knees, and tried to turn his thoughts to the divine Spirit or, failing that, to the business of obtaining a solicitor. Still, he would not have called it agitation, that merry seesawing between two faces (the women's other, hidden parts he tried not to imagine). It was only now, caught up in the noisy tumult of the city, walking along Fleet Street and thinking of the sleeve buttons, that he felt it all shifting into new complications like a cat's cradle. Maggie's voice echoing Father's: *That's good, Abraham.* The sense of being laid open, exposed. Why could he not bring himself to turn and face her? Was he ashamed? And if ashamed, was it from feeling exposed or from his own yearning?

He did not know.

And was it the boldness of her questions that had taken him so deep within himself?

The missing ledger came to mind. Of all the old ledgers, it was the one that would offer a glimpse of Father taking over the reins from the dying Ford, ceasing to make cannon, and beginning the great expansion of Coalbrookdale—a feat that Abraham could not begin to emulate. His own life seemed but an echo. And yet he had taken over the reins from Richard Reynolds; he had arranged to buy back the Goldney shares; and the bridge would be his own great labor: he could not help but draw a few comparisons.

Was he worthy?

He prayed so.

Suppose he had turned to face her. What then? He might have embraced her. The thought rushed through him like a torrent. But whether his fear was of embracing or being embraced, or feeling so dreadfully exposed, he could not say.

Continuing along Fleet Street, he stopped to admire the instruments displayed in Ramsden's. He admired the telescopes and solar microscopes of polished brass. His attraction to such earthly objects was, he knew, a kind of idolatry. Mixed into this were thoughts of Maggie's tapered fingers handling the pieces of his electrical machine. With an effort he tore himself away and continued to Lombard Street, where the Lloyds and the Barclays had established their Quaker banks within a few doors of each other.

That evening, taking tea with Sampson Lloyd and David Barclay at one end of the Lloyds' parlor, while at the other end a Lloyd daughter played harpsichord for the ladies and children, Abraham asked for advice on choosing a solicitor.

He described the two sides contending on the Bridge Committee: the influential Reverend Harries had put forward his cousin, who practiced law in London, but some titled gentlemen were pushing for a certain Mr. Hamilton. Which side should he avoid offending?

Abraham had supposed that Barclay and Lloyd would counsel him to disregard the titles, all men being equal in the Light. Instead, they recommended that the troublesome Reverend Harries should be brought into line; and as Hamilton practiced law not far away, at Lincoln's Inn Fields, they agreed to send one of the Lloyds' sons with a note requesting an appointment for the next morning.

They also advised Abraham that if he was going to wear his drab Quaker gray, he should at least have a more presentable wig. Barclay loaned him a fine wig made from the hair of Flemish girls and insisted he carry an umbrella—a clever device introduced from Paris and now the rage in London—which Abraham had seen but not used. Barclay instructed him how to open and close it.

Thus equipped, Abraham set off the next morning, the white curls bouncing at the edge of his vision contributing to his sense of being someone else. After meeting with Hamilton and discussing the wording of the act, Abraham walked to Parliament, accompanied by the solicitor, and they met in the lobby with several MPs. At the MPs' suggestion, Abraham stopped also at the Crown and Anchor, on the Strand, where much of the business of Parliament was conducted informally and where he might promote the bridge.

The place was thronged. He ordered a short beer and gravitated to the ambit of one table that was surrounded by spectators and formed a kind of vortex in the hubbub of voices and brown shadows. There in the lamplight he recognized (from their caricatures) Edmund Burke, Pitt the Younger, and Edward Gibbon, all with their rumpled newspapers and long-stemmed pipes, holding forth with great pomposity amidst a cloud of tobacco smoke and surrounded by many anonymous faces that had escaped the illumination of Hogarth's pen. Indeed, there was the cartoonist himself, or some other, scribbling in a dark corner. All that was missing was the balloons engraved over the men's heads containing their words. Abraham could not bring himself to intrude on this scene, nor even to announce himself to the MP from Dawley whom he recognized sitting at the fringes. Instead, he finished his short beer and betook himself into the fresh air. He was not cut out for hobnobbing. Anyway, he had done the important thing, engaged the solicitor and started the process.

Now, as it was a sunny day and he had only one remaining appointment—to inspect the house that Samuel had leased—he strolled to St. James's Park. There he sat on a bench and observed the fashionable promenade. He was dismayed by the sumptuousness of the ladies' gowns, by the enormous hooped skirts so wide that two could scarcely pass abreast on the path, by the gentlemen with their swords, buttons, and oversized shoe buckles glittering in the sun. It was all vastly overdone. This year's fashionable color was a sort of plum—*puce,* according to Barclay's son, who was Samuel's age—but there were splashes of rose madder and lime green (perhaps vying to be next year's color), most evident among the macaronis, who could be seen bowing elaborately and striking theatrical poses, some wearing wigs that towered easily a foot high. All very *flash,* according to young Barclay. To Abraham it was the worst sort of superfluity. If he lingered, it was only to condemn. Compared to this, Samuel's brocaded vest was positively Quakerly.

What would happen to Samuel in this Babylon?

Abraham reflected on the progression one could observe in many a Quaker family. They started out strict in all observances—some, like his great-grandfather, having taken up Quakerism during the march of the Valiant Sixty in Cromwell's time, some having endured jail and floggings for their beliefs. But each younger generation deviated a little further from the discipline of old. Now the younger Barclays had a harpsichord in their parlor.

Abraham could observe this trend in his own family. Though he held in great measure to Quaker discipline, he lacked his mother's stalwartness; and he noticed the lapses in his brother, who seemed almost to belong to a younger generation.

The sky was cloudy. Weary now from walking on city pavement, Abraham hailed a hackney cab and instructed the driver to take him to George Yard, south of St. Paul's, where Samuel had selected a house. Abraham was annoyed at Samuel's extravagance. The Dale Company was, after all, paying rent of a hundred pounds a year for a perfectly good office in Southwark, with living quarters above the forge located near Pickle Herring Stairs—not elegant, but roomy and convenient to the docks. Apparently it was not good enough for Samuel. Wrong side of the Thames. And the view of the Tower was "depressing." Samuel wanted to be within walking distance of bookshops; and he could attend the Meeting in Cheapside. Good arguments all, but. *Twenty-one years old, and he wants the moon!* And the desk. Samuel had insisted on purchasing a fine counting desk, for which Abraham had grudgingly laid out some eight pounds nine shillings of Dale Company money.

Still, it did seem for the best, putting Samuel in charge of the London office. Samuel would finish his apprenticeship in October, only at the sufferance of Joseph Rathbone, who declared it unlikely that the youngest Darby would perform any more reliably at Coalbrookdale. Mother had urged Abraham to put Samuel to work on the bridge. "He hath an inventive mind," she observed, "and might rise to the occasion." But Abraham could not imagine trusting his younger brother with such a project. The costs already exceeded his earlier estimates. And in truth, now that Abraham had accepted responsibility for the bridge, he had begun to feel possessive of it. This last he did not confide to Mother, for she might have chided him for putting his fleshy self forward.

Richard Reynolds's proposal was more to his liking. "Thou art young thyself in the works," he'd observed. "Send him to London. 'Twill give ye room from each other, and Samuel a chance to find himself." Perhaps it was true. Perhaps Samuel would show an interest in ironmaking at the forge here in London—or if not the making of it, then the selling.

Abraham got out at George Yard, which was located between Black Boy Alley and Broken Wharf—an unpaved close that meandered along the back of a timber yard, where a dog on a chain barked. Certainly not an imposing address. The house occupied the lot tentatively: a steep-roofed frame structure with gables, canted slightly and painted mostly blue. Looking at it, Abraham felt a great pensiveness. Perhaps it was only the closeness of the river, the dampness, the blue paint venturing into the slates, as if the painter had no clear direction where to stop. The house seemed more like the end of something than the beginning. Abraham tried to shake off the feeling.

The landlord, whose name was Crookshank, seemed surprised to see that Abraham was a Quaker. He showed him through the rooms, where a plasterer was at work, and assured him that the floors would be scraped and varnished in time for Samuel to take occupancy by January. And here was the counting desk, made of cherry with inlaid fruitwood and installed in the place Samuel had specified, by a window. Abraham dusted off the stool and sat down, and tried to imagine his brother faithfully keeping the accounts. The image that came to mind instead was of Samuel gazing out at the river. A sadness came over him. Sadness and a twinge of jealousy.

After finishing his business with Mr. Crookshank, Abraham walked back up to Paul's Yard. The bells were just striking five. Rain threatened. Some shops had already closed. He entertained the notion of visiting the Bull's Head Coffee House. The laughter he'd heard there yesterday had piqued his curiosity. The younger Barclays said that the Golden Lion was the latest rage: Captain Cook was seen there between voyages, a parrot on his shoulder, and the actress Elizabeth Inchbald appeared in the guise of a man. London! Perhaps he would attend a masquerade. Go as a Quaker! It was a mad whim. London surely bred a kind of madness, as coral was said to breed teeth in a baby's gums.

But when the shopkeepers began to lock their doors, quite another thought sprang to mind. Abraham wanted those silver sleeve buttons.

He dashed to the shop just as the first few drops of rain were spattering the pavement. Finding the shop open, he asked to see the pair of buttons that had caught his fancy. He compared them to others— one pair of enameled gold—but returned to his original choice. He kept seeing long, slender fingers. With the shopkeeper's help, he picked out a little oval tin box painted red and lined with white satin, and watched with fluttering excitement while the shopkeeper wrapped it in marbled paper. Abraham knew with sudden certainty that the buttons were for Maggie.

Outside, he was grateful for the umbrella, for it was raining quite hard now. Barclay's powdered wig would have been reduced to a pasty mess. Abraham felt the oval box secure in his pocket. Then, looking around St. Paul's Church Yard, he was surprised to see umbrellas bobbing everywhere—an enchanting, disconcerting sight.

# Maggie Foster

The business about cannon making at Coalbrookdale had caught her by surprise. It wasn't the cannon making itself—a relatively obscure historical fact, jogged into memory by her reading *Robinson Crusoe* last winter—but the intensity of Abraham's response.

Her question was aimed at getting a fix on his attitude toward armsmaking, at understanding his relationship with Wilkinson. She knew Abraham disapproved of Wilkinson but had no sense of how deep the disapproval went. So she asked the question partly to smoke him out. And it worked. He was certainly passionate on the subject of cannon making. Painfully protective of his father's memory. But his withdrawal afterwards—staring out the window without looking at her, trembling when she touched his shoulder, and then avoiding her before he left for London—made her worry whether she had pushed him too far.

And the episode left her more puzzled than ever about his collaboration with John Wilkinson.

When Abraham returned the following week, he seemed more relaxed. He invited her to stroll in the deer park and chatted about London. They laughed at his descriptions of the younger Barclays, the outlandish fashions at St. James, and Samuel's blue house overlooking the Thames. She had no idea Abraham was so observant or could be so funny. His eyes twinkled; he seemed at the brink of confiding some secret.

What had happened in London?

The next day he enlisted her help looking for the missing ledger. Sarah helped also. They started with the attic at Sunniside and went through every box, turning up worn-out shoes, a dried bouquet from their mother's wedding, old letters. But no ledger. Then they walked down the hill to Dale House—the smaller brick house where the family had lived before Sunniside was built—one of a short row of houses by the pond that supplied power to the Old Furnace. Dale House, Maggie knew, was where Abraham would live next year, after his marriage to Becky Smith. It was vacant now. Part of it served as an office; the rest was given over to storage. The interior was shabby now, the floors gritty. It would be extensively renovated.

"This is where I was born," Abraham said. "Mally too. Sarah and Samuel were born at Sunniside."

The three of them searched until their clothing was full of dust and they were sneezing. In the attic, Sarah found a long velvet coat that had belonged to their great-grandfather John Darby before he was Convinced in the 1690s: burgundy faded to rust at the shoulders, belled out at the bottom, braiding at the borders, wide cuffs, and a double row of tarnished brass buttons. Sarah tried it on, twirled around once, and pronounced it quaint.

But no ledger. *No plum,* as Abraham put it.

He pointed out the sturdiness of the rafters, the oak stairs. All quite solid, he said. These comments seemed somehow directed at Maggie. "When I marry," he said, "I shall live here." It was said not quite matter-of-factly. She thought she saw him blush. Oddly, she felt herself color too. Sarah gave her a darting, curious glance.

She was not making it up. Abraham was courting her. Catching her eye at the supper table. Soliciting her advice on matters of household finance. Inviting her on walks. Asking about her faith, her opinions of various Quaker practices. Offering his own views.

And worse, she was playing into it. Responding to his overtures in ways that she reminded herself she could not afford to indulge. She was annoyed at herself, but she was flattered. It had been a lonely two years. She could scarcely summon up that little smile on Trevor's lips. She felt buried in her celibacy, cut off from her sexuality. And here was this unwilling excitement. She found herself chuckling in response to Abraham's humor. The tenderness in her voice frightened her.

Sarah had already begun to notice. Even Jane, who avoided most eye contact, gave her a knowing look.

What would happen when Abiah got wind of this? Bad enough that Maggie was not a born Quaker, and only newly Convinced. More a problem was the importance Abiah attached to his leaving an heir. In the company of women, Maggie had heard Abiah voice concern that Abraham marry in good time, lest he leave sons too small to take over the Works. A reasonable concern, given that Darby males died young.

Abiah would never approve of her.

Obviously, Abraham had not confided his feelings to his mother. When he did, Abiah would set him straight pronto.

Maggie could not help fantasizing. Suppose Abraham went against his mother's wishes and married Maggie for love? It would put her in an influential position. But that was a long shot. She couldn't imagine Abraham defying his mother. More likely, Maggie would end up at odds with Abiah, a rival to Becky, a persona non grata here at Sunniside.

The risk was too great.

She toyed with another idea. Suppose she revised her story and said that she might be able to conceive after all—then married him and kept them all guessing for a few years? She had lied about who she was and where she was from. But no, she didn't think she could bring herself to lie about her fertility.

One afternoon, Abraham invited her to come with him to the Haye farm, to observe the last haying. They took the chaise, following the wagon road that led to Madeley Wood. The river was low, the air heavy, the sky milk-white beyond the funnels of smoke, and a few leaves were already turning yellow. When they got to the place where the gorge narrowed, she asked Abraham if this was where the bridge would be built. Yes, he said. He suggested they get out. They walked to the edge of the bluff, and he pointed to where the various approach roads would be.

She smiled. "I can see why you chose it."

He nodded. They looked down twenty feet at the slow brown current. A dead dog floated past, its stiff legs cartwheeling into the air as it caught on a snag and then spun slowly free.

He took her hand and led her to a log, where they sat down. "It's perfect," she said, thinking of the layers of soft brown clay and mudstone beneath them gravitating inexorably toward the center of the riverbed. She was aware of something else—how small was the gap separating him from her on the log. His presence as a man.

Abraham cleared his throat. "Tell me about Trevor," he said slowly and earnestly. "What sort of husband was he?"

"Quiet," she said. "Caring." Bitter, she wanted to add. That was a feeling they all shared. But Trevor's bitterness seemed more enigmatic than her own, more resigned, more profound. His was the bitterness of a conquered people. "Loving." Despite everything.

Abraham waited. "Forgive me," he said. "I fear I have made thee sad."

"No." She shook her head. "I mean, yes. But it's behind me."

"If I may ask, didst thou—didst ye—" Abraham reddened, fumbling for words. "Didst thou want to have children?"

"Yes," she said. "Very much." She didn't know why she added the *very much*. She wasn't altogether sure it was true. The larger sterility had removed the matter somehow from the realm of personal choice. Would they have made good parents? It was a moot question, even then.

"Wouldst thou—" Abraham looked at her searchingly.

She decided to spare him some awkwardness. "We tried to have babies. We tried for three years but couldn't conceive."

"Thou art young. Perhaps 'twas he."

She shook her head. "No. I would like to believe that, Abraham.

But no, it was my fault." *Fault?* Not the right word, but it would do. Without genetic diagnostics, it was as close as she could get to the truth in this context. She repeated her standard story—the one she had told Abiah and Polly when the subject came up, as it inevitably did among women—that Trevor had fathered a child in a previous marriage and that mother and infant had died in childbirth. When they suggested that she was young and might try again, she had added, as she did now, that a doctor had confirmed that she was barren.

She said all this partly to protect Abraham, partly to keep from running afoul of Abiah. But there was more to it than that. She had lied about who she was, and she had declared herself Convinced when she was really only sympathetic. But there was a line she would not cross; under the tissue of falsehoods was a real self she needed to protect.

Abraham was quiet, gazing across the river, scarcely breathing. Finally he turned to her and spoke softly. "I am very fond of thee, Maggie."

"I'm fond of you, Abraham." *Thee,* she almost said. Suddenly she felt teary.

He reached into his pocket and pulled out something wrapped in marbled paper, which he set gently in her lap. "This is for thee."

Inside the wrapping was a little red oval box. She opened the lid and saw what she thought at first were earrings. "Why, they're lovely! Thank you, Abraham." Excitement mingled with foreboding. "What are they?"

"Sleeve buttons."

Heart pounding, she remembered now a description in Abiah Darby's published journal of a pair of gold sleeve buttons given by Abraham to Rebecca Smith for their engagement. But these were silver. She looked at him, confused.

Abraham beamed. "For thy sleeves."

For a moment she simply registered the beauty of his expression. She had never seen his face so open. "But . . ."

"But what?" he asked.

"Well." Maggie held them in her palm, smoothing them. "How do you intend them?"

"As a token of friendship."

She looked at him steadily. "Just friendship."

"Yes." He laughed. "A loving friendship."

Okay. Not a proposal, exactly. But there was too much excitement in his voice. Did he know himself what he wanted?

She held one of the buttons to a sleeve and studied it. Two of his fingertips settled on her wrist, so softly that she could scarcely feel them.

She shook her head. "No, Abraham. These are too—too serious." She put them in his hand. "I can't keep them. Becky wouldn't understand. Nobody would understand."

He looked out at the river, worked his jaw silently. "Sometimes I feel . . ." He stopped.

"What?" she asked softly.

But he only shook his head, frowned, and put the buttons back in their nest of white satin. Wordlessly, they got back into the chaise.

As they continued along the wagon road, an ache rose in her throat. Was she depressed? Damned right. She could learn to love this decent man. She could teach him to loosen up. Did she feel like a loser? *Stop,* she told herself. She wiped her eyes, pretending to adjust her bonnet, and tried to will the ache away.

They drove past Bedlam Furnace, dodging carts and wagons, past the furnaces on the left, the Crumps' cottage on their right. After days without rain, everything was brown with iron oxide. Even the geese were rusty. No sign of Polly. Mrs. Merryweather was out tending her cabbage patch, but showed no sign of recognizing her. Cataracts, Polly had said. At the ironstone pile, the big woman was breaking ore with the men as usual, the front of her dress between her breasts drenched with sweat in a V that went all the way down her filthy apron. Hips wide and easy. How many babies had passed through that ample pelvis? And the girls raking and sorting the broken ore into baskets, their ragged hems orange with rust, how many babies would they have?

Her pain had more to do with her body than with Abraham. The pain of betrayal. Not by her body, as she sometimes thought, but by human greed. The filth funneling into the air and water appalled her.

They passed the Bird in Hand. Bedlam's din faded behind them as the road descended and then climbed up the ravine, until they could see the Haye farm: rolling orchards, horses grazing, sickles flashing in the fields.

Abraham took her around, showing her improvements he had made—the new creamery, a horse-driven threshing machine. He showed much more propriety about the farm than about the Works, and more warmth toward the workers.

Driving back, they were both subdued. As they passed the bridge site, she gave Abraham's hand a squeeze. "I want you to be happy," she said, "with Becky."

Several days later, she listened to Abiah and the Reynoldses laying plans around Becky's next visit. Abiah made a whispered reference to allowing "the young people time together." Maggie felt a twinge. Sarah's glance crossed hers.

Still no ledger. Abraham pursued the search with a grimness that masked his hurt. Apprentices were set to the task of searching every inch of the Works.

Maggie could feel his frustration. "What about the daybooks?" she offered. "Would they help?"

He shook his head. "The daybook for that decade is missing."

"Missing?"

"Yes."

"Abraham, isn't that a little strange? I mean, that they should both be missing?"

"Why dost thou say it that way?" He sounded annoyed.

"Well." It seemed more than coincidental. But she held her tongue.

"No, say it!"

Hearing the edge in his voice and seeing the hardness in his eyes, she knew they had turned a corner. She might never again experience that softness from him. She shook her head. "No." She reached to give his hand a squeeze, but he pulled it away.

**M**aybe it was hearing Jane's laughter. The distance she felt from Jane that somehow felt like hurt.

And now Abraham's anger. A sense of helpless waiting to see where it would go. She had installed all the lightning rods he could possibly use, and he was resisting her offers to help find a site for a new coal pit. So there she was, trapped once more in Abiah's sitting room, copying letters while Abiah and Sarah discussed prison reform over their tatting.

Maybe it was the weight of the day, the scent of newly cut hay in the sultry breeze that filled her with longing, and Abiah's droning voice raveling the endless strands of Quaker politics from the skeins of family histories. Or maybe—she would think, looking back on it— it was the memory of Sarah twirling around in her great-grandfather's burgundy velvet coat.

It wasn't ennui nor simple loneliness that led Maggie to do what she did. It was perhaps the profound isolation of who and what she was—an overwhelming sense of her sterility, of carrying a whole culture within her person, of being the last representative of a world that might never happen. She felt as she supposed Ishi must have felt, that California Indian who was the last remaining speaker of his language. Trevor used to say there was a little Ishi in every Indian, that the hoop was broken. To some extent it was true of all of them at Ecosophia: each individual a reservoir of culture surrounded by the ruins of society. But at Ecosophia at least they had one another. Here, she had no one. And her frustration was compounded by the tension of secrecy, and by the hard edge of intentionality that shaped her every act. After two and half years, there was a part of her raging to get out.

So there she was, upstairs, discussing prison reform and feeling imprisoned while downstairs Mrs. Hannigan and the servants were preparing dinner, the cheerful murmur of their conversation floating up the stairwell. Then came that burst of laughter—Jane's raucous voice rising above the others. Maggie felt a pang that she recognized as jealousy.

Later, when Abiah and Sarah had gone with Mrs. Hannigan to the malt mill and Rachel was upstairs changing the linens, Maggie went into the kitchen, where Jane was making bread. She stood and watched Jane knead the dough. Jane refused to look up, kneading fiercely while Maggie drew closer. Finally Jane glanced up and tossed her braids defiantly.

Maggie's heart pounded. "Jane," she pleaded. She touched the other woman's freckled forearm, half expecting her to lash out. All the things she missed about Jane—her mirth, her way of slapping her thigh—suddenly enveloped Maggie. She took Jane's hand. "Come," she said. Jane frowned, dusted the flour from her hands, and followed her outside.

The stable was deserted, the fragrance of hay thick in the shafts of afternoon sunlight.

By the time she pulled Jane into an empty stall, they both knew what it was about. They embraced. Maggie felt the strength of Jane's arms holding her, the sudden warmth of a deep kiss, the taste of fear dissolving into sweetness.

Jane tipped her face back and looked at her with eyes wide. "Well I'll be fooked!"

"Shh!" But there was no one in earshot. Andrew and Joseph were out stacking hay.

They tore off their bonnets, buried their heads in each other's necks, and kissed again. Jane looked at her wonderingly. The kissing became more urgent.

"I gave thee up!" Jane said.

Maggie nodded. Jane's leanness, her work-hardened hands, the softness of her fine coppery hair against Maggie's lips filled Maggie with explosive heat. Her whole body ached. *This is madness,* she thought, even as she cupped Jane's breasts. Did she say it aloud?

"Aye," she heard from the breath on her neck. "Aye. Aye."

An image flashed to mind of herself at thirteen with Sandi Kalowicz at CALYPOOL, fondling each other under the simulation deck at the

Laserdome until a motion detector set off a piercing siren. And someone else with sculpted lips, whose name she could not remember. She clasped Jane tight, and their hearts thudded against each other. It was a minute before she trusted herself to speak.

"I've missed you."

Jane nodded. She too seemed at a loss for words.

Finally they separated. Faced each other, leaning against the side of the stall. Dust motes danced.

"Please accept me, Jane."

"As a gentlelady?"

"As whatever. Just don't hold it against me. Okay? What I'm doing. I've got to do it."

Jane's voice took on an edge. "And is he sweet on thee? Abraham?"

"No more."

"Found out, did he?"

"I told him."

Jane nodded. "Abiah would ne'er brook it."

"No. Never."

"And now he be peeved at thee."

Jesus. Was it so transparent? Maggie nodded.

Jane reached out and stroked her face slowly. The warm rough hand slid softly down her cheek, the backs of fingers curling in the crook of Maggie's neck. "Tha be'est a strange'un."

"I know." She took the fingers and kissed them.

"And I ain't the only one to think so. I hear them talking."

A little flare of panic. "What do they say?"

"The Reynoldses think thy ways with electricity unbefitting a lady. And think thy speech improper."

Maggie nodded. "Is that all?"

Jane smirked. "The Darbys hear thee at night."

"At night?"

"Aye. In thy chamber."

"I do exercises."

"Well, they do wonder at the sound."

Maggie laughed. Kissing Jane's hand again, she tasted flour. "Your bread," she remembered.

Jane gave her a bump with her pelvis. "My bread will rise without me." She looked over Maggie's shoulder.

Maggie turned to see the steps leading up to the hayloft. She shook her head. But it was all she could do to scoop up their bonnets and put the necessary urgency into tying her own.

# Abraham Darby III

He missed the first meeting of the subscribers, having a terrible headache, which arose from his nervousness over the growing cost of the bridge. In his absence, the subscribers approved his choice of Mr. Hamilton for solicitor, approved the wording of the act, and elected Abraham treasurer.

Abraham's estimate—arrived at after consulting with Thomas Farnolls Pritchard, Richard Reynolds, and his own clerk—had swelled to three thousand one hundred fifty pounds. Much of the increase could be laid to the approach roads, which had not been included in the original reckoning. But many of the subscribers were blaming it on the cost of building with iron.

The problem was this: If his estimate was too high, then the subscribers would run from the project; if it proved too low, then the difference would come out of his own pocket.

Whether it was because he had missed the first meeting or because he was the youngest, Abraham did not feel part of the group gathered for the second meeting at John Carrandine's public house in Broseley. It did not help that, looking around the table and seeing John

Wilkinson, John Nicholson, John Guest, and John Bilbo, Abraham realized he was surrounded by subscribers named John.

"What think ye gentlemen of these tolls?" said Bilbo. At the mention of tolls, the others sat up and listened carefully while he read his proposal:

*For every horse, mare, gelding, or ass, laden or unladened and not drawing—the sum of one penny. For every drove of calves, hogs, sheep, or lambs—five pence per score, and so in proportion for any goats or others.*

The phrasing was not satisfactory to some. "Drove" was thought too vague. And what of wandering geese? The Reverend Harries wished to be exempted from paying tolls, in exchange for his giving up land for the approach road. Others clamored for exemptions. They all wanted tolls, but no one wanted to pay them.

Compared to Quakers, they were a noisy lot. And although at the first meeting they had roundly endorsed Abraham's choice of Hamilton for solicitor, they now insisted on engaging Harries' cousin. Next came a great haggling over the wording of the act. John Rose found fault with the title; John Wilkinson wanted to specify "iron," on the grounds that iron would attract more interest in Parliament, but he was overruled by those who argued it would bind them unnecessarily—an objection that Abraham himself would have raised if they had not.

Afterwards, as they all filed out, Wilkinson clapped an arm around Abraham's shoulder. "Good work, Mr. Darby. You are just the captain for our ship." Abraham recoiled from the familiarity. Hurrying to the horse ferry, he could hear Wilkinson's voice sing out shrilly behind him. "There's money in this bridge, Mr. Darby. You will be glad to have the lion's share!"

*Money!* Did Wilkinson take him for a fool? This bridge might turn a profit someday, but not in his lifetime. Not when it was costing more than three thousand pounds. No, he was not doing it for money!

The subscribers from Madeley continued chattering as they went across on the ferry. Abraham rode in the stern. Danny Day, leaning on the tiller, grumbled that he must be compensated for his losses once the bridge was built. Abraham promised to bring it up at the next meeting.

Privately, he was flattered by Wilkinson's phrase *captain of our ship,* even if he suspected that the real captaining, if it could be called that, was going on outside these meetings and among men older and craftier than he, swapping this favor for that—their venality colored by family feuds, coveted lands and wives, and endless ancient grudges going back to impoundments of water, gored oxen, and collapsed coal shafts. Still, as captain, he must stay aloof from their petty quarrels so that the ship might sail a fair course.

No, he was doing it not for money but for Mother and Father. He was doing it because it was needed, and because it was the proper thing to do.

The other voices receded into babble. He listened to the creak of the tiller, the current gurgling past the broad rudder, and felt the dark current dragging against the hull, dragging them toward the Bristol Channel a hundred miles away. He thought of the dead dog turning like a millwheel and the look on Maggie's face when she handed back the silver sleeve buttons.

# Maggie Foster

"Will tha romp with me, Maggie?"

They were leaning against the well—autumn crisp in the air, the linden tree yellow overhead. Anyone glancing out the kitchen window might suppose that they were talking casually. But their hands were grazing, full of wild heat.

Jane wanted more. Their near-tumble in the hay last month filled them both with lust. Maggie could not keep her mind off Jane. The situation had been awkward before; now it was dangerous. The glances they exchanged in the dining room; a stolen embrace when they encountered each other alone upstairs: it was too volatile. Someone was bound to catch on.

Again, her obsessiveness scared her. She had unloosed a flood of forgotten sensations—at a time when she was most frustrated in her efforts to influence the design of the bridge; when Abraham was ignoring her, and the whole plan seemed to be in trouble. Yet at this moment, standing at the well in the yellow dappled light with Jane's fingers slowly stroking the back of her hand, she felt exquisitely torn. She turned her hand over, exposing the palm, startled by her own sharp intake of breath. "Oh God." She wanted to surrender.

"Jane." *Sweet woman!* "We could get into very serious trouble. You could lose your place. I could lose mine."

Jane wrinkled her nose. "I dinna ask thee to tell 'em."

"They have eyes and ears. Even now, if anyone happens to be watching from the house, we're standing here too long. Mrs. Hannigan could be watching us right now!"

"We only be getting water." Jane grinned, holding up a bucket.

"No we're *not*, dammit!" Maggie's hands were shaking; she clamped her jaw, shut her eyes. She couldn't afford to be this out of control. *Take a deep breath.* She looked up to see Jane flushed with anger, gripping the bucket with white knuckles. Maggie wanted to grab her, feel their bodies merge. They stood locked in that ferocious gaze.

"I want to kiss you," Maggie said evenly, "but I can't. This is too hard, Jane. I'm sorry I started it. No, I'm not. But let's don't make it worse. I just—I just want the friendship."

Jane tipped her head, folded her arms. The old bravado entered her voice. "I warrant I'll have to find me a man."

Maggie smiled hard. *Bitch.* "Good."

"But 'twill not be the same," Jane added softly.

Walking away, Maggie felt the other woman's eyes on her. Was aware of how her hips moved.

Was it love?

Probably not. But it felt good.

Why a woman?

They managed a kind of truce, avoiding each other's gaze, agreeing to pretend that nothing had happened. But the question worked on Maggie all that fall. It wasn't that she was shocked or hugely surprised. Her only really long-term relationship had been with Trevor, but there had been women. What troubled her about the encounter with Jane—about her lust for Jane—was that she didn't know how deep it went. How much of it was Jane, and how much circumstances?

Why this turning toward a woman?

It did give her a little solace. During Becky Smith's visit, Maggie watched Abraham and Becky enter into formal courtship—do their little dance—and felt comfortably removed from it. She felt a pang when she saw the silver buttons on Becky's sleeves, but that passed. And as she thought about those buttons and how they were not the gold enameled buttons described in Abiah Darby's journal, she came to a realization that was both obvious and startling.

*She had changed history.*

A minor deviation, to be sure, but this was the first change she could actually document.

Had she felt more in control, this would have given her hope. But she hadn't a clue as to how she might have influenced the shift from gold to silver.

At the most unlikely times, when she was copying letters for Abiah, for example, she would think of Jane's freckled chest, the breasts white and glorious, and fantasize kissing them. Why a woman? She had done right not to choose Abraham, but why not a man, she wondered, *some* man? She thought of the things she loved about Trevor—his laconic humor, the way he moved, the way he filled his jeans, the smell of his neck; the way, when she was on top, his strong hands buoyed her, caressed the rim of her vulva so she couldn't tell where she left off and he began; the ecstasy of those long deep strokes, whether they were hers or his. If only she could relive them.

Where would she find a man like that again? Trevor wouldn't be born for another 239 years. But it wasn't just a lack of suitable men. It was her own feeling of entrapment—in these damned petticoats, in the embroidering, the endless parsing of Quaker politics, the stunted repertoire available to women. She missed running. Dancing. Just walking naturally. Slurping soup, arguing, swearing, playing her flute. Laughing out loud.

No wonder she was drawn to Jane.

She adopted a new regimen. She got Abiah's permission to take a "constitutional" by herself at midmorning. She explained it was her way of being with the Maker. On those walks, hidden by hedges, she could lift her skirts and run in place, as she used to do with Jane. But now, alone, she added a few martial arts moves, until she had put together a routine that left her panting. She returned refreshed, ready to face the embroidery hoops and Bibles.

Evenings, she did her exercises, having explained to Sarah what she was doing. Sometimes she masturbated. Often she wound down by doing an abbreviated form of t'ai chi very slowly, centering herself. This was followed usually by meditation, then sleep.

It all helped. And it helped that she could recognize, under the obsessing and fantasizing, that old hunger for wholeness, which went back to Jeremy but also to her old life. She could see the pattern now. She could remember at times demanding something from Trevor that he could not give—a sense of completion that she had to find within herself.

That recognition bridged her two worlds. It might have been disheartening to realize she had been as neurotic in the twenty-first century as she was now in the eighteenth; but it wasn't. It was a comfort.

Ecosophia seemed more and more like a dream. She remembered the texture of the fig tree's bark, Erzulie's laughter, the beauty of sagebrush blooming in the desert. But much of it was fading. She had lost "Harlem Nocturne" and even the melodies she used to play on her flute. Trevor's face was reduced to a couple of expressions, his humor to an abstraction, their lovemaking to three or four moments. The future was becoming the past.

A s for the bridge, she was completely outside the loop. The subscribers had met three times already. Abraham was increasingly involved, but he rebuffed her every effort to discuss Pritchard's new sketches.

One rainy, blustery afternoon at the end of October, when he was on his way to meet with Wilkinson and a couple of the subscribers at the Swan Inn, she intercepted him in the foyer. He had the canvaswrapped boards containing Pritchard's drawings tucked under his oilskin coat, the umbrella he'd purchased in London clamped under his arm, and was waiting for Andrew to bring the carriage around.

"Abraham," she pleaded, "how can I be your consultant if you won't consult?"

"My mother has more need of thy services at this time."

"But I could be useful. You can't just build a bridge without—" She was getting shrill. She took a breath and lowered her voice. "My knowledge of geology could help you."

Abraham was tying his hat string under his chin, peering out through the rain-spattered window. "I must go." He pushed the door open against the wind.

*Shit!* Maggie looked out in time to see the umbrella turn inside out. *Serves you right!* The carriage lurched forward with him in it. On impulse she darted outside, and from the arch in the boxwood hedge watched the carriage disappear into the sheeting rain. She felt like crying. A gust of wind lashed the hedge, driving cold pellets of rain into her face.

She returned to Abiah's sitting room, where Abiah and Sarah sat by the coal fire. Abiah's legs were elevated, wrapped in wet poultices. Maggie resumed work on the letter she was copying.

Abiah looked up from the letter she was reading. "Samuel expects to come home next week. He hath finished his apprenticeship."

"Praise the Great Name," exclaimed Sarah.

While mother and daughter discussed Samuel's letter, Maggie tried to quiet her own agitation. The quill splattered. After copying the same line twice, she sighed and started over.

Abiah peered over at her. "Thou seemest unquiet."

Maggie nodded. "Abiah, why won't Abraham talk to me about the bridge?"

"Thou art a woman."

"Doesn't he discuss it with you?"

"Rarely. Some things a young man must do by himself."

"But I have skills he can use."

Abiah fluttered her pink eyelids. "Thou art a woman."

"Abiah, you mustn't say that!" Maggie blurted. "We're all equal in the Light! You can't—" *You can't surrender technology to men!* But she stopped herself.

Sarah's eyes widened at this outburst. Abiah shut hers, the signal for silent prayer.

Maggie knew. Her rash words were the mark of an unquiet soul. Well, dammit, she *was* unquiet. She sighed. Sometimes she wished she really were Convinced. Then she could talk to God. She listened to the rain lash the windows. If she could pray, what would she pray for?

Erzulie used to say that prayer helped simplify.

Maggie had always been skeptical. "It might work for you, but I have no God of the sort that can answer prayers."

Erzulie chuckled. "Child, I'm not talking about answers. I'm talking about the asking. I just kick back and ask for what I'd want if it *could* be granted. That's the gift of prayer. It's in the naïveté."

Abiah finally spoke. Something from Scriptures, about helpmates, from which she concluded: "The bridge is a matter for men." Then, reflecting further, she added, "Samuel does not leave for London until January. He will help with the bridge."

Samuel.

It was an idea.

That evening, Maggie reviewed her notes. Next year was going to be eventful for the Darbys. In January, following his twenty-first birthday, Samuel would move to London; Sarah would go with him to keep house. Sometime in the spring, Abraham would purchase Bedlam Furnace. In May, Abraham would marry Becky Smith. In August, Samuel would marry a woman named Deborah Barnard. In September, an impasse among the subscribers would be resolved—over whether the bridge was to be built wholly of iron. Work could finally begin on the abutments.

Samuel's role in the bridge would be negligible. He would be in London during most of the planning and construction—enjoying three or four years of independence before the Dale Company's forge went belly-up under his management and he succumbed to the nervous disorder referred to in his mother's diary. As far as the bridge was concerned, Samuel's signature would appear on a few documents and his attendance would be recorded at a couple of meetings of the subscribers. But that was about the extent of it.

Unless she could change that.

Samuel might be the key. Abiah wanted to involve him in the bridge; Sarah felt protective of him. Those were powerful dynamics, if Maggie could find a way to exploit them.

Samuel was in good spirits when he arrived at Sunniside in early November. He wore a handsome blue gabardine coat with side pleats and brass buttons. He was twenty now. He had filled out in the shoulders and face, and his skin had cleared. New sideburns added a little width to his face. Perhaps because his features were coarser, he gave an impression of being more fully formed than Abraham.

He complained to them about Joseph Rathbone's business dealings, but the complaints seemed more mature this time, based on Samuel's own opposition to slavery. Some of the chain made in Joseph's forge regularly found its way onto slave ships. Abiah and Abraham tried to soften his judgment. Abiah suggested it was an issue for the Liverpool Meeting to decide.

"The Liverpool Meeting!" Samuel sneered. "Scarcely a hand is innocent in Liverpool—even among Quakers. The very bricks are mortared with the blood of slaves."

Here Abraham interceded, saying Samuel should speak more respectfully to his mother. He glanced at Maggie, evidently annoyed to find her in the midst of family matters.

In the days that followed, Maggie found opportunities to talk to Samuel and Sarah alone. They were already discussing London. Sarah looked forward to it as much as Samuel.

Samuel's interest in ironmaking was focused on the decorative aspects. He complained of the stodginess of Dale Company firebacks and fenders, and described some bold designs that he had drawn. Maggie asked to see them. The drawings, based on intertwining vines, seemed inspired by Celtic motifs.

Samuel was clearly pleased at this attention. One of the designs had received Abraham's approval, and Samuel was busy carving the wooden mold pattern. Most had been rejected, Abraham having found them too *flash*. Samuel fumed at this. "There is no room at Coalbrookdale for new ideas. In London—"

"What about the bridge?" Maggie interrupted.

Samuel snorted. "A lost opportunity! Thomas Pritchard's designs are so *ordinary*. They might as well be built of stone! The new sketches are more timid than ever."

"Why don't you try some sketches?"

"Perhaps." He shrugged. "Perhaps I will." He exchanged a glance with Sarah. "But in any case," he said, "in London I shall have a chance to try new things."

"We shall attend plays," Sarah said.

"Plays?" Maggie registered surprise.

"Of the proper sort." Sarah's intonation contained a hint of parody. She wrinkled her nose mischievously.

Sarah and Samuel shared a fun-loving quality that was missing in Abraham or their mother. They occasionally got raucous. Once they hid in a pile of leaves and surprised Maggie when she thought she was alone. She was taking her constitutional between the hedgerows—out of sight, presumably communing with God. She was in the middle of her routine, skirt hiked up between her legs like a Samurai swordsman, when they suddenly sprang up in an explosion of leaves.

"Jesus!" Maggie yelled.

They fell back into the pile, laughing until tears rolled down their cheeks. "That was a mighty prayer!" Samuel declared.

Maggie's face burned. But realizing how ridiculous she must have looked, she had to laugh too.

"What wert thou doing?" Sarah wanted to know.

Maggie tried to explain that she was "investigating the connection between mind and body." Her pomposity elicited more peals of laughter.

That prank seemed to admit her further into their little clique. Samuel showed her more of his pencil sketches, which he worked on sometimes late at night. His work had matured since the early mermaids. His subjects included butterflies and beetles drawn from life, as well as more fantastical creations—all vividly drawn, with a strong sense of structure. She praised them.

What struck Maggie most forcefully was the energy Samuel put into drawing, and how at odds it was with the Quaker strictures against art for art's sake. Art, Abiah had once explained to her, could be justified only to the extent that it provided moral instruction. A painting or novel without redeeming virtue was no better than idle music or dancing. Samuel's drawings seemed to erupt from this suppression. A dragon's coiled tail, a flamboyant butterfly, all glowed with unseemly energy. A slave master whipping his charges bared ferocious teeth. It was the fleshiness, the emotional extremes, perhaps the vividness itself that distinguished Samuel's drawings from austere Quaker engravings, from the placid figures in *William Penn Treating with the Indians* or the dispassionate geometry of the slave ship.

Abiah, answering the call of her ministry, asked permission of the Madeley Meeting to visit the meetings in the north of England. Receiving the letter that certified she was traveling under the care of the Meeting, she left in December with an old friend as a companion.

In their mother's absence, the interplay among the siblings changed. Samuel and Sarah sometimes ganged up on Abraham, and Abraham acted older. Sometimes all three seemed to perform for Maggie. Certain signs of decadence appeared. The rule of silence at mealtimes was suspended. Sarah dispensed with her bonnet around the house; Maggie followed suit. The two men smoked their long-stemmed clay pipes in the downstairs parlor, which was normally off-limits.

Abraham lectured on the reported medicinal benefits of tobacco, as well as chocolate, coffee, tea, and opium—all to be taken in moderation.

Samuel's laconic response was that Europeans alone benefited, since all these nostrums depended on the ill use of Negroes, Indians, and others who fell under the colonial yoke.

So it went, the two brothers trying to best each other, but remaining civil, while the women formed an appreciative audience. Sarah asked questions, rarely offering an opinion. Maggie followed her example. Occasionally she caught Abraham glancing at her when he thought she wasn't looking, and she sensed he was playing to her, even if his stance remained sometimes peevishly detached.

Samuel regaled them with stories of Liverpool low life involving his friend Edmund, a rakish fellow who bet on horses and frequented public houses. In one of his escapades, Edmund went to a Liverpool gambling den and drank punch with sailors from Sardinia who had necklaces of garlic. Like Joseph stripped of his coat of many colors, he lost first his ruffled shirt, then his five-shilling diced stockings, and finally emerged hatless and shirtless as the first cock crowed.

How much of this was fact and how much invented, Maggie could not tell. Sarah listened wide-eyed. Abraham seemed fascinated as much as repelled.

"Why," demanded Abraham, "dost thou continue a friendship with such a skipjack wastrel?"

Samuel wagged a palm benignly. "It is as Abraham of old entreated the Lord on behalf of the inhabitants of Sodom and Gomorrah, asking if fifty good men might be found worthy, would He spare them His wrath; and then forty-five, and a score, and so forth. So do I ask myself, whether, if Edmund has at least a few good qualities, then might not our friendship be spared my righteous indignation." He said this with such aplomb that it was only upon reflection that Abraham frowned and pronounced it blasphemous.

Samuel used his voice more playfully than Abraham, exploring its full range, delighting in the whimsical and the unexpected, gesturing expansively. Abraham became more controlled in Samuel's presence.

One evening, Samuel offered to teach them all how to play whist, and Abraham agreed to join them. Sarah put on her green gown for the occasion and asked Maggie's help putting up her hair in a French roll. They sat around the table in the upstairs parlor. Samuel explained the rules, and they divided into teams, Samuel and Sarah playing against Abraham and Maggie. They got through one game and started another. But Sarah kept trumping Abraham, and Samuel kept distracting him with Edmund's shenanigans, until Abraham interrupted with a reference to the prodigal son, which Samuel took offense at, responding with the suggestion that Abraham was jealous of his more adventurous life. At that, Abraham threw his cards on the table. "Idleness!" he declared, and stalked out, slamming the door.

Samuel and Sarah exchanged looks of feigned disbelief. Maggie deliberated whether to follow Abraham. She didn't want to take sides against him.

Sarah stamped her feet. "We've lost our fourth."

"Dost thou think it possible," mused Samuel, gathering up Abraham's cards and studying them with an eyebrow cocked for Maggie's benefit, "that my brother and I were got by the same father?"

Sarah rolled her eyes. "Thou art such a saucebox, Sammy. Mary Wilkinson is back from France. She would make a fourth. We must ask her sometime."

"I am so comely, and he is so plain."

"Let's have some brandy," Sarah said. It was a declaration. While she poured the brandy into three glass bowls, she complained that she liked playing whist, that the Lloyds and Barclays all played whist. "Why must Mother be so strict in all things?"

Samuel filled his pipe. "Mother lives not in the world. 'Tis one thing to hate war and injustice. But to hate idleness? Idleness has accomplished more in the world than slavish work. Idleness is the great mainspring of our age. It sets the wheels of Progress awhirling."

Sarah cocked her head. "But the Bible—"

"Devised by idlers!"

"Sammy!"

"I intend no disparagement. Idleness hath its own virtues. Jesus was surely an inspired idler—a carpenter called from the drudgery of carpentry."

Sarah looked at Maggie beseechingly.

But Samuel was on a roll. " 'Tis thus with the bridge. They will give thee ten dreadfully serious reasons why it should be built, reasons of economy and duty. But it is all from idleness! And pretending otherwise, they miss the point. Constrained by the guise of practicality, they think of it as simply a large object, like a large bellied pot."

"And the real point?" Maggie sipped her brandy, amused.

"Well. Once the bridge is built, 'tis there." Samuel rapped the table with his knuckles. "Where before, there was *no bridge,* just an empty space where everybody said, 'Why, we should have a bridge at this spot.' So: bridge and no bridge. What comes between is the building of the bridge. And that can happen only once. So I say, 'tis an event as much as a thing."

"Oh Sammy." Sarah gave him an affectionate, hopeless smirk. "Thou thinkest it an entertainment!"

"But it is! Entertainment for man and beast." Samuel blew a smoke ring. "Deep down, under all the seriousness, they are like children eating a Christmas pie, eager for the plum! Our brother is too dreadfully solemn to see it as sport. 'Tis why they put him in charge. He is their pack mule."

"Sammy. Methinks thou art jealous."

Samuel folded his arms. "Let Abey carry his Friday face hither and yon. If 'twere up to me, I should take some pleasure in it! Not that I shall be given the chance. But Coalbrookdale is a bit dull, is it not? It's all an eat-coke-and-shit-iron sort of business, dost thou not agree?"

"Sammy!"

"Sorry." With a nod to Maggie: "Family expression."

"Thou art the only who says it."

"I am arrived at this view so far ahead of the others," he explained to Maggie, "because I am so far behind them in patience. Being an idler myself."

Sarah took her brother's arm. "Sammy! Pray, show Maggie thy drawings of the bridge."

Samuel sucked at his pipe and frowned. "They are very rough."

But both women begged him, and Samuel bounded upstairs. Sarah smiled at Maggie. "Thou art a great encouragement to him. Mother ignores his talent. I think she fears it."

Returning, Samuel spread a dozen or so sketches on the table. Maggie examined them eagerly. Some were based on the conventional Roman arch. Others took a radical departure, capitalizing on the properties of cast iron to create airier, trusslike arches that rose above the roadway.

Maggie caught her breath. This might be what she was looking for.

Most of the designs resembled in varying degrees the Whipple bowstring truss bridge that would become popular in America during the next century. The principle was the same: trusses were used to stiffen the arch, which carried the roadway from above.

One design was particularly dramatic: the arch was heightened from a semicircle to a parabolic curve; and instead of making the truss members straight, as in timber construction, Samuel had curved them fancifully, calling attention to the uniqueness of cast iron as a building material. The arch rose from either side of the roadway like wings.

"It looks like a butterfly!" Maggie exclaimed.

"That's where he got the idea." Pride in Sarah's voice.

"Wow," Maggie breathed. It was a plausible design. She could see where the stresses would be concentrated as the abutments crept inward. And it was top-heavy enough that once it cracked and started to tip, there would be no stopping it.

"Fantastic," Maggie whispered. She examined the others.

Samuel leaned forward, ruffling his sideburn with his pipe stem. "Which one dost thou like best?"

"This." She returned to the butterfly design and tapped it with her fingernail. "This is the one."

# John Wilkinson

As winter approached and Wilkinson anticipated traveling to France, he made sure that Darby was sufficiently caught up in the bridge. The subscribers were bickering again over the choice of solicitors, Reverend Harries plotting to relocate the approach roads on his own land. The committee was a proper quagmire, and Darby was in the thick of it, being treasurer and carrying the weight of his family name. He might yet come to his senses and abandon the project, but for now his pride should hold him fast.

Let other men posture on the public stage! Wilkinson preferred a quieter role for himself. The Privy Council had overturned his cannon-boring patent; yet his lawyers continued to threaten interlopers with lawsuits that none but the richest could afford. His cylinder-boring machine remained a closely guarded secret. And his negotiations with the French would be cloaked in subterfuge.

With Darby stuck for now up to his shoe buckles—and by spring, Wilkinson hoped to have him up to his knees—Wilkinson could turn to more important matters.

Boulton and Watt were in a frenzy of promoting and perfecting the new engine. They had received their first order, a pumping engine for the Bloomfield colliery that they hoped to erect in January. Wilkinson had ordered an engine for himself to blow his furnace at Broseley, to be erected the following month. So all was proceeding at a fast trot, thanks to him. And he would have the monopoly in supplying cylinders for all of Boulton's and Watt's customers.

The French in the meantime were making overtures on the matter of the water pipes. Three separately sealed letters had arrived in a packet whose ordinariness belied its contents. One letter was written on thick creamy vellum, from the office of the French minister of finance, Jacques Necker; another was written with a soft quill on pale vellum and perfumed, from the French embassy in London; and a third, more straightforward letter was written with a steel point on thinner rag, from the Périer brothers, on behalf of the Paris Waterworks Company. The ironmaster sniffed and creased the pages admiringly as he read. The paper was as French as the words. French and Dutch papers were generally superior to English paper; Florentine was the finest of all. The texts were masterpieces of indirection. Below the surface politeness lay a kernel of meaning, and these kernels, taken together, suggested the outlines of the scheme.

The ambassador thanked him for the hospitality he had extended to Marchant de la Houlière last summer, and referred vaguely to a need for caution. Jacques Necker expressed hope that Wilkinson might do business with the French government and made a veiled reference to Indret. The Périer brothers listed their substantial needs (which included large valves as well as pipe, and eventually steam pumping-engines) and invited him to visit their office in Paris.

Houlière had done his work well.

Wilkinson set out alone in December, over the protests of Mary Lee, who begged to accompany him as far as Paris. He insisted that she keep an eye on the Works and placated her with the promise of another trip. In truth, a wife would be an encumbrance, and he was in no hurry for Mary Lee to learn French ways.

He planned to cross the Channel on his own brigantine, the *Bersham*, which was carrying a cargo of sugar cane mill rollers destined for Port-au-Prince by way of Le Havre. But once at the Bristol harbor, he learned of a salmon smack about to set sail directly up the Seine to Paris. As the winds looked favorable for such a small, fast craft, he paid for a berth in the forecastle and made it across in five hours. He arrived in Paris in two days.

In Paris, he saw *The Barber of Seville* as the guest of Houlière, who had been promoted from brigadier to major general. Houlière asked solicitously after Madame Wilkinson. They conversed almost wholly in French, at Wilkinson's suggestion, so that he might recover his fluency.

They visited the *restaurants,* where the ironmaster was prevailed on to try snails for the first time. Discomfited by the creatures in their shells garnished with butter and parsley, the warm smell of garlic filling his nostrils, Wilkinson recalled that as a child he felt a great affection for snails despite their low reputation. Behind the Backbarrow Company, where his father founded pots, was a damp slate wall shaded by a chestnut tree and covered with ivy, where as a boy he used to encounter them in their silky meanderings and touch a finger to them.

> *Snail, snail, put out your horns,*
> *I'll give you bread and barley-corns.*

He was appalled by the cruelty of his schoolmates, who impaled the innocent creatures on the blackthorn bush outside the dormitory at Dr. Caleb Rotheram's Dissenting Academy, as a cure for warts. He tried it himself once, but the blackthorn with its grisly burden reminded him of the Saviour's suffering on the Cross.

"Delicious, is it not?" asked Houlière.

Wilkinson nodded diffidently. If snails, why not slugs? No accounting for tastes. The French had no appreciation for good English porridge.

They had tea with a Madame Bougainville, whom Houlière had described as an old friend from an old intellectual family, placing so much emphasis on the *old* that Wilkinson was surprised to find a woman no more than forty, of breathtaking charm, whose laughter brought the blood to his cheeks. She entertained them with an account of a recent salon that included a lecture (or demonstration; Wilkinson wasn't sure which) of priapism, which occasioned some delectable shaking of bosom from Madame Bougainville and screams of laughter from Houlière.

The lady seemed to be personally acquainted with many of the most enlightened thinkers in Paris, including some who, like the Abbé Claude Yvon, had fled to the Dutch republics to avoid death or imprisonment for their anticlerical and republican beliefs. She explained casually that she was the illegitimate daughter of Jean Rousset de Missy, who helped foment the Dutch revolution of 1747. As a young girl growing up in Amsterdam, she had attended the salons of Baron d'Holbach and sat on the lap of the artist Bernard Picart while he made erotic engravings for Voltaire and Sallengre.

Most of these names were unfamiliar to Wilkinson. Houlière, however, apparently nervous at the direction the conversation was taking, reminded her that he owed his allegiance to the Bourbon court. She laughed deep in her throat, and Houlière responded with a chuckle.

Wilkinson offered a few witticisms of his own, which were well received. Rarely had he felt so clever. He mentioned his connection with the famous philosophe Joseph Priestley, adding modestly that he had given Priestley "some help" with his theory of dephlogisticated air. Madame Bougainville was acquainted with Priestley's work but said she preferred the thinking of Lavoisier. Wilkinson's pulse raced. Even a difference of opinion from those lips was intoxicating.

When they bade her adieu, Madame Bougainville pulled a long-stemmed red rose from a bouquet and presented it to Wilkinson, drawing it coquettishly across her face. "Monsieur Wilkinson, I should like very much to see you again." Her warmth and fragrance followed him into the night streets. How many admirers, he wondered, could afford such a hothouse rose?

Houlière answered his discreet inquiries by saying that Madame Bougainville was "well acquainted" with Jacques Necker. "A most frustrated man," he added.

"Why?" asked Wilkinson.

Houlière shrugged. "Madame Bougainville has very expensive tastes." He offered no more, and Wilkinson did not press the matter further.

T he next day, Houlière took him to visit the venerable *Machine à Marly,* the great chain of wooden push rods and rocker arms that undulated like a centipede as it pumped water for the fountains of Versailles—an impressive feat of engineering in its day but destined to be replaced by a steam pumping-engine. "Perhaps," Houlière said, "you will supply us with one of the new engines devised by Monsieur Watt. Eh?"

Wilkinson was thinking of Madame Bougainville's laughter.

They visited the newly completed Nevilly Bridge, whose elliptical, squashed-looking arches Wilkinson found quite as ugly as those of the new Black Friars Bridge in London. They ended up at the offices of the Périer brothers—Jacques Constantine and Augustin Charles— short, earnest men with dark eyes, who might have been twins, except that one face seemed compressed horizontally and the other vertically, as if they had lain at right angles in their mother's womb.

Sprawling across one wall was an enormous plan that showed the existing network of reservoirs, vaulted tunnels, aqueducts, and wooden pipes and troughs that conveyed water by gravity through most of Paris, the heart of the labyrinth going back to ancient times, when the city was all cow paths and springs. Tracing-paper overlays showed the elaborate new waterworks that the brothers were designing. They explained in detail how fire engines would pump water from the Seine into four brick reservoirs high on a hill, so that all Paris could be served with sufficient pressure to carry drinking water into the upper floors of buildings. Ha! A frivolous objective, Wilkinson thought. Typically French! But he could well understand why such a system would require iron pipes, as well as valves and engines.

The Périer brothers were assisted by a senior clerk who spoke almost entirely in numbers. In addition there was a man whose specialty was money; another in charge of making arrangements; and yet another, with a face as blank as a pudding, who seemed to be representing the French crown.

The Périers let it be known that they were not altogether decided whether to use iron or ceramic for the larger pipes. They called on the clerk who spoke in numbers to bolster this argument or that. Wilkinson held his tongue, although every fiber longed to cry out, "Iron!" These gentlemen were playing a game he knew only too well, and they were clearly experts. He must hold with the hare and run with the hounds.

"Well," he said jovially, with a shrug. "All possibilities should be considered. You might wish to consult my friend Wedgwood."

It was not the response they had anticipated. A darting of glances confirmed his suspicion that they were settled on iron. Now he asked what allowance they had made for the rate of failure of ceramic pipes, as compared to iron. He referred to the cracks and insufficient firings that could cause a clay pipe to collapse after a few years "into something like putty." While they argued amongst themselves, Wilkinson examined more closely the plan on the wall. If Paris were to adopt this new system using iron pipes, then London would follow. Antwerp, Brussels, Vienna, Petersburg. Iron pipes would sprawl across the great capitals, carrying water into the upper stories of buildings everywhere! Iron engines pumping, iron bridges spanning rivers, iron horse trams carrying people and cargo. The world would be transformed by iron. It was a dizzying certainty. He gripped the head of his cane and breathed this knowledge into his lungs. Then, like the performer Johnson, whom he had seen at Covent Garden riding first two and then three horses at a gallop, he reined in his thoughts and dedicated himself to the task at hand.

He turned to find the others huddled around Monsieur Numbers, who was being forced to revise his calculations. They had settled on a ratio of four to one: that is, four ceramic pipes would fail for every one of iron. The cost would be about the same. Was this ratio sufficient, in Wilkinson's view?

Wilkinson wrinkled his nose skeptically, but reserved comment, observing that he was of course biased. "However," he added, "even if we accept that ratio, which may be generous, your reckoning must include the actual cost of failures—which goes far beyond the cost of the pipe itself. First, you have to find the leak. Hmm?" A majestic sweep of his cane took in the gargantuan tangle. "Under cobblestones laid on sand. Hmm? Under canals. Ha! Through public parks. 'Tis not so easy. Only then can you dig up the failed section and replace it. And with ceramic, you cannot replace only one length, because they are cupped one into the other—unlike iron pipes, which can be bolted together at their flanges. Therefore you must excavate forty or fifty feet."

In the end, the case was made unequivocally for iron.

The pudding-faced man stepped forward and bowed with a courtly flourish. "Our Majesty Louis XVI greets Monsieur Wilkinson, and invites him to visit the royal arsenal at Indret."

For an instant Wilkinson thought it might be the young monarch himself, but recovered his senses in time to make the appropriate response. "Sir," he said. "May His Majesty be advised that John Wilkinson accepts his invitation most gratefully, and offers sincerest greetings on behalf of himself and the New Willey Works, and"—he cut a little curlicue in the air with his cane—"the Shropshire iron trade." He looked forward to seeing the Quakers' faces when he announced this at the next quarterly meeting of the ironmasters.

The following morning, they set out for Indret, six passengers in all—a journey that would take the better part of three days. The arsenal was to be built on an island in the river Loire, just inland from Nantes, on the Brittany coast. They traveled in a gilded coach-and-eight flying the royal colors, with advance postilions sounding cornets to clear the way, scattering chickens and geese as they thundered through the Paris suburbs.

Wilkinson's stomach felt empty, unballasted. His meal had consisted of a single honey-glazed squab with croissants, melon, cheese, and coffee—dainty fare for a man accustomed to a full English breakfast.

Once he inspected the site and they reached an agreement, he would not return to Paris but save time by sailing home direct from Nantes. He voiced his one regret to Houlière, that he would not be able to see Madame Bougainville, and was immediately sorry, for Houlière said with a giggle, "We will make a Frenchman of you yet!"

Wilkinson scowled out the window in time to see a cart overturn in a ditch, apples spilling everywhere, the driver waving a fist at their coach as it rumbled past. Poor devil. In England, the common man at least had some recourse in the law.

Wilkinson's fellow passengers consisted of Monsieur Money, sitting on the other side of Houlière, and three senior military officers, who occupied the facing seat. Of the three, the highest ranking was the fleet admiral, directly opposite Wilkinson—a tall, ruddy fellow with watery blue eyes and white muttonchop whiskers that gave him an almost ethereal air, who wrapped himself in a deep-blue wool military cape trimmed in gold braid and talked about naval engagements during the Seven Years War, and clucked to the homing pigeons in the wooden cage at their feet. At the other end of the seat was the general who would be in charge of building the cannon works. He was a square-built man with a pocked face and sarcastic wit. Though he tried to question Wilkinson about the invention for boring cannon, he was unable to contain his arrogance and ended up talking about the land battles of the Seven Years War, of which he seemed to remember only French victories. Sitting between the admiral and the general was another general, an Alsatian with one leg who wore pince-nez and a faded horsehair wig and asked a few good questions about air furnaces. About the Seven Years War, in which he had apparently lost the leg (the pigeon cage occupied the space where his foot would have been), he said little, listening to the others and nodding, enveloped in a great sadness.

When they stopped for the night at inns, they slept in two large beds usually supplemented by a cot. At the first stop, a pigeon was released bearing a message penned by Houlière concerning some "special arrangement." The pock-faced general, not to be outdone, released a bird the following day on the pretext of military business, but Wilkinson suspected it was a sham.

Most of the conversation took place between Wilkinson, Houlière, and Monsieur Money. The three senior officers reminisced among themselves, mainly about their colleagues' careers. Observing how little interest they displayed in ironmaking or commerce, Wilkinson felt his usual contempt for military men. They were babes, for all their plumes and preening. None of them had ever had to meet a payroll.

The only point on which the admiral showed any ardor was the tendency of the French cannons to explode. "For your expertise, sir, France would be forever indebted." He drew himself straight as a ramrod.

It was Houlière and Monsieur Money who described the scope of the new arsenal and got down to the business of the *quid pro quo*— the order of the pipes Wilkinson could continue to supply even in the event of an embargo on military goods, should the two countries go to war (which seemed increasingly likely). In exchange, Wilkinson would supply technical advice, including the secret of boring cannon from the solid.

Only one point proved troublesome to Wilkinson, and unfortunately Houlière and Money kept insisting on it. They wanted him to send Will to oversee construction of the arsenal. "Your brother is young, eager, unmarried," Houlière coaxed. "Let him stay for two years."

Wilkinson resisted. He could not spare Will for even a year. His brother was a dependable overseer at Bersham, more valuable than he knew, and content for now in his subservient role. Would he remain so humble after a glimpse of the world? Would he not be corrupted by French ways?

The subject was dropped while Houlière amused them with yet another story. The Frenchman was more formal in the presence of the other officers, who were his superiors in age and rank. However, he was so adept at dropping names from the court at Versailles, referring to intrigues that only an insider would know, that by the time they were halfway to Indret, the officers were currying favor with him.

The stories that centered on the foibles of officers Houlière related in English. But when he portrayed ladies associated with the court or described amorous rivalries, he lapsed into French enough to pique the curiosity of the pock-faced brigadier general, who took a grudging interest in such gossip.

Love, thought Wilkinson, is the currency of the bored. A pathetically inflated coin. Gazing out the coach window at the bare December orchards and bleached stubble of cornfields of Brittany, he thought of his first wife, Ann, dead some twenty years. But he could recall neither her features nor the sensations of love. And he could summon none of his early feelings toward Mary Lee, only the excitement that her fortune had brought him. Comfort, yes. A steady mind, good cheer, a tiredness in the haunches. The familiarity of meals taken together with few words exchanged. But not the thrill of that rose, not the shiver of laughter that stirred his blood. By God, he was forty-eight years old. He did not have long before he would be plagued by toothache and gout. A restlessness swelled in him.

Laughter from the others interrupted this reverie.

"*Mais c'est vrai!*" said Houlière.

The three officers were chortling. The old Alsatian slapped his good thigh. Monsieur Money rolled his eyes.

Wilkinson asked the cause of their mirth.

General Pock-Face responded in French. "Our friend Houlière thinks he knows the reason the Parisians wish to have water upstairs!"

Houlière shrugged, insouciant. "You have but to ask the ladies. They will tell you."

"What reason is that?" demanded Wilkinson.

Houlière switched to English. "It is quite simple. The water is for the ladies' ponies."

"Ponies?" asked Wilkinson.

"*Oui, oui.*" Houlière spread his knees to demonstrate, seeing Wilkinson's puzzlement. "You have not this narrow tub, to wash the private pieces?"

"Yes, yes. I suppose." Wilkinson chuckled with the others, but he remained baffled.

When they arrived at Indret, Wilkinson was taken on a complete tour and introduced to various engineers. Indret, it was explained, had been a sleepy coastal hamlet before the earthworks were started two years ago. He was impressed with the magnitude of the preparations, which included improvements to the island itself as well as an ingenious system of dikes with gates designed to impound the tide. Leave it to the French to do things on a grand scale!

Beyond this, he was appalled. The samples of coal they showed him were too soft to make good coke, and the French method of coking in open piles was quite primitive. Little wonder they used coke only for malt making. In these and other matters, such as air furnaces, they were more backward than he remembered from his last visit to France. Or was it simply the rapidity of change in England these past few years? Here in France, time seemed to stand still. It would go against them in the coming war.

"You will help us, then?" Houlière asked, the second evening. They had had much discussion. The others had gone to the inn outside Nantes, and Wilkinson's host had brought him to this stone château, hinting at some "surprise." The two men stood on a balcony with a stone balustrade overlooking an expanse of salt marsh bounded on either side by rocky headlands—a view that was to burn forever in Wilkinson's memory, for reasons unknown to him at that moment.

Wilkinson sighed. He thought of his father's adage. *If the French would ever give up their fiddling and dancing*...Confronted by the sorry state of French ironmaking, he felt like Jesus Christ being presented with the lame and the blind. At the least, he should hold out for more money. He offered his companion some Hispaniola snuff from the little oval ivory box he carried in his waistcoat pocket.

"I fear," said Wilkinson, when they were done sneezing, "that you require more help than I have time to give. It is much more than learning my technique for boring cannon. You must learn to fire with coke."

"Ah, but you have only to send your brother Will."

*Ah, but!* Wilkinson thought. His obstinacy hardened. All the arguments that Houlière had presented were true: Will's presence here would guarantee the work against interruption, Will was young enough to benefit from the experience, and Will would give Wilkinson a foothold in the French market. Still, Wilkinson had the foreboding that nothing would be the same again with his brother.

"Monsieur Wilkinson." Houlière bunched his hands impatiently and spread them like a chicken stretching its wings. "We are *so close* to an agreement."

It was true. They had prepared a draft of the contract, on which they largely agreed. Seeing the pleading in those liquid brown eyes, Wilkinson realized what was at stake for Houlière: the man's reputation with two ministries and the court of Versailles; his career; another row of curls in his wig. The ironmaster leaned his elbows on the railing, gazed at the moon's reflection in the salt marsh, and let the silence stretch between them. He would send William for only three months. Ask for more money. Insist on a sinecure for one of Priestley's sons, who showed little talent for ironmaking but who was interested in carbonated water. In short, he would drive a hard bargain.

"I believe," said Houlière, "it is time to introduce a certain visitor who has come all the way from Paris to see you."

Wilkinson turned to see a woman silhouetted in the doorway, the lace of her full gown lit by lamplight. He heard the rich music of her laughter.

The next dozen hours robbed the ironmaster of his resolve, his brother, and his reason. That part of his character that was flinty and implacable melted in the lady's hands like ice, and the part of his body that was soft and flaccid was coaxed into sublime rigidity.

She kept the lamps burning low and insisted that they remove their clothing entirely, except for a long black silk scarf she wound about herself provocatively. This surprised him, who was accustomed to rummaging blindly amongst petticoats and nightgowns. Never had he seen a woman so revealed. Nor had he known such hands—such skillful, teasing, probing hands. Hands capable of endless variation, moving over him with the scarcely palpable stirring of a lazy zephyr or cupping his ballocks with unexpected vigor. Her fingertips and tongue were at times indistinguishable. At her command he entered her—without armor, for she assured him he had nothing to fear, and her dandling fingers made it impossible to resist. She lifted both her knees higher than he thought any knee could go—to her ears, in fact—and conveyed him this way and that, only to force his withdrawal, until he was quite beside himself.

When he was spent, she rolled from the bed and opened a wardrobe chest that had accompanied her from Paris—an upright cabinet of the sort that generals take with them into the field, in this case fruitwood inlaid with ebony and mother-of-pearl. She took out a narrow stool that contained an oval silver bowl, which she called a *bidet*. She asked him to fill the bowl with water from a nearby pitcher, which he did happily, surprised to find some lines of old French poetry engraved across the bottom of the bowl. He translated them to himself:

> *Arise! Let us go see the dew-pearled plants*
> *with your lovely rosebuds crowned with buds*
> *and your delicate carnations watered*
> *yesterday evening by a caring hand.*

It was signed FROM YOUR GREATEST ADMIRER, J.N.

When she was finished with her ablutions—which he scarcely dared watch—she opened a drawer in the chest and removed a vial of scented oil, a red leather riding crop, and other objects, which she applied to him with some enthusiasm, until to his wonderment he had grown large again.

She counseled leisure this time. "You cannot smell the flowers from the galloping horse, Monsieur Wilkinson." She said it sternly, and flicked his thigh with the riding crop.

What happened next was beyond anything Wilkinson had ever experienced. She pressed against him with such obvious pleasure, and prolonged the act with such skill, allowing him entrance and then not, applying pressures here and there, lashing his buttocks until they glowed with heat, wrestling him this way and that and climbing astride him from above and below with such amazing agility, that he could not stop bellowing and snorting like a donkey. Then she got him on his back and crouched over him with her legs spread and dipped herself on his rigid member—*la plume,* she called it—once, twice, thrice: rocking each time, moaning like an apparition, her throat quivering; unleashing torrents of such pleasure within him that he thought he would choke to death on his own spittle.

Before the explosion could take place, he felt a hard pressure between his legs, which must have been her thumb driving deep into the fleshy root of his ecstasy, stopping it before it could erupt. Slowly then, so slowly that she seemed at first motionless, she eased herself from him, the parting of flesh clasping flesh like a fruit being peeled. Slowly, tantalizingly, she eased herself from him.

My God!

"*Je demande l'autre plume,*" she whispered.

His back was arching, eyes bulging. "What other plume?" he rasped.

She chuckled. "You must sign." Encircling his penis with her fingers, as if holding a quill, she waggled it.

"Sign?" What the devil was she talking about?

"In a moment," she explained, "Marchant de la Houlière will come to the door with the agreement for you to sign. It will take only a minute. Then you and I may continue."

Wilkinson started to protest, but she knelt beside his *plume* again, lifted one white thigh, and plunged him again into paradise.

Madame Bougainville moaned sharply, twice.

A knock sounded at the door.

Deftly she rolled from the bed, handed Wilkinson his breeches, helped him into his shirt. Sweat was pouring from him. His legs wobbled like India rubber. She buttoned the front of his breeches. "Ah, but he is so big!" she exclaimed with a pat.

*Ah, but,* thought Wilkinson ruefully.

"When this other business is finished," she whispered, "you must allow me to sit on your lap. Please hurry, for my sake!" She fled to the closet and shut the door.

Still shaking, Wilkinson opened the door for Houlière, who was holding a lap desk. They exchanged muted greetings. Wilkinson sat on the edge of the bed, his buttocks stinging, and forced himself to read the agreement. The terms were all as they had agreed, with one clause added: William Wilkinson was to come to Indret for a period of at least one year. Will was to receive a salary of twelve thousand livres, which amounted to five hundred pounds. Too generous! Will would come back corrupted. A ragged sigh escaped from Wilkinson's breast. But he nodded.

Hesitating before dipping the quill, he wondered if he himself should be the one to come to Indret.

What came to mind was that oval silver bowl, the lines of poetry shimmering through the water. The initials J.N. The *bidet* had been a gift, he realized, from Jacques Necker.

And the lady? She might be Necker's mistress. And might become his, too, with the finance minister's blessings. Who could understand these French games? The thought of her waiting in the closet quickened his pulse.

But she was not a woman to be tamed.

Then he thought of all his undertakings, the furnaces spouting black smoke, and the bridge, and how if he did not keep a close watch on Darby, the scheme would miscarry. He remembered the flurry of matters that clamored for his attention, even as his heart pounded like a blooming hammer under his sweaty shirt, its ruffles damp with the perfume of love.

He heaved another sigh. "Marchant de la Houlière," he whispered. "You must not allow my brother William anywhere near Madame Bougainville."

The Frenchman nodded once, crisply, with a wink that was like a salute.

Wilkinson signed with his usual flourish:

*John Wilkinson*

# John Wilkinson

U pon his return, he called on Darby to make sure the young Quaker was pursuing the act in Parliament and tending to his tasks as treasurer. Again, Wilkinson promoted the idea of a hotel to be erected at one end of the bridge. And in talking to others in a position to influence Darby, he again encouraged them to put in a word with Darby and to make the case for iron. Finally, he was satisfied that it was all moving forward. Darby was caught up in the whole affair, trussed up as tight as a rabbit on a roasting spit.

In the meantime, Wilkinson was busy lining his own pockets, filling orders for cannon. New Willey had never been busier: the boring mill shrieked into the evening; the sky was black with smoke; the slag heaps bled ocher liquors into Tarback Dingle. Only occasionally did memories of Madame Bougainville send a shiver down his spine. He spent the balance of his time preparing foundations for the new engine, which Watt was to erect in the coming month.

One day in January, when Wilkinson was in the engine house supervising construction of the cooling pool in which the separate condenser would be submerged, he looked out through the rain (falling elsewhere as snow) to see Darby's carriage. It surprised him. Darby rarely deigned to visit. As it turned out, the visitors were Darby's younger brother, Samuel, and his sister Sarah, accompanied by none other than Mrs. Foster, *l'électricienne formidable*.

Mrs. Foster, in her forthright manner, with little in the way of preamble, stated the purpose of their visit. Young Samuel had come up with a new design for the bridge. There were, she said, "compelling reasons" why his design compared favorably with Pritchard's.

Wilkinson saw that Samuel was holding a long tube under the flap of his greatcoat to protect it from the snow. Managing to conceal his amusement at the presumption in this, and swayed by Mrs. Foster's large green eyes and commanding presence, Wilkinson conducted his visitors to the office. He ordered a counting table cleared so that Samuel could unroll his plan. The young man hesitated, looked around furtively at the scriveners. He was a queer bird, this youngest Darby.

Mrs. Foster spoke up. "We need someplace more private."

"Very well." The ironmaster took them into his own office, behind the clerk's platform. Apologizing for the clutter, he cleared his desk of some drawings of steam valves, and Samuel unrolled his drawing.

Wilkinson stared. At first he could see little order in the whole business, with its soaring lines. Well, there was order of a kind. But how to make a bridge of it? Then he saw it was topsy-turvy: the roadway was suspended *beneath* the main arch. How odd. Nothing could be further from the classical principles of bridge building. It made the Black Friars Bridge or the Nevilly Bridge look Roman by comparison. He looked up at his guests to see if perhaps it was a joke.

Mrs. Foster was watching him expectantly. "This is more than a bridge, you understand. It is a statement."

A *statement!* Wilkinson's belly shook with laughter. He could not help himself. "I daresay," he chuckled, "if one man can construct a copper duck to quack and eat, then another can make a bridge talk! Ha! My dear lady—" He paused to look again at the absurd drawing. "My dear lady." He could only shake his head and chuckle.

Samuel Darby's face darkened. He seemed about to snatch the drawing away, but the ladies soothed him.

Mrs. Foster responded with surprising spirit. "Mr. Wilkinson, I promised to give you compelling reasons why this design of Samuel's should be considered. Are you interested in hearing them, or do you just want to entertain yourself at our expense?"

Wilkinson frowned. "Forgive me, Madame," he said in a tone that she could not have failed to recognize as patronizing. "Just what are these compelling reasons?"

"First, if you'll notice, this bridge would be impossible to build using wood and stone. Look at those curves. It shows off the advantages of cast iron."

This was certainly true. The wooden patterns themselves would tax a joiner's skill.

"Whereas," she added, "Mr. Pritchard's bridge could be built as easily of wood."

She had a point. Even now some of the subscribers were complaining it could be built more cheaply of timber or stone; and Darby seemed about to cave in to them. A hateful possibility, which must be avoided at all cost. "Yes," Wilkinson agreed. "Quite so. Go on."

"Well," she said, "you'll notice too that it uses more iron. Perhaps twice as much as Pritchard's design."

The ironmaster shrugged. " 'Tis extravagant, I should say."

"Exactly."

Wilkinson felt a smile creep across his face. This was a bold lass. "Aye, madame. 'Twould be an advertisement for excess."

"It would be a celebration of iron."

*Yes!* Wilkinson felt his pulse quicken. "But whether the subscribers would agree to such a celebration is another story. And your brother"—he turned to young Samuel—"is hardly given to extravagance." But as he said this, another thought occurred to him. "Have you shown this to Abraham?"

Samuel shook his head. "We wished thee to see it first."

"Ah." Wilkinson raised his eyebrows questioningly.

"My brother," said Samuel, "has a very narrow view of the bridge."

Wilkinson was pleased to detect a note of petulance in this. "Your brother," he agreed, "is a cautious man." He smiled crookedly at the drawing before him. He observed how the rigidity was accomplished, how the weight was distributed—and he began to admire its originality. To be sure, it was not to his own taste. Like the snails he had sampled in Paris. But the structure, however lofty, looked stout enough to endure the Severn's rampaging floods. "Very original, Mr. Darby. But why build it so high? The upper part of the arch carries little actual weight."

Samuel smiled. "Why is Winchester Cathedral built so high?"

*Quite so.* Wilkinson nodded. *Quite so.* A cathedral to the new age. What was it Darwin said? A hymn to Man.

Samuel appeared more at ease now. He continued excitedly. "Imagine it seen from the river. Imagine Lincoln Hill on one side and Benthall Edge on the other."

"Imagine," said Mrs. Foster, "the visual impact."

*Visual impact.* An imaginative phrase. Why not? It would be a spectacle, a triumph. It would be, as she put it, a *celebration* of iron. People would flock from London to see it. More, he supposed, than would come to look at Pritchard's design. All those slack-jawed pilgrims struck dumb by its visual impact!

And here was Abraham Darby's young brother visiting him in secret. What was the meaning of that? Hmm? Wilkinson's mind raced. And what was Mrs. Foster's interest in Samuel Darby? He smelled intrigue, and more. Certainly it was an opportunity to be seized.

"Well, sir." He gave the drawing a thump. " 'Tis a capital design. No mere pigwidgeon, this! Ha! Indeed so." He reflected a moment. "We must have a model!"

## Maggie Foster

**R**iding home, they were all three elated. Maggie leaned back in the carriage seat, her eyes shut against the low afternoon sun dazzling off the newly fallen snow. Her cloak was open and the sun warm on her chest while Samuel and Sarah chattered opposite her.

It had gone well with Wilkinson. Maggie had not expected to like him, but she admired the Broseley ironmaster's spontaneity. Not that she completely trusted him. He had ended up embracing Samuel's design almost too eagerly. Did he really believe that Abraham and the committee would be won over by seeing a scale model? Was it simply the decisiveness of a man who gets things done—or did he have some secret agenda?

Sunlight against her eyelids. Andrew was driving west to the Build-was Bridge. She was glad to be upwind of the gorge. She liked Wilkinson, she decided. Everything at Sunniside seemed to move at such an agonizing pace, between Abraham's ambivalence and the Quaker devotion to consensus. At Ecosophia, too, decisions took forever. But sitting there in Wilkinson's office, watching him write the contract, listening to the scratch of his quill, she had felt a thrill of hope.

"...hereby commissions Samuel Darby," intoned Wilkinson, speaking of himself in the third person, panting obesely, "to build a model of said bridge."

*Bingo!* Propagate a few whims! She had never been around anyone like Wilkinson.

That power was seductive. The ironmaster, in his bluff, cheerful way, had asked Samuel a few questions and then written out a contract. He was jovial yet businesslike. The model had to be built to the same scale as the model that Pritchard was working on, so that the two could be readily compared. Samuel was to be paid twelve guineas, half of which he would receive upon completing a fully detailed drawing. The finished model was to be in Wilkinson's hands by Midsummer's Day. That gave Samuel five months. The whole thing was to be kept secret until Wilkinson decided the moment was right. Timing was everything, he said.

While he walked them out to their carriage, Wilkinson talked about iron—mostly to Maggie. He became rhapsodic as he leaned closer to describe sotto voce the crystalline properties of cast iron. "I would like to see you again, madame," he said, kissing her hand as he helped her into the carriage.

"He hath French ways," Sarah observed after the carriage pulled away.

Samuel smiled lopsidedly. "He hath a face that would ripen cucumbers."

They rode past stacks of cannon—the same cannon they had observed on their way in but seeming less ominous now, lost in the excitement.

They called at the Wilkinson home, a blocky faux Norman structure of brick and stone known as the Lawns. It was smaller than Sunniside, with most of the lawn in back. They were received by Wilkinson's wife and his twenty-year-old daughter. The ostensible purpose of this visit to Broseley was to play whist with the daughter.

Maggie observed in Mary her father's prominent nose, mercifully softened by youth. She was the child of Wilkinson's first marriage and his only legitimate heir. In a few years she would marry a clergyman named Theophilus Holbrooke, be disowned by her father, and die giving birth. Chattering blithely about France, she showed them the parasols she had brought back for herself and her stepmother.

After they played a couple of rubbers of whist, Samuel announced he was impatient to go back to Madeley. Sarah stamped her foot in mock protest but relented. On the way home, Samuel unrolled his drawing excitedly several times to point out problems he would have to solve before beginning the model. Once, gazing out at the ice-fringed river, he let out a little whoop.

Sarah radiated pleasure. "What a wonderful birthday present," she said. Samuel had turned twenty-one the day before.

They crossed the Buildwas Bridge, the inky river zigzagging like a brush stroke through the snow. The sun dipped behind them as they turned east toward the gorge. A chill fell, and Maggie huddled under her cloak. When she looked up, she was surprised to see tears glistening in Samuel's eyes.

"What's wrong?" she asked.

He struggled a moment before he could answer. "No one, except Sarah, hath"—he patted his sister's hand—"hath ever believed in me."

Maggie put her arms around him. Sarah joined in the hug, and the three of them rocked together.

"Thank thee," Samuel said.

"Don't thank me," she protested, but then thought of those abutments slipping slowly into the riverbed and felt a surge of guilt, with his sideburns springy against her cheek and Sarah's arm around her. They disengaged themselves as the hoofbeats rattled across the wooden bridge at Birches Brook. The fading violet light gave way to the glow of lime kilns and smelters. " 'Twas your drawing that did it," she said.

Samuel shook his head. " 'Twas thy arguments that carried the day."

After supper, he bounded upstairs to his study. Maggie went to the greenhouse. She was still flying high from the day's success. Sitting on the brick floor in the darkness, inhaling the earthy fragrance and pretending she was back in Ecosophia, she talked herself down. *I did good,* she told Trevor. Erzulie. Carl. The smell of tomato vines brought them closer.

She was disappointed when Sarah arrived with a candle and asked if she could join her. The two women sat in silence, the candle flame reflecting in the glass. Finally Sarah spoke.

"I have my doubts about John Wilkinson."

Maggie's throat tightened. "What in particular?"

"I cannot stop thinking about all those cannon."

Maggie felt her heart thud. She had put the cannon out of her mind. "Me too." It was not altogether a lie.

"And I dislike going behind Abey's back."

*Great.* Maggie felt a sinking sensation: the whole plan falling apart. "So. You think we made a mistake."

"I know not what to think. Sammy is so pleased. 'Tis such a brave plan." She shook her head fiercely. "Thou canst have no idea how important this is to him, Maggie!"

"And you're afraid for him."

"Yes."

"What would you like me to do?"

Sarah was silent. Waiting for her response, Maggie felt a gathering resentment. Why hadn't Sarah voiced her objections earlier? Finally Sarah spoke.

"Mind thou dost not raise his hopes too high." She sighed. "And yet that will be difficult, with Sammy." She put a hand on Maggie's arm. "I do not fault thee, Maggie. I beg thee only listen with care to thine own heart. Listen to that small, still voice."

They sat in silence a while longer. Then Sarah gave Maggie's arm a squeeze and left. Maggie watched the candle flame disappear from sight. She kept getting new glimpses of Sarah. Sarah had a wise heart. And she was right: their pact with Wilkinson was—Maggie couldn't think of the word. Suspect. Yes, suspect. And it was true: she had to find a way to protect Samuel.

Abiah was back from her journey. She had carried her message with varying success, sometimes *owned by the Spirit* and sometimes not. She brought tidings from Becky Smith and from other Friends in Sheffield and York.

Meals were again eaten in "awful silence," the men's pipes disappeared from the downstairs parlor, Sarah's green silk dress went back in her armoire, and Maggie resumed her secretarial tasks. But the atmosphere at Sunniside changed that spring in surprising ways.

Samuel was maturing before their eyes. He arranged with Abraham to work in the mold room, where he could learn more about casting complex shapes. And as soon as he came home from the Works, he disappeared into the attic. He sometimes skipped meals, went days without shaving or changing his clothes, and had to be reminded to attend Meeting. He was cheerful despite his red-rimmed eyes. His earlier sarcasm had given way to whimsical irony. His bouts of depression were less acute; instead of skulking around the house, he took long walks or mused abstractedly at windows.

Sarah was clearly proud of him. She herself put more energy into the household, taking over some of Abiah's functions at the malt mill, helping organize the social calendar, becoming more focused in her letter writing aimed at prison reform. Her posture improved.

Maggie kept Sarah's warning in mind. The sight of Samuel dozing during Meeting, a lock of hair falling across his forehead, awakened a kind of maternal pride in her. She had no right to that pride, she knew, since her success would require his failure. Nevertheless, a plan was taking shape in her mind—a way of protecting him against that failure.

Abiah was preoccupied as usual with her ministry, writing letters about her recent travels; still, she too noticed the changes in Samuel. Once, observing him staring intently into space, she said that he reminded her of their father.

Abraham bridled at the comparison. But he could hardly complain. With Samuel's anger in abeyance, Abraham seemed freer, younger. He could be heard humming to himself or bounding up the stairs two at a time. In January he and Becky received approval from their respective Meetings to marry. The wedding would take place in Yorkshire, in May. Everything was proceeding on schedule.

Almost everything.

A week after their trip to Broseley, Samuel announced to Maggie that he was not moving to London.

"Not go to London?" Maggie echoed.

He grinned and shrugged. "So I can build the model."

"What did you tell Abraham?"

"That I need to stay to learn more about casting, and that I can help him with the bridge. He was agreeable. London can wait. I shall go after Midsummer, when I have finished the model."

Maggie was stunned. This was more basic than sleeve buttons. Samuel's move to London in January was to have been a turning point in his life.

History was about to change.


H er plan for protecting Samuel was to get him involved in another project before the bridge was even completed—before it had a chance to fail. Get him involved in a project that would succeed. Perhaps a smaller bridge at a more stable site.

It was not just on Sarah's account. Maggie had developed a real fondness for Samuel. Overlooked in the first shock of Samuel's decision not to go to London was a simple human response that came to her later: she was glad Samuel and Sarah were remaining at least for the summer. She would have missed them.

Intervening to stave off Samuel's ruin, in the course of carrying out her mission, involved some further risk. The risk of unintended consequences. But she was beginning to realize that everything she did involved that risk.

She and Samuel slipped notes under each other's doors.

*Dear Lady Green Eyes*—written at the bottom of a sketch—*dost thou think this curve is sufficient?*

*Go for it!* she wrote back.

"Go for it?" he asked, puzzled, when on the following night she tiptoed up to his study.

She grinned. "It means proceed."

"Dost thou like it?"

"It's fantastic."

She meant it. He was taking more seriously than she expected the use of natural structures, studying insect wings and tree leaves under a magnifying glass to incorporate those patterns into the bridge, for strength. " 'Twill save iron," he explained. But she sensed more was involved.

As the drawing evolved, the curved members making up the bowstring trusses became more veinlike, defining lozenge-shaped spaces. The effect was reminiscent of the Art Nouveau movement at the beginning of the twentieth century. If Samuel's bridge succeeded, it could revolutionize British design, bypassing that whole ponderous, pedestal-based Greco-Roman aesthetic that clunked Frankenstein-monsterishly through the nineteenth century.

When, by the end of February, Samuel had reduced the mass by almost half, she grew uneasy. He had eliminated nonsupporting structures and was beginning to subdivide the lozenge-shaped spaces into triangles.

One night she came upstairs and found him playing with a shape cut from pasteboard. It was an equilateral triangle, with sides given a slight S-curve. He was trying it at different locations within the large pencil drawing. He looked up and grinned. He was wearing the red breeches that he sometimes wore after the household was asleep—what he called his cavorting breeches. "Mark, Maggie!" he said, showing how the triangle could be used to fill the various spaces. Maggie's heart started racing. It wasn't just the bowstring-truss bridge he was anticipating.

What if Samuel studied bees' honeycombs under that damned magnifying glass? What if he put those triangles together to make a tetrahedron? He was dangerously close to the structures that Buckminster Fuller began developing in the 1930s.

"What thinkest thou?" He handed her the triangle.

She shrugged. "It's okay."

"Okay." He frowned. "I never know what thou meanest by 'okay.' "

"Not bad. Not good. Just okay."

"Just okay." He pouched his lips in and out, sucked his teeth, and scratched one sideburn. Waited for more from her.

Maggie sighed. She liked being Lady Green Eyes, liked having her opinion count. But at the moment she was scared. Struggling to act casual, she handed the triangle back to him. "I don't think you should make it any lighter, Samuel."

"Why not?"

"Well, for one thing, what John Wilkinson liked about your design was its mass. He likes that heft."

"John Wilkinson!" Samuel sneered. "What does John Wilkinson know about bridges? 'Tis Abey and the subscribers who shall decide."

"John Wilkinson is the one who's commissioning you to build the model, young man!" Instantly she regretted the "young man."

Samuel glowered.

"I'm not arguing with you." She lowered her voice, aware of the sleeping household below (and Jane, on this floor). "It's just that we sold the idea to Wilkinson on the basis of its mass. And Wilkinson has influence."

"Influence?"

"He can promote it to Abraham and the subscribers in a way that we can't."

Samuel fumed. "Thou art speaking of politics!"

"Exactly!"

"But I would have my bridge judged on its own merits! What dost *thou* think?"

Maggie sighed. "Well, for starters, how will you connect these pieces to one another?"

"Bolts."

*Bolts!* Jesus. She sat down on the floor. Bolts might be a good thing. More rigidity. But . . .

"What's wrong, Maggie?" Samuel climbed down from his stool.
She shut her eyes. She had to think this through. The room felt airless. Samuel's butterfly wings proliferating through time and space brought to mind that classic metaphor of chaos theory: the butterfly flapping its wings causing an endless chain of consequences.

"Maggie?"

"I need a little time to think about this, Samuel."

"Tomorrow?" He offered her a hand up.

She nodded, taking the hand. "Tomorrow."

She lay awake most of the night, unable to get those triangles out of her mind.

Samuel Darby figured in the historic record as a mere footnote. But suppose he were to come up with the geodesic dome a century and a half before Buckminster Fuller?

What would be the impact on human society? Domes instead of skyscrapers, circles instead of squares.

But to be more realistic. Samuel's design was already conspicuously daring. What if Abraham refused to go along with it? And what about the subscribers? Paul had observed once that early attempts like this at using new materials tended to be conservative, allowing wide margins of safety. Samuel was pushing it pretty hugely.

And if by some miracle the subscribers went along with such a lacy design, then its failure would send the wrong message. The bridge would fail because of its rigidity in the presence of geologic movement, but that would not be the perception. The failure would be attributed to the bridge's *lightness*. She thought of the collapse of the Tacoma Narrows Bridge in 1940, the Kansas City Hyatt Regency Hotel skywalk in 1981, and the buckling of the Akashi Kaikyo Bridge in 2012—failures typical of a more confident stage of engineering, where margins of safety could be reduced according to presumably more precise calculations. It was too soon for that kind of failure. The lesson in this present would simply be *more bridge*.

It occurred to her that she could show Samuel how to allow for geologic movement. She knew enough to help him design a sliding foot. It would be a lesson in lightness. Domes instead of skyscrapers.

But Samuel was pushing the limits of cast iron too far. Such a bridge might accelerate the demand for structural steel. Which in turn might hasten the advent of skyscrapers, battleships, and tanks. She thought of how the Eads Bridge, still a hundred years in the future, would prompt Andrew Carnegie to increase steelmaking capacity.

Her mind was getting muddled with possibilities.

The clock downstairs struck three.

She told herself to get some sleep.

*You can't think of everything.* Scalpel, not an ax. That was why the mission was kept so narrow. But was there any such thing as narrow, once you opened up the fabric of history? She could almost hear that fabric rending. The tick of individual fibers bursting.

What time was it now? In another two or three hours she would hear the rooster crow, the creak of Jane's tread on the winding staircase. She tried thinking of Jane, but the fire was gone. Jane was seeing a man now, a maltster in Dawley.

Samuel was not going to London. History was changing. Soon, her carefully memorized dates would no longer serve as a reliable road map.

Erzulie used to say she got to sleep by praying. It helped her let go. *Just kick back. Say what you want.*

*I want the bridge to fail. I want Samuel to succeed later, at something. Something lighter, humbler.* She tried to shape it as a prayer.

*Please. Let humility prevail. Let me be humble.* Tears ran down her cheeks. She fell asleep.


**B**y the time she finished breakfast, Maggie had her thoughts in order.

1. Make Samuel's bridge look strong. It must fail by its grandiosity.

2. Encourage his use of bolts. They would make for a more rigid bridge frame and concentrate the stress. When the first frame mem-

ber snapped, the stress would be transferred more readily to adjacent members.

3. Keep the agenda narrow.


When Samuel got home from the Works that evening, she invited him to walk with her in the deer park. She had rehearsed what she wanted to say.

"Hast thou decided?"

He produced the triangular piece of pasteboard from his pocket.

She nodded. She talked about the limits of cast iron. How it was brittle stuff, crystalline, untrustworthy when poured thin. "Suppose you get a gas bubble or a hairline flaw? A thin casting like that could crack." The emphasis she gave the word *crack* caused a doe to look up, ears alert.

"True," he agreed.

"Trust me. You're better off building it too strong than too weak."

Samuel pulled at his sideburns and pouched his lips. Finally he nodded. He started to crumple up the pasteboard, but she took it from him.

"I'll save it. Maybe it'll be useful in your *next* bridge!" She smiled, tucking the triangle in her apron pocket. "The next one will be your bridge, Samuel. Something smaller. Light and airy. Just play it safe with this one, all right?"

Samuel chuckled. "Play it safe. My Lady Green Eyes hath a rare gift for the original phrase."

# Abraham Darby III

A braham and Samuel were silent as they walked down the foot-path to the Works, through dense fog the color of tobacco. Wearing oilcloth capes and carrying their leather dinner pails, they listened to the cinders crunch underfoot. They could scarcely see their feet. Samuel seemed not altogether awake, having burned his candle at both ends of the day. And Abraham was reluctant to share the uncertainties that bedeviled his thoughts as they proceeded toward the glow of the furnace. This fog had lingered in the gorge for days, growing ever more bitter on the tongue and bringing a sharp pain to the lungs if one breathed too deeply. Still, Abraham took pleasure in hearing the sound of two pair of feet.

He was pleased with Samuel's decision to delay his move to London. Now that Samuel was taking an interest in the Works, Abraham felt less alone. His brother provided an ear for his smaller complaints.

It was the larger questions that Abraham was reluctant to confess—his doubts surrounding the bridge: whether to build it entirely of iron, as Wilkinson insisted, or to follow the more cautious combination of iron and stone now being advocated by many subscribers. This was the question that kept him awake, pacing the floor of his study, along with another question: What did it mean that no one else was interested in building the bridge? At first he took it as confirmation that he was man enough for the job. Now he wondered if he was the only man foolhardy enough.

These doubts he kept to himself, lest he appear indecisive in the eyes of his younger brother. He felt a tenderness toward Samuel that he had not experienced since they were small lads, before Father died: when Abraham used to dress Samuel, who could not yet read, and tell him stories from boarding school.

They stopped at the Old Furnace before going their separate ways—Abraham to the office, Samuel to the pattern-making shop. Abraham said, "Whitbread's brewery claims that the new cylinder we sent them is nearly three-quarters of an inch out of round. I must have a word with Wagstaff." He made a face. He did not mention Whitbread's reference to Wilkinson's new machine, which offended him deeply. Nor did he communicate, beyond the grimace, his reluctance to reproach Wagstaff.

"Wilt thou take it back?" Samuel asked.

Abraham shrugged. "If it be truly off by that much, then we shan't be able to correct it. I hate the idea of shipping it back." He frowned. "I shall have to send a man to confirm the claim, then bore a new one for Whitbread and turn the old to scrap."

"Should Wagstaff not have taken its measure more precisely?"

Abraham nodded. "Most assuredly." Samuel's response was the same as his own—unlike that of the clerk, who, with cool, unblinking eyes, rarely blamed or commiserated. Again Abraham took comfort in Samuel's presence. Turning to go, he was warmed by the thought that a man could do well with a wife at home and a brother in the Works. Water in one's own cistern.

Wagstaff was foreman of the boring mill, a gruff fellow twice Abraham's age, set in his ways, barrel-chested and partly deaf, so that it was difficult to get him to budge. Any suggestion for improvement caused him to glare in the most baleful manner and puff himself up like a toad.

And of course it was just while Abraham was remonstrating with

Wagstaff that John Wilkinson strode into the boring shed. Wilkinson proclaimed that he was on the way to Bedlam Furnace to purchase pig iron but had detoured here "with an idea in mind." Perceiving that Abraham was occupied, the Broseley ironmaster made a show of staying out of the way, but he was difficult to ignore as he strolled jovially among the cylinder cradles and prodded screw jacks with his cane.

"Old," Wilkinson observed with a smile, when Abraham joined him.

"Old?"

Wilkinson nodded, giving a crank a careless twist. " 'Tis good enough for the common engines, I suppose."

" 'Tis not so old," Abraham protested, trying to conceal his irritation. "This whole boring mill was built new by Richard Reynolds just twelve or thirteen years ago."

"Ah. Then I venture to say time moves differently for you and me, Mr. Darby. 'Tis the *idea* that is obsolete." He took Abraham's arm. "You would be better off if the machine itself were older, I warrant, for then you could justify changing it!" The armsmaker laughed a shrill, demonic laugh that caused Abraham's guts to contract. Wilkinson went on to talk of the "arithmetic of change" and cackled again, just as horribly. " 'Tis the future!"

Abraham shook off Wilkinson's hand. Whitbread's letter had referred to Wilkinson's new boring machine and its supposed ability to bore accurately to the thickness of a worn shilling. Abraham wished to hear no more of Wilkinson's cleverness—least of all from Wilkinson. He thought longingly of the teapot simmering back in his office, where he had left a licorice root steeping, and he recalled how it was talking to Wilkinson like this in December that he had come down with that terrible grippe.

Wilkinson leaned forward confidentially. "Have you given any more thought to Bedlam?" He would be happy, he said, to make discreet inquiries of the owners concerning their future plans, taking care to say nothing about Abraham's interest in it.

The keenest interest, of course, was Wilkinson's, although

Abraham had been considering the purchase himself for the past year. Of all the works, Bedlam was closest to the site for the new bridge. Its extra ironmaking capacity would permit him to keep making pots while the bridge was being cast. And although Bedlam had higher costs, the demand for pig iron was steadily rising.

Still, Bedlam had drawbacks. He voiced them to Wilkinson. The most obvious was flooding—as nearly happened during the flood of 1770, and again during the landslip three years ago.

Wilkinson countered that floods of such magnitude as 1770 could be expected only every twenty or thirty years. "If you can buy the furnace cheap enough to recover your costs in five years, you minimize your risk."

This hardly sounded like the voice that spoke to Noah. Still, Abraham saw his point. And yet flooding was not the only risk, he observed. For although it was true that demand for pig iron was now rising, with the supply of American charcoal iron cut off from the great iron plantations of New Jersey and Pennsylvania, what if the rebellion were to end next month?

"Tut, tut!" said Wilkinson. "I have obtained from the French a very substantial order that will require more pig iron than I can produce at New Willey. So I shall be a ready customer."

Heat rose to Abraham's face. "Thou surely knowest I will not bloody my hands supplying iron for cannon!"

Wilkinson seemed startled by his vehemence, but quickly recovered. "Blood in this case," he said cheerfully, "is not as thick as water. The contract, my dear fellow, is not for cannon but for a great lot of pipes for the Paris waterworks."

Abraham was chagrined.

"The fact is," Wilkinson went on, scarcely disguising his triumph, "I shall have my hands so full, betwixt pipe and engine castings, I shan't be making many cannon in future."

"What if England and France go to war?"

"Why, then 'twill be your gain too, sir, for the price of iron will rise like a rocket."

"I refuse to profit from war!"

"Then you must forswear making pots, sir. For all boats rise on the same tide. As iron for cannon rises, so will the price of pots!"

Abraham struggled to keep his voice steady. "At Coalbrookdale, John Wilkinson, we try to hold our prices down!"

"Aye. So you do, for your largest customers." Wilkinson chuckled. "And I do not fault you Quakers on point of business, for thus do you keep the pot trade to yourselves. But alas, I have no wish to provoke you, sir. *Au contraire.* I only suggest that I can guarantee you a market for your surplus pig iron."

"Why dost thou not purchase Bedlam thyself?"

Wilkinson shrugged. " 'Tis on the wrong side of the river."

"The bridge will shorten the distance."

"True, true. Still, I should then be left with a surplus—and must needs choose betwixt pots and guns." He hoisted an eyebrow puckishly. "Would you have me make more guns, sir?"

"I would not."

"Then would you have me turn to pots?"

"I—well. That is thy business, John Wilkinson."

"Well, sir, if I may be bold—whom should you prefer to see end up with the surplus, you or me?"

Abraham frowned, smelling sophistry in this argument. But before he could think of a rejoinder, Wilkinson again softened his tone. "To put it plainly, my friend, your purchase of Bedlam would help wean me from cannon. If thou canst find it in your own interest"—had Abraham's ears deceived him? was Wilkinson addressing him with *thou?*—"then 'twould be a boon to mankind. Ah, thou lookest surprised. But even I will concede that the world is awash in cannon, and we all want peace."

Abraham studied Wilkinson's plump face, trying to gauge its sincerity. Did Wilkinson really wish to quit making arms? Behind those flushed jowls, those gray steely eyes, did the Light yet shine? "I will think upon it, John Wilkinson."

" 'Tis all I ask." Wilkinson smiled fiercely and clapped him on the shoulder. "Now I must be on my way." He conducted Abraham outside the boring shed with the geniality of a host bidding farewell to his guest—and just in time, for Abraham could feel a needle twinge of headache entering his right brow.

Wilkinson untied his mare. "You must visit me at New Willey. Even as we speak, that fellow Watt is busy erecting an engine to blow my furnace. 'Twill power the bellows directly! None of this fiddle-faddling about with waterwheels. We should have it up and running by next week. He turns out to be quite a genius, the Scotsman. Difficult fellow. Prickly, but first rank. Splendid, really. You must see his engine."

Abraham nodded. "I should like that."

"Perhaps you might ask Mrs. Foster to accompany you. She is an idea'd woman, is she not? Watt might find her amusing. Ha!" Wilkinson's foot was in the stirrup. "Shall I make discreet inquiries, then, at Bedlam?"

Abraham nodded, wishing in no way to delay Wilkinson's departure into the fog. The latter swung his bulk into the saddle with a great creak. The big mare snorted and danced back apace, poor animal. "Perhaps, sir," said Wilkinson, "I will feign some interest on my own behalf."

"That is thy business."

"Perhaps I will mention a low figure, to test the waters." The mare danced in a circle.

"That is up to thee, John Wilkinson." He was relieved when Wilkinson doffed his tricorn with a flourish, turned the mare, and faded into the lurid glow.

Back in the safety of his office, drinking his licorice tea, Abraham reflected on the exchange. He relived his chagrin at having assumed the French order was for cannon. He fretted over what he should have said and what he should not have said. Could he afford Bedlam? He must reduce the expenditure of cash to mere numbers. He must think of the future. Think of the great expansion Father had undertaken in the fifties. Of what risks Father took building the pond at Horsehay, when for days men dithered about in rowboats staunching leaks with sandbags and coaldust, and when everyone laughed and said it was doomed to fail! So must Abraham keep an eye to the future.

Another question intruded rudely. Should his disapproval of Wilkinson be mitigated now by duty toward the man's soul, by the opportunity to wean him from arms? (Odious image: a cherubic Wilkinson nursing at a cannon.) In truth, it was not simply Wilkinson's armsmaking that raised an alarm in Abraham's breast; it was the man's effusiveness, his innuendos, his way of larding everything with secrecy. Wilkinson did nothing in the open. And each of his subterfuges seemed interlocked with another, so that one felt drawn into the larger, darker machinations. How did one meet that of God in such a soul?

Gazing through the wavy glass at the ghostly line of fillers tipping their loads into the blazing furnace head, Abraham recalled how as a lad he used to watch that same procession, shielded from the sparks by his father's bulk, holding his father's hand and feeling such security with his own small hand enveloped in the great warm one. He longed for that security now. Father would know how to respond to Wilkinson's sophistry.

Sitting down at his desk, Abraham took up the little silhouette of Rebecca in its oval frame and kissed it—a luxury he permitted himself only rarely, for kissing a picture recalled the idolatry of the papists with their painted saints. Although the profile was only snipped from black paper, the memory of golden hair and soprano voice it elicited was as salutary as any headache powder or saintly relics.

Then Maggie flashed to mind. Her long slender fingers smoothing the sleeve buttons. The crease in her brow when she refused him. Why could he not think of Becky without also recalling that scene by the river?

And what was Wilkinson's interest in her? *An idea'd woman,* he called her.

Wilkinson was fastened onto him like a wood louse!

On impulse, Abraham went to the cabinet and plucked out the ledger for the 1750s. He found the entries—he knew them almost by heart now, he had read them so often—showing so many tons of pig iron sold to the Wilkinsons on this or that occasion. Written in Father's even hand, they were reassuring, yet puzzling. How could

Father be sure that the Wilkinsons were not casting his pig iron into cannon?

That evening, finding Mother alone in her sitting room, he raised the question with her.

"Oh, he knew." She smiled and shut her eyes with certainty. "He knew."

"But how?"

"He had his ways. Of that thou mayst be certain, Abey. And thou wilt find thine, as thou walkest in the Light."

They went on to discuss wedding arrangements. Now that Samuel had put off his removal to London, Mother wondered if the wedding might not be better moved to June (for complicated reasons involving various families) and if they might not have it here in Madeley. Abraham was happy to leave that whole business in female hands.

The next day, he visited Horsehay. Richard Reynolds offered more practical counsel, approving the purchase of Bedlam, inasmuch as demand was rising, and asserting his willingness once again to stand surety for Abraham's debts. Bedlam would help with the bridge. As for the problem vexing Abraham, he supposed there was no absolute way of knowing where pig iron might end up after it was sold. A man could not watch every pig he sent into the world. He himself struggled with the same question, for he regularly sold pig iron from Horsehay and Ketley. "I would not knowingly sell it for cannon. In the end, I must decide whether the buyer can be taken at his word. If I am clear in my own conscience, the rest is up to the Great Author. 'Tis all one can do."

"Can John Wilkinson be taken at his word?" Abraham ventured.

"That is something which thou must decide, in thine own conscience."

Abraham nodded. He would talk to Wilkinson again. Visit New Willey, see James Watt's new engine, and hope to satisfy his doubts.

"And the bridge?" he asked Richard, before he left. "Should it be made wholly of iron, or of iron and stone?"

But on this question, Richard offered no opinion—just a twinkling of the eye that said that this too Abraham must decide.

# Maggie Foster

W hen Abraham invited her to accompany him to New Willey, Maggie took it as a good sign. Who knows, maybe he was thinking of her again as his consultant. As they stood waiting on the cobblestoned ferry landing, she saw hints of spring glimmering through the smog: willows bearding the slag heaps with pale chartreuse.

Abraham unhitched the horse from the chaise in preparation for the passage. "Hast thou seen John Wilkinson, since he came visiting with the Frenchman?"

"Only once. When Samuel and Sarah and I went to play whist with Mary." She left a question in her voice.

"He seems to think thou art inclined toward matters philosophic."

What had Wilkinson said to Abraham? she wondered. Anxiety gave way to annoyance. When was the last time Abraham had shown any interest in discussing "matters philosophic"?

"Didst thou speak of steam engines?"

"I don't think so. Mostly he talked about iron." Abraham's questions were making her nervous. She scanned his face, but his mouth was pursed in much the same way Abiah pursed hers: so enigmatically judgmental, you found yourself checking the corners for life.

Maggie was finally putting two and two together. "I gather it was John Wilkinson's idea that I come along."

"Yes. He fancied thou might enjoy talking with James Watt."

"James Watt?" Maggie's stomach did a flip-flop. "You mean, Watt will be there? I thought it was just his machine." Why hadn't Abraham said something earlier? He was so damned reticent.

"Watt is at New Willey erecting the engine."

Great, she thought. James Watt was absolutely the last person she should be talking to! She watched Abraham and the ferryman secure the horse and the chaise. A boy pushed the ferry off with a pole. The river was swollen, the color of milk chocolate. Maggie sat on a bench in the square prow. The horse was confined in the middle of the small flat craft, in a slatted box stall that kept him from turning, and the chaise was parked behind him. The grizzled ferryman leaned on a tiller eight or ten feet long, using the current deflected against the rudder to propel the boat, which was tethered by a long chain anchored near the center of the current. Abraham spoke soothingly to the horse.

Maggie studied the battered wooden prow, its layers of white paint stained with rust like everything else in the gorge. Why had Wilkinson wanted her to come along? Did he want to talk to her about Samuel's bridge? What the hell had he said to Abraham?

And Watt. She would have to be careful. James Watt was too much at the center of technological change for comfort. She was on thin ice now. The slightest influence on him could have unimaginable repercussions. Surely no single innovator—other than Newcomen or possibly the first Abraham Darby—was more responsible for thrusting Britain into the industrial lead.

Without Watt's separate condenser, steam power might remain confined to pumping water; Britain's rapidly evolving textile industry might depend wholly on water power; ships might continue sailing by wind through the whole of the nineteenth century. Without Commodore Perry's steamships threatening Tokyo with cannon,

Japan might not be opened to the West. Without railroads, the vast interiors of Asia and Russia and North America might remain insulated by their deserts. Indigenous human cultures might be spared, jungles and prairies kept intact.

She fantasized assassinating Watt. Get him alone, get a choke hold on him. Use his shirt collar for leverage, her crossed forearms pressing the carotid artery into the larynx. These moves were part of her training in self-defense. A few seconds without blood to the brain would disable him; thirty or forty seconds would bring unconsciousness; four minutes, and the higher brain functions would be irreparably damaged. *Nothing personal, Mr. Watt.* She could maybe even cover the traces of violence. Massage the bruises before the color changed, put food in his throat. Claim he'd choked. No Heimlich maneuver for you, Mr. Watt. Sorry.

The ferry docked, and Abraham hitched the horse. Maggie rode while he walked the horse up the Benthall rails.

Practically speaking, the problem with her macabre fantasy—even assuming that she could bring herself to kill another human being— was that she would be too late. Watt had obtained a patent. And Wilkinson had produced an accurate cylinder. The engine was too far along.

A more fundamental objection was her commitment to nonviolence. Her world had been laid waste by war and by the violence of corporations looking only at the bottom line. *Bottomthink,* as it was called. She was not about to engage in bottomthink now. Self-defense was one thing: even poor little Ecosophia was armed for defense, with its land mines and its ancient surface-to-air missiles. But the consensus was clear there, about this mission: Ecosophia was unwilling to bequeath to the world a new reality based on a violent act.

She must say nothing to Watt that would jog his imagination. However, if she could use the occasion to score points with Abraham, then it might improve her chances of getting him to accept Samuel's design.

They had arrived at New Willey and were approaching the engine house when they heard a loud banging and saw steam billowing from the door. Horses reared. Abruptly the banging stopped. In the relative stillness, another sound seized their attention: the agonizing screams of a pair of horses that had reared, tipping over the wagon they were pulling. They were now kicking helplessly—one horse, in its struggle to pull free, dragging the wagon laden with pig iron over the trapped legs of the other, which lay flailing on its side. Men fearful of the flying hooves stood back in a circle. Abraham handed her the reins and jumped from the chaise.

"A knife!" she heard him say to the driver, who seemed frozen with panic. "A knife!" Someone produced a knife.

With sudden grace, Abraham darted in close and cut one of the traces. Maggie could hardly bear to look, sure he would be struck by a flying hoof. But in another instant he had the rearing horse free and was turning his attention to the other, whose legs remained trapped and whose screams were so piercing. He cut the other trace and directed the men to lift the wagon, which had been emptied of its load. But when the weight was removed, the horse was unable to stand on its bloodied legs, and its cries continued, high-pitched, almost whistling. A terrible sound. Abraham seized its bridle and examined the horse's legs. Again Maggie flinched, fearing the hooves.

The horse would have to be killed. The driver, who was apparently the owner, was provided a pistol from the counting house, and he fired a shot into the animal's head. The horse expired with a great racking shudder that undulated the length of its body.

Maggie could not put the screaming out of her ears. Someone was taking the reins, putting an arm around her. It was Abraham. She wanted to tell him something, but her throat was paralyzed. She sobbed for breath.

"I was afraid you'd be killed!" she cried.

She felt a wave of relief. Then all she could think was *He doesn't die until 1789!* Then that other, frightening realization. *History has changed. He could have been killed!* Grateful for the arm encircling her, she surrendered momentarily to her confusion.

"What ho!" piped a cheerful tenor. Ruddy face beaming over Abraham's shoulder. "Greetings, Mrs. Foster! I am delighted that you could come." Wilkinson talking breathlessly, his wig askew. Excited as he was, he seemed not even to notice the horses.

She let them help her from the chaise. Blood was pouring from the horse. She looked away, her legs weak, thinking of the shudder that passed through its dying body. Abraham was hatless and his clothes bloody, but he appeared uninjured.

Wilkinson escorted them to the engine house, where the horse's scream still echoing in her mind was drowned out, once they were inside, by the rhythmic thump of bellows from the other end of the building. Men were walking around in the mist assessing the damage. A cloud of dust was descending into the steam. The air reeked of hot metal and lard, and something she couldn't identify. Wilkinson pointed out James Watt, a wiry, stoop-shouldered man in shirtsleeves barking orders as he climbed some steps.

"This," said Wilkinson, "is the engine."

Maggie looked up. Superficially it resembled a Newcomen atmospheric engine: a vertical cylinder towering ten feet or so, its top disappearing into the gallery above, and the long oak walking-beam tipped to an extreme. Sunlight from small windows knifed through the thick air, tracing the black mass of the cylinder and the delicate brass pipes and valves, rendering the whole scene as dramatic and numinous as a Pre-Raphaelite painting of ruins after a storm. More pipes and valves than on a conventional engine; this was more complicated. But she was still too shaken to absorb the particulars.

" 'Twas extraordinary." Wilkinson shook his head reverently. "An amazing demonstration." He led them up the steps to the second floor, where Watt was preparing to examine the top of the cylinder for damage.

Maggie's breathing had almost returned to normal. She could hear Abraham's bronchial wheeze. She was proud of him.

"Madame," Wilkinson observed. "You look pale."

She nodded. "That horse . . ."

"Ah. Yes. Poor beast." He clucked. "And you—" He turned to Abraham and appeared to notice his soiled clothes for the first time. "I fear ye will suppose me a rude host. We must get you cleaned up."

He led them back down the steps and toward the bellows. Maggie supposed he was taking them to a washbasin. Instead, he showed them a second pair of bellows, now idle. They were actually blowing-tubs of the sort used at Coalbrookdale, consisting of a pair of iron pistons that forced air into a brick reservoir so that the blast entered the furnace in a constant stream. Wilkinson said they had been working admirably, powered by the new engine. Shouting to be heard, he explained that once the new engine was working properly, the waterwheel would be devoted wholly to powering his boring mill. He seemed to have forgotten about the water for Abraham.

" 'Twill be the first fire engine in the world," he told them as he led the way back to the engine, "to blow a furnace directly. The first to be used for *any* purpose other than pumping water." He was obviously very pleased with himself.

He went on about how it would now be possible to build blast furnaces twice the size of existing furnaces. "Which is fortunate," he added with a chuckle, "because the demand for pig iron will rise like a Bristol tide once people discover all that can be done with it. Once they see that bridge, eh, Mr. Darby!" He clapped a hand on Abraham's shoulder and winked behind his back at Maggie.

Maggie felt a sudden aversion to Wilkinson. "So what went wrong?" she asked.

"Wrong?" Wilkinson snorted incredulously. "Ha! Why, my dear lady! It performed jollily for nearly two minutes!" This said, he confessed that indeed the engine was making too long a stroke, causing the piston to crash against the cylinder top. "Mr. Watt is attempting to discover the reason."

After conferring briefly with Watt, Wilkinson returned to say that Watt had decided to remove the cylinder cover so that the piston could be examined for scouring. They were asked to step back while Watt's assistants splashed buckets of water on the cylinder to cool it. Clouds of steam rose from the hot metal. "Not too fast!" Watt yelled.

Maggie found her own bucket of water and helped Abraham scrub the blood from his waistcoat and breeches. The image in her head, she realized, recalling those flailing hooves, was Picasso's *Guernica*. By the time she finished scrubbing, she was over the shock of what had happened.

The men were removing the nuts that held the flanged top to the cylinder. Watching them work, and listening to the talk between the two ironmasters, Maggie was impressed with how many problems were being encountered here for the first time. The chief problem was the need for precision at this large scale. But there were other challenges: joining materials with different coefficients of expansion, finding lubricants and gaskets that would hold up under high temperature and pressure. Not having synthetics or much experience with petroleum products, they used materials mostly from the barnyard: manure-soaked pasteboard for gaskets, rendered lard for lubricating the gudgeon, linseed oil and goose grease for lubricating valves. She listened to Wilkinson extol the superiority of grease from a Christmas goose over grease from a summer goose.

Wilkinson prevailed on Watt to join them. The inventor's face was covered with grime, and he needed a shave. He wore a tool apron and a leather cap with a long bill turned backwards. A little smaller than the hats worn by furnace men to keep cinders from falling down their backs, it resembled a baseball cap, which, with his general scruffiness, gave him a strangely modern look.

At Wilkinson's request, he agreed to explain his engine.

"For the benefit of the lady," he began (with a wink for all the men), "this"—he rapped the cylinder with a wrench—"is the cylinder." A pock-faced assistant chortled.

Maggie listened carefully while Watt, in his rapid Scottish brogue, rattled off an explanation that would have been impossible to follow if she hadn't already known: about how the various "wee tappets" opened and closed the different valves; about how steam was piped from below the piston into the "separate condenser" and condensed back into water so as to create a vacuum, which allowed the steam above the piston to drive it down; about how a new charge of steam was admitted into the cylinder, repeating the cycle. All the while he pointed to various push rods that worked from the beam, operating more "wee tappets" that opened and closed different valves. Then, with a glance at his pocket watch, he asked if they understood.

Maggie nodded. "The separate condenser sounds wonderful. You must save a great deal of energy."

"Energy?" Watt looked quizzically at her, then at the two men— as if for translation.

She blushed. "Fuel. You must save a lot of coal, not having to cool down the whole cylinder."

"Exactly!" cried Watt. " 'Twill use only a quarter as much."

She asked if they might see the separate condenser. She felt a restraining pressure on her arm. Abraham whispered, "Maggie, Mr. Watt is busy."

But Watt insisted. " 'Tisn't much to see," he warned. They followed him down the steps to the ground floor, level with the bottom of the cylinder. There, under a movable cistern cover, they could see the round top of the condenser under a couple feet of water.

Abraham asked how much steam was released into the water.

"None!" snapped Watt. "I fear ye miss the point, man!" He clapped his arms to his sides and explained again the function of the separate condenser. Abraham's face turned red. Wilkinson, feigning a coughing fit, suggested they leave Mr. Watt to his business.

"Oh dear," Maggie interjected. "I've kept you from your work, asking silly questions." She went on in that vein, thanking him.

Watt sputtered in protest. Abraham recovered his composure, and Wilkinson stepped forward, smiling. "Good, good," he said. "And now, Mrs. Foster, I have something else to show you and Mr. Darby." With a bow to Watt, he escorted them away. "Something quite amazing," he added, and gave Maggie a little pinch on the arm.

# John Wilkinson

"A mazing" was perhaps an overstatement. Wilkinson's purpose was first to get them out of Watt's hair—what with the damned engine nearly knocking itself to pieces. He would show them the cannon-boring mill.

He needed to buttonhole Darby. Get him alone. Persuade him that now was the time to make an offer for Bedlam. The sooner Darby purchased Bedlam, the more deeply he would be ensnared in the bridge; and as the young man intended to marry in May, which would likely prove a great distraction, Wilkinson resolved to heed the advice of that old Roman reprobate, Publilius Syrus, to "strike while the iron is glowing hot."

As for the Quakeress, Wilkinson wouldn't have minded getting her alone as well, for she had quite captivated him on her last visit. Her enthusiasm for iron and steam enginery was rare in the female tribe, her intelligence like an untended garden growing voluptuously every which way. He would like to buttonhole her too. Yes indeed.

"Come, come," he said, leading them briskly from the engine house. He had no exact plan in mind, but trusted himself to seize the opportunity as it arose. *Carpe hominem,* Isaac Wilkinson used to say, and the *diem* will follow.

He was happy to be out of Watt's presence. He had only so much patience for those wee tappets, which required constant adjustment, and for Watt's endless calculations. Perhaps Smeaton was right; it was said that he declared the new engine too complicated. Watt's other engine, at the Bloomfield colliery, was acting up as well. And Watt, although a genius to be sure, was an arrogant fellow who had the social grace of a hedgehog. Complaining that the war would spoil everything. A brooding hermit who spent his evenings in his chamber writing letters to his new wife, doubtless filled with complaints about his host. He chewed with his mouth open, moaned of headaches, and seemed happiest rooting about alone in the mechanical thicket of his own making.

The Scots were a surly race, as stubborn as the Dutch. Quick-tempered. And although Wilkinson counted himself an enemy of provincialism—his own boyhood in Furness having left an accent in his speech considered odd here in Shropshire—it seemed to him that Watt was living proof of the adage that the noblest prospect a Scotsman ever sees is the high road that leads him to England.

"Is that a cannon?" Mrs. Foster asked as they walked past the shop where the wooden cannon patterns were turned.

"Quite so, madame. A thirty-two-pounder, destined for His Majesty's Navy." He might have added that it would likely be used against her Colonial brethren.

She examined the carved crucifix that would decorate the breech over the words NEW WILLEY CO. "Why a crucifix?" she inquired.

The artisan busy with his carving tools responded impertinently, with scarcely a glance up. "To remind the tars they be fighting for a Christian cause."

This amused Wilkinson. "And what cause is that, sirrah?" he demanded, standing directly behind the fellow.

"Why—" The man recognized his employer's voice and his neck reddened. "Whatever cause His Majesty's Navy be fighting, I warrant."

Darby frowned and stalked out.

"And you, Mr. Wilkinson," Mrs. Foster asked as they followed Darby. "What do you intend by the crucifix?"

"Oh, the Navy insists on it! So does the East India Company! 'Tis as Voltaire says. Every butcher wants his flags blessed, and solemnly invokes the Lord before he goes out to exterminate his neighbor!"

"And you? What do you think?"

"Of the crucifixes? Ah, well. Who am I to judge? They are removable. I take them off for the Turks. I add a double eagle for the Russians. I am no idealist. 'Tis the idealists who do most of the mischief in the world, fighting this holy war or that." He had no wish to pursue this subject. "Come," he said, catching up with Darby and propelling them past piles of cannon to the boring mill, where he provided Darby and Mrs. Foster with waxed cotton wool to plug their ears against the screech of four cannon turning.

Darby looked more ill at ease than ever, rolling his eyes like a colt. Wilkinson leaned close to him. "I know you have no love of weapons, my friend. But 'tis an ill wind that does not blow somebody some good. These, you see, were the inspiration behind my new cylinder-boring machine." He explained that the guns on the machine now were three-pound swivels. "They will go to Rigby and Sons, for sale to Liverpool merchants."

"Merchants?" Mrs. Foster asked.

"In a manner of speaking. With the Africa trade and West Indies trade cut off, most of the owners have taken to cruising under letters of marque." He saw that she still did not understand. "They turn privateer. Pirates, if you will. These are cruel times for honest trade."

Darby paced about restlessly. "I should prefer seeing the machine for boring cylinders!"

"Ah," said Wilkinson, "I fear the cylinder-boring machine is at Bersham. But as I explained, 'tis these cannon lathes that inspired it. And you are free to examine them as you wish."

With obvious reluctance, Darby examined the machines more carefully. "But how doth thou manage to rotate something as large as a cylinder?"

"Ah. That, my friend, is the great secret." Ha! Darby had swallowed the bait. Served him right.

Eventually, Wilkinson vowed to himself, he would make a man of holier-than-thou young Darby, and a humbled one in the bargain! Having no father of his own, Darby was fortunate to encounter such a teacher as Wilkinson. The bridge would be Darby's opportunity to experience firsthand some of the crushing weight of life. 'Twould be an opportunity for him to develop character, and to perform a service for his people. Yes, let the Quakers bear the burden of it, yoked to the common good. Let the third Darby pick up where the second one left off after pissing his tallow. Short-lived as rabbits, these Darbys; they were forever turning up their toes and dying. It was their religion that did it to them. Too much virtue sapped the strength, like too much bloodletting. A man needed to hold fast to his wits and his ballocks.

He escorted his guests to the adjacent polishing shed to show them an immense forty-two-pound carriage gun. Destined for the fortifications at Gibraltar. Upon his orders, the polishers stepped aside and two small boys clambered from the bore, their hands and knees ruddy with polishing rouge. Inviting Mrs. Foster to peer down the barrel, he tried for a glimpse of ankle. "A gun like this cast in bronze," he told her, "would cost eight times as much. Cast iron, you see, has altered the nature of war. 'Tis no longer a gentleman's sport. Iron has made possible an abundance of cannon hitherto unknown. Someday England shall rule the seas so perfectly as to eliminate war altogether!"

This suggestion seemed to trouble Mrs. Foster. Or perhaps she was tired. He suggested as much, and invited her to sit down on an empty cannon cradle, which he ordered a fellow to dust with a clean cloth. Excusing himself from Mrs. Foster, he took advantage of the opportunity to speak to Darby. Pulling Darby a little distance away and removing the cotton wool from his own ears, he addressed the young man earnestly.

He said he had talked with the owners of Bedlam and determined that it could be had at quite a bargain provided Darby moved quickly, for with the price of pig iron rising, they were likely to change their minds. Again, he mentioned the French contract for water pipes and declared himself a ready customer.

Darby worked his jaw muscles. "How do I know that my iron will go into pipe and not cannon?"

It was so stupid a question, Wilkinson hardly knew how to respond. "Why, sir, I should be happy to keep your iron separate from the rest."

"And not use it for cannon."

"Indeed, sir. If that is your wish. I will make it my policy to stack all your pigs in one pile, apart from the rest."

"As thou didst with my father's iron."

"Why, exactly so, my good fellow," Wilkinson assured him, seeing he was quite in earnest. "You shall have the same treatment as your father. You have my word, by heaven."

"I would not ask thee to swear."

"Then by my word as a gentleman." Such were the foibles of human conscience, that a man believed what he wanted to believe, with little regard to facts! Wilkinson would go through the motions of keeping Darby's pigs separate. But more iron for water pipes would mean more iron for cannon! In the end, it was all the same. Iron was iron. And yet Darby, for all his pretended objections, appeared mollified.

"If you are agreed in principle," said Wilkinson, "then may I suggest we set a date." Wilkinson pressed forward. Isaac used to say it was one thing to have the shoat's head between one's knees and another to get the ring clamped in its nose. "I should be happy to accompany you on Thursday next. Or would Wednesday be better? I should think the sooner the better."

When the particulars of time and place were settled, Darby let out a sharp sigh of exasperation and excused himself to fetch some headache powder from his chaise. Wilkinson watched him hurry away and slapped his belly with glee.

Returning to Mrs. Foster, he invited her to stroll around the pond with him. They would be in sight, he assured her, for Darby to see them upon his return. He offered his arm, and they sauntered along the footpath that led around the pond, until the shriek of the boring mill diminished to a hiss, barely audible over the pulse of the furnace. Beyond the smoke, the sky was bright as a boiled onion, the sun reflected in the pond's dark water. By now their distance around the pond offered a degree of privacy. Darby was nowhere yet in sight. Wilkinson stopped and took both her hands in his. "The truth is, Mrs. Foster, I have been wanting to talk to you alone." He tried to gauge by her hands how compliant she might be. They were warm, slender hands; strong but amenable to his holding them in a manner now that just exceeded politeness.

"About Samuel's bridge?" she asked.

"Yes, yes, of course. How is the model progressing?"

"Fine. He's started on the large drawing. I think he's about half finished. But . . ." She sighed, and those large green eyes fixed on him soberly. "Well. Mr. Wilkinson, be honest with me."

"I am always honest, my dear."

"Well. Assuming we can get Abraham to go along with the design, what about the subscribers?"

"You wonder if they will accept something so novel."

"Exactly. Are we trying to do too much?"

"Ah well," he chuckled. " 'Tis not classical."

"We do not live in classical times, Mr. Wilkinson."

"But that is what men admire, those ancient verities. The subscribers shall want some convincing."

"Can you convince them? That's what I want to know." Stepping back but not breaking free of his hands, she gave him a look that beseeched him, or perhaps challenged him.

Those eyes were most extraordinary. Mysterious depths. What explained her ardor for young Samuel's design? What explained anyone's ardor? My God! He wanted to consume her. But the question that she posed so gravely demanded a response.

"That remains to be seen." He nodded pensively. " 'Twill not be easy." Then, perceiving himself at an advantage, he threw caution aside. "Madame, I adore you!" He embraced her.

"*Mister* Wilkinson!" She struggled.

He released her—whether voluntarily or not was unclear, so

insistent was the fingernail pressed into his windpipe. He coughed. She would not be won easily, he could see that. "Forgive me," he said when he had regained his voice. "I am"—his voice caught again—"a very passionate man."

Her cheeks were splotched with color. "That doesn't give you the right to paw me."

"No, no, you are quite right. I forgot myself. Do forgive me." He rubbed his throat. "But let me come to the point."

"The point?"

He nodded. "If I may speak candidly, I understand you are a widow."

"Why, yes."

"Then I should like to know, are you spoken for?"

Her eyes widened. "Spoken for?"

"Yes. Again, forgive my boldness."

"Forgive *me*, Mr. Wilkinson, but aren't you married?"

"Madam, I am a freethinker."

"Please, Mr. Wilkinson." She gave his hand a squeeze. "It's been a long day. And it's the bridge I'm concerned about."

Darby appeared by the boring mill, waving and hallooing. Damn him! Wilkinson waved and hallooed back, then turned to Mrs. Foster. "What would you have me do?"

"Get Samuel's design accepted! I'll take care of Abraham. You take care of the subscribers." She fixed on him a look of fierce determination. "Can you do it, Mr. Wilkinson?"

"I can." Wilkinson cocked an eyebrow. "And will. Provided you . . . take care of me." It was a bold stroke, a calculated risk.

An expression he could not fathom flitted across her features—not disgust, perhaps uncertainty. It was a frown that said she understood his meaning. Then the frown became a smile, she doubtless acknowledging where her interests lay. She glanced back to see that Darby was still some distance away, then did something astonishing. Stepping forward and unfastening a button or two on his ruffled shirt, she reached inside. Encountering his linen undershirt, she seized it in both hands and ripped it asunder—buttons popping everywhere—

and swept her palm across his belly like a ship on a tropical sea, splooming the little hairs, swooping south as far as his navel and then careering north to cup a hairy breast and waggle it. She withdrew and stepped back.

"You've got yourself a deal, Mr. Wilkinson," she said, her head tipped saucily.

Wilkinson felt a longing chill where her hand had been. But before he could utter a word, they heard Darby close at hand.

"Tuck your shirt in!" she hissed.

He got his shirt buttoned and stuffed into his breeches just before Darby hurried up. A button lay on the path; she stepped on it in the nick of time.

# John Wilkinson

**W**ilkinson was waiting for Darby at the Bird in Hand at half ten, as they had arranged. Having arrived early, he was enjoying a second breakfast of kidney stew, bread with cheese, a pickled egg, and brandied pears with clotted cream, all washed down by cider while he read a newspaper account of British victories in New York. He hoped Darby had not seen it. If the war was indeed over, then Bedlam was no prize.

Thoughts of Mrs. Foster swam pleasantly through his mind. She had proved herself a wanton, after all! He shuddered with pleasure at the memory of that hand running across his belly, and the hand mingled now in his imagination with the dexterous Madame Bougainville's final exquisite ministrations. Lips lapping like a tide, giving pleasure beyond pain; lapping, lapping, having thrown off her wig, her shaved head bobbing beyond the snowy mountain of his belly, which was arched in the moonlight while he inched away from that lapping, desperation giving way to ecstasy. His thoughts were thus distracted when Darby entered the public house accompanied by Richard Reynolds.

Wilkinson was disappointed to see Reynolds. He fancied himself Darby's advisor in this transaction. But he put a jovial face on it, shaking hands with both men and exchanging pleasantries.

The Quakers of course declined food and drink. They disapproved of the Bird in Hand for the cockfighting that went on in the cellar and the sale of contraband stolen from barges—a pity, because fresh oysters from Chepstow were said to be arriving by coracle any minute. They sat primly—Darby dark and sallow, Reynolds ruddy with bushy white brows—both of them straight as ramrods while Wilkinson sopped up the last of the kidney stew with a crust of bread and turned his attention to the pears. To Darby's inquiry about the new blowing engine he responded exuberantly, mouth full, that last week's problems appeared to have been solved. Watt had got the tappets properly adjusted and was devising a better way of controlling the pressure. The new engine, he assured them, would save a great deal of coal. And Matthew Boulton had come up with a clever scheme for winning new customers. Instead of selling engines, they would be selling power—royalty payments to be based on actual coal saved.

Reynolds perked up his ears at this, for he relied heavily on pumping-engines at both Horsehay and Ketley. Wilkinson relished the idea of selling him cylinders bored at Bersham.

" 'Twill change our lives, this new engine!" Wilkinson chuckled. "Erasmus Darwin is already hot upon steam chaises." He gobbled down the last of the fruit, wiped the cream from the corners of his mouth delicately with a thumbnail, and suggested they lose no further time getting down to the business at hand. "Considering that we are in the Bird in Hand," he added. Ha! Neither man found the pun amusing.

Quakers. Wilkinson despised them. Alone, Dick Reynolds was a likable enough fellow, willing to laugh at a joke. But here, setting an example for young Darby, he looked as if he had swallowed a poker.

Nevertheless, as the three men began to discuss the business of listing the provisos to be included in the purchase agreement, Wilkinson had to admire their thoroughness. They had thought of everything: contingency clauses against inaccuracies in the inventory of raw materials, renewals of indentures and leases and rights-of-way, indemnities and warranties. Ferriday and his partners would get out with only the rust under their fingernails. Wilkinson had little to add. He suggested that Darby lose no time installing his own accountant. But they had seen to it; an accountant and an overseer were to arrive from Coalbrookdale at noon.

Their discussion finished, the three ironmasters left the Bird in Hand and rode past squatters' cottages with flooded gardens, and into Bedlam Furnace. "It helps our cause that the river remains so high," Wilkinson observed, with a wink at Reynolds. Darby eyed the current dubiously. Wilkinson did his best not to laugh.

The problem with Bedlam, quite apart from its being cramped and prone to flooding, was that its fuel costs were especially high. It belonged to the newer generation of ironworks, which included New Willey, Horsehay, Lightmoor, and Ketley—erected twenty years ago, during the frenzied expansion of the iron trade that accompanied the Seven Years War. They all depended on pumping engines. But where Horsehay had the benefit of quite a large pond, Bedlam depended on water pumped almost continually from the Severn. The fact was— and a lovely fact it was, in Wilkinson's view, though he forbore mentioning it—Bedlam owed its very existence to the profits of war. For only in wartime was such an arrangement profitable. *Ha! The poetry of money speaks louder than words.*

When all the papers were drawn up and signed and the deal was completed, the owners looked relieved. Doubtless they had got wind of the British victories in New York.

Wilkinson clapped an arm on the Quakers' shoulders as they stepped from the narrow office. "Between the two of you," he observed, "you now own ten furnaces. Why, together you account for a third of the iron produced in all Britain!"

But they would not join in his jubilation. Their faces said that Pride goeth before a fall.

Quakers! He rode with them in silence, westward along the wagon road toward Coalbrookdale. Secretly it was himself he congratulated, for he had the most to gain from Darby's purchase—and without the risk. In the event of peace, prices would drop and Darby would be squeezed. In the event of war, prices would rise with demand, but Wilkinson could always install a second blowing-engine and turn out more pig iron at New Willey. In the meantime, the purchase of Bedlam took Darby another step closer to the bridge—to not merely building it but building it of iron.

Once again Wilkinson had proved himself a consummate politician. Perhaps he should join the Church of England, purchase a lordship, and stand for Parliament. That would show the old turkey-cock. Not only Isaac but Bacon and that Johnny-come-lately crowd in South Wales. 'Twould show them all. But he would save such honorification for his dotage. For now, there was more to be got by his wits.

At the bridge site they dismounted to observe where saplings had been cut and bracken trampled—likely by the surveyor's men. But they saw no stakes.

"We should mark it!" Wilkinson proclaimed. He stood upwind of a mossy stump and pissed on it, smiling broadly at the Quakers.

While his companions emptied their bladders more discreetly, Wilkinson cut a slender elder sapling with his penknife and peeled the bark from it. "Here," he said, presenting it to Darby. " 'Tis you, sir, should choose the exact place."

Darby glanced at Reynolds, who offered only an amused smile. Darby, after some deliberation, planted the wand amongst the ferns—a pale little sentinel in the wilderness.

# Maggie Foster

The date for Abraham's and Becky's wedding had been moved from May to June. And now it was to take place in Madeley instead of Yorkshire.

When Maggie heard of the change, she felt the same lurching sensation as when Samuel had announced the postponement of his move to London. But this time the feeling was more pervasive, a queasy mixture of excitement and uncertainty that came with the realization that from this point on she could no longer trust the historical record. She was on terra incognita, every detail in her road map suspect.

By mid-April, the wedding preparations were well under way. Quaker ladies arrived at Sunniside most mornings—Becky Smith and her aunt Rebecca, and others coming and going—taking over the house with sewing and quilting and endless talk. Maggie let herself get caught up in it. The feminine politics were clear: her inclusion in the preparations reinforced the shift in her status from employee to household companion—a good thing, since Abraham had all but dropped her as his consultant. She figured that if her articles of indenture were renewed next December, it would depend on the women, on Abiah and Sarah, and now on Becky too.

At first, all the expenditure of energy around the wedding seemed absurd. It brought to mind Granny's lavish wedding in Bergen, New Jersey, in 1976—exactly two hundred years ago in the future—all of it recorded in still photographs and camcorder, digitally remixed by Granny herself forty years later with the help of a personal techie and copied onto a few centimeters of plastic by pulse laser: a weird montage of bridesmaids in chiffon dresses wearing lipstick and corsages and smiling the toothy smiles that were fashionable in America and Japan of that era; a long buffet table with champagne bottles nested in tubs of chipped ice; the camera panning across sliced beef, shrimp, and carved watermelon to end at the big cake; crepe paper and stretch limos. It all seemed so exotic, profligate, so far removed from anything at Ecosophia. Closer to this.

Some of the talk at Sunniside reminded Maggie of the women at Mrs. Merryweather's. It may have been more pious and stylized but was still threaded with gossip, much of it devoted to matchmaking. Becky was particularly zealous in her attempt to fix Sarah up with one of the Lloyds of Birmingham, who was of marriageable age.

Sarah demurred, saying she was too plain. At twenty-three she seemed to think of herself as a spinster. Maggie wondered if the youngest Darby daughter was already seeing herself in a caretaking role for her mother and Samuel. Maggie no longer thought of Sarah as plain. Sarah's features were sharp, like Abiah's; she had dark eyebrows that met in the middle (which Becky advised her to tweeze) and a little gap between her front teeth. It was an expressive face, radiating more calm and more humor than when Maggie had first met her two and a half years ago.

Maggie too was the object of matchmaking efforts. Abiah recalled that she herself was thirty and widowed when she married her Abraham. " 'Tis not too late for thee," she observed, pointing out that Maggie might do well to consider a widowed man with children. But Maggie protested that for now, at least, marriage seemed too complicated.

Sarah nodded at this. "Complicated. Aye, yes. That speaks to my own heart."

In all this talk—the networking; the advice about how a wife could assert her authority in indirect ways; the suggestions for dealing with company clerks; the tips on parenting—there was a cohering feminine culture that transcended the particular marriage. A culture that was missing in Maggie's own early adulthood.

Here in eighteenth-century Shropshire you had a clear patriarchy; death was omnipresent; individuals' expectations were defined by traditions. And below this public surface was a matriarchal weaving together of private lives. None of this was true of Ecosophia, where women had as much voice as men, death could often be forestalled, and everything was new. What was missing at Ecosophia was that coherence. Maybe it went beyond gender.

Ecosophia was not a society. It was too small and too new. Nor was it even an outpost of the larger society, like those Roman garrisons that survived for years while the empire was disintegrating—or, for that matter, like the pleasure-dome bunkers where it was bottom-think-as-usual as long as the jacuzzis could be heated and the supply network defended against rival chieftains and nomadic motogangs.

Ecosophia was orderly and communal, but it lacked a cosmology. Lacked even that pathetic faith in technology that seemed to sustain Granny. Technology had failed. There was a vision of the planet as an ecological whole, but it was a tragic vision, because the planet was doomed as a human environment. Maggie could not imagine this kind of energy going into a wedding at Ecosophia.

Samuel finished his final drawing and took it to Wilkinson, who paid him six guineas, the first half of his commission, and pronounced it "a work of genius." Samuel returned with the drawing, elated. He handed Maggie a sealed letter, which Wilkinson had addressed to her.

It was the first time in her life that she had received a letter. She waited until she was alone to read it.

It was folded in quarters and sealed on three sides with red wax. Written on thick, creamy paper in a neat hand that she recognized immediately, it began with some flowery words of praise, referring to her "twin orbs" and to the affinity for iron that they shared, and included a couplet entitled "Ode to Iron," which he had penned in her honor:

> Oh purest Iron, who calls thee base
> When Thou art the ferrous of them All?

He referred cryptically to their "arrangement," whose outcome he "fervently awaited." *I remain, Madame, Your Most Obedient Servant. John Wilkinson.*

Maggie smiled. Whatever qualms she had about their "arrangement," the letter took the edge off her dread. John Wilkinson might be repellent, but the man was not without charm.

She started to hide the letter alongside her notebook wedged under the armoire. The hiding place seemed secure enough. But she changed her mind, with the realization that she herself was now part of written history, at least theoretically. Her notebook, if it were ever found, would be difficult to decipher. The letter, however, was quite legible and implied an intimacy between herself and John Wilkinson that she could not afford to be found out by the Darbys. When no one was looking, she burned it in the kitchen fireplace.

As for the intimacy itself, she had mixed feelings. She was prostituting herself. Yet she had few resources at her disposal. It seemed not too great a price to pay to get Samuel's design accepted. And whatever mortification she felt was offset by hilarity. Whenever she thought of the look on Wilkinson's face when she ripped open his shirt, she nearly laughed out loud.

*Pussy power.* Erzulie had used the phrase. *Girl, you just might have to resort to pussy power.* When Erzulie said things like that, Maggie couldn't always tell when she was serious.

Samuel started right to work on his model. He carved the abutments from blocks of pine, painting them to look like stone, mounting them at either end of a five-foot plank. He experimented with different materials for the bridge frame. In the beginning he told

Maggie he wanted to fashion the miniature members accurately enough to erect them in exactly the same manner and sequence as the full-sized castings. But it soon became obvious that the model was too small for that. The curved castings and their flanges could not be carved with that sort of precision. Maggie prevailed on him to use glue.

Back in CALYPOOL it would have been a cinch to transform computer drawings into solid shapes. You used lasers to scan a matrix of polymer resins. Here, the task required a physical dexterity that pushed Samuel's patience and skill to the limit. He worked intently, hunched over his table, measuring with calipers, tracing drawings on wood, carving and sanding pieces so delicate they sometimes snapped in his hands. He tried shaping some from pipe clay, taking them to Jackfield to be fired, but the clay shrank and warped unpredictably in the kiln. For most shapes, wood was preferable.

Maggie and Sarah encouraged him. When his back ached, Maggie kneaded his shoulders. And they talked him through his frustrations, persuading him to repair broken pieces and to use a mixture of sawdust and glue as filler where necessary.

" 'Twill look wretched!" he complained.

"Paint it black when thou art finished," said Sarah.

"It'll look great," said Maggie.

By the end of April, he had completed the lower part of the span, up to the roadway, and was starting on the bowstring trusses that arched above. One of the arches was complete in its main structural elements, with some of the smaller stiffening members in place. The model was now perhaps a third complete, enough to suggest the soaring drama of the whole.


Following several days of rain, the weather was suddenly beautiful. Blustery winds scoured the smoke from the dale, leaving the air sweet and the tile rooftops crisp in the sunlight.

The women hung out the bedding and beat mattresses. Blankets flapped in the wind.

To Maggie, those big puffy stratocumulus clouds piled high in the northwestern sky signaled a high-pressure front moving in from the North Atlantic. They were spectacular. From a satellite they would have appeared as ragged crescents of white wandering across the British Isles—to judge from archival satellite photos she had seen from the 1970s. (By 1990, the view was not nearly as clear, needing computer enhancement; and by the time Maggie was receiving her training in 2034, she had to compuhance with false color just to distinguish landmasses.)

Industrial pollution was already beginning here. Coal smoke was starting to kill the peat. Acid fog withered the vegetation around smelters. But the effects were still local. Seen from a low orbit, the planet would be a riotous swirl of greens and blues. Most of South America and sub-Saharan Africa would appear as emerald jungle or savannah, broken only by blue lakes and rivers catching the sun like crystal. The vast conifer forest of North America would stretch from the west coast across the Great Lakes all the way to Hudson Bay, and virgin grassland would sprawl from Saskatchewan to Texas, dotted with vast herds of bison. Seen from outer space, Earth would sparkle like a sapphire, a reservoir of life.

If only the people here could see the planet as a whole—could see how finite and precious it was!

But people did have that image during the last third of the twentieth century. Granny had it. Two or three generations had known what they were destroying.

What accounted for their paralysis?


Samuel came home from the Works early, declaring he had heard the first cuckoo sing—a time-honored pretext in Shropshire for playing hooky. They got Abiah's permission for Maggie to take the afternoon off, packed food in a basket, and the three of them—Samuel, Sarah, and Maggie—set out on a footpath that led diagonally up Lincoln Hill. Samuel brought along his drawing in its leather tube. Having the path to themselves, they took off their hats and stuck violets in their hair. Samuel and Sarah sang until they were out of breath. The three stopped to rest, gazing out at the opposite slope of the dale, which was cloaked in the pastel green of new leaves above the rooftops sparkling below. Maggie was struck by a feeling of déjà vu.

"I need to keep walking," she told them. By this time she was the one carrying the picnic basket. Taking a steep shortcut up the path, skirts hoisted between her legs the way Polly had taught her, she relished the feel of her calves pumping and the pungence of wild garlic after the rain. She stopped to peel off her stockings. Somewhere below, she heard Samuel's voice insisting he could see a crow on a lightning rod at Sunniside. She continued walking until their voices were lost in the sounds of the Works and now the cries of blackbirds and the ringing of sledges and wedges from the limestone quarry ahead. Sweat rolled down her bare legs. Again she was haunted by the feeling that this was all familiar.

She stopped at another overlook, enjoying the breeze. She could see the Severn stretching west as far as Buildwas, the profile of the Wrekin rising in the northwest. At her feet was a profusion of violets.

She thought of the climb up Fajada Butte, the Anasazi trail. Here the scale was much smaller, everything wetter and greener and crowded together, the air exhilarating in her lungs. She luxuriated in it, held out her skirt, letting the breeze cool her thighs, and inclined her face to the sun.

She would like to be here with a lover. All winter she had fantasies of a romp with Jane outdoors, in the spring. But Jane was seeing her maltster regularly now, "a lusty fellow with big hands," as she described him with a little flash of malice or at least mischief in her eyes. So the Jane fantasies were safe now, but not as much fun. Sometimes Maggie fantasized sitting next to Abraham on the log, the oval box in his hands, excitement in his voice. Imagined them kissing, falling slowly into the ferns, her hands snaking down his naked buttocks. That too was safe. Sometimes she felt like that tin box, with its lid pressed tight. She flapped her skirts.

Wilkinson. She saw the portly ironmaster cavorting like a satyr among the wild garlic behind her. It was just ludicrous enough to have some erotic appeal. She felt voluptuous, overlooking Coalbrookdale. Felt her juices gather.

Pussy power.

A distant giggle. Sarah and Samuel were coming up the path. Sarah, following Maggie's example, had her dress hiked up, and Samuel was tickling her legs with a fern frond. He grinned, seeing Maggie. "The picnic rock lies yonder." He pointed to a clearing farther up the path.

It was a flat limestone shelf that commanded a panoramic view of the gorge. To the left, they could look down into the limestone quarry, a huge open pit, at the bottom of which men toiled with sledgehammers and teams of mules. Beyond was the river, stretching east past the Calcutts. Sails bellying in the wind. Gulls' wings flashing. The gorge was, well, gorgeous. And from this perch three hundred feet up, its geology was more evident. The limestone outcropping belonged to the Wenlock escarpment across the river, whose steep western edges were lit by afternoon sun. The river these days was a trickle compared to the glacial melt that must have roared through this notch seven or eight thousand years ago, emptying the lakes and causing the Severn, which used to empty into North Wales, to reverse its direction.

Samuel shook the leather tube and removed his drawing, which he spread flat and anchored with stones to keep it from blowing away. He pointed to the bridge site below. "Imagine how 'twill appear from here."

" 'Twill be a marvel, Sammy!"

"It'll be fantastic."

"And seen from the river," he went on, " 'twill divide the scene horizontally, into sky and earth. 'Twill change the gorge in men's eyes. Give the gorge a different *meaning*. Why, I think they must rename it Ironbridge Gorge."

The words sent a shiver through Maggie.

They were silent, feeling his joy. He lay back on the rock, looking at the clouds. He started to say something, stopped himself, then started again. "Sometimes—I hardly dare voice this, lest it go away.

Or lest—" He shrugged. "Sometimes I feel something moving through me. Spirit, I like to think. As if I were but a spring, or a mill-race, through which the water pours."

Sarah looked radiant. She threw herself down beside him, partly on him, caressing his chest. It seemed almost sexual. Maggie tried to look away, but could not stop watching.

Abruptly Sarah sat upright. "What a wedding gift it would make for Abraham!"

They laughed, and fell quiet again.

Samuel seemed more content than Maggie had ever seen him. Whatever frustrations he was experiencing with the model, he was at least making progress. Observing his gangly frame sprawled on the rock, the wilted violets scattered in his dark stringy hair, Maggie sensed that his old anger had evaporated. He possessed a new confidence. Her thoughts came back to what Sarah had said.

"The model. Is that what you mean?" she asked Sarah.

"Make it a wedding gift?" Samuel asked.

Sarah nodded, eyes bright. "It simply popped into my mind."

A look passed between them, an excitement.

"It might better catch his fancy," Sarah added.

"It might." Samuel nodded slowly, pulling at his sideburns.

"He could hardly reject it!" Maggie exclaimed.

Samuel shook his head. "Yes, he could. He may think it too flash."

"But if it be given as a gift," said Sarah.

"Aye. He might be readier to accept it."

Maggie kept quiet, listening to their assessment, her own excitement growing. "And it would explain our secrecy," she could not help adding.

Then Sarah made a face. "But the model belongs to John Wilkinson."

They looked at Maggie.

"I'll take care of Wilkinson." She felt her cheeks glow.

Samuel nodded reflectively. "Good. I should like to be free of him."

" 'Tis a relief for me." Sarah snuggled against him, with a smile at Maggie.

They basked in the happiness of the moment.

A flock of starlings took off from somewhere below and wheeled about in unison, swooping over the water from Madeley to Broseley and back again with majestic precision.

"How do they do it?" Maggie mused.

" 'Tis the mind of the Creator," said Samuel.

"But how," Maggie asked, "does the mind of God enter the brains of all those birds at once?" She was thinking of instinct, electromagnetic fields, brain waves.

"The mind of God," said Sarah, "includes the birds."

Maggie shut her eyes. Coming as she did from a mechanistic world that had reduced everything to rubble, she liked the idea of the mind of God moving through the birds.

"Hark!" cried Samuel, sitting up suddenly and pointing below. "I see it!"

"What?" asked Sarah.

"The bridge!"

"Oh Sammy!"

Samuel's eyes were shining ecstatically. "Didst ye see those birds fly under it, and over't? Mark how the sun shines on the arches! And that coach-and-four driving across it with the dog chasing after! 'Tis a flaming wonder!"

"Sammy, please!"

"Mark ye! Passenger barges come all the way from Bristol to gawk! See the ladies with their French parasols."

"Stop," cried Sarah. She threw herself on Samuel, tickling him.

"Sammy," said Maggie. "Get hold of yourself."

He went into a coughing fit. When he recovered, he was pale.

"Let's go back," Sarah said.

Walking back down the path, they were quiet. Maggie was not sure exactly what had happened. At first she had thought Sammy was teasing. But brother and sister both seemed shaken. Had he actually hallucinated?

Their plan was a good one. She just wished it didn't depend quite so heavily on Samuel.

And there was Wilkinson for her to contend with. He was not going to like being cut out of the deal.

# Abraham Darby III

**H**e dreaded this evening's meeting of the subscribers. They were deadlocked over the question of whether or not to build the bridge wholly of iron. He himself was undecided. He had worked late at Bedlam, missing supper, and was now riding west along the wagon road, in the direction of the Swan Inn. The way was dark, the twilight sky so clear that it reflected little light from the furnaces, and the moon had not yet risen. He let the gelding pick its way.

Abraham felt overwhelmed by the complexities surrounding him. Bedlam. Whitbread's threat to take their business elsewhere. All his doubts concerning the bridge. All the money. All the arrangements for the wedding.

"Do not worry thyself," Becky told him before she returned to Yorkshire. "The wedding will go smoothly."

She was right, of course. The wedding had been taken up by such a flurry of female energy as to be carried forward with the momentum of a hoop rolling downhill.

If only the bridge could move forward so easily. Summer would arrive soon, and with it the drought. Time to start building the abutments. And every time he turned around, he saw new expenses. Most recently it was the scaffolding—the cost of timber and labor. And rope. He was sure he had not budgeted enough for Manila rope. He was beginning to believe that the more conventional of Pritchard's designs, which made use of stone, was the most practical.

Lost in these thoughts, Abraham suddenly had an ominous feeling. He looked around in the wooded shadows. Was someone lurking? Then, as he reassured his steed, speaking calmly and patting Blacky's neck, he knew where he was. He saw the pale willow wand.

Now he recalled last night's dream. He had been wandering around a place that was like Bedlam but not quite Bedlam, everything aslant except for a platform built of planks laid across timbers that, he somehow knew, came from Danzig. As he climbed the steps, he realized he was wearing no clothes, although the workers, going about their jobs with wheelbarrows, appeared not to notice. Peering into their barrows, he saw that they were carrying babies. "What are they?" he demanded of the nearest worker, who, looking up, proved to be Wagstaff.

"Why these be Darbys," said Wagstaff. As if it were the most natural thing in the world.

"Where art thou taking them?"

"Them were not included in the budget," came the reply.

"Merciful God!" said Abraham, and fell to his knees, knowing with terrible certainty that the babies were being taken to the furnace. He rushed to stop the wheelbarrows, but Wagstaff was already out of sight, and now Abraham understood that the wooden platform was part of the scaffolding to be used to erect the bridge, and Richard Reynolds was standing over him holding out a noose and inviting him to put his head in it. "Just for a bit," Richard kept saying, "to try its size."

Now, looking up, Abraham saw that the scaffolding was a gallows. "Why?" he asked in a quavering voice.

"Because," said Richard gravely, "the price of rope is rising."

And it was no longer Richard's face but that of John Wilkinson, who was offering him something that he knew was evil and that he must refuse. He woke up gnashing his teeth.

Now, gazing at that wand, he was angry. He dismounted, waded into the bracken, tore out the wand, and flung it as far as he could into the river.

Wilkinson! Damn him!

Finding the log where he and Maggie had sat, he knelt, laid his forehead on his clasped hands, and gave himself over to anguish. He tried to pray, to beg forgiveness for that moment's hatred in his heart, for cursing Wilkinson. He prayed for humility and charity. But the tempest of his feelings pressed around him, and he could not open himself. Blacky snorted. The ordinariness of the sound served to calm him.

A rriving at the Swan Inn by Dales End, Abraham sat down at a small table in the side room, where he could eat alone without encountering the subscribers as they trickled in. He ordered a pigeon pie, which he did not finish. He was still upset. He wished now that he had invited Samuel, and resolved to encourage his brother to become a subscriber. The others had gathered by now around the long table—a dozen or so men—and when he joined them, he felt quite alone.

Some of his discomfort was owing to the barge owners. In general they were an obstinate lot. They had been invited to subscribe at the suggestion of the indefatigably conniving Reverend Harries, for reason of politics, and were now complaining that iron would cost too much, but did not wish to raise the budget. Harries himself thought the budget too high, so the bargemen were his allies.

Abraham kept silent. He, of course, feared the estimate was too low. He wished Thomas Pritchard were here, for the architect had helped with the calculations, but Pritchard was absent.

John Potte, one of the barge owners, stood up and startled everyone by pounding sharply on the table with the hilt of his sword. Swords, though commonly worn by gentlemen in London, were a rarity in Shropshire. And Potte's countenance was difficult to fathom, in part because he had a glass eye that roved in an unsettling fashion and a large wen on his forehead that added to his ferocity. "Who amongst us," Potte demanded, scowling around the table, "can explain why this firking bridge should cost so dear?"

John Nicholson spoke. "Mr. Potte, in the name of courtesy and our common ease, I beg you put away your cutlass."

Potte rammed the blade into its scabbard noisily. "I repeat my question, sirs! Who amongst us can explain why a bridge of iron should cost so much more than one of wood or stone?"

Abraham's heart drubbed like a blooming-hammer. Although Potte had refrained from fixing Abraham in that meandering gaze, the challenge was clearly directed at him. Abraham studied his own face reflected in the polished brass sconce on the opposite wall. The others waited for him to speak. He was about to open his mouth, about to speak once more of the uncertainties attendant on erecting so large a structure, the uncertainties of designing and casting its members, carrying them to the site, and joining them over water. But these very worries seemed only to support Potte's case, and for the moment Abraham found himself quite overwhelmed. Could he in fact afford to undertake this project? *Abey, Abey, Abey.* Potte was facing him now, glaring ambiguously. Abraham dropped his gaze to the account book in front of him, an inexpensive four-column ledger with a green pasteboard cover that he had purchased in Birmingham for fourpence, the price still legible in pencil. He was aware of the surrounding halo of faces waiting. He tried to calm himself.

John Wilkinson's voice broke the silence. "Mr. Potte, you understand that these castings will be very heavy, requiring more scaffolding than the usual bridge."

"Then God's teeth, sir!" Potte roared. "Let us build the usual bridge!"

A clamor of voices rose in agreement. Some spoke reasonably, arguing that the tolls would bring a profit to the investors only if the cost was kept low, or that the virtues of iron could be exploited most happily in combination with timber or stone. Others argued for stone as opposed to timber, or for timber as opposed to stone. All the while, the Reverend Harries darted around the edges of the fray like a border collie working a flock of sheep. Among the men present that night, nearly half seemed to side with Potte—against iron.

Abraham kept silent. Richard Reynolds had prepared him for such an impasse. "Thy success," he warned, "will depend on striking a balance between thine own need for capital and the investors' need for security. The greater the risk, the greater reward they will expect in profit." But as Abraham listened to the voices on all sides, it was not the subscribers' security that concerned him but his own. His was the greatest risk by far. The noose from his dream came to mind, and with it the realization that John Potte's objection offered him a way out.

It would be no less a Darby bridge, that more conservative of Pritchard's designs, which used stone built around an iron hub. It would be acceptable, surely, considering the great burden of his debts! With his pencil he doodled a pound sign of prodigious thickness.

"Gentlemen," said Wilkinson, tipping his bulk forward from his chair. "I fear you are missing the point. This is a talking bridge. 'Twill shout our wares as surely as a pie jawer shouts his. Build it half of stone, and you give it but half a voice!"

"It shouts your wares, sir," spat Potte. "Not ours!"

Another of the bargemen agreed. " 'Tis the ironmasters should pay the added cost!"

Wilkinson was quick to parry. "But gentlemen, you have as much to gain from it as we do! What cargo but iron do you most carry? Will you not invest in the industry that sustains you?"

"But iron should cost no more than timber!" protested John Rose, an old friend of the Darbys—well-intentioned, but unfortunately wrong.

Abraham winced. Again he felt surrounded by Johns.

"We solicited for proposals, did we not?" John Rose continued, cheeks flushed. "We advertised in the Birmingham and Shrewsbury newspapers, and posted boards in market squares, and no proposals were received. Not a one! Mr. Darby's price is fair!"

But now the Reverend Harries leaned forward and peered over his reading spectacles with an unctuous smile that showed his long incisors. "Perhaps," he said. "But we are in rather a captive situation, are we not, gentlemen, here in the Severn Gorge? Hmm? The solicitation for competing bids was, I dare say, a formality. With all due respect to the ironmasters present, 'tis common knowledge that Mr. Darby has received the blessings of that worthy fraternity. And we all know that he is best situated to provide the castings. Who would be likely to bid against him? Mr. Wilkinson? Mr. Reynolds?" Harries threw back his head in silent laughter. He all but cocked one ear, waiting for a response.

Abraham stared motionless at his own reflection in the sconce. This was precisely the point that had troubled him all winter. Was he the only one foolish enough? A yardstick was lacking; there was no one else's rigorous effort to calculate the costs and risks. Those who advised him did not stand in his shoes. Pritchard, desirous of having his design chosen, was inclined to understate the costs. Wilkinson lost no opportunity to press the case for iron. And Richard, though he would act as banker, would not be risking his own money. Looking down at the pound sign, Abraham saw that he had doodled a gallows on it.

Rope. The cost of rope from the Philippines was certain to rise if the French and American privateers grew any bolder. Abraham's chest tightened. The odor of the candles was suddenly oppressive. *Abey, Abey, Abey.*

It all came down to family. What would Mother say? What would Father have done? Simply asking those questions raised the answer. A darkling presence fluttered behind him somewhere, a greatcoat reflected in the brass like the angel of the Lord come to stay Abraham's knife raised over Isaac. Deliverance in the form of the ram. Abraham's heart began pounding as it did at Meeting when he felt led to speak.

John Potte slammed his fist on the table and jumped to his feet. "I say, put the bastard out to bid again! Begging pardon for me language, gentlemen. Put it out again. And this time make it clear as daylight that we shall entertain proposals for a bridge built of any material!" He sat down with a clatter.

Harries grinned. " 'Twould tell us the cost of timber or stone!"

"Aye!" someone agreed. "And hence the true cost of iron!"

"But—" John Rose stood up again, to the rescue, cheeks flushed. "But 'twill delay us by a year! We shall lose the building season!"

By now Abraham's heart was in his throat, his palms moist.

"Mr. Rose speaks with reason, gentlemen," said John Wilkinson. "We must start in summer whilst the river is low." He went on, arguing the case for iron.

Abraham rose, waiting for Wilkinson to finish.

"Ah." Wilkinson smiled. "I yield to Mr. Darby, who can answer your doubts better than I."

Abraham tried to keep his jaw from shaking. "I agree," he said in a stern voice, looking around the table, "with John Potte."

The Johns all stared at him in astonishment. Potte cupped his ear and consulted with his neighbors to be sure he had heard correctly.

Abraham repeated his declaration. His voice became surprisingly even. He even smiled. "I agree with John Potte. If it please the subscribers, I hereby rescind my agreement to build the bridge. Let us release ourselves from the present obligation, so that we are free to solicit more proposals."

Wilkinson looked at him in amazement. An uncertain smile twitched across Harries's face.

Abraham continued. "Let us advertise once more for proposals—for a bridge to be built of any combination of material. Wood. Stone. Whatever combination the builder might choose as strongest and most economical." He sat back down, buoyed by a great swell of contentment.


The next morning, Abraham awoke with a sense of liberation. Sounds floated up from the kitchen; a cock crowed. Last night's meeting flashed to mind. Wilkinson's stricken countenance. Abraham's own exuberance as he galloped up the dale.

Wishing to savor this feeling, he dressed and tiptoed downstairs. He instructed Mrs. Hannigan not to expect him for breakfast, saddled Blacky, and rode to the Haye farm. There he watched the foals and visited the dairy barn to see the new Guernseys. He helped Thomas Sparrow ruddle the ewes, smearing a handful of powdered rust on each to mark them from the rest of the flock. He breakfasted with the

Sparrow family, listening to their talk and finding comfort in its simplicity. Someday perhaps he would leave the Works in Samuel's hands and retire here with Becky to farm.

An orphan lamb wrapped in wool flannel bleated from a box at one end of the kitchen fireplace. He left with the lamb tucked inside his shirt; it had been years since he took a lamb home to Sunniside. The fog had lifted in the meadow; the foals were starting to gambol. Yes, someday he would abandon the stink of ironmaking. Samuel showed promise. The lamb squirmed against Abraham's stomach. He remembered the feel of the worn gold piece in his hand as a young lad, and how sullen he had remained despite Thomas Goldney's efforts to cheer him.

Arriving at Sunniside, Abraham arranged the lamb snugly in a basket and gave it to Mrs. Hannigan to keep by the hearth. Samuel had left for the Works. The women were busy upstairs. Abraham realized he was not eager to tell his mother what had happened at the meeting. He would tell Samuel first. Sammy would understand. He rode down to Dale House to check on the renovations. The second floor was now completed, the roof having been raised to give more headroom. He walked around inside, smelling the new wood and plaster. He watched the joiners installing new paneling in the study. He thought of the curtains that Sarah was making, how Mother had at first disapproved of the lace, on grounds that it was a superfluity, and how they had all tried to persuade her that it was a small luxury—in vain, until Sarah reminded her of the gold cuff links that she once gave their father. Then, to everybody's surprise, Mother offered to pay twenty-three pounds for the new carpets.

By now it was half past ten. Abraham stopped at the New Furnace casting house to invite Samuel to accompany him to Bedlam. Sammy, with his droll sense of humor, would enjoy hearing of John Potte's swordsmanship and John Rose's misguided attempts at rescue. Such entertainment might encourage Sammy to become a subscriber. Darby men should stick together.

Samuel at first declined, saying he was taken up with readying the mold for the first of three large try-pots, but Abraham prevailed on him to trust that task to his assistant. " 'Tis a beautiful day," he added. And Samuel relented.

This reversal amused Abraham; it was usually he who lectured Samuel on the virtues of industry. Proof that his instruction had done some good! He could scarcely wait to tell his brother what had happened. There was an element of confession in it, he supposed. A sharing of mischief. The look on Wilkinson's face; Potte cupping his ear in disbelief. It became funnier the more he thought about it.

They rode past Dales End. "The Bridge Committee met last night," Abraham commented as they turned past the Swan Inn.

"Was it a great bore?"

"No." Abraham chuckled. " 'Twas most entertaining." But he held his story for when they arrived at the bridge site, where he purposed to stop and relate it with suitable gestures. He observed that Samuel was sitting too far back in the saddle, as usual, so that Toby trotted irritably, stiff-legged, neck up. But Abraham forbore criticizing. Samuel was not a great hand with animals. Not a farmer—as Abraham considered himself to be, at heart. He thought of the lamb on the hearth. Samuel belonged in the Works. Perhaps Samuel should not to go to London at all, but take up his career here in the midst of the furnaces. These were all pleasant thoughts.

When they arrived at the site, Abraham looked for the willow wand and saw that it was indeed gone. His throwing it in the river was no dream. The sunlight dappling the bracken and new hawthorn blossoms was pleasant. "Come, brother, let us tarry," he said, dismounting, "and I shall tell thee about the bridge meeting." He was amused again at the reversal of their dispositions: it was Samuel who seemed preoccupied with work—doubtless ruminating over the try-pots— and himself wishing to follow a whimsy.

Dismounting, Samuel studied the hillside, cocking his head this way and that. "I have an idea, Abey."

"Only one?"

"Dost thou notice how level the ground lies, within yonder thicket?"

Abraham saw that the ground under the thicket did appear level for a distance of several rods.

Excitement entered Samuel's voice. "Why not level it a little further, and build a pair of air furnaces right at this spot? Bring sand for a casting floor. And instead of transporting the castings from Bedlam, we could pour them here!"

It was a perfectly mad idea, Abraham thought. And it would negate one of his reasons for purchasing Bedlam. But it did solve a problem, for otherwise the ungainly castings would have to be carried overland by some conveyance yet to be decided, perhaps long timbers supported by several low wagons and drawn by oxen, and even that short trip from Bedlam would introduce the risk of fractures. It was, in fact, a brilliant idea. Still, Abraham found himself impatient. He did not wish to entangle himself in such talk at this moment.

"And the people," Samuel exclaimed. "The people could witness the casting. What a spectacle, to see the molten iron from across the gorge!"

"A worthy idea, brother," Abraham said in the most generous tone he could muster.

"But no plum."

Abraham smiled. "It is perhaps premature."

" 'Twould allow a more ambitious bridge."

"More ambitious?"

"Aye. More ambitious than Pritchard's. More soaring!" He moved his hand in a great arc. "Thou art smiling, brother, but surely this is not a time for half measures."

Abraham saw he was in earnest. "Samuel," he said gently, " 'tis possible the bridge will not be built of iron at all."

Samuel guffawed. "Aye! As the Pope is not a papist!"

Abraham laughed with him. "But come, brother," he said, motioning him over to the log. It was time to take Samuel into his confidence. They had not discussed costs. "Come. Sit with me, and I shall relate the story of last night's meeting, and thou shalt know my mind perfectly concerning the bridge." He thought of Maggie sitting next to him: her hand in his, and the dead dog floating past. Samuel listened while Abraham told the story, painting with suitable flair the background rancor of the bargemen and mimicking Potte's saber attack. He gave the various arguments, interspersing them with his own concern for costs, such as that of the rope.

"But surely," said Samuel, interrupting, "these are trifles!"

"Trifles?" Abraham frowned. "The rope alone might cost thirty-five or forty pounds. And that is my point. In a project of this magnitude, such trifles add up!" He ended by describing the astonishment of the subscribers when he offered to rescind his agreement. "Thou shouldst have seen the look on John Wilkinson's face! He looked as if he'd swallowed—"

"And the committee agreed to it?" Samuel asked.

Abraham smiled, annoyed. "Of course! What else could they do?" Somehow Samuel was missing the point.

"So the agreement is rescinded?"

"Yes! With my blessings!" he added, puzzled by the tone in his brother's voice.

"But what if a meaner proposal is accepted? Suppose someone agrees to build the bridge of wood, at lower cost!"

Abraham shrugged. "Then I suppose 'twill be built of wood. Or stone," he added.

Samuel stared with furrowed brow. "How canst thou say such a thing?"

Abraham laughed, realizing that something was wrong—a forced laugh that ended awkwardly. "Canst thou not understand my strategy, brother? If the subscribers have doubts about my estimate, 'tis best to satisfy those doubts. That is the whole purpose of advertising it anew."

"But wood!"

"Or stone. It would be a proper bridge in any case. The point is this. If someone proposes to build it of whatever material—for, let us say, two hundred pounds less—and will guarantee the cost, then the subscribers will have the advantage of choosing between iron and . . . and something else. And if the proposals come in higher, then it gives me—"

"But suppose they choose something else!"

The vehemence in Samuel's voice had climbed beyond peevishness. How was it that Samuel could not see the wisdom of this strategy? And why did he not accept his older brother's authority? "The bargemen are a stubborn lot," Abraham explained, withdrawing into reason. "They need reassurance. They merely want two proposals from which to choose. Iron and—"

"But it *must* be iron!" Samuel jumped up.

"Stop shouting, Samuel." Abraham struggled to keep his own voice from rising. "In the first place, I do not seriously think anyone will come forth with another proposal. The whole purpose of advertising anew is to permit me to revise my estimate. In the second place—"

"I thought thy purpose was to reassure the bargemen!"

"That too." Abraham's face was hot.

" 'Tis thee that wants reassuring!"

For a moment he thought his brother might strike him, so inflamed was Samuel's face. It loomed so close, Abraham had to make an effort not to flinch. "Sammy," he said evenly, "this is a complicated matter. Methinks thou art too new to the Works, and too young, to apprehend all the subtleties of it."

Samuel stalked into the bracken and stood with his back to Abraham. Presently he threw back his head and let loose a great long howl like the roar of some wild animal. The sound sent a chill down Abraham's spine. He remained seated on the log. In his mind's eye he saw them both as puppets on a stage—he on the log, sullen, and Samuel with his head thrown back and fists clenched. Abraham fixed his ears on the distant shouts of the bow haulers. Such passions were repellent, his own anger as unbearable as Samuel's. A swarm of gnats was dancing over the stump where Wilkinson had pissed. Abraham's shoes wanted polishing. He thought of the time that Sammy let Abraham's frog escape from an old butter crock that Abraham pretended was a jail. How furious he had been to find the crock empty; how it was not until Father's funeral that the brothers had taken each other's hands again. His anger had cooled now, and out of this coolness he supposed he must soothe poor, wretched Sammy.

"If thou wilt but hear me, Samuel," he said, standing. "I should like to explain so thou canst understand." But Sammy was mounting his horse, his face expressionless except for its pallor. "Sammy," Abraham began, the air thick in his lungs. "Wilt thou hear me?"

But Samuel galloped off, back toward Coalbrookdale.

APRIL 1776

## Maggie Foster

She was helping Abiah at the malt mill when Sarah burst in, breathless. "Sammy has run away!"

Abiah looked up sharply.

"What happened?" Maggie asked.

Sarah waved her hands helplessly. "I know not! His words were all higgily-piggily. Abey said something that set him off."

"Where did he go?" Abiah asked.

Sarah shook her head violently, tears filling her eyes. "I know not!"

"When?" asked Abiah. "When did it happen?"

"Not five minutes ago. I ran here. I should have ridden after him." The last was a wail.

The three women hurried up the hill to Sunniside, Sarah adding what information she could. Samuel had stopped at Sunniside to get a few things from his room, then galloped off again, his face white as chalk.

"You don't know what triggered it?" asked Maggie.

"The bridge! He said it might not be built of iron!"

"Who said that?"

329

"Abraham! I mean, Sammy! Sammy heard it from Abraham!"

Maggie tried to pull more details from the confusion—what exactly Abraham had said—but Sarah's focus was on Samuel. "He called Abey a"—Sarah's voice dropped—"a *stupid get,* and took off like a demon." She wrung her hands. "I should have followed him!"

Maggie put her arms around her. Sarah seemed small, the brim of her bonnet pressed against Maggie's collarbone. All Maggie could think of was what this meant to their plan. What Abraham said. None of it had to do with Sarah's pain, which she felt through a filter of numbness. "Samuel will be all right," she soothed, wanting to believe it.

Samuel's bedchamber was in disarray—his money box turned upside down, clothes scattered on his bed. Maggie wondered if he had taken the drawing with him.

"I could not understand half of what he said," Sarah told her. "He ranted about the bridge being made of *whatever.* He cursed, and he mumbled, and paid me no mind."

Abiah sent Joseph to the Works for Abraham.

During the next hour and a half, while they waited and speculated where Samuel might have gone—London, perhaps—Maggie found an opportunity to go up to Samuel's study. She was relieved to find the drawing secure in its leather tube. The partly constructed model remained untouched, under his table, concealed by a cloth. Wherever Samuel had gone, at least the drawing was safe.

A braham appeared at the sitting room door. "Has Samuel come home?" His face tightened, seeing their expressions.

His account of what happened was orderly—too orderly, almost officious, until he got to Samuel's scream, when his voice caught. " 'Twas a beasty howl. A most piteous sound."

Abiah shut her eyes. "Why, observing thy brother in so pitiable a condition, didst thou not pursue him?" Her voice had a hard maternal edge.

Abraham explained that there was business for him at Bedlam, that he reasoned that Samuel would come to his proper mind and might wish, moreover, to be alone. It all sounded equivocal. When he finally expressed impatience with Samuel for causing them such worry, Abiah reproached him.

"Thou art," she said severely, "thy brother's keeper."

"But he is so secretive," Abraham protested. "I do not know his mind."

"Secretive?"

"Staying up till all hours."

Sarah responded indignantly. "He stays up late working."

"On what?" asked Abraham.

Sarah hesitated, glanced at Maggie. " 'Tis a surprise."

Maggie nodded. "A wedding gift."

Abraham frowned at the floor. Dogs were barking in the distance. Sarah peered out the window but saw nothing. Abiah returned to the subscribers' meeting, wanting Abraham to clarify his position. His position remained ambiguous, however, or was shifting under pressure. By the time he finished, it appeared that his willingness to consider building the bridge of timber or stone was mainly a ploy to increase the budget. But Abiah's questions had lent legitimacy to Samuel's response. Whether it was her intent to put him there or not, Abraham was clearly in the doghouse.


The next morning, Samuel still had not returned.

Abraham paced around the dining room, trying to put the best face on things. "At least he had the presence of mind to collect his coat and his money. At least he was sufficiently rational..." He trailed off before the women's silence.

After Abraham left for the Works, Abiah marched upstairs. Sarah and Maggie followed. By now the disarray in Samuel's room seemed ominous. Abiah rehung clothing on the cast-iron hooks, taking inventory. She regarded a pair of yellow silk stockings with disapproval. "So he took his red breeches?"

Sarah nodded. "Aye."

Abiah announced she was going to Ketley Bank to consult with Richard Reynolds, though he was ill. Sarah and Maggie crowded into the chaise with her. Abiah let Maggie drive. They followed the horse tramways north through Lightmoor.

"Liverpool," said Sarah abruptly.

Abiah looked at her. "Was it something he said?"

Sarah shook her head. " 'Tis only a feeling."

"Praise the Maker if it be true," said Abiah, "for he would be in good hands with the Rathbones."

"Perhaps." Sarah's glance told Maggie she was skeptical.

The doctor was leaving as they arrived. Rebecca Reynolds told them that Richard had just been bled but would see them. Reynolds received them cheerfully from a couch in his study. He was in no great discomfort, he assured them. The doctor, theorizing that he had a cold in his spleen, had applied leeches; but whether he was suffering from an overabundance or an insufficiency of splenic essence was unclear. "These modern quacksalvers," Reynolds chuckled, "bandy high phrases about like shuttlecocks."

After listening with concern to Abiah's account, he offered to send a trusted man to Liverpool to make inquiries. Abiah thanked him and said she would consider his offer if Samuel did not return that evening.

Reynolds lay back on his pillow. "So. 'Twas the bridge."

Abiah nodded.

"Well, I must tell thee." Reynolds chuckled to himself. "Samuel is not the only one alarmed by Abraham's decision. John Wilkinson is jumping about like a cat on hot bricks."

"And thou, Richard? What is thy opinion?"

Reynolds raised his shaggy eyebrows. "Actually, it may be a good strategy. The committee has been deadlocked for months. And Abraham is carrying the greatest burden."

"And should it be iron or not?"

"Oh, iron, without a doubt."

Abiah nodded resolutely. " 'Tis what his father wanted."

"But this is Abraham's project, Abiah. He must choose."

Reynolds's blue eyes regarded her carefully. "A young man must find his own path."

Abiah nodded. "I try not to interfere."

Reynolds smiled.

So much unspoken between these two, Maggie thought. She remembered seeing them conferring in whispers during the Goldneys' visit a year ago.

On the way home, mother and daughter discussed Reynolds's offer to send a man. Sarah observed that even if Samuel was headed for Liverpool, it would take several days for them to receive word. The journey to Liverpool required two or three days on horseback, depending on the weather. Half that by stagecoach. And even if he was headed for Liverpool, he might not go to the Rathbones.

"Where would he go?" asked Abiah.

"I know not." Sarah shrugged. "But 'tis too long to wait. Someone must go look for him. Richard's man will not do, no matter how trusted. Let me go, Mother."

Abiah deliberated. "The way is dangerous. Thou must needs take Joseph or Andrew."

"Or me," Maggie volunteered. "I could go with her."

Sarah looked to her mother.

Abiah was noncommittal.

When bedtime arrived and Samuel still had not returned, Abraham, feeding the lamb in his lap, voiced regret for the "misunderstanding," as he now called it, between himself and his brother. And he said very clearly, for everyone to hear, that he hoped the proposals would come in high, so that he could afford to build the bridge entirely of iron.

Abiah glanced up from her mending. "Thy father would approve." But there was a coolness in her voice. She gathered up her Bible and her mending to go to bed, first stopping to gaze out at the carriage lane. She turned to Abraham. "Tomorrow morning, Sarah and Maggie will leave for Liverpool to search for Samuel. I wish them to take the phaeton."

"The phaeton belongs to the Lloyds."

"They said we might use it."

"Who will accompany them?"

"No one. Andrew is too old to be of much assistance, and Joseph is too young. They will have each other."

They left after breakfast, with a hamper of food and a small trunk that included a change of clothing for Samuel and a little tin box of amber cough drops. Abiah would post a letter advising Mally to expect them.

Sarah asked Maggie to drive. Cautious at first, Maggie held the horses to a slow trot. The phaeton, with its huge wheels and two horses hitched in tandem, handled very differently from the chaise. But the roads were dampened only slightly by a misting rain, and the phaeton invited more speed, so once the fog lifted, she let the horses fall into the brisk trot that seemed to suit them. Sarah knew the way. North past Lightmoor and Ketley, through Wellington toward Market Drayton, then follow the Roman road to Whitchurch and then north again to Wrexham and on to Chester and Liverpool.

"At least the drawing is safe," Maggie observed.

Sarah gave her a withering look. "I would rather Sammy be safe."

Maggie reddened. "I'm sorry. I only meant, if we find him—that is, *when* he turns up—"

Sarah finished the sentence for her. "Then he shall have the drawing to return to."

"Yes. Exactly." She thanked Sarah silently. But she was also pondering the question now in her mind. What did she want? For Samuel to turn up safe and sound? She thought of her own affection for him, the notes they slipped under each other's doors, her wish to protect him. But she could not ignore a darker thought. She wanted his safe return *so he could go back to work on the model.* Heartless, but it was the truth.

Suppose he came back unable, for whatever reason, to complete the model?

Another, crueler idea surfaced. Of all the disasters she could imagine befalling Samuel—a psychotic break, serious physical injury, or irreparable disgrace, any of which could put an end to their plan—death might be preferable. It might give his design just the boost it needed.

Sick!

She focused on the horses. North of Wellington, as they left the coal measures and entered farming country, she got the horses to break into a canter. They were long-striding animals, one chestnut, one dappled. She had to slow down for villages and for droves of cattle and sheep, but slowing down made the bursts of speed even more intoxicating. She liked working the horses from almost a crouch, feeling the road in her hamstrings. She liked that she and Sarah were on their own: two Quaker ladies getting double takes from the slower vehicles they passed in this outlandish rig.

Once, she put the horses into a gallop. "This is great," she said. "Why doesn't anybody ever use it?"

"Samuel wants to. Mother thinks it a bit flash for Quakers."

Back in CALYPOOL, riding in APCs, she must have gone faster than this. And even in a sun trike, if you really cranked on a hard surface, you could get moving nearly this fast. But there wasn't the thrill of the horses—the clatter of hooves, the brute power, this collaboration with another species, making the relationship with Gaea a little less lonely.

Sarah kept fretting over Samuel. "What if I'm wrong? What if he's not gone to Liverpool?" Every time they stopped to rest the horses and make inquiries, Sarah worried that he had taken off in some other direction. "London," she fretted. "What if Sammy went to London?" It got on Maggie's nerves.

A few people claimed to have seen a young Quaker on a bay mount, but the details were sketchy or contradictory. A publican described a young man with sideburns, but said he rode a white horse. A tollkeeper described Toby perfectly—a bay gelding with brindled hindquarters—but said the rider was a one-armed man.

"The one-armed man stole Sammy's horse," Sarah agonized, "and left him for dead!"

"Or else Sammy has lost an arm," Maggie said cheerfully.

Sarah rolled her eyes.

"Sorry."

Highwaymen were a real concern, Maggie knew. But at least it was flintlocks. A highwayman would not be so quick to shoot—if not for fear of the gallows then for fear of a misfire.

"Our uncle," said Sarah, "was killed on this very road when he was thrown from his horse."

"Well, at least Samuel is a good rider."

"Abraham says not. And suppose he had a fit?"

"He hasn't had a fit in years, has he?"

Sarah shrugged. "He did not always know when he had one."

It was true: Samuel might be dead. Maggie could not keep her mind from running to the next thing. *What better memorial to a young man cut off in his youth than the bridge he designed?* They could hire someone to build the model. Rally around the tragedy. Push Abraham's guilt buttons. Get Abiah behind it.

"I wish I had tried harder to stop him," Sarah said.

"I wish," said Maggie, "that I had helped him more with the model. He was having such a—"

"The model!" cried Sarah. "Sammy may be lying in a ditch somewhere, and thou canst think only of the model!"

Maggie glowered at the horses' backs slick with sweat. Their ears were up, feeling her tension through the reins. Her shame boiled into anger. "Stop blaming yourself, Sarah! Stop blaming me!" Thinking *She's right, I'm a monster!*

"Stop the phaeton," Sarah said. It was an order.

Maggie pulled over, gripping the reins, steeling herself against more accusations. But Sarah was calm. She asked that they pray. In the silence, Maggie felt tears gather. She hated herself. Finally the constriction in her throat became unendurable, and she burst into tears. "I'm sorry!"

She felt Sarah's arms go around her. She let herself be held, let her pride dissolve.

Sarah spoke softly. "Forgive my rash words."

"No, you're right. I really am obsessed with the bridge."

"And I with Sammy. We are both overwrought."

Sarah took a turn driving. Maggie sat back and watched the hedge-rows go past, white with blossoms. Farmers plowed their fields. She did care about Samuel. She thought of how happy he had looked that day, sprawled on the picnic rock with violets in his hair. And how, once the news that he was delaying his move to London had sunk in, she realized she was grateful to have them at Sunniside for the summer. But now, who knew what would happen?

Sarah talked about her childhood. She confessed to a fear of horses arising from an accident when she was five. She observed that Maggie said little about her life in the Colonies. Maggie told her it felt so long ago that it all seemed invented. "Like something I made up."

Sarah asked what had happened between Maggie and Abraham, and was not surprised to have her suspicions confirmed. "I should have liked to have thee as a sister-in-law," she said. They talked about babies, marriage, duty, and—incongruously—how Sarah admired Maggie's posture. "Thou art taller than most men, and yet carry thyself so upright and graceful." Sarah laughed. "I used to imagine thou wert a princess in disguise. Or a long-lost sister come to change my life."

It was confession—whimsical, but a confession nonetheless. Laughing with her, Maggie felt shy.

Five o'clock. Shadows lengthening. Maggie's shoulders ached. She was driving again. The horses, lathered, tired more quickly between rests. She watched for signs of limping, as Abiah had taught her. Nine hours they had been traveling north, the road hilly, rutted, and badly drained. But now they were headed west on the Roman road, which was noticeably straighter and smoother. Major weirdness: here, right at the cusp of the First Industrial Revolution, the Roman roads were the best. Whitchurch by dusk. Stay with Friends. And to-morrow, if the weather held, they should make Liverpool.

Granny had gone to Liverpool once, on the Beatles Tour. The name conjured something dark and squalid.

The terrain changed. Coal and ironstone diggings gave way to peat bogs, heath, and signs of glaciation. Maggie had hoped for more trees, but most of the land was given over to crops or grazing. Not just industry gobbling up the forests but agriculture too. Overpopulation beginning here in the Old World. Land everywhere across the globe was being seized by the powerful and treated as a commodity.

A few big trees stood out on the landscape. Sarah pointed to an immense oak in the stream valley ahead. "We always stop by that tree." When they got to it, Maggie brought the phaeton to a halt under the immense canopy. The air was peaceful. The leaves, not quite full size, were a pale, tender green, unfolding. Despite its size, the tree was still in good health. The cool light scattered through the branches was suffused with life.

Sarah looked up. "In all Madeley there is no tree this big."

Together, holding hands, they could not reach halfway around the trunk.

"How old do you suppose it is?"

"Ancient. They say the Cuckoo Oak is four hundred years old, and 'tisn't near this big. Father told us this tree might go back to William the Conqueror." Sarah smiled. "I used to get *conqueror* muddled with *conker*. A chestnut."

Minnows darted in the stream below. Maggie took the leather bucket from the back of the phaeton and scrambled down a worn path to fill it. Returning, she held the bucket for each horse in turn, bracing herself against the toss of their heads. Cold wet seeped through the gray flannel of her dress, cold droplets tingled against her neck and soaked her breasts. She laughed. Looking up through the boughs, she felt herself taken up in that lambent meeting of leaves and sky, as though she had joined the powerful capillary flow that reached to the topmost leaf, felt herself taken into the pure light. For a moment she swayed, light scintillating against her closed lids. Everything in the world connected in that swaying, as though all separateness was illusion. She was startled by a loud snort, a rolling eye, the thrust of a wet muzzle nearly jerking the bucket from her arms.

"Thou must miss the trees in America," Sarah remarked when they were on their way again, Sarah driving.

Maggie nodded, leaning back. How could she confess that she had never seen such a tree in her life?

She wanted to tell Sarah who she was, as she once longed to tell Jeremy and Jane. The impulse only fed her loneliness. She tried to return to that other sensation, of being drawn into the light, everything marvelously connected—but it was gone, flattened into an idea.

She asked Sarah, "How much do you remember of your father?"

"Quite a lot. Actually, only bits. The conker oak. How he used to come home from the Works smelling of sulfur. I rather fancied the smell, until my sister Mally told me it was like a fart." She laughed. "Even then I liked it. Father was always working, coming home tired. I suppose 'tis why most of my memories are from journeys. Quarterly Meetings. We were coming home once at dusk, and Father pointed to the glow of Coalbrookdale in the distance, took my little hand in his, and said it was like a bunch of roses. He said it so simply. And he wasn't a man for poetry. I shall never forget it."

Maggie thought of her own father's hands. It was the one memory she knew did not come from the little blue laser disk, because she could remember the feel of them. Squarish hands, the knuckles crowded by curly black hairs. She could hear him saying *Poor bubby*.

"I remember him as a sad man," Sarah said. "But that may be because I saw more of him at the end. I was eleven when he died. Abey was thirteen, away at school. Mother was traveling, following her ministry. I took care of Sammy and nursed my father as he died."

It was dusk now. They were outside Whitchurch. A stone post marked the turnoff to Shrewsbury. Sarah reined the horses to a sudden halt. "Look!" She pointed.

Perched atop the signpost was a Quaker hat. Sarah jumped down, ran back. Maggie saw her shake something from the hat, wipe it in the grass, and examine it. Running back to the phaeton, Sarah looked overjoyed.

" 'Tis Samuel's! Mark where I sewed the string with green thread!"

On to Whitchurch. Maggie drove while Sarah examined the hat and chattered excitedly, declaring she was not at all surprised that Samuel had lost his hat, considering his state of mind. A passerby must have found it and left it, out of kindness, on the signpost, where it would be found. It was probably another passerby with a dislike for Quakers who added the horse turds. Proof in any case that Samuel had come this way. A sign from the Author of Light.

Maggie could have offered a more pessimistic interpretation. Maybe Samuel had had a seizure. But Sarah was determined to look on the bright side.

Who could say? Maybe it *was* a sign.

# Maggie Foster

The next day, as they drove north from Wrexham along the Welsh border, Sarah pointed out the plume of smoke from Bersham Furnace—built by Quakers, now owned by John Wilkinson. They began passing wide-wheeled wagons weighed down by cannon. "Cargoes of death," Sarah observed, "headed for Liverpool." She frowned at a row of carriage guns that would likely end up on privateers. "Sammy is no keener than I am on Wilkinson, thou must know."

The words pricked Maggie's conscience. She still did not know how she was going to finesse Samuel's withdrawal from the commission. Twice she had started letters to Wilkinson, only to tear them up. She told herself she needed to do it in person. The fact was, she was ambivalent about giving up the alliance with the Broseley ironmaster. The model was his idea, after all. He would be offended. Which put a premium on the other part of the deal that was the dirty little secret she kept from Sarah and Samuel.

And there was the matter of the six guineas that Wilkinson had already paid. He would want his money back. Samuel had probably spent it or lost it. She couldn't bring herself to mention it now.

"Thou seemeth worried."

Maggie nodded. "Just thinking about Sammy." She wished she could confide some of this to Sarah. But once she began opening up the truth, it would be hard to stop.

Arriving at Chester, they followed the Mersey estuary west past windmills and salt marshes, until they could see Liverpool's church spires across the water. The brackish smell of tidal flats gave way to a salt breeze. By the time they got to the ferry landing at Birkenhead, they could smell the saltworks and the sugar refinery and see the gold domes of municipal buildings.

The ferry crossing took nearly an hour. They saw square-rigged oceangoing ships approaching the harbor under full sail—an impressive sight. The ferry itself was maybe forty feet long, with two masts. Maggie had never been on such a ship. She had never seen the ocean, although she couldn't let on. She found it all exhilarating. The smell of the sea breeze, the rolling deck. And Liverpool was not at all the dark ugly city she had imagined, it was a sun-dazzled sprawl of white buildings with tile roofs. The harbor was crisply defined by granite fortifications and piers.

Sarah made inquiries of the ferrymen at both sides, but none of them recalled anyone of Samuel's description. At the Liverpool shore Sarah and Maggie received help disembarking into two feet of water, where the phaeton's tall wheels were a great advantage. Sarah drove to her sister's house, past pleasant row houses, many with geraniums in their windows. She stopped at a narrow brick house overlooking the harbor. From behind the house came the sounds of Joseph Rathbone's forge.

Mally greeted them at the door. She was a matronly woman of twenty-eight, with the pointed features that were the hallmark of Abiah's side of the family, and she had a habit of clasping her hands at chest height. Yes, yes, she was expecting them. Mother's letter had arrived today. She introduced herself to Maggie before Sarah could speak, and shepherded them inside in a flurry.

"Is he—" Sarah began.

"No." Mally frowned. "Samuel has not shown himself here. I am not surprised."

Mally instructed the housekeeper to have the stableboy tend to the horses. She led them upstairs to their room, chatting in a businesslike way about the inquiries she and Joseph had begun making. Joseph would be happy to accompany Sarah and Maggie tomorrow morning to a place called Babbidge's, a chophouse where Samuel used to eat. "Joseph would take thee there this very evening," she added, "but he must return to the foundry after supper. 'Tis just as well. Ye must be exhausted from the journey. Better to rest, and ready thyselves for supper. We have a pineapple from Jamaica—a rarity these days." She clasped her hands with extra enthusiasm and, after a brief exchange of family news, bustled downstairs to attend to supper.

As soon as Mally left, Sarah threw herself on the bed and pounded the pillow.

Maggie massaged her back. "You really thought Sammy would be here, didn't you?" She felt Sarah's muscles gradually relax.

"Not really." Sarah sighed. "Maybe a little." She groaned. "Mostly 'tis my sister."

"Mally's a real mother hen."

"She's protective." Sarah rolled over. "Being the oldest and having no children of her own." She got up, walked to the window, and looked out at the sun, a red disk descending into the Irish Sea. "Tomorrow is not soon enough. I will ask to go tonight."

"What will she say?"

"She'll be opposed. And Joseph won't hear of it."

"Then don't ask. Just tell them. We're going tonight."

Sarah pondered this. "Just *tell* them?"

Maggie nodded. "You're a grown woman. I'll help you rehearse."

Sarah was right. Joseph would not hear of their going alone to Babbidge's.

"I forbid it," he said, when Sarah announced her intention after supper. "Liverpool is not Coalbrookdale. 'Tis a dangerous city at night, and since the riots last August we are all walking on eggs. We shall have time aplenty to search for Samuel tomorrow, in the daylight." He turned to Maggie. "Perhaps this evening thou canst amuse us with tales of James Watt's steam engine. I am told thou art well versed on the subject." The corners of his eyes crinkled. He was a large, balding man whose formality was softened by a pleasant, fleshy face.

Maggie turned to Sarah. She knew this was the part that Sarah dreaded. They had role-played it in whispers.

"Joseph," Sarah said, "I value thy counsel, but fear I must do as my own judgment bids." Babbidge's, she told him, was a respectable enough place for two ladies together. They would be in no danger. Samuel's safety must come before their convenience. She began to appeal to Joseph's compassion, and for a moment started to whine, but caught herself and declared firmly that they must go. Maggie was proud of her.

Joseph finally relented. "Very well. Thou hast come this far, I suppose. But take care to avoid the waterfront." He sent word to the stableboy to harness the horses.

Mally did not hide her disapproval. "Ladies," she warned, "have no business out at night alone."

"We have each other," Sarah said.

The Rathbones followed them to the phaeton, Joseph going on at length about the riots last August and how it was even worse now, since the predations of American and French privateers had interrupted trade. Sailors were unemployed. There was a great anger afoot. "Thou wouldst be well advised," he warned Maggie as he helped her into the phaeton, "not to announce thy nationality. 'Tis bad enough being a Quaker. My brother William's house was attacked by the rioters."

Mally's clasped hands soared in lamentation. "They cut open the feather beds and scattered feathers everywhere. All for his opposition to slavery."

"Samuel," Sarah reminded them, "is sometimes outspoken in his opposition to slavery."

"And known to take strong drink," said Mally with a frown. "The two do not mix. Not in Liverpool."

Sarah drove, since she knew the streets.

"Good work." Maggie grinned.

Sarah nodded. "Thanks to thee. Thou didst open the way."

A̲t Babbidge's, no one had seen Samuel. Sarah and Maggie were sent to a somewhat less reputable place named Casteen's, in the direction of George's Dock, where ships from the West Indies moored. The proprietress of Casteen's introduced them to a ruddy, muttonchopped little Irishman called Skittles, who claimed to know Samuel, or at least a young man by that description who "fancied the prancers." Skittles called himself a "doodle-doo man," meaning he had something to do with cockfights. He looked a little like a rooster himself, with his disheveled red wig, skinny neck, and cold little round eyes. He was quick to accept Sarah's offer of a pint of short beer, and quick to pick up on her urgency.

"Information has its price," he confided with a wink, suggesting that a dinner of beef stew might stimulate the natural keenness of his mind. Sarah obliged him. He took off his wig while he ate, revealing a pale, freckled head. Between spoonfuls he told them that they had come to the right fellow. "Skittles has many an oar in the water," he said, "and knows old Liverpuddle like his own mum, he does. Skittles'll find the young gentleman, he will. Aye, ferret him out—if the body snatchers don't snab him first."

"Body snatchers?" asked Maggie.

"Aye, yer ladyship. Press gangs. This being Liverpuddle, the press gangs be as busy as the devil in a high wind."

"Doing what?" Maggie asked.

"Why, snatching able-bodied men for His Majesty's Navy."

Sarah exchanged a look with Maggie that said this was one danger she had not considered. Samuel, had he been wearing those red breeches, would have trouble persuading anyone he was a Quaker.

"Pray, sir, tell us where to look."

After some verbal strutting and meandering, Skittles squinted at the ceiling and opined that the place to try was the Puss and Boot, which he described as a "tat-shop for Guineamen." It was located on Crooked Lane, near the Old Dock, next to the mast yard, and had a gaming room and a cockpit. " 'Tis no place for ladies," he warned, "being a snug-lay for snudges and sharpers, and snafflers of prancers. But as Skittles has business there this evening, he can be encouraged—faith, a small fee would help—to keep a sharp eye peeled for the young gent."

Sarah, overjoyed, handed him half a crown, which Skittles considered thoughtfully and balanced on edge by his plate. "As I be a wagering man, I should like to know what it be worth to yez if I produce the gentleman himself in full feather."

Sarah promised him a pound. With a nod, Skittles flipped the half crown in the air, caught it in his wig, and clapped it on his head. The two women left him to his dining.

By now it was dark; the lamplighters were making their rounds. But Sarah and Maggie decided to drive past the Old Dock and at least have a look at the outside of the Puss and Boot. Sarah oriented herself by the Merchants Exchange and the burnt caramel smell of the sugar refinery along Castle Street, which led toward the Old Dock. There were no streetlamps in this neighborhood, but against the pallor of fog hiding a rising moon they could see the rigging of ships nearby.

"The Old Dock is where the Guineamen moor," Sarah explained.

They found Crooked Lane, the mast yard, and, a few doors down from it, the Puss and Boot. As they rolled slowly past the sagging, half-timbered facade with its tiny leaded panes, they heard shouting inside. "Keep moving," Maggie urged. Then came a crash that sounded like a table tipping over. Looking back, they saw the door swing open and a man being heaved onto the pavement, followed by another. Sarah clucked the horses into motion.

"What do you say?" Maggie asked when they were a safe distance away, trotting in the direction of the Merchants Exchange. "Come back tomorrow, during the daylight, or wait for Skittles to make his rounds?"

"I do not trust Skittles."

"I don't either, but he's our only lead."

Sarah slowed the team to a walk. "Our leading must come from the Maker."

Outside the Merchants Exchange, streetlamps shone on the cobblestones. Sarah pulled over, and they sat in silence. From the harbor came the clanging of buoys. Maggie was thinking that the odds of finding Samuel were slim. Skittles had been equivocal as to whether he knew Samuel. In any case it was possible that Samuel had never made it to Liverpool.

Sarah spoke. "We must go back, in the Divine Light. We must go inside. Speak truth to power."

Jesus. Maggie looked at her and sighed. This was the lady she was coaching to be more assertive? But instead of saying *You're crazy,* she said, finally, "Okay. But you do the talking."

Leaving the phaeton at a hostelry on Sugarhouse Lane, the two women proceeded on foot, holding their Bibles, their bonnet brims drawn chastely tight. As they passed a shop's bay window, Maggie saw in the moonlight a row of small branding irons and other iron implements laid out in a neat row. She stopped and stared, feeling horror in the pit of her stomach.

Sarah took her arm. "Aye. This is where ships are outfitted for the Africa trade."

Maggie tapped on the glass. "What's that?"

"A thumbscrew. 'Tis a most abominable invention for torturing slaves. Have ye not these in America?"

"Why would they torture them?"

"If the slaves be obstinate. Joseph's brother says if that key be turned, the bar tightens on the thumbs, causing great pain. If it be tightened further, blood spurts from the ends. And when the key is removed, the Negro can do nothing to end the pain. Nor can other slaves assist him."

"My God."

"And that"—she pointed to another device—"is for opening the jaws of Negroes who attempt to starve themselves."

Maggie felt her tugging at her arm.

"Come," said Sarah. "I cannot bear to look at those things."

Maggie wrenched her gaze away with difficulty. It was the casualness of the display that appalled her. This was 1776. The Age of Reason. Mozart was writing his violin concerti, and Thomas Jefferson and others were penning high-blown phrases. *Life, liberty, and the pursuit of happiness.* And here was Western technology being applied routinely to breaking the human spirit.

"Didst thou not encounter such devices in the Colonies?"

Maggie shook her head. "No." Slavery, at least by that name, had slipped into the amorphous abstraction of history. Slave labor was, however, a continuing fact from the late twentieth century into her own era. The methods of control were generally more sophisticated. Factories and food-processing plants that could be assembled or broken down in a matter of hours and shipped anywhere. But there were also death squads, torture—even devices of this sort—that furnished the raw material for the punishment veeries at CALYPOOL: You are the chosen ones, but this is what happens to children who do not play the bottomthink game.

When they arrived at the Puss and Boot, one of the men thrown out earlier was sitting up, holding his head and muttering. They edged past and pulled open the heavy door. Inside, the air was thick with the smell of unwashed bodies, beer-soaked sawdust, rum, garlic, tar, tobacco, manure—the smell more palpable than the dark beams and dingy plaster walls that contained it. They were the object of stares. A large raw-boned man who seemed to be the publican was hammering a tap into a barrel. He looked up, mallet poised, in the fashion of a man expecting trouble, then ignored the women while he tipped the barrel into its cradle.

"Hast thou seen a young Quaker named Samuel?" Sarah asked.

The man wiped his hands on his apron and spat into the sawdust at his feet. "I seen no Quaker by any name."

"Please. It is my brother. He might not look like a Quaker. He is twenty-one years of age and hath side-whiskers."

The publican spat again and waved them away. "Begone, ladies. Yez no business in this place, have ye now? Begone." He pointed to the door.

Sarah stood on her toes, trying to peer into the back room, where men were playing darts, but by this time several men had crowded around them, blocking her view. A man with a pocked face and blackened teeth pointed a finger in their faces, leering. "Quakeresses!" The word made the rounds amidst laughter.

"Have ye come to make us repent?" someone shouted.

"Please," said Sarah. "We are searching for my brother."

"I'll be yer brother!" A red-bearded man with a ring in his ear threw an arm around Sarah.

"Aye," said a man behind him. "I'll be another!"

"Tha'll have to thee-and-thou 'er!" someone laughed.

" 'Tain't all I'll do!" roared the red-bearded man.

Maggie slipped her own arm around Sarah. "Let's get out of here. Now!"

"But Sammy may be in here." Sarah raised her voice, calling toward the back room, "Sammy!"

At the sound of a woman's voice, some of the men in back joined the throng. Getting out was not going to be easy. The press of bodies was suddenly formidable. The bonnet brim added to Maggie's claustrophobia. Feeling a hand on her shoulder, she turned and saw a huge man beside her.

He grinned down at her with golden eyes set in a bronze complexion—quite a beautiful man, actually, his breath smelling of cloves, his dark hair tied into a ponytail, his shirt open to the waist, exposing a braided leather lanyard and a wall of muscled flesh against which he began to clamp her in an easy one-armed hug. Maggie fought back panic.

"Take your butt-faxing hands off me!" she cried. But he only laughed, pressing her against that garlicky flesh. Her vision was swimming in hot darkness, as at the bullring, but this time there was no small hand to steady her.

"Stop!" she yelled, forcing herself to breathe. "Help!"

Sarah was being pulled from her grasp. "Stop!" Sarah cried. "Have pity!"

There were too many of them, and no room, in these close quarters, to use her assailant's strength against him; scarcely room to swing a punch. The damned bonnet was askew, blocking her vision further. She could knee him, maybe. Bite his chest. But she didn't want to enrage him without an escape route. Now a goddamned hand was up her dress.

Suddenly the air shook with a deafening blast. Plaster rained from the ceiling through a cloud of acrid blue smoke. The publican was waving a pistol in the air. He brandished a second pistol. "Hold!" he screamed, covered with plaster dust. "Every man-jack jelly-bag of yez, mark me words! If I can't have order in this piss-factory, I'll cancel the fooking cockfight and keep my cut of the purse!" From the stunned silence in the room rose a swell of grumbling. The publican waved the pistol toward the door. "Quakeresses!" he hissed. "Out with yez! Out!"

Maggie grabbed Sarah's arm. "Let's go!"

The men parted reluctantly for the women to make it to the door.

Outside on the pavement, Maggie tried to hurry Sarah away. But Sarah resisted. "Samuel might be in there!" she said. "Mother has gone in many a such place and testified." She waved her Bible. "Spoken her heart, answering that of God in everyone."

"Not in that place, Sarah. And not at night."

"But—"

"Sarah, please, come on! Do you have any idea what could've happened to us if—"

They had got no more than a dozen paces, arguing in this way, when the door burst open and the big man with the ponytail leapt out. Maggie yanked Sarah by the hand. "*Run,* goddammit! This is not the Madeley market!"

They ran down the street, shouting for help. The bonnet restricted Maggie's vision, but she didn't need to look back to know that the man was gaining on them. She might have been able to outrun him alone, but Sarah was tiring. Finally there was no choice. The big man's boot heels were right behind her, the sound of his breathing. "Keep running!" she told Sarah, and gave her a shove forward. She smelled the cloves, estimated his bulk. Thinking of Mr. Ho's *Your moment of greatest vulnerability can be your greatest strength,* she stopped, dropped her Bible, and turned in a single movement, blocking him with her hip, seizing his arm with both hands, and pulling him over her back in one long plunge. He was almost too tall for the maneuver, but his momentum carried him. She brought the arm down hard and smooth and straightened her legs with a pop, and he sailed in an arc, landing on his back with a very satisfying crash. She whirled in time to catch the man with the red beard in the stomach with her right elbow—a lucky hit, square in the solar plexus, followed by stiff fingers knifing into the diaphragm. Red Beard bent in half, gasping, eyes bulging, and crumpled to his knees. Lucky for him. It spared him a kick in the balls. She was tempted to deliver it gratis, since he was the one who had started the attack. But Red Beard was making pathetic retching sounds. The big man with the ponytail was lying on his back stunned, eyes and mouth open. The wind knocked out of him.

Skittles had been right. This was no place for ladies.

Sarah stared in disbelief. "How didst thou manage that?"

Maggie picked up her Bible. "The power of the Word."

They set off at a rapid walk, Sarah trotting to keep up. But by the time they reached the hostelry, Sarah was pulling at her to stop. "We never saw the back room!"

"Sarah." Maggie looked at her incredulously. "You must be kidding."

"Sammy could be in there."

"Sarah, sweetie. Sammy could be anywhere in Liverpool. It's a big city; there must be dozens of places like the Puss and Boot. We'll come back tomorrow, in the daylight."

They were still arguing when they arrived at the hostelry. "Don't you think he would've come out," argued Maggie, "hearing all that ruckus about Quakeresses?"

Sarah's eyebrows knitted. "Suppose—suppose he was not able?"

"Sarah. Let it go. We've already pushed our luck. Let's call it quits for tonight."

Reluctantly, Sarah agreed. They were waiting at the stable door for the hostler to bring out the phaeton, when Sarah, peering at the various stalls, noticed a horse with brindled hindquarters. "Toby!" she called. The animal lifted its head. She ran to examine it. "Maggie, it 'tis Toby!" She clapped her hands. "We are on the right track!"

The hostler confirmed that a young man of Samuel's description had arrived three days ago—"boozed or mazed," to judge by his behavior—and had not returned for his mount.

Sarah drew Maggie aside. "Well?" she demanded.

"All right." Maggie nodded. "But this time we need a plan."

They agreed to pay the hostler the three shillings he claimed was his due. Sarah gave him another sixpence to groom and walk Toby, who was in pathetic shape. While he attended to Toby, they discussed their next step in whispers. "I'll go back alone," Maggie said. "Disguise myself as a man." Reluctantly, Sarah agreed.

Among the items of clothing they had brought for Samuel was a gray shirt large enough to fit Maggie. Samuel's breeches, however, were too small.

"The hostler," said Sarah, pointing to the pantaloons he was wearing, loose trousers with a button flap at the waist. "Perhaps he owns another pair."

The hostler indeed owned another pair, which he was all too happy to sell for two shillings. It seemed an exorbitant price, but Sarah readily paid it. For another sixpence she got him to throw in the old floppy hat he was wearing, and the grimy rag around his neck.

They drove the phaeton into the dark alley behind the hostelry, where Maggie changed clothes. She used Samuel's stockings to bind her breasts, then slipped on the gray shirt and the filthy pantaloons. She tied back her hair. The neck rag and floppy hat completed her disguise.

"What do you think?" she asked Sarah. "Will I pass?"

"Thou makest a comely man. But thy face appears too fresh."

Maggie smeared dirt on her face, and at Sarah's suggestion darkened her eyebrows with carbon black from the phaeton's lamp.

Sarah studied her up and down. "Thou must needs squint thine eyes and walk like a sailor."

Maggie took a practice stroll, trying to recover her normal walk. Since becoming a lady, she had made an effort to take smaller steps and not swing her arms. Now, under Sarah's critical gaze, she was pretending to be a lady pretending to be a man.

"Feet farther apart," Sarah told her. "Imagine a rolling deck."

Maggie grinned, but Sarah cocked her head critically. "What is it, Sarah? Am I doing something funny?"

"Maggie. It might be best if thou didst not smile so much."

"Okay."

"And do not say 'okay.' "

"Okay." Maggie winked. "Just kidding."

"Maggie, have a care. If thou art found out, at the very least thou couldst be jailed for impersonating a man."

Right. She was acting giddy. The truth was, she was terrified of going back in that place.

They hugged before Maggie left on foot. "I will hold thee in the Light," Sarah called softly after her.

The plan was for Sarah to keep driving in a loop between the Merchants Exchange and the Old Dock, so that every ten minutes or so she would get a good look at the entrance to the Puss and Boot. If Maggie didn't come out by ten-thirty, Sarah was supposed to summon the constable.

As Maggie again passed the bay window, she tried not to look at the display of grisly hardware, but its horror reached out to her. Somewhere in this world, shackled in a slave ship or tilling the soil on a plantation, were Erzulie's ancestors.

What had brought Samuel to this place?

Church bells chimed ten o'clock.

No sign of their attackers outside the Puss and Boot. Maggie waited, slouched in a doorway, until a trio of sailors approached. She entered behind them. Once at the bar, she strained to hear how people ordered. A cock crowed in the back room. She pushed a thrupenny across the zinc counter and muttered gruffly, "Pint o' short" from under the floppy hat. Her hands were too clean, she realized. Too delicate. She kept her fingers bunched. The publican slid a mug at her, with some change. She sipped her beer and gazed around the room. No sign of the men who had chased them. Good. No clock in sight, so she would have to listen for the church bells.

In the back room, men were calling out wagers as cocks crowed. Maggie edged through the crowd. Swarthy faces, exotic beards, pantaloons ballooning above bare calves, a curved knife tucked in a belt. Nice to see a little ethnic diversity. She liked the freedom of moving in pants, even these filthy things, and perhaps too the illicit excitement of passing undetected through this strange male world. Was she courting danger? She hoped not. And was impersonating a man a capital offense? It was not too late to leave. She had been lucky before, taking their pursuers by surprise. *Admit it: you liked the feeling of that guy crashing to the pavement. Not just the smooth execution, but the crash. The bastards got what they deserved. Not very Quakerly of you, Maggie.* Anyway, she would not take chances. She would look for Samuel and get out of this place.

She was about to pass through the wide doorway connecting the two rooms, stooping slightly for the heavy oak lintel, when the ponytail appeared practically in her face. She stopped short. The big man's head was obscured by the lintel while he stood talking animatedly to a couple of sailors. Heart pounding, she pulled her hat down farther. She strained to catch what he was saying but caught only one word, "Quakeresses," followed by laughter. Continuing through the crowd, she overheard two men talking:

"The Spaniard says them two Quakeresses attacked him when his back was turned. Swears on 'is mother's grave 'twasn't women at all!"

"Not women?"

"Nay, nay! 'Twas two fellows! Pranked out as doxies. But blades, sure as ever pissed!"

Great. Now the Spaniard would be looking for a man—if he believed that much of his own story. She looked around for Samuel. The room was packed: men waving money in one another's faces, shouting to be heard over the din, exchanging scraps of paper. Oddsmakers pranced back and forth, chanting a singsong argot that sounded nothing at all like English. The birds crowing, the suffocating smell of feathers, shadows leaping across the walls. Samuel could be somewhere in this confusion and she might not see him—especially if he didn't want to be found.

She saw Skittles strutting about, carrying a bunch of receipts in his wig, hopping up on a stool to display first one fighting cock and then another, chanting their virtues and stamping his feet while an accomplice kept a tally of the bets on a piece of slate. At intervals, a door opened to the cellar, and a man brought up another pair of birds to exchange for those Skittles had touted. When the wagering seemed nearly finished, two birds got loose—perhaps not by accident—and flew at each other so viciously that the crowd fell back with a shout. Skittles held up a handkerchief spotted with blood, his chanting rose in pitch and volume, and there was another round of frenzied betting. A bell rang in the cellar, the cocks were taken below, and the last receipts were harvested. While a man stationed at the cellar door collected admission with a different singsong chant, everyone crowded down the steps to get to the pit, many of them farting first—apparently as a matter of decorum—until the room was empty except for a few feathers floating in the lamplight and a few stragglers, among whom, to Maggie's dismay, was the Spaniard.

No sign of Samuel in the exodus. Unless he was already in the cellar. The thought of going down those steps filled her with fear.

From the cellar, two bells rang. Those who had detoured to the taproom or urinal now rushed down the steps. The Spaniard was studying Maggie curiously. Would he follow her downstairs? She was deliberating what to do next when she noticed something lying in the shadow under a bench against the adjacent wall. It could have been a pile of rags. But as she went closer, she saw a hand and made out the shape of a man facing the wall. She saw that he wore red breeches.

It was Samuel. He was scarcely recognizable, his face was so swollen. His skin was cold to her touch. She found a weak pulse. She tried opening his eyes to check his pupils. One eye was swollen shut; the other appeared dilated.

*Get him out of here.* She dragged him into a sitting position, got behind him, and struggled to get him onto the bench. He was a dead weight. She was aware of the Spaniard's eyes on her. On her hips? As soon as she got Samuel upright on the bench, she knelt, slipped his arm over her shoulder, centered his weight carefully, and used her legs to lift him in a fireman's carry. Samuel weighed probably no more than she did, but she would fall if she did not keep the weight centered.

The Spaniard's golden eyes followed her as she ducked carefully under the lintel. "Your friend?" he asked.

She nodded. She could feel her hat slipping. *Just get him the fuck outside.* She kept the rhythm of that urgency in her head as she made her way through the taproom. *Just get him the fuck outside.* "Boozed 'is jib, did he?" someone asked. The man with the blackened teeth wobbled in her path, grinning and pointing his finger in her face: "Quake—" he said. She twisted past the ravaged face.

The publican looked up. "Whither ye taking Edmund?"

"Outside."

The publican laughed. "I was going to charge him rent."

Asshole.

The Spaniard said something to the publican. One of them called out, "What's yer name?"

*Just get him the fuck outside.* "John Lennon," she called over her shoulder, the hat slipping off as she pushed open the door, the air cool on her sweaty face. She saw the phaeton up the street, thank God. She waved, started walking, her heart thudding in her ears. Hooves clattered toward her, and Sarah peered down.

"Is it Samuel?"

"Yes."

"Praise the Maker!"

"Right. But let's get out of here!" She was struggling up the steps, trying to keep Samuel's weight balanced, when the tavern door flew open and a pair of boot heels hit the pavement.

"Go, Sarah!" she yelled, falling to the floor of the phaeton with Samuel in a heap. The phaeton lurched. Maggie got to her knees in time to see the Spaniard grabbing for the lead horse's bridle. The whip cracked, the horse reared and seemed about to step over the traces, but Sarah brought them under control. After a moment's hesitation, in which the Spaniard retreated but then made a grab for the phaeton's side rail, Sarah cracked the whip again, the horses lunged forward, the phaeton swayed in its leather slings, and the man fell on the cobblestones, cursing.

As they took off at a gallop, he scrambled to his feet. *"No sois mujeres!"* he screamed after them. *"Yez men! Hombres!"*

They laughed. Maggie stood up and yelled back, cupping her hands, "We're women! *Women!*" She pounded her chest. *"Mujeres!"* She cackled maniacally.

# Maggie Foster

On the way back to the Rathbones, Sarah stopped the phaeton long enough for Maggie to change back into her dress and discard the trousers. "Hurry," Sarah urged. They continued on their way, Maggie scrubbing at her face. Samuel showed no sign of consciousness.

The candles were still burning at the Rathbones. Mally met them at the carriage house, declaring she had been frightened out of her wits. Joseph carried Samuel inside, where they put him to bed under heaps of blankets and sent for the doctor.

Samuel appeared to be in shock. The cause was unclear. His face and neck were badly swollen, his lips black, but there were no bruises. They applied cold compresses to his face. He was still unconscious when the doctor arrived, but his skin had lost its earlier chill—thanks probably to the blankets—and his heartbeat was stronger. The doctor was mystified. He advised keeping Samuel warm and promised to return the next day.

By noon the next day, the swelling had diminished, but Samuel's eyes remained shut. He seemed engaged in a silent dialogue, eyes moving back and forth behind the lids. Mally made a decoction of hot water and tincture of rhubarb, following the doctor's prescription, but Samuel was not awake enough to swallow it—or was refusing. It was hard to say.

"Get him to drink plain water whenever he's able," Maggie told Sarah after Mally left the room. If Samuel had lain under that bench for more than a day, he would be dehydrated. Sarah, who did not leave his side, got him to drink several teaspoons of water.

By evening, he showed signs of recognizing them. Now that the swelling had subsided, they could see bumps on his face. At the center of each red welt was a tiny black dot. Briefly they entertained the possibility of smallpox—although all the Darby children had been inoculated, in the manner introduced from Turkey. But the doctor, examining the welts under a magnifying glass, said they appeared to be insect stings.

Samuel tried to whisper a word but could not. He touched his throat.

The following day, he was fully conscious. He managed to swallow some thin gruel and responded to questions in a whisper. He was surprised to learn that five days had passed since his quarrel with Abraham. He remembered the quarrel but had no memory of making his way to Liverpool. Later, he said he remembered waking up to find himself falling over Toby's neck into cold water. The rest of his journey was a blank.

"What wert thou doing," Mally demanded, "in a gambling den?" She went on to scold him. Did he know he had nearly lamed his horse? Did he have any idea how much they had all worried? Would he not at least take the amber cakes for fits that their mother had prepared?

To all his sister's questions, Samuel shut his eyes and shook his head. He asked to be left alone.

That evening, Joseph questioned him sternly. "Dost thou know, young man, how much money was in thy purse?"

Samuel closed his eyes.

"Wilt thou not report it to the constable?"

Samuel shook his head and pretended to go to sleep.

"Please," Samuel begged Sarah and Maggie when the Rathbones were out of hearing. "Get me out of here."

They set out the next day at a slow pace, with Toby tethered behind the phaeton. They took the overland route, to avoid the ferry, and made it only as far as Chester. Samuel sat between them huddled in a blanket, and spoke no more than a dozen words.

The next morning, continuing south along the Welsh border, they saw more wide-wheeled wagons laden with Wilkinson's cannon. Samuel sat with brow furrowed, deep in thought. At Wrexham, the sight of the market square jogged his memory. He recalled stopping to purchase a sweetmeat and asking what day it was, and then thinking he was being followed by John Wilkinson, who was dressed in black and whose ivory cane had a small human skull carved on top, but every time he turned to confront him, it turned out to be somebody else.

"That was an illusion, wasn't it?" He sounded uncertain.

"Yes," Maggie said firmly. "John Wilkinson was not following you."

Samuel pondered this for several miles. "But why would someone who *looked* like John Wilkinson be following me?"

Sarah rolled her eyes.

"Good question, Samuel," said Maggie, very seriously. "Or to put it another way, why would you imagine John Wilkinson was following you?"

The question was lost on Samuel, who was back in his own world. No, Samuel was not ready to return to Sunniside. They still had no idea what had happened to him. And he offered not a peep about the bridge—which seemed ominous to Maggie.

This was her worst-case scenario: Samuel coming back screwed up; Abraham leaning toward iron. Everything grinding inexorably toward the Pritchard design.

By the middle of the next day, Samuel had accepted the possibility that he had imagined John Wilkinson's following him, although Wilkinson apparently continued to dog his thoughts.

"The bridge!" Samuel finally exclaimed. "What about the bridge?"

Sarah shot Maggie a warning glance.

"It's fine," said Maggie casually. "Just fine." And waited for his next question.

After many silences layered with questions, Samuel got the gist of what had happened at Coalbrookdale during his absence, including the main thing that Maggie wanted to impress upon him: Abraham's rescinding of the agreement had turned out to be a strategic retreat aimed at increasing the budget.

"It might even work in favor of your design," Maggie observed.

Sarah was pinching her, hard.

"Anyway," Maggie concluded, "there'll be plenty of time to talk about the bridge."

It was Samuel who brought up the quarrel. He recalled his rage and how it had carried him toward Liverpool—although he could not say why—and how something had happened along the way that changed everything.

Several times he referred to that moment when he found himself tumbling over Toby's neck into a stream, where the poor animal must have stopped to drink, and how the shock of the water brought him awake "more fully," he said, "than I have ever been."

When they came to the huge oak south of Whitchurch and got out to stretch their legs and water the horses, Samuel seemed deeply affected. He walked around under the massive boughs, tipping his face up and raising his arms as though to feel something in the air.

Maggie was filling the bucket. The stream was crystal clear, every pebble visible, the green canopy above them filtering light. The leaves had opened and grown darker. Samuel was standing beside her. She saw that his hand trembled. His eyes were shining as he stepped into the water.

"Sammy!" cried Sarah. "Thy shoes!"

His voice was filled with wonder. "This is the place!" he whispered, fingertips brushing the water. " 'Twas so cold." He laughed. "I thought, when I fell in the water, 'What am I doing here?' And then I apprehended that I might have been killed, might have struck my head on a rock or broken my neck and been drowned, and I thanked God and Toby for preserving my life!" He looked up into the cool light, his face radiant. "I heard a voice saying 'Thou art!' and I could not tell whether it came from within or without. Thou art! And I knew without thinking, knew with a great certainty, that 'twas God speaking in me, saying *Thou art!*" He looked around, tears coursing down his cheeks, and took a great breath. He looked at the two women as if he were seeing not them but something beyond them. Then he laughed like a child.

Sarah brought the blanket from the phaeton. Samuel, sitting under the tree and wrapped in the blanket, spoke in an urgent whisper. "I thought Abraham had failed me, that he even sought to hurt me. I took it unto myself. I saw all my dreams come tumbling down. And I feared my own anger. Feared I might—strike him."

"So thou fled," said Sarah.

"Yes." He nodded. "Telling myself once again I had failed. Guilty as well as angry. But now, I see 'twas a failure of imagination."

"On whose part?" Maggie asked.

"Abraham's. I could not see 'twas not malice but a kind of self-imprisonment. As if he were imprisoned for refusing to tithe. But Abey hath locked himself up in a cage within a cage. A cage of petty restraints, avoiding this, avoiding that. Fearing Mother's disapproval. Father's memory. Surrounding himself with iron bars, great and small, as if they all had equal weight."

This was the most energy he had put into speech for days. He leaned back against the tree and pulled the blanket up to his throat, which obviously pained him. Maggie was about to ask how the bridge figured in this, but Sarah motioned her to be quiet. They waited.

"I knew not why I was headed for Liverpool. But in the end I suppose it was to sort the petty evils from the great. Is it so great an evil to dance? I have seen sailors dance the hornpipe who seemed closer to God at that moment than any other.

"Is it an evil to wear pretty clothing, or build a bridge that pleaseth the eye? At the beginning of my flight, I purposed to gamble, get swivel-eyed drunk, and find a woman who would, as they say, take in the beef."

Sarah and Maggie exchanged wondering glances. Samuel smirked ruefully and lowered his eyes. "I am young. I am not an old man!"

They nodded reassuringly.

"But it was not just to play the rake. This, at least, is what I think now." He puffed his lips in and out. "It was to draw a line for myself between the petty evils and the great—for if ever there was a great evil, 'tis the traffic in souls that has built Liverpool. And having drawn that line, I should know my own self and hold that self true in the Light!" He stopped, peered at Sarah. "Am I making any sense?"

Sarah said he was.

Samuel shook his head and shrugged. "I fear I am but trying to make sense of nonsense. In any case, confusion took me to—"

He fell silent, studying the blanket. Eyes moving back and forth.

"To Liverpool?" Maggie asked.

"Thou went to the Puss and Boot," Sarah coaxed.

"Aye. And no sooner did I walk in the place than I was offered a wager." He shuddered.

"Thou didst gamble on the cockfights?"

"No. 'Twas stranger than that, Sarah. I had scarcely sat down when by Divine Providence a couple of Guineamen sailors came in carrying a whiskey bottle with a rag stuffed in the mouth and offering to take wagers if any man could swallow the contents. Inside the bottle were seventeen wasps.

"I took it as a sign from God, and as I looked at those wasps buzzing and creeping inside their glass prison, I said to myself, 'There are the little evils which thou wouldst consume,' and in my mazed state I felt an excitement seize me, not unlike a gambling fever—for of all the vices I am prey to, gambling is the one I know how to govern least. So I agreed to do it on a wager of two shillings sixpence."

Sarah looked anguished. "Thou nearly killed thyself for two and six!"

"I reckoned the odds were in my favor, for I took a large swallow of gin and held it in my mouth, supposing to half drown them. But they stung my lips. And then I fancied I could befuddle them by sucking the air from the bottle—"

"Oh, Sammy!"

"But they stung my tongue and—"

Sarah squealed.

He managed a wan smile. "It sounds foolish, I know."

"It sounds demented," Maggie said. But she patted his knee. "Anyway, we're glad you're alive."

Sarah sighed. "Pray, change into dry clothing, Sammy."

Putting together what Samuel had said with the hostler's account, they surmised that Samuel had been unconscious for two days. He might well have died under that bench.

D usk was falling by the time they passed through Wellington and entered the coal measures, but since they knew the roads, they pressed on. Sarah drove. For miles they had been watching the glow of the gorge become more intense.

"Roses," muttered Samuel.

"Roses." Sarah smiled at Maggie.

Maggie felt a rush of affection for the younger woman. Something had changed in this journey, between them.

The stars disappeared as they entered the veil of smoke: coking fires glowing red along the turnpike, the furnaces of Ketley, Horsehay, and then Lightmoor spouting fiery columns that conjoined with Coalbrookdale's glow ahead. They were once again inside the bouquet.

"He denies it, of course," said Samuel abruptly, as they followed the horse rails south.

"Who?" asked Sarah.

"Joseph. His forge supplies the Guineamen."

"What?" demanded Sarah. "He makes leg irons?"

"Not leg irons. But chain. That is the line he draws between great and petty evil. He will enslave men, but leave the torture to others."

"Surely there's a difference," said Maggie, "between making chain that *might* be purchased for the slave trade and supplying the trade directly."

Samuel grimaced. "Art thou finding virtue in ignorance?"

"Not virtue," Maggie said. "But it may be out of his control. How do you know that Darby pots don't end up on slave ships? Some of them probably do. Those big kettles. Or they're traded for slaves."

"Yes, thy point is well taken. As long as slavery exists, we all have a hand in it."

"But why," asked Sarah, "dost thou accuse Joseph?"

"Joseph hath not the luxury of ignorance. His is the round-linked chain made especially to hold shackles. I have seen the men come in for it who make the leg irons and wrist irons. Thou canst hear the smiths working only three doors away."

The women were silent, listening to the pulse of the Old Furnace get louder.

Maggie's uneasiness about Samuel shifted. He seemed to be in his right mind, but was changed. Until now her influence over him had depended on her ability to affirm him as an artist. Now that he was caught up in this other vision, who could predict what he would do?

They turned into the carriage lane, the cedars looming on either side. A dog barked. Lights burned in Abiah's sitting room window, where a silhouette bobbed into view, first one, then another.

"Maggie," said Samuel suddenly, "didst thou talk to John Wilkinson about my commission?"

"Not yet. I didn't know—"

"I shall finish the model. But I must be free of Wilkinson."

Maggie nodded. "I'll get right on it."

# Abraham Darby III

**E**ver since Samuel's disappearance—from that first morning when Abraham had tiptoed down the hall, opened Samuel's door a crack, and seen the empty bed—Abraham had been fearing the worst for his brother.

Not knowing Samuel's fate, Abraham felt disconnected from his workaday life. When he nursed the lamb with the glass teat bottle, he thought of Samuel the lost sheep, but thought of himself too as an orphaned creature, abandoned by those he loved. Once the lamb was on its feet and scampering after the servants, who had done most of the feeding, Abraham felt more alone than ever.

Scarcely an hour passed when he did not imagine some disaster befalling Samuel, or recall that terrible howl, or reconstruct his own words so that Samuel might hear them differently. He prayed ceaselessly for Samuel's safe return. Prayed for Divine forgiveness in Jesus' name, and for forgiveness in his own heart.

Yet he was angry. Angry at Samuel for the humiliation he had suffered from Mother's reproach (surprised also at the strength of her opinion that the bridge should be of iron, which caused him some disgruntled reexamination of his own opinion). He was angry at Samuel for behaving so explosively, for causing them all to worry, for making himself the center of attention as usual. He was also angry for having these feelings when Samuel might be coming to harm. Angry at being made to feel such guilt.

*What hast thou done? The voice of thy brother's blood crieth unto me from the ground.*

From his mother and sister, Abraham felt a disapproval that trembled in the air like a whiff of camphor from a bedding chest. When Sarah and Maggie left in the phaeton, he knew it was he who should have gone. He very nearly rode after them.

Walking into his office, he imagined his father turning his back on him and dissolving into the bookcase, the hem of his greatcoat disappearing into the row of ledgers, the soles of his shoes winking into the darkness of leather spines.

He took refuge in his coming marriage. In a letter to Becky:

*Thou mayest be pleased, my dearest Becky, to know I have made certain inquiries concerning our honeymoon lodgings, the location of which I am determined to keep as a surprise, but which I fervently hope will be to thy liking.*

Excitement entered his belly as he thought of the lodgings he had hired at Chepstow, with romantic overlooks of the cliffs near Bristol. As he thought of the bed they would share.

Would marriage overly incline him to the flesh?

Under this pious but somehow delicious question lay a more practical one. Would he know what to do? As often as he had watched the rams mount the ewes and the stallions mount the mares, he was not completely clear how the act was accomplished in the human species. As the man, was he not expected to know? And was it seemly to pray for such guidance?

He considered expressing these doubts in a delicate way to Becky. *I pray that*

But the ink dried on his quill as he struggled for words, and his thoughts returned to Samuel.

*I pray that we receive word soon as to Samuel's whereabouts. Mother is beside herself with worry.*


Finally, a letter arrived from Mally, saying that Sammy was found. A second letter was more enigmatic, complaining of a certain "willfulness" exhibited by Sarah, under the influence of Maggie Foster.

The evening that the phaeton rolled into Sunniside—Samuel seated between the women and looking pale in the lamplight—Abraham felt both joy and trepidation. Samuel, upon seeing Abraham, said scarcely a word.

After two days they exchanged a sort of apology, when they were alone together in the stable, feeding Toby the oats sweetened with molasses that Abraham had prescribed to restore the horse's weight.

"I regret thy misunderstanding," Abraham told Samuel.

"And I regret thine," Samuel replied.

When they were gathered that day for silent prayer at the Old Furnace, Abraham felt moved to speak. He evoked George Fox's injunction to Friends to *keep atop of that which will cumber the mind, and dwell in love and peace one with another.* After delivering himself of this message, listening to the thump of the bellows, he was at first pleased but later gnawed by doubts as to whether he had been moved by the Spirit or by calculation.

Within a few days of Samuel's return, Abraham was filled with impatience. Samuel showed no inclination to return to the Works. He spent all day in idleness, in his study working with great secrecy (presumably on the wedding gift, which Abraham could hardly criticize) or talking with the women who were gathering to help with the wedding preparations (and who now included the younger Barclays, arriving by coach from London). The women encouraged his idleness with their proclivities, asking his opinion concerning their dresses and matters of no interest to a man, and assaying to find him a wife.

Samuel a husband! It was a ludicrous thought.

" 'Twould be better," Abraham remarked to his mother, "if he would first become a man."

Her response surprised him. "Marriage might settle him," she observed.

At Meeting, she spoke of love and charity. *And the greatest of these is Charity.* Words he took as a gentle rebuke to the annoyance smoldering in his own bosom.

The truth was, Abraham was deeply disappointed. He had pinned too many hopes on Samuel, fancied turning the Works over to Samuel—only to find him the untrustworthy Sammy of old.

He was further piqued by Samuel's refusal to tell him what had happened in Liverpool. Samuel was not unable, like Lazarus come back from the dead, to reveal his experience; he was simply unwilling. Unwilling to confide in his own brother. He seemed willing enough to talk to the women, to judge from the rapturous voices in Mother's sitting room.

One day, seeing Sarah and Maggie walking together in the chestnut grove, Abraham confronted them. "Why will Samuel not speak to me?"

"Give him time," Sarah said. "Sammy will speak when he is ready."

"But he speaketh to thee!"

"Not that much."

"And to thee!" He frowned at Maggie.

"He may just need a little space."

"Space! Time and space! What else doth he need?" Abraham demanded. He intended sarcasm, but Sarah and Maggie exchanged a look. Maggie nodded, and Sarah spoke.

"Opportunity," she said.

Abraham scarcely heard the word, for impatience. They tried to calm him, but he shook them off and strode away.

That evening, approaching the door to Abiah's sitting room, Abraham heard their voices. He stopped and listened. Samuel was speaking passionately. How enormous were the profits, and how great the suffering of Negroes. How slavery was the "monstrous keystone" to all the other West Indies trades—cotton, tobacco, indigo, sugar, chocolate, rum. How Quakers were caught up in it, with their chocolate and their banking. "Quaker hands," he cried, "are as bloody as any!"

Mother's voice responded. "If thou holdest such strong feelings, wilt thou not help me write letters?" She spoke about the minute being carried to Yearly Meeting, which declared that those Friends who owned slaves should be cast out of the Society.

Samuel answered with scorn. "I am appalled that such a resolution should even be necessary among Quakers!"

Abraham was incensed that Mother should have to bear this impudence. It was all he could do not to burst into the room. But they fell silent. At that point he might have walked in and joined them in their silence. Instead, he waited.

Samuel said something, a plaint that Abraham could not hear. Maggie spoke, then Sarah. They seemed to be counseling patience.

Finally, Mother: "Well then. Thou shouldst tell him thyself."

*Tell whom?* Abraham wondered.

"He will not listen to me," said Samuel. "Abey never listens to me."

"Thou must needs ask," their mother said. "Thou must needs give him the opportunity. Wait for the right time, and listen with an open heart."

Abraham's ears burned. The voices again ceased. But he could not bring himself to enter. He tiptoed back to his study, mortified to have eavesdropped. He wondered what opportunity he was to be given.

It seemed to Abraham that his brother had changed. Samuel's movements, which had always been languid, were somehow more precise. His body seemed more compact. His voice had lost that theatrical resonance; was quieter and yet often more urgent.

Samuel spoke for the first time at Meeting, held in the Madeley meeting house. Abraham, seated on the oak bench, did not realize who was rising to speak until the shadow fell across his lap. His own heart pounded from the fear that his brother would behave in some manner that would embarrass him.

For a long time Samuel remained silent, swaying, eyes closed, sunlight backlighting one ear and one downy side-whisker. He swayed so long that Abraham avoided looking at his face, terrified that Samuel might once again throw his head back and unloose that bone-chilling howl.

But when Samuel spoke, his voice was so thick with emotion as to pour forth almost in a melody. "Sometimes! Sometimes—forgive me, O Creator—sometimes I think that my life is for naught, that I have arrived too late in a world too finished to admit my labors. I think, in my vanity, that no act I can perform is needed, wanted. Sufficient!"

He heaved a great sigh. Then held out his hands, palms up. "These hands! They are useless in mine own eyes. And yet they are stained with innocent blood! Help me. Thou who art all-knowing, help me find labor in the service of beauty and truth, according to Thy purposes. Thou who knowest all that I can never know!" He swayed a while longer, but apparently he was finished. He sat down.

Compassion swelled in Abraham's bosom uncontrollably. He held back a sob, until the blood pulsed in his ears. He was relieved when others offered vocal testimony. John Rose spoke of the "Ocean of Darkness and the Ocean of Light." Another spoke of love and the Divine light in every person. Another compared the Light of Christ to the lamp in the deepest coal pit, without which man labored in darkness. Yet another spoke of that which remained unfinished in the world. And to this Richard Reynolds added that Creation was not fixed but, rather, a process without an end, and that in loving the Divine we carried Creation in our hearts.

After the rise of Meeting, many people gathered around Samuel to take his arm or press his hand. Outside the meeting house, Maggie and Sarah embraced him. Everyone agreed that it was a gathered Meeting, that the Divine spirit had moved powerfully through them.

"Samuel," whispered Abraham, taking his brother's hand, "come back to the Works."

The next morning, Samuel appeared at breakfast dressed for work. The brothers walked down the path in silence. Abraham wondered if this was the "opportunity" Samuel was seeking. Probably not, since it was he, Abraham, who had invited Samuel. The opportunity, he imagined, was yet to come.

Between them, the bridge remained a subject to be avoided—or approached cautiously, with trepidation, at least on Abraham's part.

Abraham was careful to voice satisfaction when no proposals came in response to the advertisements for a bridge of timber or stone. " 'Twill allow us to build it of iron," he observed one morning, as they were about to part ways at the Old Furnace.

Samuel's eyes twinkled at this, despite the early hour. He nodded but said not a word.

Pritchard's model arrived, delivered by his brother, who had built it. It was constructed from mahogany and handsomely varnished. Abraham invited Samuel to his office to inspect it. Samuel should have approved of it heartily, for it was the bridge made wholly of iron. Instead, examining it at length, Samuel sucked his teeth and put on an expression of such indifference that Abraham was compelled to ask what was the matter.

Samuel smiled lopsidedly and shrugged. " 'Tis so ordinary," he said. "Surely the world's first iron bridge should have more visual impact."

*Visual impact.* The phrase was one that John Wilkinson had used. It left Abraham exceedingly disgruntled.

Samuel's newfound superiority, his air of mystery, even that spiritual awakening that everyone had observed, fed Abraham's confusion and vague sense of betrayal.

All these thoughts mingled uneasily in his head. But the wedding, only days away now, began to claim his attention.

# John Wilkinson

John Wilkinson eagerly awaited Mrs. Foster's arrival at New Willey, anticipating that their bargain would be consummated sooner than they had agreed originally—sooner than the lady herself expected.

Wilkinson had been busying his brains with schemes of far greater consequence. Boulton was pestering Watt to make the leap to rotative motion, declaring he could sell a hundred such engines. *Quod mola facere potest rotativa motione!* Soon all England would run on steam, thanks to Wilkinson's new cylinder. The Lunar Society was fawning on him, or at least acknowledging him. And the French scheme was going jollily, Will having got to France just ahead of the war fever now raging in Parliament.

As for the bridge, the issue of whether it was to be built wholly of iron seemed about to be resolved. If Mrs. Foster was correct, then Abraham Darby's wedding would furnish the occasion for settling whatever doubts remained within Darby's timorous breast—for they now wished to relinquish the commission and present the model as a wedding gift.

Wilkinson, reflecting on it, supposed it was a clever enough strategy. Abraham, if he was impressed favorably by the gift, would recommend it to the subscribers. This would guarantee a bridge made of iron—which was Wilkinson's utmost concern. As for the lady herself, she assured him that the arrangement between them was a private matter, which had nothing to do with the commission except insofar as he must succeed with the subscribers. *I will not disappoint you, Mr. Wilkinson, if you will not disappoint me.*

It was this last point that prompted Wilkinson to answer her letter in the manner that he did. He claimed to have *grave reservations* about her request and suggested they meet here at New Willey to discuss the matter further. In truth, Wilkinson had doubts that the subscribers would go along with Samuel's outlandish design. It was difficult to get them to agree on anything. And since he was far more interested in the guarantee of iron than in any particular design, he was quite prepared to sacrifice Samuel's design if that was what it took. In short, the odds were that Mrs. Foster would be disappointed. Thus he was determined to obtain her favors now, while he had power over her.

The vague objections he raised in his letter to releasing Samuel from his commission were a pretext for getting her here alone.

Everything was in readiness. The room looked pleasant. It was the same small windowless anteroom where he had entertained Sniggy Oakes, but he had taken steps to make it more suitable for the occasion, had ordered a couch brought in with a satin coverlet. Next to the couch was a low table set with fine china, wineglasses, and oysters on the half shell laid out on a bed of ice on a silver tray. Under the couch were warm bricks, on which lay a plate of olive oil containing iron dildos in various sizes. Inspired by Madame Bougainville's *accoutrements,* and crafted by his own hand, the iron phalluses were polished to silky smoothness. He could not understand the upstairs maid's insistence on satin padding. " 'Tis not the same as iron," he complained, but she said it was not natural in any case, and demanded half a crown for her troubles. He fancied Mrs. Foster would prove more venturesome. Such thoughts teemed in his brain while he waited. The brick walls were hung with tapestries, one depicting a unicorn with its head in the lap of a virgin. Centered above the couch was a life-size oil portrait of the ironmaster himself wearing a toga and a resolute countenance that he hoped was not too forbidding.

He had left strict orders not to be disturbed, and stationed a man outside the door with orders not to admit anyone even if screams were heard. "Even if you hear cries for help!"

Rape was the last resort of scoundrels; gentlemanly seduction was what Wilkinson had in mind; but in his experience a great deal fell somewhere between. And although he judged the lady a whore from their last exchange by the millpond, he understood that fickleness of the female mind which must sometimes be overcome by manly lust.

She arrived at two o'clock, as promised. Receiving her in his office, the ironmaster escorted her into the anteroom. He was wearing his blue satin suit with an orange ruffled shirt and saffron stockings, and the large three-tiered wig he had purchased in Paris for nine pounds six. Mrs. Foster wore her usual Quaker drab; but, upon finding herself in so private an apartment, she removed her bonnet and shook out a mass of curls as formidable as any artifice of the friseur. While she admired the portrait, he discreetly locked the door.

She claimed to have little experience with raw oysters. She made a face, but bravely ate one, then another, and declared she might develop a taste for them. They drank some Bordeaux and became quite mirthful, toasting Darby's forthcoming wedding and Samuel's design. She startled him by removing her shoes, which testified either to the informality of the Colonies or to the effects of the wine. He pretended it was nothing unusual and tried to keep his eyes from wandering to her stocking feet.

They sat beside each other on the couch with their knees almost touching, the beeswax candles casting a fragrant light across the glossy oysters and ice.

He spoke of iron. He spoke of iron as metaphor, the lifeblood of civilization, the font of science and art. He told her of the poet he was commissioning to write a mighty ode to Iron, a man named Blake whose skill as an engraver had been brought to his attention by a dealer in copper.

Wilkinson chuckled. "The fellow is so destitute that his poor wife must sell his copper plates for scrap before the ink is dry. Hearing of his straits and wishing to offer my patronage, I sent him two lines of my own composition and offered him a penny a line to elaborate on my theme." He recited the lines:

*Iron, iron, burning bright*
*In the furnace of the night.*

"A penny a line doesn't sound like much," she said, not seeming to notice his hands straying onto her skirts. "You paid Samuel six guineas for his drawing."

"Ah, but for the poem I am in no hurry; the man can take years. And what is poetry but mere words? The bridge, madame, shall be iron!" He let his hand rest on her knee and wondered whether the oysters were having their desired aphrodisiological effect.

"But the poem," she said, "may survive long after the bridge has fallen. Crumbled, I mean," she corrected herself, reddening. "Turned to rust." Fanning her face with her bonnet, she asked if it was not warm (which of course it was, owing to the bricks radiating heat under them).

"Alas, yes." He shuddered at this melancholy thought. "I detest rust. My brother-in-law, Priestley, has a morbid fascination for it. But whenever I contemplate the injustice of rust, the relentless attack of dampness upon iron—" He shook his head. "Why, do you know, my dear lady, that pure iron does not exist in nature, except in meteorites? Iron ore is nothing but rust, and must be reduced from rust back to iron! That is your tragedy, madame, worthy of Sophocles, the way everything conspires to wrest that great metal back to the earth whence it comes. Gold and silver do not suffer such indignity. Nor even base lead! Stout iron, made by man, suffers endlessly—like the Saviour Himself, pierced by iron nails. And that is why iron is the noblest element of all!"

He gazed into her eyes passionately. "The heathen savages lack all knowledge of ironmaking! When Cortez ran out of iron for horseshoes, he shod his horses with silver!"

He offered her another oyster, going so far as to hold it to her lips, but she pushed his hand away, laughing a coarse laughter that inflamed him enough to carry the play further, but then she straightened and assumed a more serious demeanor.

"I think," she said, "we should get down to business."

"Yes!"

"You said in your note, Mr. Wilkinson, that you had grave reservations about my request."

"Yes, yes." Wilkinson swallowed the oyster himself and wiped his fingers on his shirt, mindful of his satin suit. He took her hands in his, gazed deep into those remarkable green eyes, and sighed. "Have you any idea, dear lady, how distracting it is for a man in my position—laboring under the invisible hand of competition and the yoke of Reason—to receive a difficult request from a lady with your charms?"

"Is it such a difficult request, Mr. Wilkinson? We only want to make Samuel's model a wedding gift."

"But you are asking me, in effect, to tear up the contract, are you not?"

"Correct. But it needn't affect the rest of our deal."

"*Au contraire,* my dear." Wilkinson, knitting his brows, alluded to the nature of contractual agreements, questions of propriety, first claim, etc. He threw up his hands as if it were all quite impossible.

"What are you getting at, Mr. Wilkinson?"

"Only that I fear by nullifying the contract, we shall have no agreement at all."

"So you won't support Samuel's design?"

"Ah, I did not say that. I only mean we shall have to renegotiate our arrangement."

"I see."

"But I have every confidence in our ability to overcome the obstacles"—he twiddled the gray wool of her skirt with his thumb and forefinger and waggled his eyebrows suggestively—"that lie between us."

"I see." Mrs. Foster grew pensive.

"The afternoon is young, and we are quite safely alone."

She said nothing at first. Her face was flushed. She seemed to be making up her mind. They were both perspiring from the heat. He refilled their glasses and inched closer to her on the couch.

She reached out, took his index finger in her palm, and squeezed it. An obscene gesture. It took his breath away. "How is it going with the subscribers, Mr. Wilkinson?"

*Subscribers be damned!* He was in a rutting fever. But he controlled himself. "I am confident they can be won over. The bargemen understand better now the case for iron."

"The case for iron. But what about the case for Samuel's design?" She gave the finger another squeeze.

"That, madame, is the great challenge."

"But you're working on it?"

"Aye, yes. But if you will forgive my candor, madame, I need you first to work on me." He waggled the finger slyly.

She did not appear to take offense. Instead, with a smile, she peeled off one of her stockings and drew up her leg so as to make a tent of her skirt, and then took his hand in both of hers and pulled it a little ways under the tent. Wilkinson's heart pounded. God's nose! He scooted closer, but she kept hold of his hand.

"So, Mr. Wilkinson," she purred. "Where are we at? Relax your hand." She kneaded his palm, working each finger in turn—he supposed in the manner called *massage* by the French colonists in India—coaxing it around and around her bare foot, slipping his pinky between her toes, using the whole hand so sensually that he surrendered all volition and let it go as limp as a scrub rag. "Well," he managed. "I believe the committee will come around to Samuel's design." Around and around.

"I hope so, Mr. Wilkinson. That's the important thing. Accomplish that, and I'll show you a good time." She brushed his fingertips across—could it be her thigh? "But you have grave reservations."

"Perhaps not so grave," murmured Wilkinson, lost in that slow circling.

"Questions of propriety."

"Well. There is, of course, the matter of the six guineas."

With her free hand she pulled a small purse from her bodice and laid it before him. "Here are your six guineas."

"But, but I would happily waive the six guineas, you see, if you would—as you put it—show me a good time. Now!"

"But we have a bargain. And you have objections."

It *was* her thigh against which she was brushing his hand. His hand sought to enlarge its scope of that hidden, humid world, but was somehow prevented. Wilkinson startled himself with a snort. His brain seemed mazed in those languid circlings.

"Take the six guineas!" he panted. "Let it be my portion of the gift."

"But Samuel wants it to be his gift. I'm afraid he won't budge on this point. It was the only way he would agree to return to work on the model."

"*Samuel* won't budge?" cried Wilkinson, pulling his hand away. "We've got the bargemen to worry about, titled gentlemen, clergymen—and *Samuel* won't budge? 'Tis I who should not budge!"

"He wants to be entirely free of you."

"Indeed! Am I such a pariah in the eyes of a stripling—whose talents I am trying to encourage?

"I know, I know," she soothed. "Think of it as Samuel's problem, Mr. Wilkinson."

"He is a strange young man!"

"Yes. And you're so angry. Here. Let me listen to your heart." She leaned forward and pressed an ear to his chest, and he felt the ecstasy of buttons being unfastened, her hand plunging. He groaned. Then she squirmed off his lap, leaving a great coolness of flesh. She took his hand and kissed it. Her tongue traveling across it sent a shiver of excitement down his spine. "Any more—objections?" She crooked her knee again and brought his hand once more under her tented skirt.

"None."

"Then you renounce all claim to the model?"

"Yes, yes!" Impatient, he tried to advance toward the damp warmth he could feel beyond his straining fingertips, but she had his wrist somehow locked. "Unequivocally." With his free hand he wiped the perspiration from his eyes. "I shall tear up the contract." By now, his patience was stretched to its limit, the fire in his loins concentrated all in a hard lump, deep-rooted and straining at his satin breeches.

"I will have you, madame!" he cried, throwing himself forward. "The game is up!"

She blocked his hand's sudden thrust, but he pressed forward to pin her under his bulk. There was fear in her eyes. Ha! She wriggled free and leapt up from the couch. He lunged after her. She spun around and clasped him in her arms—a change of heart, he thought—but suddenly he lost his balance, his feet slipping out from under him, and he landed on his back with a clatter that collapsed one end of the table and left him half-somersaulted backwards on the silver tray with the oysters, ice, and shattered glasses. There was an acrid odor, a flame at his ear, something on fire, which he realized was his wig. "Help!" he shrieked. "Help!"

# Maggie Foster

**M**aggie's first impulse, seeing Wilkinson upended amidst the oysters and other debris, was to laugh. Then she was afraid he was hurt. Then relieved to see he wasn't. Then she thought, *I've blown it.* And in the next instant his wig was on fire, and he was thrashing around screaming like a lunatic. He snatched off the wig and flung it from him. Maggie managed to stamp out the blaze before it could ignite a nearby tapestry. Then the stink of burning hair filled her nostrils, and she was throwing herself at the door, clawing at the latch to open it, because she had the sudden, vivid memory of a woman burning to death in the desert, the horror of burning flesh. She pounded and screamed, "Let me out!" Screamed at Wilkinson to unlock the door, even when she could see it was not the horror, only the wig smoldering on the floor. She gasped for air.

Wilkinson looked at her, dazed. "What happened?"

"Unlock the goddamn door!"

Pale, he fumbled in his pocket, produced a key, and opened the door. She saw a window beyond and felt relief at seeing daylight. Why daylight? In some memory, blackness, and boulders lit by a fireball.

Wilkinson was looking at her blankly—somehow off-kilter. His eyes large, his head unexpectedly bald. *Okay, okay. Relax,* she told herself, and took a deep breath. The woman burning to death, her name was Tina. Surely it was only from a veery, but it seemed so real. The smell of gasoline and the fireball. Maggie took another deep breath and became aware of her body, her bleeding knuckles.

Wilkinson looked pathetic standing there. One eyebrow was singed. His fancy blue outfit was soiled, the yellow stockings splattered with wine. "You poor man," she said, putting an arm around him. "You must have been terrified."

"What happened?" He was baffled.

"You must have slipped." She brushed fragments of glass from his waistcoat.

"But—"

"The ice. You probably stepped on a piece of ice."

"Ice. Of course." He limped around the room, relighting a couple of the salvageable candles and surveying the charred wig, the broken table, and the scattered remains of oysters and wineglasses. "Dear, dear," he clucked.

The party was over.

Maggie retrieved her stocking from the debris. Wilkinson's ardor was dampened, to say the least. What now? She put on her Quaker bonnet, tucked in her curls. She counted Sarah's six guineas from the purse and put the coins in his hand. Cold silver. "The contract," she reminded him.

Wilkinson groped in his waistcoat pocket, took out the contract, unfolded it, lit one corner from a candle flame and dropped it onto the brick floor. She did the same with Samuel's copy. They watched the ashes curl.

"So," she said. "The only thing left is our, uh, arrangement."

Wilkinson looked at her ruefully. Or perhaps it was just the singed eyebrow that produced the effect.

She had to rekindle his interest. She was counting on him, and the wedding was only five days away. She ran to the door and pulled it closed, then took his hand and led him back to the couch, sat him down, straddled his lap. She couldn't bring herself to kiss him, but she did reach a hand below his paunch. She heard a sharp intake of breath.

"Oooh," she said. "Is that silk?"

"Satin," croaked Wilkinson, his jowls florid.

All in the line of duty. It was the best she could do, under the circumstances, and given the revulsion she was beginning to feel toward Wilkinson. Take refuge in comedy. She felt his little cock swell under the satin from a button to a sausage, climbed off his lap provocatively, hoisted a leg for a split-second flash that made his eyes pop. "Gotta run, Mr. Wilkinson." She blew him a kiss from the door. "Don't forget. The subscribers."

Samuel did not look up from his work when Maggie came into his study that evening. She sat on the stool, admiring his concentration as he glued a piece into place. She liked the smell of the hide glue simmering in its little brass pot. Its thick, sweet fragrance was an antidote to the odor of burnt hair that clung to her though she had washed and changed clothes.

"How fared thee with John Wilkinson?" he asked.

"Good."

Samuel looked up from his work. "So I am free of his commission?"

"Free as a bird."

"Good." He selected another ceramic piece and filed one edge so it would fit. He blew off the dust. "Was he angry?"

"At first. But in the end he was on our side. He'll do everything he can to persuade the subscribers—"

"I don't want him on our side! The man has blood on his hands! Think of those cannon headed down the Severn on barges. 'Tis a parade of death."

Maggie sighed. "You're right." Samuel's passion forced her to acknowledge what she had been trying to put out of her mind. Wilkinson might be a charming buffoon, but under that mask of affability was something else she had glimpsed when he lunged at her: brutality. Wilkinson represented, after all, not only those cannon but the parade of ever-more-sophisticated weapons systems that had laid waste to her world. And somehow Samuel was clearer about it than she was.

"Well, in any case," she said, "you're free."

Samuel smiled. "Thou art my angel, Maggie." He brushed hide glue on each end of a piece and gave it to her to hold while he applied glue to the mating surfaces.

She watched him press the pieces together, then took over, holding them, serving as a second pair of hands while he went on to the next piece. "It's beautiful," she said, and was not exaggerating. The arches soared from their painted stone abutments, the second arch nearly completed now. The span, despite its top-heaviness, or maybe because of it, had an exuberance, the strength and delicacy of a butterfly pausing to sip nectar. It was not yet painted. Some pieces were ceramic, others wood. Nevertheless, squinting through the filigree, Maggie was able to lose the scale, forget it was a model. She could imagine it arching across the Severn Gorge. Samuel's hand loomed beyond the arches, his face gigantic.

She imagined more: a series of cracking sounds and groans, like ice breaking on the ponds, a shudder reverberating through the bridge as it tipped, slowly at first; but once it started to go over, there would be no stopping it. In all likelihood the collapse would happen during a flood and heavy wind, when the combined delta force would be greatest. She imagined the bridge toppling downstream, the force of the water cracking it further, even tumbling it over.

River trade would be disrupted for weeks, while men tried to break it apart and haul pieces of it to shore. A lesson in humility for Western Industrialism.

This craziness would be over soon. Assuming the plan worked, assuming Abraham and the subscribers agreed to Samuel's design, then her mission would be essentially completed. She could begin to live something like a normal life. Maybe move to London with Samuel and Sarah, help drum up business for Samuel's forge.

As for screwing Wilkinson, she didn't *have* to enjoy it.

Normalcy. It seemed so elusive. She envied Samuel his freedom.


T ina.

All afternoon—or night, which was it?—Maggie had heard, from her hiding place in the rocks at the foot of the mesa, the motorcycles revving, the drunken yells, and the woman's cries while she was being raped and tortured. It must have been night, because now Maggie remembered the flickering shadows from the fire. Then an eerie silence that may have lasted only a minute. She looked out from the cleft in the rocks to see them pouring something. She smelled gasoline. Heard the whoosh of flame erupting in an orange ball, saw Tina's screaming face illuminated for a moment, the bikers silhouetted around her. Heard her shrieks and smelled her hair burning. Maggie bit her own hand to keep from crying out, willed herself to remain hidden in the rocks.

No, it was not a veery.

How old was Tina? Early forties? A big woman, or she seemed big to a skinny seventeen-year-old; a Chicana, with distinctively sculpted mouth and nose. Tina had helped Maggie. They had traveled together for days—no, weeks. They had stolen food, trekked across the mountains. It all came back. Walking at night, sleeping in shadows during the day—for safety, because of the motogangs and the corpo recon-odrones. Tina told stories about growing up in the Zones after the Petroleum Wars, after the accidental nuclear exchange that took out the San Fernando Valley. She was searching for her son. Everyone Maggie met on that long trek was looking for someone.

When they heard the motorcycles in the distance, Tina crawled outside the cleft. Why? Maybe to brush their footprints from the sand. And she was seen. There was a yell, a motorcycle came gunning toward them, and Tina ran, dodging behind rocks, until they caught her. Six or seven men with faces tattooed or scarified.

It all got confused with the veeries. Somehow, arriving finally at Ecosophia, a waif who had lived by her wits too long and seen too much, Maggie forgot most of that eighteen-month journey from California to New Mexico. The horror left her. But the smell of burning hair had brought it back. How she had shut her ears against the screams, pressed her forehead against the grainy sandstone. Afterwards, she approached the charred body, its hands like claws, seeping lymph. She pretended not to see the shallow breathing.

She had blamed herself all these years, for hiding, surviving, for not acknowledging the remnant of life remaining in that body. She had not asked the question, *Tina. Can you hear me?* Afraid to see the charred lips move.

And yet what could she have done? Medically there was nothing. End her suffering. But Tina was probably beyond pain.

Bury her?

But Tina was still alive.

*You were seventeen. You did the best you could. You survived. And it's over. You are loved.*

*Who loves me? Trevor. Erzulie. People who live in a future that may never take place.*

She lay in bed, unable to sleep. Unable to get the smell of burning hair out of her nostrils.

Was it fear of losing her past? Surviving?


"Thou canst understand," Samuel said as he passed the water jugs to them, "why no one goes up there."

The hot humid air enveloped Maggie and Sarah at the top of the steps leading to the attic loft above the loam shed. Maggie passed a jug to Sarah. "It sure hits you like a hammer," she observed. It was mostly the heat by now; their olfactories were becoming inured to the stench. She had thought of this place last night, while she was trying to go to sleep. Unable to get that other smell out of her nose. Trying to think of anything she might have overlooked, before the wedding.

Samuel left for work. The Rhemish jugs were his idea, along with the bandannas, which they soaked with water and tied over their lower faces to filter the dust. The two women were wearing their oldest dresses, with their canvas malt-mill aprons. They looked around, letting their eyes grow accustomed to the gloom. Most of the light came from cracks between the floorboards. Everything was covered by a thick blanket of dust and soot, except where it had sifted through the cracks or where air currents had caused it to drift. Near the stairs opening, a few boxes looked recently deposited. But a few feet beyond, the dust lay undisturbed—confirming Maggie's suspicion that the apprentices had never searched here.

They began sorting through the piles. "Mold patterns," Sarah said, her voice muffled by her bandanna. She held up a wooden frying pan, wiped off the soot, and noted that it was cracked. "They save everything." She pointed out box molds of a sort that were no longer used.

Maggie felt the cool wet cloth suck in and out with her breathing. The clutter was organized loosely into piles with aisles between— much of it in boxes. She had no clear idea why she was doing this, except that the missing ledger remained a loose end. She was following a hunch.

Perspiration rolled down her sides and prickled where her bonnet brim hugged her forehead. Stopping every few minutes to wet their handkerchiefs, they moved everything they could, and kept it in roughly the same order. Occasionally something was identified with a note chalked on a broken tile or scrap of paper. There was no ledger.

Abraham, during the search of the Dale House attic, had voiced the theory that the ledger had been in use somewhere in the Works when a calamity took place, a fire perhaps. It may have been scooped up and tossed in a box, and then got buried under other things. A reasonable conjecture, but Maggie suspected that someone had deliberately lost it or destroyed it.

The farther they got from the stairs, the thicker the grime. Maggie's nose itched, her hands were parched; sweat stung under her breasts; dust crept down her neck. They had emptied one of the Rhemish jugs and started on the other.

Sarah sneezed. "Mark thee," she said, after examining a pattern for a bellied pot. "This is the old type, if I am not mistaken. Thicker than the ones made today." She had assembled the pieces of a four-part box mold, including the pattern for molding the core, and was comparing the inner and outer surfaces. "It goes back to my grandfather's day, before he discovered he could cast pots thinner, firing hotter with coke." She examined the bottom, holding it in a shaft of light. "A. Darby, 1709," she read.

Maggie was impressed with Sarah's technical knowledge, although it should not have surprised her. Sarah had grown up with ironmaking; and following Abraham's death, in 1789, Coalbrookdale would be run by three women—Sarah, Becky, and Samuel's wife, Deborah, constituting the so-called Petticoat Government—until once again a male Darby came of age.

Sarah sat down on the box mold, her elbows propped on her knees, and looked at Maggie. "I fear we have gone past the place where we were likely to find it."

Maggie looked at what remained unexplored: a discouraging tangle of what seemed rubbish, no real aisles among it. Still, she wanted to exhaust this possibility. "I'd like to finish," she said, "as long as we've come this far. I don't mind working by myself."

"Why art thou so interested in finding the ledger?"

Maggie shrugged. "Maybe I'm doing it for Abraham." She wiped her face and neck and rinsed out the cloth. "He's curious. He wants to know more about the Dale Company's business dealings thirty years ago."

"Abraham is curious?"

"Yes." She thought she heard irony in Sarah's voice. "Well, okay. I am too. Aren't you?"

"I am only amused," Sarah drawled, "that everyone wants for Abraham that which they want for themselves. Samuel doth wish to give Abraham what Samuel wants. And thou dost wish to discover for Abraham what thou wouldst discover."

Maggie felt herself blush. "Maybe you're right, Sarah."

"And what dost thou expect to learn from the missing ledger?"

The question was long overdue. Abraham had never asked it, filled as he was with his own expectations. Now Sarah was asking, with that characteristic directness which required an honest response.

Maggie took a deep breath. *Here goes.* "I want to know whether your father was making cannon."

"Father? Do you mean my father, or Richard Ford?"

"Your father."

Sarah furrowed her brow. " 'Twould kill Mother."

"Sarah, your mother must already know. She was involved up to her ears in Coalbrookdale back then."

"But why bring it up now? The pain it would cause. And to what purpose?"

"I don't know. But don't you want to learn the truth?"

Sarah wiped her neck and studied the rag.

Maggie's own motives were far from clear. She wasn't just trying to discover the truth. Suppose Samuel's design was rejected? Suppose the decision narrowed to the two Pritchard designs? And what if she ended up having to steer Abraham *away* from iron? Maybe she was hedging her bets. "Aren't you just plain curious?" she asked Sarah.

"Thou art a complicated woman, Maggie. Dost thou never crave simplicity?"

"Yes." The question was more disarming than Sarah could know. "Yes, I do. But what was it Samuel said, about virtue that depends on ignorance?"

"Well," said Sarah. "Mother hath always assured us that Father put a stop to cannon making the year Richard Ford died. It was told to me as a girl, whenever we discussed the Quaker Testimony against War."

"And Ford died in, what, 1745?"

Sarah nodded. " 'Twas the year they married. She would not hear of gun making. Father followed the leadings of God and put an immediate stop to it."

"Immediate?"

"Yes!"

"But the ledger is missing for that period."

"Yes?" A rising note in Sarah's voice, of challenge.

"Well . . . Doesn't it make you all the more curious?" It was this line of questioning that had piqued Abraham.

"In truth, it does. Mother speaks little of that time, except to praise Father." Sarah gazed at her filthy hands in her lap, deliberating. She looked up. "I want to trust thee, Maggie. There was a time, thou surely knowest, when jealousy entered my heart, when Sammy would call thee Lady Green Eyes and ask thy opinion on everything. And I, being only his sister—poor in learning, and plain—found myself casting doubts on thy motives. All that changed when we went to Liverpool. Thou hast shown thyself a sister to me, more than my own sister. Truly I have come to love thee."

Gazing at the younger woman's dust-streaked face, Maggie felt the burden of her own deceit, felt unworthy of such generosity. "Come on, then," she said finally. "Humor me. Let's finish up, and get out of here."

They soaked their handkerchiefs again and put on their bonnets. This last pile appeared futile. Sarah was right: they would have found the ledger by now if it were up here. But as they worked their way into the pile, Maggie began to see a logic in the chaos. An enormous piece of timber lay across the pile, tangled in rope, blocking their progress? "Something funny about this, don't you think?"

" 'Tis careless. Putting so large and useful a timber in so out-of-the-way a place."

"Too careless." Maggie looked around for something to use as a lever.

The purpose of the timber was revealed when they pried it aside, untangled the rope, and dragged away a rotted tarpaulin to expose what was underneath. There they lay, in a neat row: wooden cannon.

Sarah and Maggie lifted the first one into view. Sarah gave an anguished cry. "So they saved them! Of all things to save—" She shook her head furiously. "Always, when I was a little girl and saw the cannon stacked up at the Willey wharf, I thanked the Divine Spirit that we did not make such things at Coalbrookdale."

She kicked the pattern. "How many men hath this thing killed?" Furiously, she wiped dust from the breech end. But it was blank on both sides. No name, no date. Scrambling into the pile, she dragged out the next one. Finally she located the dates. At the muzzle end of each was a small brand that said C'DALE, followed by further brandings: 6 LB CARRIAGE, 1742, R.F.

"Richard Ford," said Sarah. "Not my father!" But when she got to the fifth one, her face fell. The words gave proof as unequivocal as any ledger:

C'DALE, 9 LB CARRIAGE, 1748, A.D. JR

Three years after Ford had died.

Sarah brushed her fingers across the letters, as if to verify their reality. She looked older than her twenty-four years.

Abraham had hoped for fair weather for his wedding. But yesterday afternoon the swallows were flying close to the ground, a sign of rain, and this morning's sky was marbled ominously in the west.

Carriages had been arriving from London, Birmingham, Bristol, Liverpool, York. It was yet early, but boys from the Works, wearing blue sashes, were already on hand to see to the horses and carry messages back and forth between Sunniside and the other homes where guests were being lodged.

Now a fine rain was falling. Abraham walked through the long open tent erected on the lawn to shelter the banquet tables. Along one side of the tent, men were placing blocks of ice in a trench lined with straw. The musty smell of the canvas filled him with both excitement and dread. By nine o'clock the kitchen was bustling. Carts stood, laden with baskets of broccoli and cucumber, legs of lamb, sides of beef. The carters were waiting for directions from Mrs. Hannigan. The rain stopped, but the sky still threatened. Women sat on benches trussing geese, tying asparagus in bunches, and skinning rabbits next to a cart filled with the limp white bodies of swans. Mrs. Hannigan, her face shiny red, hurried about, wiping her hands on her apron and instructing everyone.

Abraham felt superfluous. He had spent all yesterday shaking hands with new arrivals, talking more loudly than usual, his voice strange in his ears. He answered the usual questions about the Works as he escorted visitors in wagons that were cleaned up and outfitted with benches for that purpose. He responded cheerfully to all the predictions of weather, agreeing with those who supposed the sky would clear in time for the festivities. It had rained in Wales, according to the guests arriving from Welshpool and Shrewsbury. The older guests talked about the weather at past weddings and funerals.

Abraham was kept too busy with all this to brood further on his doubts.

Was he prepared for marriage? The careful steps by which he and Becky had announced their intentions now seemed precipitous. Both were in good health. And he loved her, he was sure—as sure as he was of anything. But what if something were not right? What if something went terribly wrong? *Abey, Abey, thy middle name is Maybe.*

One minute, he loved the prospect of marriage, and the next, he dreaded it. One minute, he was rehearsing his vows—*Friends, in the Fear of the Lord, and before thy Assembly, I take this my Friend Rebecca Smith to be my Wife*—and the next, he thought it all too hasty.

Yesterday, he galloped most of the way to Horsehay to call on Richard Reynolds. He confessed only some of his anxiety to Richard, not all. Richard assured him such doubts were natural. "Trust in the Lord," he said, smiling his steadfast smile, and Abraham was calmed by it as always.

Abraham had hoped to raise that other question—rather, that dark body of questions that he could not quite bring to his lips. Concerning the marriage bed. He got as far as asking Richard, "Is there anything, brother, that I should know before the wedding?" *Night,* he wanted to add, but could not say the word. "Any advice thou wouldst give me—of a personal nature?"

Richard considered the question solemnly. "Apart from faith in the Great Name?"

Abraham nodded. "Apart from faith in the Great Name."

Again Richard smiled. "I fear thou wilt find my answer too simple. But thou knowest me well enough, it shall come as no surprise. I do affirm, brother, that nothing is so important in a household as plain order. A place for everything, and everything in its place."

Abraham frowned at his shoes. It was partly the question of place that concerned him. Where *was* it, in the human female? In the four-legged species it was under the tail, forward of the anus. Was it the same in the upright species? While his brother-in-law expounded on the virtues of order, Abraham pondered the question. *If there be no tail, where then doth it lie?* But none of these questions could he coax past his lips. "Thank thee, brother," he said.

"Trust in the Maker," Richard said as they parted.

Abraham rode off praying for that trust, but at the same time he asked himself: Was it possible that Samuel would know?

Samuel was his junior by five years but might have had experience with women. The possibility was both annoying and intriguing. At supper that evening, Abraham's eyes kept returning to Samuel, watching him chew his food, as though the mastications of that long jaw might offer a clue. Afterwards Abraham followed his brother upstairs to talk to him alone, but again could not bring himself to betray his ignorance.

And now, on the morning of the wedding, seeing Samuel wearing his brocaded vest amongst a flock of guests, Abraham found the vest an affront, an attempt if not to embarrass Abraham, then to call attention to Samuel's creaturely self—and he felt only irritation.


H ave a care, Maggie," Samuel warned as they carried the model down the attic stairs.

The model was light enough that one of them might have carried it alone, but it made an awkward burden, the wooden base being five feet long and the bridge nearly two feet high, and the bridge was so delicate.

Sarah, who had gone ahead to make sure the coast was clear, beckoned them into the upstairs parlor, where the gifts were spread out on the table. Displaying the gifts in this fashion was an idea Maggie had picked up from Granny's wedding. But it was Sarah who had lobbied for it and obtained Becky and Abiah's approval and who was taking a proprietary interest in these final preparations. After Maggie and Samuel had positioned the bridge on the table, Sarah arranged the other gifts around it. "I can hardly bear to cover it," she said.

Sarah and Samuel both seemed to have put the discovery of the cannon patterns behind them for now. Samuel, upon seeing the dates, had responded as Sarah did, with angry disbelief. "All that piety!" he kept saying. He sat back on his heels. "All I can think of," he said finally, explosively, "is Mother's damned dream!"

Sarah said nothing, only put her hand on his.

Samuel wanted to tell Abraham immediately, but the two women persuaded him to wait until after the wedding, when Abraham returned from his honeymoon. Sarah made him promise. " 'Twill only muddle things."

Maggie had felt the discovery weighing on them palpably, especially in their mother's presence. But it seemed forgotten today in the excitement, and now they were focused on the model, which looked magnificent, painted with Japan black.

Sarah stood back to admire it. "Oh Sammy! 'Tis like nothing ever seen!"

Samuel grinned. He put an arm around each of them.

The completed model had surprising power. In its airiness and its spirit of exultation it was like a French Gothic cathedral, if anything.

Maggie felt torn, contemplating the paradox before her—the undeniable beauty of this flawed structure that she hoped would change the world by its failure. And yet, standing here with Samuel and Sarah, the three of them linking arms, she felt it as their triumph.

She marveled at her influence in their lives. And it was reciprocal; she had opened herself to them. She longed for a time when she could reveal herself more. She would find a way, when all this was over. It might take years. After she was sure she had succeeded.

Samuel frowned. "Suppose Abraham finds it too flash?"

"He'll like it," Maggie said.

"But suppose."

Sarah's advice struck Maggie afterwards as remarkably astute. "Sammy. Even if Abey doth not appreciate thy gift immediately, thou must trust it will find favor in other eyes. Our brother shall be won over in due time by Mother and the rest of us."

"That's a good point," Maggie agreed. "Give him time."

"Trust in the Maker," said Sarah.

Samuel seemed reassured. He helped Sarah draw the cloth cover over it, and they tied the red ribbon in a bow.

Standing with Becky before the assembled guests and saying his vows, Abraham felt a great nervous tremor in his limbs.

*Friends, in the Fear of the Lord, and before Thy Assembly, I take this my Friend Rebecca Smith to be my Wife, promising, through Divine Allegiance, to be unto her a loving and Faithful Husband, until it shall please the Lord by Death to Separate us.*

Looking around the meeting house, he saw everything and nothing. The guests crowded into the gallery were a blur of hats and shadowed faces. Men's hands clasped over canes; women's bonnets all turned toward him.

The rosy flush in Becky's fair neck spread up her face as she said the words in her clear, tiny voice. *I take this my Friend Abraham Darby to be my Husband, promising, through Divine Allegiance, to be unto him a loving and Faithful Wife, until it shall please the Lord by Death to Separate us.* She wore a gown of silk in a pale plum floral design, over discreetly hooped petticoats that had satin flounces and a sash. There had been a great deal of conferring, Abraham knew, over the size of the hoops. She wanted her dress to appear "elegantly plain." Abraham had never seen her so beautiful.

Outside, the sky had indeed cleared. A sign, everyone said. The solemnity gave way to festivity and the ringing of the Dale Company bell. With boys running ahead to announce their coming, their carriage decorated with paper pennants, they rode to the Old Furnace, where the workers gathered for cakes and ale greeted them with lusty cheers. Then they proceeded down the dale, past the New Furnace and the mills and forges all steaming in the sun to Dales End, where an ox was being roasted and fiddle and fife were playing.

"Mother," said Abraham, "will disapprove of the music."

Becky giggled. "She will pretend not to hear it."

Abraham pointed out the famously fat man named Small Jake, who appeared at such occasions, when food was free, and who raised his hand in benediction.

The barges now began ringing their bells. Abraham called Becky's attention to three coracles. "The Rogers brothers are going to perform."

Under the skillful direction of their occupants, the three coracles began weaving in and out amongst each other as if around a maypole. Then, with their tiny round boats tethered together like a flower with three petals, the brothers stood, balanced, each with one foot planted in the boat of the next, which occasioned a lusty cheer from the spectators. Each man now stepped into his brother's boat, and the next, until the flower was made to rotate slowly like a horse gin. It was an astonishing feat of balance, considering the instability of the coracles and the strength of the current.

Becky clapped her hands with delight. "Oh Abey, I feel like royalty."

It was such an un-Quakerly thought that they both laughed. The smell of the ox roasting stirred Abraham's appetite, and yet he was too excited to eat. His thoughts were advancing to the honeymoon.

Their carriage completed its loop, stopping first at Dale House, where a delegation headed by the company clerk presented them, in the rose garden, with a cast-iron plaque. The Worshipful Company of Wheelwrights delivered a proclamation, and the Shropshire coalmasters presented the bride and groom with an ornate ceramic soup tureen. Abraham squeezed Becky's hand and whispered in her ear, "I am impatient for this to be over." She shushed him.

They got back into their carriage and proceeded up the road to Sunniside for the reception. The road was crowded now with carriages belonging not only to Quakers but to various lords and ladies, to Dundonald, Gower, Forester, and other gentry, to two Members of Parliament, the vicar of Madeley, and assorted ironmasters. The carriages moved aside to let Becky and Abraham proceed. They passed John Wilkinson with his wife and daughter in a polished black gig, his wife holding a silk parasol. The Broseley ironmaster smiled fiercely.

Wilkinson ambled among the other guests on the lawn at Sunniside, keeping an eye out for Mrs. Foster while he greeted his fellow ironmasters, amused as always to see the likes of Ferriday comporting himself as a gentlemen. Wilkinson fancied that he himself cut a splendid figure, with his red-and-orange floral waistcoat with silver trim and his black tricorn topped with a snowy egret feather. Seeing the solicitor general engaged in conversation with the MP from Bishop's Castle, he joined them long enough to inveigh against the new coal tax, then helped himself to some almond cakes and scanned the crowd again for Mrs. Foster. He saw his wife and daughter showing off their French parasols to Lady Forester. The sunlight fell pleasantly across the lawn, which was still damp from last night's rain. Under the great tent, the banquet tables were being readied. The almond cakes were most tasty. Where was Mrs. Foster?

Seeing Thomas Farnolls Pritchard carried past in a litter, Wilkinson hailed him. Up close, Pritchard's face looked starkly older than when they had seen each other last, and Wilkinson realized it had been quite some time. The architect's skin was sallow under the rouge, the furrows deep around the mouth, his wig too large. Wilkinson recoiled.

"Have you seen my bridge, Mr. Wilkinson?"

"Yes, yes. Darby has got it set out most prominently in his office. A sign of keen interest, eh, Mr. Pritchard?"

Pritchard nodded morosely. He complained of the deadlock among the subscribers and of Darby's vacillation on the matter of building the bridge wholly of iron. Pritchard said he had little time remaining to carry out his commission. He motioned Wilkinson to lean closer so he could whisper. "I fear, sir, that I am dying."

"Yes, yes, yes," Wilkinson said impatiently, withdrawing from the other man's breath, which was alarmingly fetid. "Poppycock, my friend," he scolded.

He reminded Pritchard that no proposals had been received in response to the advertisements; he promised that young Darby's vacillation was coming to an end. He did not mention Samuel Darby's model, of course. As for Pritchard's presentiment of death, it had been going on for so many years now, it seemed a ploy for commanding attention, much as a fellow announces he must depart from a meeting in one minute and then takes thirty to make his point. Still, the skull under that withered flesh reminded Wilkinson of his own mortality.

He did not believe in the immortality of the soul; he believed in deeds. What could a man leave, besides an heir, to carry his name beyond the grave? The bridge was as fitting a monument as any—and he cared not a fig whose design was used, only that the bridge be built of iron, and—if he were wont to luxuriate in it—that generations afterwards thank John Wilkinson for that fact. He told Pritchard of course he would put in a good word with Darby. (Promises were cheapest to the dying.) Poor fellow. Wilkinson took another couple of almond cakes and looked around for Mrs. Foster.

By now no Quakers were to be seen. Something was afoot. Seeing his wife and daughter engaged in talk with the vicar of Madeley, Wilkinson made his way to the house. He lingered behind the boxwood hedge long enough to overhear the maid explain to a guest that the bride and groom would come down shortly; they were now opening their gifts.

*Aha!* thought Wilkinson. He should not miss this for the world. He waited for the other guest to leave, marched up to the front door, and said breathlessly, "I hope I am not too late for the opening of the gifts." Presenting his card to the maid, he bustled upstairs, where he found the parlor crowded to overflowing. He joined the people gathered at the door and murmured greetings to those he knew. His eye immediately picked out Maggie Foster; she was standing with Samuel and Sarah Darby near a table laden with gifts.

Among the gifts not yet opened was a bulky shape covered with cloth and tied with a red ribbon. Ha! That would be Samuel's bridge. A child of six or seven kept pointing to it and asking when they were going to open "the big one," a request that in less sober company might have produced some outright laughter. The Quakers only shifted their eyes humorously.

Wishing to get closer and observe Darby's response, Wilkinson eased his bulk through the door. With muttered apologies he sidled farther into the room, until he was nicely positioned. Not since William Goldney's funeral had he been among so many Quakers. Looking around at their drab apparel, he thought what a whey-faced lot they were. Well, their faces were ruddy enough, and the bridal couple was radiant, as befitted poor young fools enjoying their day in the sun. But in general the Quakers seemed determined to prove how unhappy the world was. Or how unjust, that some men could afford fine silks while others wore only rags. Pshaw! It was arrogant in its own way, putting themselves in charge of keeping God's accounts! Presbyterians took a more humble view, perceiving that things were pretty nicely determined. Predestination, and all that. Rathbone. There was a good fellow. A Presbyterian at heart, under those dun-colored togs.

"Open the big one!" the child cried.

"Hush!" whispered the mother.



At Samuel's urging, his present had been left till last. Becky and Abraham together unfastened the red ribbon. Maggie felt a hollowness in her stomach as Abraham lifted the cloth.

"What is it?" asked the youngest Lloyd.

"Why, 'tis a bridge," someone exclaimed.

Becky gave a little squeal and clapped her hands, but stopped and glanced at Abraham, whose face had darkened.

Maggie told herself that his furrowed brow signified critical interest.

Samuel stepped forward, exuberant. "Now, brother," he laughed, "canst thou understand our secrecy!"

Abraham responded through clenched teeth. "I understand! I understand perfectly!"

Samuel's jaw dropped.

Maggie and Sarah spoke at once. "Abey—"

But Abraham cut them off. "Later! I will deal with Sammy later!"

Few of the guests could have overheard this whispered exchange, although the tension must have been obvious. Abraham, his face flushed, turned to the crowded room. "Friends, the tables are set outside. Let us—"

"No!" cried Samuel, raising his voice. "If thou wilt rebuke me, do it now!"

"This is my wedding, Samuel!" Abraham hissed. "Do not mock me with thy conceits!"

"Let them see it," cried Samuel, "as thou invited everyone to see Pritchard's bridge!"

Maggie tried to catch Samuel's eye. He was forgetting everything they had talked about. She saw Abiah whisper something to Becky but couldn't catch the words.

"What art thou afraid of?" Samuel demanded.

Becky, blushing, thanked the guests and again invited them to proceed to the banquet. Most began a polite exodus for the door.

"Brother! Brother!" Samuel reached for Abraham's arm.

Abraham pulled away furiously. His elbow must have grazed the model, because a section of arch made of pipe clay broke off and fell to the table with a clink.

Samuel looked stunned; then his shoulders bunched. Suddenly both the brothers' bodies were tensed. They were facing off like two dogs, hackles raised. It was a nightmare. Maggie could hardly register what was happening.

Sarah leaned forward and spoke in a low, urgent voice to Samuel. "Sammy. Remember what we said. Abey might need more time. Ye are both wroth. This is not the moment."

Good girl. But Maggie wondered if Samuel could hear. Richard Reynolds reached a hand out to each. Neither would take his eyes off the other. "Charity," Reynolds reminded them soothingly. "Faith, Hope, and Charity . . . And the greatest of these is Charity."

Most of the guests were leaving the room, following Becky's request and wishing to spare the family embarrassment. A few men remained, clumped near the door, listening.

Abraham, at Reynolds's urging, mumbled an apology to Samuel for having damaged the model, but again their voices rose.

" 'Tis *so* a Quaker bridge!" insisted Samuel.

" 'Tis not!" said Abraham. " 'Tis vainglorious! Puffed up with thine own pride! Thomas Pritchard's plain iron bridge is more Quakerly."

Samuel looked to the ceiling wildly.

"Look at these!" Abraham went on, pointing to the soaring arches. "Canst thou imagine Father approving such superfluity?"

"Do not bring Father into this!"

But Abraham shook his head stubbornly. "Everything I do, I submit to his judgment."

Samuel lost whatever restraint remained in him. "Judge thyself!" he screamed. The room froze. Abraham's face was ashen; Becky looked as though she might faint. "Judge thyself!"

Abiah rose to her feet and said in a loud, stern voice, "Let us pray."

But Samuel whirled and pointed at his mother. "Our father made cannon!"

Abiah tottered as if she had received a physical blow.

"Thou knowest it to be true! Father made cannon long after Richard Ford died! Even after thou wert married to him."

Abraham grabbed Samuel's brocaded vest. "Liar!"

"Look in the loam-house loft. Thou wilt find the proof. Cannon patterns! Proof every word be true!"

Abraham turned back to his mother, who buried her face in her hands. He turned to Richard Reynolds.

Reynolds put an arm around Abiah with an awkwardness that confirmed the accusation. His shoulders rose, then fell helplessly. "I had thought at various times to tell thee, Abraham. But . . ."

"Is it true?" demanded Abraham.

From Abiah came a ragged intake of breath that was the beginning of a sob.

"True?" John Wilkinson's jovial tenor rang out suddenly. "Of course 'tis true! Why, my father purchased guns from Coalbrook-dale."

Abraham's lips contorted, showing his teeth. "From Richard Ford!"

"No, no, no, no, my dear fellow. From your father! Ford was two or three years in his grave. I was but twenty years old, but I recall we purchased three-pound swivel guns for the Liverpool trade. I supposed you knew." Wilkinson seemed genuinely surprised. But the surprise turned instantly to gloating. "I can attest to his skill as a cannon maker, sir. Good, for a Quaker. And honest. Ha! Aye, he was an honest cannon maker!"

"I do not want thy opinions of my father!"

"The pity!" Wilkinson pointed his cane at the bridge. "For by your leave, sir, I reckon your father would have liked this." He winked at Maggie.

Abraham in a sudden fury brought his fist down on one of the butterfly arches. Samuel's face went white. Abraham's hand was bleeding. Wilkinson, with a cackle, handed his cane to Abraham. Maggie made a grab for it, too late. In a frenzy Abraham smashed the bridge to pieces.

"You bastard!" she screamed at Wilkinson.

Ignoring her, Wilkinson held out his hand for his cane when Abraham stopped, panting. "So," Wilkinson said. " 'Tis decided! You shall go with the plain iron."

# Maggie Foster

Samuel's body was fished from the Jackfield Rapids three days later.

Danny Day, the ferryman, had seen him walk into the river and disappear in the swollen current. The news, traveling swiftly up the dale and spreading among the guests, gave the wedding a final funereal note, but not before the bridal couple had been bundled into their carriage and sent off on their honeymoon.

Jeremy Crump was among those who found the body and brought it to Sunniside in a cart. Maggie, lying in bed fully clothed and with the shades drawn, heard the voices congregated outside, heard Mrs. Hannigan run up the stairs and knock on the door of Abiah's sitting room—it was not the housekeeper's familiar rapid tap but something more somber and uncertain—and then she heard Abiah's footsteps hurrying downstairs. Maggie knew, even before she heard Abiah's cry.

She heard Sarah rush downstairs. Her own feet carried her down more slowly. As she stepped out the kitchen door, she saw Mrs. Hannigan weeping, Jane's face white, Abiah with her hands to her face, Sarah reeling back from the cart. All as in a dream.

404

Jeremy had grown so, she hardly recognized him. He was standing with some other young men, who were holding their hats, while a flock of dirty-faced children took peeks and ducked behind one another. Someone was gasping repeatedly, Sarah. Then all sound stopped as Maggie forced herself to look in the cart.

Samuel was barely recognizable, his body bloated and white, his bloodless mouth torn open. And something had happened to the eyes.

"Eels," said Jeremy apologetically.

The tongue was gone, too. A blackness rose from her chest, and the gravel drive swam up to meet her. From somewhere she heard wailing. She felt herself carried through space. Faces in a circle calling her name. Erzulie holding out her arms. Maggie floated through filaments, like Jeremy's coracle threading through the willow shoots. Her body passed upward through twisted strands and pale leaves, into light. The warmth at her temples became hands rubbing.

"Maggie?" Sarah peered at her earnestly.

Maggie craned her neck to find herself lying on the horsehair settee in the downstairs parlor.

"Thou didst faint," Sarah said, her cheeks streaked with tears.

It came back to her, the eyeless corpse. He wasn't supposed to die for another twenty years! Her mouth shaped the name, as if to make it real. "Sammy."

Sarah nodded, her face breaking. Maggie pulled her down, felt hot tears on her neck, and her own racking sobs. "It was my fault, Sarah."

She could feel Sarah shaking her head. "Thou didst love him."

*Did I?* But the grief answered *yes.* Maggie's whole body was shaking. She thought of that look on Samuel's face before he fled, and when she cornered him outside the deer park. She shuddered, and Sarah responded. The grief moved back and forth between them as they held each other. Sarah's warmth on top of her. Suddenly all Maggie wanted was that warmth.

They were sitting up now, Abiah standing beside them. Mrs. Hannigan arrived with tea and whispered to Abiah, "They be awaiting outside with—with the cart, ma'am, not knowing what to do, with—" The housekeeper hid her mouth with her apron.

Abiah straightened. "Have Joseph and Andrew bring ice. We'll lay him on a board under the linden tree for now."

The burial took place the next day, because the body had started to decompose. The Dale Company's master pattern maker and two apprentices worked much of the night on the coffin; they carved a silhouette of Samuel's bridge into the mahogany top, based on the drawing that Sarah provided them with. Twenty or so people gathered at the Quaker burial ground, including the Fothergills, who had stayed to support Abiah, and Mally, who stayed while Joseph returned to Liverpool.

Before the casket was lowered into the grave, Abiah recited the Twenty-Third Psalm. "I shall not want," she said. The sweet, dizzying scent of roses barely masked the other smell. Under the words of the psalm, Maggie heard the tiredness in Abiah's voice, the texture of old pain and loss, all those old babies. She heard Richard Reynolds weeping unexpectedly, heard all their snuffling against the dark heartbeat thump of the furnaces, the New echoing the Old, and the ring of the blooming-hammer resounding up the dale. The shovels began. She picked up a handful of dirt, dropped it onto the coffin, and watched the carved butterfly arches disappear forever into the earth.

Why didn't I stop him?" Maggie kept asking Sarah.
Walking in the deer park, they came to the spot where Samuel had climbed over the iron fence and fallen to the other side. The pine needles were still scuffed, and the dried mud still showed the gouge like a check mark where his heel had landed and twisted.

"He ran too fast."

Maggie shook her head. "I could have caught him." *And I should have!* "He stopped, and I could have reached out and touched him, he was that close. But the look on his face—"

"Like a mask," Sarah said.

"No," said Maggie, "like a wounded animal."

They had had this conversation before—once or twice in bed—as if by repeating it, they might make sense of it.

*I should have tackled him.* But she could not bring herself to lay hold of him. She had waited for Sarah to catch up, while Samuel scuttled along the hedge and threw open the gate to the deer park. Why had he gone in there? And once he was in, why had she delayed pursuing him? Was it the assumption that he was trapped or the hope that he would get away? They watched in disbelief as he clambered up the tall wrought-iron fence and half-jumped, half-fell to the other side and continued, limping, down the orchard slope.

"I don't see how he got over," Sarah said, looking up at the sharp cast-iron finials. "He was not a good climber."

"He had to get away." Maggie scanned Sarah's face, looking for reproach.

"Thou wast protecting him."

*Yes.* "From what?"

"Protecting his dignity."

Maggie nodded. Maybe so. *And maybe protecting myself, from having to continue to play God.*


Abraham returned from his honeymoon furious that Samuel had killed himself. Furious that it happened on his wedding day. Furious that they had already buried Samuel.

Little was said. Abiah talked about only the most mundane matters: the newel post had to be repaired, letters written, legal transfers of property signed. After the initial shock, she became once more stoic. Maggie once tried to give her a hug, but felt resistance. And the revelation of the cannon molds seemed to have been cauterized into silence.

Maggie avoided Abraham. His anger only made her angrier at him. She felt sorry for him but could not forgive him. Even Sarah hardly spoke to him. For several days after the funeral, they saw little of Abraham, as he settled into Dale House with Becky.

Marriage seemed to agree with him, but underneath was an

irritability. He started coming to Sunniside on small errands, launching into brief rants—mostly about politics. The brick tax, levied to pay for the war in the colonies, and the proposed coal tax.

Once, when he was taking some remaining things to Dale House, he summoned her into his study.

"Dost thou wish to have this?" He indicated the electrical machine, tapping the glass globe. His tone was so imperious, it was hard to know how to respond.

"Don't you want it?" she inquired evenly.

"That is not the question."

"Well, what—" What *is* the damned question? she wanted to ask.

"Dost thou wish to have it?" he repeated impatiently.

She shook her head. "No."

He whirled away.

Once, when he had stood facing away like that, working his jaw, she had reached out and touched his shoulder. Damned if she would touch him now.

*I*t isn't Abraham I need to forgive, she wrote in her notebook. *It's me.*

# Abraham Darby III

For several days after his return from Chepstow, Abraham avoided the loam-shed loft.

His whole life had changed. He was a married man, living at Dale House. His father's ghost no longer visited him. There was a new grave in the burying ground, and a new anger in his heart. Yet none of it seemed altogether real.

Finally he could no longer resist the pull. He went to the loam shed, climbed the steps. There in the jumbled gloom of the attic, a frenzy of hand marks through the thick carpet of dust exposed the naked wood: COALBROOKDALE, 9 POUND CARRIAGE, 1748, A.D. JR. Abraham's own fingers were drawn to the engraved words scrubbed at the date to make certain the last digit was an eight and not a zero. There was no mistaking it. He sat with head bowed, then suddenly struck the wood with his fist. Surprised at the pain. He fled down the steps and outside, eyes burning, breeches covered with grime, taking long strides, half-running. He climbed the limestone wall behind Dale House and went up the terraced orchard, taking the path that Samuel was said to have taken, until he arrived at the deer park fence, where he stood wheezing, gripping the iron bars, overwhelmed finally by grief.

In the days that followed he begin to perceive the viciousness behind his own actions. Sammy might have behaved foolishly; his efforts were certainly misguided, his bridge design even—as Abraham had persuaded himself—idolatrous. But all that was forgivable. What Abraham could not forgive in himself—what he could not confess even to Becky, and could scarcely bring himself to acknowledge—was that his elbow swinging into Samuel's model had not been purely an accident. It was done in the heat of anger, to be sure, but there was also an instant of cold calculation. The cruelty of that moment weighed on him.

The cold became visceral, as though his constitution had accumulated an excess of phlegmatic humor. He took to wearing a woolen undershirt, even in August, and still he shivered under his waistcoat. Becky sewed him a vest of flannel-lined gabardine, but the chill persisted. His armpits perspired coldly. At night he found respite in the warmth of the bridal bed, the wondrous unfoldings of flesh, but even asleep in Becky's arms, he dreamt he was suffocating in the furnace, trying to scratch his way through the scaly mustard-colored walls, his fingers bleeding, and woke, and thought of Samuel floundering in the water, and the cold seeped back into his ribs.

He was glad to be gone from Sunniside, and yet he sometimes stopped there to talk, though avoiding the subject that haunted them. His voice sounded strident, the voice of a stranger.

At Dale House, he paced in his study. He missed the view from Sunniside, missed Mrs. Hannigan and the big kitchen fireplace. Some nights, he climbed the orchard slope and visited the deer park, looked through the bars at the deer with their ears erect in the moonlight, and pressed his forehead against the cold iron. *How could Samuel have done this to us?* And still Abraham did not confront his mother.

It was Sarah who insisted they talk: the three of them in Mother's sitting room, Mother and Sarah seated, Abraham standing by the coal stove and hugging himself for warmth.

"Why?" he demanded. "Why didst thou lie to us?"

Mother opened her mouth, but no words came forth. She was trembling. For the first time, she seemed vulnerable.

She began by defending Father. She spoke of his financial straits when he was building Ketley and Horsehay, of how deeply indebted he was to the Goldneys. "He supposed that if he continued—" She stopped, screwed up her face, and then burst into tears. "*We* supposed," she said finally, "that if we continued making cannon for a few more years, then we should never have to make them at Horsehay and Ketley. The day we put an end to it was the happiest day of my life." As she made that familiar declaration, her eyes showed a trace of the old pride, only to fill again with anguish. "When ye were young children, it seemed easier for ye to comprehend the spirit of it to say it happened the moment thy father took over the Works. I always supposed when ye were old enough, we would tell ye the truth. But as time went on, it became difficult to undo the lie." She went on in this vein, contrite and yet insisting the lie had been made for their children, to set them a good example.

Abraham scowled. " 'Twas a false example."

He berated her, not satisfied until she was in tears again. "All my life . . ." His voice cracked. "All my life I thought him a saint." Futility and pain gathered in his throat. Sarah wept for the loss of Samuel. A sacrifice, she called it, to false gods.

By the time it was over, they were all three weeping, exhausted. Darkness fell, but the candles remained unlit. In the silence Sarah arose to put her arm around her mother and her brother in turn. She drew them together. "Good work," she whispered.

An odd thing to say.

# Maggie Foster

Summer took place outside of time. It did not so much elapse for Maggie as disappear in the grieving, in the residue of her failure, and in the drawing close to Sarah. All their lives seemed to be falling in space like the fragments of Samuel's bridge, still in motion, yet suspended in time. Nothing had come to rest.

Maggie had been sleeping in Sarah's bed since the wedding, when Samuel was feared drowned and Sarah was afraid to sleep alone. They slept together during the first paroxysms of grief, and continued sleeping together in the quieter weeks that followed, until sharing a bed became their custom.

Sometimes, when they cuddled, Maggie longed to deepen their caresses. But she restrained herself, kept the boundary. She wanted to maintain the purity of this comfort, which she needed so much. And still she wondered what to do with her secret self, cradled in this new intimacy.

Sometimes, lying on her side with Sarah's arm draped over her, Maggie remembered the weight of Trevor's thick forearm across her chest, remembered how she used to kiss it and savor the solidity of it and hold on to it sometimes with both hands. How it felt to be possessed and possessing at the same time. The wonder of such communion. As if, whatever distance she and Trevor kept between them during the day, they had license to feel proprietary at night.

They had not done so badly together, she and Trevor. Considering the sadness at the center of their love. And when she thought back to the awkwardness of their leave-taking, their annoyance with each other in those last days, she could see it came from their unwillingness to face the loss. It seemed so long ago now. But there were echoes of it in the way she and Sarah shared their grief. Echoes too of that childhood sense of being outside her body, hovering somewhere high in the quonset hut, examining blooms of rust and looking down at herself playing with her raggedy doll—looking down now on the two women sleeping in each other's arms, detached in her isolation.

Sarah's grief was at times a wall that shut Maggie out and that kept Maggie from her own feelings. At other times it was Maggie's secret that was the wall. Sarah was afraid to be alone. Maggie finally had to insist on her own need for solitude. She went for walks. Once, she put her notebook in her apron pocket and wandered through the chestnut grove. When she opened the notebook, a triangular piece of pasteboard fell out. It was Samuel's triangle, the one she had saved for his next bridge. There would be no next bridge now. How would the world have been different if Samuel had lived? She tore the pasteboard into little pieces and scattered them in the grove.

What did Sammy's death mean?

It meant she had changed history. In at least one way. Sammy's death was her doing. She had caused it.

What other changes had she put into motion?

Somewhere in London was a young Quaker woman named Deborah Barnard, who would never marry Samuel. Never become Deborah Darby. Never bear his three children. Never move to Sunniside in the 1780s to take care of Abiah in her old age and assume her mother-in-law's ministry. Never become part of the "Petticoat Government" of Coalbrookdale. A branch of the Darby family tree had been erased.

Somewhere in London was another woman, named Susannah Appleby, who would have been befriended by Sarah while Sarah kept house for Samuel. Susannah would never become Sarah's lifelong companion, never be known affectionately as Sukey. Never be invited to come live at Sunniside upon Sarah's return. Never live out her old age in a house Sarah would build for her known as The Chestnuts.

Maggie looked around the grove. Could this be The Chestnuts?

Everything was in flux, unpredictable. What was she going to do with her life?

And how long could she bear to keep her secret?

# Abraham Darby III

**H**e had not spoken to Richard Reynolds since the wedding. He was angry with his brother-in-law. Some of that anger might have been directed at his father, were his father alive. Even so, there were questions unanswered. Richard had been part of the deception.

It was Richard who, with the approach of Michaelmas, proposed that they sail down the Severn for the quarterly ironmasters' meeting, in Stourport. They sat on the foredeck of a barge carrying hollow ware. The air was mild. Richard wore his coat open; Abraham, however, was wrapped in his woolen greatcoat. They watched the crew pole the barge through the Jackfield Rapids and stood back while the mainsail was raised.

"Brother," Abraham said when they were well downstream. "Didst thou ever make cannon at Horsehay and Ketley?"

"No." Richard tipped a shaggy eyebrow in quizzical consternation. He exhaled in a manner that suggested he had been expecting the question. "No. Thy father and mother always counted it a sign from the Maker that Ketley and Horsehay both prospered during the Seven Years War without resort to cannon."

"And yet thou didst profit indirectly from the war, didst thou not?"

"Aye, yes. As did the whole gorge." Richard smiled grimly. "And as thou wilt profit from this one. A rising tide carries all boats."

"Profit, yes." Abraham nodded, thinking those were almost Wilkinson's words. "Still, as a Quaker I should prefer not to." The declaration rang false. He knew he would not forsake the profits—not when the bridge was going to strain his every resource. What Richard said next was not the gentle rebuke that Abraham expected.

"Abey, permit me to observe that thou hast clung to thine innocence for too long! Hath it escaped thy notice, brother, that all Coalbrookdale was built with money taken by force of arms? With treasure stolen from the Spanish, stolen in turn from the Indians? We cannot *be* innocent!

"As for us Quakers, we are not nearly so holy as we like to think. Consider those Bristol businessmen who purchased Willey Furnace to turn it to cannon making. Wilkinson's silent partners. Three of them were Quakers!"

Abraham had known this. One of those facts that occupied no comfortable place in his mind, it now carried new meaning.

Richard continued, more agitated than Abraham had ever seen him. "And slavery. Dost thou expect that the Friends who dutifully give up their slaves will also give up their interests in the Africa trade? 'Tis not just Joseph Rathbone! 'Tis half the Quakers in London and Bristol!"

Abraham was stung not by the particulars, which, taken separately, were all familiar, but by the passion in Richard's voice that freighted the whole with new meaning. He felt his own virtue crumble around him like the dried husks of insects. He gathered his greatcoat tighter and looked out at the Severn valley, at the bow haulers scrambling along the bank, at the glint of summer-hardened oak leaves shining in the sun, now that the barge was clear of the smoke from the gorge. He saw that the birches and sycamores were turning yellow. He heard the creak of the rigging.

Richard's hand grasped his knee. "We cannot pretend to innocence, Abey. We can only try to do good."

Those words returned to Abraham at various times during the winter, undergoing a slow transformation of meaning that accompanied the disappointment thickening, congealing in him. He put on an extra stone of flesh. Marriage had broadened him, Becky teased. The chill loosened its grip on his vitals.

From a trip to London he returned wearing a blue-and-silver brocade vest, not unlike the one of Samuel's that he had condemned. He surprised Becky with a sample of wallpaper in a Florentine design resembling that in the Lloyds' parlor, and he proposed papering the downstairs parlor. It was time, he said, to indulge their more modern tastes. They purchased scarlet runners for the stairs and a pair of girandole mirrors for the new whale-oil lamps. The brocade vest kept him snug and warm.

Orders for iron increased. Pots aplenty and firebacks. The new canals had opened up the Midlands. And although the Dale Company was losing cylinder work to New Willey, the price of pig iron was rising steadily enough that even Bedlam could turn a profit. The bridge began to occupy his thoughts.

Maggie Foster beseeched him to use Sammy's design. But he pushed aside the rolled drawing without looking at it. " 'Tis enough," he added tartly, "that I am building it of iron." He turned on his heel. As usual, she was exceeding her bounds.

Over time, he imagined the bridge would secure a special place for him in the Darby line—a vainglorious conceit, but one he indulged in private. Over time, he suspected he would see little distinction between doing good and doing well.

# Maggie Foster

**W**hatever attraction she had once felt for John Wilkinson was lost in loathing. The qualities she admired in him—his power and exuberance—were all overshadowed by that look of demonic glee when he handed Abraham his cane.

Wilkinson alone seemed untouched by Samuel's death. A few days after the funeral, a bouquet of flowers had arrived along with a letter addressed to the family expressing "sincerest sympathy" for the tragedy that had befallen them. No acknowledgment of his role. Abiah threw the flowers into the pigsty.

A subsequent letter to Maggie begged for an opportunity to realize his hopes of serving her. She burned it.

She took some solace in knowing where Wilkinson's greed and intransigence would lead him. Boulton and Watt would sue him for infringing their steam-engine patent. His daughter and only heir would die, disowned. His brother Will, upon returning from France, would charge him with theft, and after a bitter quarrel lasting for years the two brothers would send gangs of men with sledgehammers to break up each other's ironworks. The Welsh housemaid by whom Wilkinson would sire three illegitimate children in his eighties would abandon him, renouncing his fortune to marry another man for love. Upon his death, Wilkinson's estate would be eaten up in legal wrangling. His final humiliation would be that his iron coffin would prove too small for his girth and have to be left ajar, encased in wood.

And yet Maggie felt little satisfaction. Felt no less soiled. She was, after all, complicit. Wilkinson was part of the secret she kept from Sarah. It was hard to hate him without hating herself.

Sarah said something in Meeting that helped. She talked about forgiveness, the difficulty she had finding forgiveness in her heart. She quoted James Naylor, one of the founding Quakers: *There is a spirit which I feel that delights to do no evil, nor to revenge any wrong, but delights to endure all things, in hope to enjoy its own in the end.* Maggie could not find that forgiveness in herself just yet, but entertaining the possibility of it helped.

She decided that she had to tell Sarah. Still, two days passed before she gathered the courage.


I betrayed him, Sarah."

"But thou didst encourage him."

"I encouraged him to make his bridge too heavy. It would have toppled in three or four years."

They were sitting on the picnic rock overlooking the gorge. Most of the leaves were down. The air was crisp. They wore wool shawls.

"Thou believest that?"

Maggie nodded. She explained about the substrata, the shifting mudstone.

"But why?" asked Sarah.

"I wanted it to fail."

"How canst thou say that?" Sarah was aghast, waiting for Maggie to continue.

"I have a vision of the future. Okay? It is a future overpopulated with people. The forests are gone. The air is not safe to breathe. The sea is poisoned." She went on to describe the violence and desolation.

"Thou paintest a bleak picture. 'Tis not my vision of the future."

"It is the future I come from, Sarah."

"Come from?" Sarah's eyes were wide.

"I'm not asking you to agree with it, Sarah—maybe not even to accept it as fact. I know it sounds unbelievable. But I need you to know how strongly I hold that vision. It's *my* truth." She could feel Sarah turning this over in her mind.

"Dost thou not believe in progress?"

Reluctantly, Maggie shook her head. "Most of what people call progress is material progress, fueled by greed. No, I believe in struggle. Your work against slavery, that's one kind of struggle. But progress? Look what's happening to Africans while Quakers deliberate. Whole villages are being torn apart, millions of people kidnapped, cut off from their culture. Even if you could stop the trafficking in slaves tomorrow, the damage would continue for hundreds of years."

"Dost thou believe mankind is evil?"

"No. Just very stupid. We're like rabbits or any other creature that will overrun everything if given the chance. And we're too lazy to stand up against greed."

"What thou sayest may be true. Yet I prefer hope. I wish to believe in a future where men have learned to live in harmony."

Sarah was skirting the more pressing questions. "I want that too," Maggie said. "But I see more and more violence, constant war."

"That is a very hard view."

"I've had a very hard look."

Sarah's eyes searched Maggie's face. "Dost thou truly wish me to believe thou art from the future?"

Maggie took a deep breath. She was not going to step back from it now. "Yes, I'm from the future. That's who I am. I couldn't change it if I wanted to."

They were silent, the two of them sitting with their knees up, hugging their skirts, looking out at the gorge. Sarah frowned, seemed about to ask something, stopped herself. Finally she turned to Maggie impatiently.

"But what does this have to do with Sammy?"

Here was the painful part. Watching a fish hawk flying over the river, Maggie wanted to be that bird, wanted to be anywhere but here. She forced herself back to Sarah's steady gaze. "It's why I wanted the bridge to fail. I want to stop that trend." She explained what the bridge meant, the trend toward large-scale iron structures, the conquest of nature. "I would have wanted any iron bridge to fail," she concluded. "Not just Sammy's. But that night a year ago, when the three of us stayed up late and you got Sammy to show me his design, I looked at it and saw its vulnerability and realized that this was a unique opportunity."

Sarah's shoulders fell. "Merciful Maker in heaven!" She covered her face and rocked.

Maggie longed to reach out to her. When she finally did, Sarah looked up with eyes glistening. "He trusted thee!" Sarah said. "I trusted thee! Is that what we were to thee? A unique opportunity?"

"Sarah," said Maggie, "I love you."

" 'Tis a strange love!"

Maggie tried to explain her conflict. Her admiration for Samuel, her guilt. It came out sounding so self-serving, so bogus. How could she expect Sarah to buy it, let alone forgive her? But she kept talking, spilling everything—how she had plotted to get into the Darby household, how she had connived with Wilkinson behind their backs; all those shameful admissions—not knowing whether Sarah was hearing any of it. Not knowing where her own life was headed. And still she kept talking. Embarked on the truth now, she had to trust herself to it. She told of her plan to get Samuel involved in another project that could succeed before the bridge failed. How her affection for Samuel and Sarah had grown. How burdensome her secret had become. It all poured out in a torrent.

At some point Sarah reached out and took her hands.

Maggie was silent, eyes shut. When she began again, it was at a slower pace. "When we were in the loam-shed loft, you told me Liverpool changed something for you. Well, it changed something for me, too. When I watched you inform Joseph that you were going out that night to search for Sammy, I was the only one who could see your fingers; you were twisting them horribly behind your back, but your voice was calm. And I was so proud of you. At some point I realized it was more than pride. Much more."

Sarah nodded. "I remember hearing my voice rise, then catching myself." She looked down at her lap. "I was performing partly for thee."

The Severn was mostly in shadow now. A few sails still caught the sun. The air had got cooler, although the limestone rock retained heat. Maggie's throat hurt from talking. Her buttocks hurt from sitting on the rock. But now that she had started, she could not stop talking. She voiced doubts about her mission. "I was supposed to use argument, moral suasion. I don't think any of us back in Ecosophia gave enough thought to the deception. How corrosive it would be." Hearing herself say this aloud helped her understand.

Finally, Sarah put a hand over her lips to quiet her. "My head is too full," Sarah said.

They sat in silence, cross-legged in front of each other.

The glow of the smelters rose toward the darkening sky. Maggie finally blurted, "You don't hate me!" It was not quite a question, but she needed an answer.

"No." Sarah shook her head with a faint lopsided smile. "No. Thou art more complicated than I would choose—certainly for myself. But thou hast acted truly in thine own way. Sammy was right to love thee. And I love thee."

Maggie shuddered with relief. She leaned forward and rested the top of her head on Sarah's chest. "I love thee, Sarah."

Sarah put her arms around Maggie and rested her chin on Maggie's head. They sat like that for a long time, containing each other.

# Maggie Foster

She had a recurrent image of Paul Stanski, with his halo of white hair, gazing out at the bridge while it was being constructed. Paul slapping his hands to his sides in disgust and saying, "Oh shit."

It was only a fantasy. Nobody in Ecosophia would have a clue as to how things had turned out. The Paul in her mind had come to resemble the church warden who once examined her fingers for calluses and warned her to keep to Christian ways. *Remember, you are wielding a scalpel, not a cleaver.* For all his disavowal of the fraternity of old white men, Paul remained a patriarch; in her fantasy his disappointment was the disappointment of a father. The curious part was that every time she flashed on him saying, "Oh shit," she had an impulse to laugh.

At first she felt guilty, thinking the impulse impish at best, even malicious. But the laughter was so persistent that she finally had to listen to it. Beyond the element of childish rebellion, and beyond her relief at being out from under the burden of her mission, the laughter told her that what Ecosophia had attempted was absurd.

This realization came to Maggie only after she had detached herself from the bridge. Perhaps it was, as Mr. Ho used to say, a matter of abandoning focus.

The winter after Samuel's death, everything at Sunniside seemed altered. It was just the three women now, grieving and going about their business: Sarah and Maggie drawing together; Abiah turning inward.

Abiah continued in her ministry, but without the same certitude. When she spoke in Meeting, it was often simply to quote Scriptures. At home, although she said nothing to acknowledge the new relationship between Sarah and Maggie, pretending not to see the occasional stolen kiss, she stopped asking only one of them to accompany her on journeys and began to treat them as a couple. Or she took other companions and left them alone in the house, sometimes for weeks on end.

Maggie continued to perform secretarial duties, though she was no longer officially employed. When Samuel's estate was settled, Sarah gave Maggie half her share of the distribution of money held in trust for Samuel, declaring that Sammy would have wanted it that way. She insisted too that Maggie receive the chestnut grove, where she might someday build a house. Mally, who had come down from Liverpool in December to assist with the legal affairs, objected to the chestnut grove's leaving the family, but Sarah prevailed.

Mally also expressed disapproval of the fact that Sarah and Maggie were sleeping together, noting that the period of "natural mourning" had passed. Abiah may have taken her aside and spoken to her, but in any case Mally said no more about it.

The servants treated Maggie as a member of the Darby family. It helped that Jane had married her maltster and gone off to live in Dawley. It helped too that shared beds were common in those days. Mrs. Hannigan accepted the arrangement as one more family idiosyncrasy.

For Maggie it was a winter filled with contradictions. Nothing had gone as she anticipated. She was thirty-three years old, had failed, and had absolutely no idea what she was going to do with her life. But there seemed no urgency to know, just yet. In letting go of the mission, she felt an emptiness. But within that emptiness, a realignment was taking place, something gathering within her that she could not name. She had failed but did not feel defeated. For the first time since she left Ecosophia, she could let things happen. That was what Erzulie used to say. *Time to let things happen.* Maggie felt a deep quiet. Helping Sarah to heal was part of her own healing. And all the time she was listening for that small still voice.

C onstruction on the bridge began with excavation for the abutments in the summer of 1777, just after the anniversary of Samuel's death. In July, the pilings were driven for the cofferdams. In August, the horse gins began pumping out water, while a gang of laborers leveled the mudstone and clay at a point several feet below the waterline. In September, the masons laid the first course of foundation stones.

All this was happening a year or so earlier than the historical record had indicated, owing apparently to the deadlock over iron being settled earlier. Maggie looked in vain for some other aberration. She watched the construction from a point higher up on the bank. Sometimes Sarah joined her. Becky, who was pregnant, also came to watch. (The baby would be a boy, would die in infancy, if history took its course.) Abraham could often be seen conferring with the foreman. He carried himself differently now; he had put on weight, and his gestures were more decisive.

Work on the abutments continued during the autumn and part of the winter. Thomas Farnolls Pritchard died on schedule, in December of 1777, but his design was the one they were going with: the semicircular arch, with its radial braces and signature ogees, all of it stubbornly conservative. Maggie made a last try at tweaking the Pritchard design by arguing the case for bolts with Abraham, who seemed agreeable, but the idea got buried in committee. The castings would be joined by the same mortise-and-tenons and dovetails that had been used to join timber for generations. The bridge would be as overengineered as ever, with five pairs of ribs where three might have sufficed.

She had not changed the bridge one iota. Just moved it up a few months. The baby died of a fever.

T he abutments were completed in the spring of 1778. Two years had elapsed since Samuel's death.

Maggie and Sarah had sewn a narrow pink ribbon into each other's bonnets, to form piping where the brim joined. It was a small outward declaration of friendship. But it was a special friendship "to anyone with eyes to see," as Sarah put it. The Reynoldses and others close to the family regarded them as young spinsters who enjoyed each other's company and stayed in remarkably good humor despite their lack of husbands. People sometimes remarked on the light Maggie and Sarah seemed to radiate.

They had to be careful not to give off too much light. But they had surprising freedom as long as they confined their public show of affection to the hand-holding that was common among women. Sarah had got past the initial resistance she felt to their pleasures in bed. Lovemaking undertaken "in simplicity," as she put it, was surely the gift of a loving Maker. This was no small departure from prevailing Quaker orthodoxy, which railed against the flesh, or at least took a dour view of the body. But Sarah soon noticed the similarities between moments of sexual ecstasy and the raptures of those who surrendered to the Holy Spirit. Sometimes, transported by Maggie's ministrations, she cried out to Jesus. As Maggie saw it, they were practicing a new, more humanistic Quakerism.

And Sarah was not the only one changing. Seeing worship more and more as a vehicle for human love, Maggie began to lose some of her inhibitions in Meeting. She became more open to the occasional irrational supplication to Divine love, more open to the quavering voices and upturned eyes. She began to feel transported into the bosom of something she was willing to call God. Most of all she felt it in the shared silence. She learned to tune out distractions and open herself to the silence that went beyond language.

Finally it happened that she was sitting in Meeting and words came into her head. It was a declaration. *I have a vision.* She saw her whole world laid out in the future: the despoiled land, the poisoned water, the nomadic hordes. *I have a vision.* Her heart was pounding. *A world destroyed by greed.* Air poured through her lungs. Then she was standing, without having made any choice to stand, and her voice was issuing from her throat in a kind of wail—from which she felt at the same time distanced, responding with mild surprise to this woman she had become for the moment, who was standing with arms raised trembling over her head, fingertips ecstatic, breath coming in gulps as if she were in labor.

"I have a vision!" she cried. Fingertips cold as ice. Words pouring out between gasps. Words rushing from somewhere deep within, painting the terrors in bright colors. Then she was aware only of her own consciousness returning. The meeting house around her. Slant of sun across the circle of faces. A few heads were bowed. Most faces were rapt, staring at her. Some weeping. She was aware of her arms dropping slowly to her sides, a peaceful feeling descending around her like a soft brown cape; light on her eyelids; gravity guiding her gently, the feel of the polished wooden bench as she sat down.

Sarah, tears running down her face, looked at her in wonder.

Word of Maggie's vision spread through the Quaker network. Prior to this, Maggie and Sarah had been spending several hours a day in Abiah's sitting room, writing letters and politicking—much as they had before Samuel's death, but more purposefully than Abiah, or at least with a different purpose. Abiah's diatribes had been puritanical, inward, and in their own way self-indulgent. The younger women's efforts were aimed at securing social change, and particularly at putting an end to slavery. It amounted to a ministry. After Maggie's vision, Abiah—who had begun to retire from her public role—gave them her full support.

"Thou must obey the Spirit," she told Maggie. "Ye are both called." She wrote dozens of letters describing *A Divine Visitation*, likening Maggie's utterances to the Book of Revelation and the opening of the Seventh Seal. Sometimes, after writing furiously on her lap desk, she stopped and gazed at Maggie with a look of awe.

"It may never happen again," Maggie told her.

Abiah nodded, with a strangely alert crease across her brow. "Still, thou must remain faithfully open to the Word."

"Shall we continue working on our queries?" Sarah asked Maggie, referring to the queries on slavery they were planning to present to Madeley Meeting.

"Yes! Slavery is at the heart of it!" Maggie was surprised by her own passion. "A people who enslave others enslave themselves. They become blind to their greed. And in their blindness they do violence to Nature and themselves."

She had never put it together before. All those cotton and sugar and indigo plantations separated from any sense of the sacred. Bottomthink. The turning of people and land into commodities.

As they continued working on their queries on slavery, Maggie challenged some of Sarah's ideas about the superiority of industrial society over so-called primitive cultures and about what constituted intelligence. Sarah had no direct experience with Negroes except for a pair of children who had been brought forward once at Quarterly Meeting and for whom Quaker ladies sewed clothing. Sarah somehow assumed that Negroes were all "childlike." She was amazed to learn about Erzulie, whom Maggie described as a philosophe whose knowledge dwarfed her own and who was possibly the wisest person she had ever known.

"To learn of this is a great gift," Sarah said.

It was true, Maggie realized. Her friendship with Erzulie was a great gift. Far more important than knowing what the backside of the moon looked like. She was not introducing new technology, but she was introducing new grounds for empathy. True, it could all go awry. Somehow produce new Hitlers, new horrors. Yet she would take her chances with empathy.

"Pussy power," she murmured.

Sarah looked at her questioningly. "Pussy power?"

Maggie smiled. "Something Erzulie once said. I'm beginning to understand it differently."

The queries were plain and clear. Framed as questions designed to provoke discussion, they began by asking Quakers to examine not only the cruelty with which slaves were treated but also the corrupting effects on the slave owners; to consider the imperative not only of ending slavery but of undoing the damage already done. The queries then moved to the realm of action, asking what steps Quakers might take to bring an end to slavery and redress the wrongs.

In the Madeley Meeting, Sarah argued persuasively to prevent the wording from being weakened. Maggie was proud of her. The queries were approved and sent on to the Quarterly Meeting held in Shrewsbury.

At Shrewsbury, Maggie spoke. Word of her vision had preceded her, but this time she spoke briefly and to the point. "Friends," she said, "slavery will cast a long shadow into the future, blighting everything it touches. It is a War. It is a War of White against Black, and eventually Black against White, and must be opposed like all War."

She waited for more words to come. But that simple declaration was enough. She sat down. Someone who had never considered slavery in that light spoke in response. After further discussion, the queries were approved. They would be sent to the Yearly Meeting in London, in June.

In April of 1779, the giant ribs were poured, on a casting floor prepared at the bridge site. The iron was melted in a pair of air furnaces built for the purpose. A crowd gathered around the sand floor for each pour. One rib was poured at night, for *spectacle,* as Abraham put it. The liquid iron spurted simultaneously from the two air furnaces and filled the sixty-five-foot-long arc with an incandescence that lit up the riverbank and brought cheers from the Broseley shore. Richard Reynolds pronounced it sublime. After the huge castings had cooled, they were stacked on the riverbank for visitors to admire, while work continued on the approach roads.

**M**aggie got Sarah to see parallels between slavery and the oppression of women. Together, they began working on a new set of queries. Sarah was excited, but she thought it best for them to wait until the slavery queries had been accepted by Yearly Meeting, and then build on that success. "It takes time," Sarah said, "to appeal to the Light within." After some argument, Maggie admitted the wisdom of this.

In general, Maggie was impatient with the Quakers—with their slowness, their self-righteousness, with the hypocrisy sometimes veiled in muddled pronouncements. Still, the Quakers showed courage every once in a while, and they had a strong network. What she hoped to bring to the process of reform was more clarity.

At Yearly Meeting in London, Sarah spoke simply and eloquently at the Women's Meeting on behalf of the slavery queries. The queries were then introduced before the full Meeting, where discussion was lengthy and, by Quaker standards, volatile. One of the Barclays, who was involved indirectly in the slave trade, spoke against the queries; others too thought them provocative. But discussion kept coming back to the queries themselves, whose clarity sent ripples of excitement through the large meeting house, with its tall narrow windows and painted white balustrades. Maggie nearly rose to speak—impatient with the condescension toward Africans, with the deep cultural smugness that underlay even the most liberal declarations, impatient also with the dominance of the assembly by men. But she held her tongue, knowing she would be speaking from anger. Her heart was pounding, but it was a different pounding. She waited, and the pounding went away. Someday she would speak again, perhaps even in that prophetic voice. But *thou must not run ahead of the Guide.* For now, it was time to listen.

In the end, the queries were accepted with some amendments. They would be printed and distributed to the various Meetings for discussion throughout England and Wales. Sarah and Maggie were invited to travel to Yorkshire in October, to speak at the Women's Meetings.

It was a start.

Now that she was no longer focused on the bridge, Maggie could see it more clearly.

By the spring of 1779, the Severn Gorge was the hub of industrialization in England. Watt's new engine was the talk of London. Bigwigs flocked to the gorge to see the blowing-engine at New Willey, the iron rails at Horsehay and Coalbrookdale, and the great castings stacked on the riverbank. France had entered the war, seizing some islands in the West Indies; Spain too had entered the fray, laying siege to Gibraltar: all this boosted the demand for iron enormously. There was a lot of talk about the "free market" on the heels of Adam Smith's new book, *The Wealth of Nations,* which had already gone through several printings. But it was obvious to Maggie that the market was anything but free. Families like the Crumps, driven from the Commons, were free to choose between pathetic wages and starvation. It was not the "invisible hand" of competition that dictated; it was a government of the wealthy.

Richard Reynolds had ordered a Boulton and Watt engine for Horsehay, and Abraham was considering one for Bedlam. The whole Severn Gorge was lit up like a crucible. Visitors reported seeing the glow from the outskirts of Birmingham.

Maggie could see changes in the six years since her arrival. Increased iron production required a huge increase in coal, which led to deeper mine shafts and consequently more pit collapses; more ruthless despoliation of land. More cash in the local economy, yet more poverty. She could see her own era approaching: more drinking and transience among the new industrial workers; more gambling, prostitution, and domestic violence. Polly Crump said she hardly dared go to Jackfield, because of the bow haulers. Jeremy lost a finger in a fight with a bargeman outside the Severn Trow. For all that, there was a pervasive enthusiasm for the new. Modernity was the new secular religion, and the bridge stood at the center of it: a cathedral.

Maggie had come to see her original mission differently. Whatever the flaws in her judgment, the mission itself was flawed. None of them at Ecosophia had much understanding of history; they were mostly scientists and technicians. What they had attempted was in a sense just one more technological fix. They were naive to think they could coax industrialism onto a more benign path. Industrialism would not be coaxed. There was too much energy behind it, too much momentum. And, as the Luddites would discover in another quarter century, too much military force at its command.

Industrialism would spread over the globe, assuming various guises—constitutional monarchy, democracy, fascism, communism—but under all those masks would be the blind momentum of industrialism itself, served by a priesthood of technocrats.

Maggie had never understood the paralysis that gripped Granny's generation and her parents' generation—how, in the midst of the greatest extinction since the Cretaceous era, they were unable to take the simplest steps to preserve the environment. Now she could see that technology was following the mold of Christianity, offering solutions to problems great and small even as it created new ones at a rate too fast to process, yet always holding out the promise of salvation. A *deus ex machina*.

If she could stretch her mind in a new way, look at the world not as Granny had—not as a commodity to be used but as a gift to be treasured—then she might be humbled by that gift, might quake with humility. Might be a new Quaker.

She was at a spiritual Opening. She could feel it. She wished Erzulie could be here. She wished Trevor could be here. She wanted everyone to be with her, here and now. And, in a sense, they were. She could feel that too.

Industrialism might be unstoppable. And the development of large-scale steel structures might be an inevitable part of it—inseparable from sun trikes and laser surgery. But what if consciousness could be transformed, beginning perhaps—who knows?—with the Quakers?

What if slavery could be eliminated in America *before* the invention of the cotton gin?

What if greed could be answered by an affirmation of the sacred?

Those were big ifs. But you had to start somewhere. All her life Maggie had felt she was too late. The planet was totaled. She had blamed her parents, her grandparents. But people must have been feeling the way she felt for generations. And occasionally an individual arose with a clear sense of what had to be done in his or her own time, and society was transformed or at least moved a little bit in its path.

She stood at the edge of such a vision. She was not a George Fox or a Mahatma Gandhi or a Martin Luther King. She was an ordinary person, but she at least had this glimpse of the world as a finite whole, infinitely connected. This realization that it was time for humanity to grow up, time not to stop praying—on the contrary—but to start answering its own prayers. If she had any tool for change, maybe it was that vision.

Maybe that was all you ever had. And you just did what you could, in your own time—knowing you might fail, knowing, like Erzulie's father, that your efforts might seem insignificant, but doing it anyway. She might never have children, but she had this.

All that spring, the huge ribs lay on the riverbank, advertising the drama to come. In May, the timber arrived from Poland. In July, with the river low, the pair of scaffolding towers was erected in the shallows at either side. A barge was leased. Abraham could be seen on horseback, barking orders, conferring with foremen and rigging crews. The rope was coiled in readiness, the castings all numbered with white paint. Visitors from Birmingham and Bristol arrived to watch.

Now, on this hazy, humid day in August, with the scaffolding in place and men swarming around with levers and ropes and harnesses, the tempo increased to a feverish pitch. Teams of oxen hitched to blocks and tackle hoisted the first rib slowly aloft. Messages were relayed by speaking trumpets as the foot of the rib was swung around by means of the barge, then planted on the abutment on the Broseley side. The dangling tip was lifted slowly skyward.

By this time, several hundred spectators were gathered along the riverbanks or watching from small boats and barges. Maggie and Sarah had given up their places on a barge reserved for subscribers and their guests. It was Sarah's idea to watch from the horse-ferry landing. Now, standing next to Sarah on the cobblestoned landing, Maggie felt dim memories jogged by the smells of sausages frying, horse sweat, and wild garlic—but it was like trying to recover a faded dream.

They could see Abraham standing by the Madeley abutment, a speaking trumpet in his hand, conferring with Richard Reynolds. On the opposite side of the river, near the Broseley abutment, John Wilkinson was recognizable, rotundly outfitted in scarlet and leaning on his cane.

A man standing behind Sarah and Maggie with a tankard of ale kept saying they were watching "history in the making." He looked familiar. Maggie realized it was the publican of the Bird in Hand. He had grown a mustache since she had seen him last, yet he looked familiar in some inexplicable way.

Finally, the crowd grew quiet. A horn was blown. The oxen began to pull, and the second rib slowly rose from the Madeley side. The Rogers brothers, who had been putting on a show in their coracles, turned their attention to the ribs. Maggie felt an airiness rise in her chest.

The moment was approaching when, six years ago, she had inadvertently crossed over from one energy state to another. She supposed it would feel strange, but she was not prepared for the intensity of it. Everything around her suddenly had an uncanny resonance: the scaffolding, the cobblestones, the crowd assembled. The commonplace smells were suddenly exotic, the subtle fragrance of Sarah's hair under her bonnet suddenly intoxicating.

Sarah looked up. "Art thou okay?"

Maggie swallowed. "I feel a little weird." She wanted to explain what was happening, but words would have interfered. It was like trying to slip back into a dream, with everything elusive, a confluence of sensation and memory. Why had she come to this precise spot? Was it Sarah's idea, or hers? It was not too late to move a few yards away. Her hand tightened on Sarah's, but she could not bring herself to move.

A stir passed through the crowd as the free ends of the two great ribs were raised and brought slowly together. The crowd held its breath. A mishap might crack the flanges: the warning had gone around, adding to the drama. A boom was swung, with a man suspended in a harness preparing to make the final connection.

The two ribs came together to form a semicircle. This was the moment. Sarah, no doubt thinking of Sammy, made a snuffling noise. Maggie put an arm around her. "Ironbridge Gorge," she whispered. Sarah nodded and dabbed at her eyes.

The man in the harness secured the two iron tips. Watching him, Maggie felt a lurch of vertigo. She dropped her gaze to Sarah's bonnet, fixed it on the pink piping sewn into the brim. Then, looking up at the concentration on the man's face as he tapped the wedge in place—How could she see him so clearly?—watching a drop of sweat trickle down his nose, she was suddenly caught in a dizzying ambiguity, memory enfolding her into that dreamlike moment when six years ago she heard the voice saying, *Withdraw! It's not too late!* This was the moment when she had surrendered to the urge to reincorporate, felt gravity take her. Felt the cobblestones under her bare feet.

And she could hear the voice now, insistent, in her left ear. Everything was scintillating. The dog, a brown-and-white mongrel, was looking at her strangely and growling, its hackles raised. Was it possible that at this instant she could reenter the energy state that would return her to Ecosophia? The voice grew more urgent. *Withdraw! It's not too late!* She recognized the publican now as the man with the bloody nose who had groped for her. She imagined herself falling backwards slowly, holding her breath, falling into the calm of the Circle, darkness imploding slowly over the crown of her head, sensation draining away. It was too vivid. She stopped herself.

She did not want to leave. *This* was her time. She squeezed Sarah against her hard enough to feel her bones.

*Withdraw.*

The moment passed. The dog stopped growling. The air stopped shimmering. The man in the harness finished tapping in the wedge. Straightening his legs carefully, he trusted his weight to the new junction. He stood up, balancing. And when he raised a hand to signal the operators of the boom to take him away, it was the cue for the crowd to unleash a great cheer.

Sarah wiped her eyes, slipped her arm around Maggie's waist, and they hugged each other, hard, side to side, while all around them the crowd cheered.